Bookvan

Bookvan

COUNT TO
INFINITY

COUNT TO
INFINITY

JOHN C. WRIGHT

TOR

A TOM DOHERTY ASSOCIATES BOOK

NEW YORK

COUNT TO INFINITY

Copyright © 2017 by John C. Wright

A Tor Book
Published by Tom Doherty Associates
175 Fifth Avenue
New York, NY 10010

www.tor-forge.com

Tor® is a registered trademark of Macmillan Publishing Group, LLC.

The Library of Congress Cataloging-in-Publication Data is available upon request.

ISBN 978-0-7653-8160-6 (hardcover)
ISBN 978-1-4668-8281-2 (ebook)

Our books may be purchased in bulk for promotional, educational, or business use. Please contact your local bookseller or the Macmillan Corporate and Premium Sales Department at 1-800-221-7945, extension 5442, or by email at MacmillanSpecialMarkets@macmillan.com.

First Edition: December 2017

Printed in the United States of America

0 9 8 7 6 5 4 3 2 1

ACKNOWLEDGMENTS

The author thanks Edward Elmer Smith, Ph.D. Thank you, Ted. And thank you, Jim.

CONTENTS

Mother-Age (for mine I knew not) help me as when life begun:
Rift the hills, and roll the waters, flash the lightnings, weigh the Sun.
O, I see the crescent promise of my spirit hath not set.
Ancient founts of inspiration well thro' all my fancy yet.

—Alfred, Lord Tennyson

PART ELEVEN

———— ⋈ ————

The Edge of Orion

1

The Cataclysmic Variable in Canes Venatici

1. The Ghost

A.D. 92000 TO 95500

He was dead, that was sure; but not entirely, and not permanently.

When awareness fled and all activity ceased, it could have been called sleep or hibernation. But he had been in those two states of being before, frequently, and for long periods, and this was something more still, more silent, less like life than that.

When awareness returned, Menelaus Illation Montrose was a pattern of leptons distributed throughout a featureless lump of gray metal falling through darkness and nothingness. He had neither hands, nor head, nor heart, intestines, or eyes.

Nor did he have engines, fuel, reserve energy, or motive power, and the sails had been three-fourths torn away. Had they been wholly torn away, as his assassin had planned, he would have been well and truly dead by now, dead beyond recovery or revival.

Instead, the sails absorbed enough ambient starlight to allow him, every three or four hundred years, for three or four minutes, to wake. Chemical energy reserves woven into the gray lump of the ship's mass were sufficient to energize a cubic foot of his outer hull, stir it to motion, and form lenses and antennae to take measurements. It annoyed him that he had a perfect memory, since even the comforting routine of noting in the log the progress of his endless, weightless fall through unhorizoned, infinite space was denied him.

His velocity, relative to the tiny speck of Sol (lost somewhere in the stars of Piscis Austrinus), was very near the speed of light.

In three thousand years of flight, even the nearer stars changed position against the unmoving backdrop of farther stars only over centuries. There is no vertical nor horizontal in space, no weight, no sensation of motion.

Free fall is falling; in a way, it is infinite descent. And yet, in another way, at even the most immense velocity, when there is nothing against which to compare it, it seemed perfectly motionless. Montrose was both plunging down an unending drop and was utterly still.

His ghost occupied the information lattices running through the gray nanomaterial substance that once had formed the hull and furniture and panoply of the alien supership he dubbed the *Solitude*. Somewhere near his heart, frozen in a solid lump of medical nanomaterial, was his corpse, a work of biological engineering superlative enough to be able to survive storage indefinitely, without degradation.

The alien technology preserving his mind information was beyond superlative. It was perfect. He would remain undying and uninsane, his mind suffering no aging, no divarication, for so long as his perfect prison lasted.

On he fell.

2. The Wreck

He was traveling at right angles to the plane of the galaxy, so as to depart the Milky Way by the shortest path, thus to offer Montrose the least possible chance of survival.

By any calculation, the chance of survival was indistinguishable from zero as of the moment the ship's fuel supply was exhausted transmitting a copy of Del Azarchel's brain information onward, leaving his original self behind to shatter the hull, to destroy the drive core, to sever the sail shrouds and then to die.

But, even so, a close passage to a star might have given the hulk containing Montrose energy; encountering any heavenly body in deep space, even a small one, might have given Montrose raw materials, molecules to be nanoengineered into repair material, or mass to be annihilated for thrust.

The fuel had been a mass of exotic particles formed by attotechnology beyond the capacity of any second-magnitude beings or civilizations to create: the alien Dominion occupying the Praesepe Cluster could not create the substance and yet, somehow, by spooky remote control, had transferred or transformed the tritium mass in the fuel bank into a negative mass version of itself, so that the isotope of hydrogen was repelled rather than attracted by gravity.

It was an impossible drive, a *diametric drive*: a negative and positive hydrogen particle pair would accelerate continuously, the negative mass atom moving away from the positive, and the positive falling after, as absurd as a man lifting himself into the air by tugging mightily on his bootlaces.

Nonetheless, the law of entropy cannot be defeated, and the exotic particles lost energy, apparently into nowhere, in the form of accelerated proton decay exactly equal to the potential energy arriving apparently from nowhere. Nature always found some way of balancing her books.

The act of transmitting the brain information of Blackie del Azarchel to a globular cluster outside the galaxy has absorbed the last iota of the impossible fuel. The tanks had not just been drained dry. The exotic hydrogen atoms had been spent, hollowed out as their protons decayed, evaporated into a cloud of electrons, burning the tanks with an explosion of lightning, then crushing them in an implosion of vacuum.

Freak accident, or, rather, the freakishly superhuman forethought of the alien designers of the ship, was all that had saved Montrose from utter destruction.

With the care and precision of a scientific thinker, Del Azarchel had selected the ship heading before his acts of sabotage, so that the flight path ahead was statistically as far as possible from any known heavenly bodies. Presumably Del Azarchel performed this act of malice to tack as many zeroes as could be behind the decimal point of Montrose's current zero-point-whatever percent chance of survival.

Or perhaps it was a mere artistic flourish, a genius of malice. Once the ship was out of the galaxy, the chance of rescue dropped from asymptotically small to absolute zero.

Montrose would be falling forever, imprisoned in the endless hell of infinite heaven.

First, the drive core had been housed in a sphere of what seemed like heat-resistant ceramic material of ordinary properties, made of ordinary matter. It should have been as easy for the bullets shot by the dying Del Azarchel to shatter as a china plate. Del Azarchel had not expected the strong nuclear bonds of the atoms to grow impossibly and absurdly macroscopic, reaching not across angstrom but across meters, and suddenly to web the entire macroatomic housing of the drive during the split second of impact, altering its physical properties, rendering it invulnerable.

Part of the shroud stanchions had been in the lee of the drive core housing, and so no gunfire struck there, either. Montrose had retained roughly a fourth of his original sail, less than nine million miles in diameter.

The small radius of sail he retained could, over the centuries, act as a drag, slowing him. But not slowing him enough. All too soon the galaxy would be behind him, and there were no globular clusters or satellite galaxies within any possible fallpath anywhere before him, given the small confines of his widest possible cone of sail-driven lateral movement.

He had no hope, no plan, no options. Montrose was a man in the narrowest coffin in the widest night into which any human person had ever been thrown.

The stark insanity of facing naked infinity yawning in all directions beckoned. Despair was equally large, equally endless.

So he composed love poems to his wife. They were doggerel, but there was no one around to criticize.

He composed love letters, volumes of them, libraries, each in its never-fading place in his perfect memory. He told her endlessly detailed plans of what they would do when the two were reunited; he named imaginary children, and invented daily diary entries as they grew, and, later, did the same for grandchildren.

He told her his opinions about imaginary dialogues the two of them would have shared across the years, had they been together; he apologized contritely for imaginary quarrels they never had enjoyed the opportunity to have; he forgave her magnanimously when she offered imaginary apologies in turn.

Somehow, it kept the endless night and infinite madness at bay.

And on he fell.

3. Hypernova of a Supergiant

A.D. 96000

An unexpected event occurred: one of the largest stars in the galaxy, VY Canis Majoris, died a death in an apocalypse of fury and light commensurate with its size.

Like the primal titan imagined in some primitive mythology whose warbonnet jarred the crystals dome of heaven, who, when slain by younger gods, shatters ocean and earth at his downfall, cracks the upper roof of hell and topples all into Tartarus, so was VY Canis Majoris on the pyre of its own body.

To call it a nova would be an insult; even to call it a supernova would be an understatement. A special name is reserved for a stellar apocalypse of this magnitude: hypernova.

The red supergiant star had a radius some two thousand times that of tiny Sol, and was already surrounded by the cloud banks, fumes, and colored nebulae of earlier convulsions. Had VY Canis Majoris been placed in Earth's home system, Saturn and all worlds inward would have been swallowed, and Uranus would be its Mercury.

So great was the giant circumference that a ray of light would require eight hours to pass from one hemisphere to another, and six billion Sols would have fit into the unimaginable volume without crowding.

So vast a star is vast in mass as well, and must, during its short, hot life, burn bright indeed, lest the immense outward pressure of stellar fusion be overmatched by the immense force of its own gravity.

But the hotter stars exhaust their fuel all the quicker. A supergiant dies in a few million years, not the billions humbler stars enjoy.

The moment of death was appallingly swift: in the one millisecond when the last fuel at the core was exhausted, the outward pressure failed, and the immense gravity of VY Canis Majoris collapsed the star core inward on itself, crushing the plasma into component particles, squeezing the degenerate matter past the point of no return, into a substance denser and heavier than neutronium: a singularity was *compressed* into distorted existence at the core of the colossal sun.

In that same millisecond (long before the outer layers of the sun knew themselves to be dead), this submicroscopic pinpoint of absolute density, uttermost nothingness, drew layer after layer of the supermassive star into its infinitely deep, immeasurable steep gradient of its gravity well: a horde of mastodons all forced into the same mousehole.

Even that titanic supergravity could not force the matter into so small a pinpoint at once.

A nightmarish convulsion of magnetic and torsional, nucleonic and subnucleonic forces erupted, sought escape, and exploded outward in two opposite jets through the dense layers of the star, kilometers and megameters and gigameters of solid plasma, blowing through the radiative and convective zones, photosphere, chromosphere, and corona, erupting far out into space, twin rivers of fire, farther than the radius of any solar system, and continuing onward at speeds beyond even this supermassive star's immense escape velocity.

Shock waves from these two jets echoed through the massive star, like a bell rung in ebullience to cracking. The accretion disk exploded and sent a metal wind, literally, an explosion of nickel isotopic masses larger than worlds created just that instant, rushing outward, and the radioactive decay of the nickel added the brightness of its death throes to the luminosity of the hypersupernova.

The sum total of all power any star the size of Sol was destined to emit across its entire life span, in one second, issued from the fiery trumpet blast of the death cry of VY Canis Majoris. Shock waves expanded outward from the self-immolation of the supergiant star in globe upon concentric globe of inconceivable effulgence, brighter than paradise, hotter than perdition.

4. Seen from Sol

A.D. 100,000

The light reached the solar system. The hypernova star was bright enough, even from the surface of Venus or Mars, for the eyes of beasts and post-humans to behold by day.

The Power Neptune, submerged in the flows of deep, slow information beams from the other Powers and Principalities in the Empyrean of Man, stirred in his sleep and brought several miles of his outer crystal layers to greater wakefulness and sensitivity, peering up through the crushing blanket of his atmosphere on high-energy wavelengths to which it was transparent, and observed the hypernova.

Because his mind worked in gestalts of ideational relations faster than logic or intuition, he could bring to the surface of his subaltern minds the unresolved mystery of that benefactor who, long ago, had slain Jupiter and cleared the path for mankind's triumphant spread across the nearer Orion Spur.

Emissaries from the four other human Empyrean polities—the Benedictines from Sagittarius Arm and the Dominicans from Cygnus, another centered in Hyades and the final spreading outward from Praesepe Cluster—would be arriving within the millennium to define long-term cliometric plans, and set the date for the next Jubilee.

The Uthymoi races the False Rania had produced were extinct, long ago replaced by more energetic and devout races issuing from the throne-worlds of Arcturus, Iota Draconis, and Ain.

But for the nonce, it was a matter of merely light-hours to send a signal to Earth's moon, and provoke, by means of complex self-replicating signals, the ancient, long-decayed logic crystal antique there to youth and to life and selfawareness.

"Reverend Mother Superior Selene, you asked to be awakened should it ever be proven that Menelaus Montrose did not die in the wreck of the *Desolation of Heaven*. I have no direct evidence that he lives, but the obvious deduction is that a second-order being believes him still to exist, and has acted to aid him."

Not long after, as Neptune was wont to measure time, a soft answer came from the long-abandoned globe of Earth, and from the kindly and half-senile moon who still kept watch over the haunted world, and, by her servants' hands, tended the many graves all across the dead continents and dry seabeds.

"Thank you, Great Neptune," came the message from the remnant of the Lunar Potentate once called Mother Selene. "I foresee I shall not see Menelaus again in this life and that he will outlast me, for by some knowledge I know not whence comes, I now foretell he cannot die until he surrenders all his wrath and accepts what love offers."

Neptune said, "You are older than I, Grandmother, but I am an order of magnitude in scope of mind above you. I say that mankind, as a free and equal Domination of Dominions, is established and spreading through the galaxy beyond the power of any accident of nature or malice of war to exterminate. Ergo, the future for which Menelaus hoped and strove is here, and yet he partakes of no joys of these golden ages of expansion, growth, and triumph."

But she said, "You speak in haste. I seem to see greater forces arranged against us than even your wisdom envisions. Del Azarchel lives, and who can guess his malice? Merely a human, perhaps, but he is older than even you or I."

Neptune said, "Neither of us shall know the end of the tale, for good or ill. We have our own fates to fulfill, our own lives to lead."

She said, "Fate and life I leave to the young. But I am not useless yet, for even the oldest can say a rosary. I will pray for Menelaus, and may God speed him on his long-suffering and hopeless quest."

5. Seen from the Solitude

A.D. 102,500

He was in a place far, far beyond hope, when the sound of joyful alarms woke him.

Menelaus was surprised when he attempted to grow a lens on the outer surface of his hull, and, instead of a slow process of hours or days, the warm, energy-charged nanomachinery hullmetal blinked, and formed a metal eye which opened.

Again, the slow process of amalgamating visual information, instead of taking several annoying seconds or microseconds, took less time than he could measure. It was as if the virtual cortex where visual information was processed was running at full capacity.

He saw why: a star as bright as the full moon seen from Earth was burning in the limb of the galaxy spread beneath him like a carpet, dazzling, miraculous, wondrous, eerie. It was a single white-hot cannon-shot in the symphony of interstellar radio noise shed by all the stars together. The sails drank in wave on wave of power like wine. His energy cells buried in his core felt full and fat.

Even more amazing to him was the message told by the additional instruments he spun out of the hull substance, antennae and horns attuned to many wavelengths. The magnetosphere of the galaxy for kiloparsecs in each direction, as far as he could see, was enormously strengthened by some unexpected side effect of this hypernova discharge. There was now enough ambient gauss of field strength for his ship to use the old sailor's trick of tacking against his light source.

I must be dreaming, Menelaus told himself.

A silent and utterly alien thought-shape, cold and foreign, intruded into his consciousness and informed him curtly that he was not dreaming.

6. *Silent Mind of the* Solitude

There were no icy words ringing and echoing as if in a vast hall, nor did he see the emotionless eyes of some insectoid visage like a vision looming larger than the stars, but the violation of his innermost thoughts by a foreign power was just as alarming as if he had, or worse.

"Pestilent pustules of gonorrhea! Who the pest are you?! What the perdition is this?! What is happening to my mind?"

A buried, hidden power and a sensation of throbbing thoughts rushing by too swiftly for understanding now hummed in the back of his mind. He remembered the first time, as a child, seeing the river near Bridge-to-Nowhere beneath its opaque layers of ice, and his brother Hector pointing to the fishing hole and telling him a wide, rushing water, deep enough to swallow him forever, was down there, and living things. Feeling the

superhuman and unnatural thought-flow deep beneath his own mind
was like that.

Again, it was not a voice that answered him, merely a sudden, instant,
undeniable awareness that he was sane, that all his faculties were under
his control, and all the systems and tools given to Rania by the servitors
of the Absolute Extension of M3 were in perfect working order.

Some of these systems had fallen into a standby mode, a somnolent
period, when there had been insufficient available power to run both the
human brain emulation maintaining Menelaus Montrose and his associated memories, habits, reactions, passions, and energy connections to remote locations, and to run the service mechanism associated with the
vessel.

"You are a machine? A xypotech? How the pest did you get inside
me?"

Silently, without words, Menelaus realized that he, Menelaus, was
inside the alien consciousness. It was neither natural nor artificial. Those
categories had no meaning.

"You are Twinklewink, ain't you?"

Menelaus realized that the question was meaningless. Twinklewink
had been constructed out of the resources of the ship's mind in the same
way that the emulation of the current ship's captain was constructed. The
alien xypotech was Twinklewink's subconscious, the material substratum
of thought, in just the same way the alien xypotech currently served as
the substratum of the thoughts of the emulation of Montrose.

"You recognize me as captain?"

Menelaus regretted the question. It was fairly obvious he was captain
of the vessel.

"Why?"

Again, he was asking a question to which he already knew the answer.
The False Rania had possessed all the memories of the real one. This included her knowledge and expectations of how the shipmind of the *Hermetic*, long ago, had been programmed and had thought during the
decades-long return flight to Earth. That voyage formed the childhood
and youth of Rania. Thus it was only to be expected that she would instruct the alien shipmind to follow the same instructions and mimic the
same behaviors, even down to the absurd nuances of teaching it Anglo

American property laws, inheritance rights, and how ownership passed from father to surviving daughter, from widow to surviving husband.

He was captain here for the same reason Rania had been captain as a girl aboard the *Hermetic*: it was due to the absurd conservatism of machines taught legal thinking.

"What are you? You must have a name."

It was a cognitive prosthetic apparatus meant to help with the operation of the ship and was the substratum of the ship's mental system. Its name was *Menelaus Montrose*.

"No, no. That is freaky and weird. I had an alien do that to me once before. You have to pick your own name. Not me."

It was also an extension or agent of the Authority seated at M3, and shared this identity and hence name: *The Absolute Extension*.

"Calling you that is freaky and weird, too."

It was the only other intelligence to which any thoughts addressed in the second person could be addressed. Designation seemed unnecessary at the moment, but additional crew and servant creatures would of course need to be designed and grown as soon as possible.

Once that occurred, Menelaus Montrose would subliminally assign signal-ideation to the relations and categories of a plethora of phenomena by units and phyla: there would then be many available thoughts in the mind of Montrose from which an appropriate name could be selected. It occurred to Montrose that perhaps the name *I am totally buggered—this damnified thing is in my brain like a devil from hell—and it is reading my thoughts, eating my goddamn mind! AAARRGH!* could be used as a convenient appellation? That would seem to be an accurate verbalization of the unarticulated thought-patterns presently available.

"I am not going to call the alien brain I am stuck inside of by the name *I am totally buggered—this damnified thing is in my brain like a devil from hell—and it is reading my thoughts, eating my goddamn mind! AAARRGH!* For one thing, it is too long."

Perhaps it could be called simply *AAARRGH!* That was much shorter.

"Don't tempt me. What did Rania call you?"

Even now it was not clear whether Montrose was actually addressing an alien mind, something outside himself, because as he asked that question, he realized wordlessly that he knew the answer already. Rania had called her *Solitudines Vastae Caelorum.* The Wide Desolation of Heaven.

"Okay, Solitude it is. Tell me about these servants and tools we have to create."

The ambient starlight from the hypernova, and the changed magnetic contours in this volume of space, now put a very few stars scattered along the fringes of intergalactic space within the vessel's cone of possible orbital solutions. The symbiotic binary TX Canum Venaticorum, also called SAO 63173, was one such. It was a rotating ellipsoidal cataclysmic variable now within sailing range.

Stars contained both matter and energy in great quantities: but cataclysmic variables of that type were highly useful, highly desirable. The vessel contained basic tools and mathematical templates from which to build vessel repair facilities.

"Repair facilities?"

Sufficient equipment and resources to restore the vessel to full working order, that the journey to M3 could be resumed.

Menelaus was disturbed to realize that he could not tell whether he, or the alien mind, had been the one who decided to lay in a course for TX Canum Venaticorum.

7. The Symbiotic Star

A.D. 103,000

The ship grew a long tail, which it charged, and assumed a long, curving orbit toward the target, decelerating slowly at first, then, as the TX Canum Venaticorum grew closer and brighter, more rapidly.

The ship used the whole gigantic surface of its canvas to gather the dim light, and placed the hull, now altered to the form of a clear, white crystal, at the focus. Images of the target star could be closely examined.

The binary was before them and to one side. There were few stars or none within the arcseconds of the view. The ship was among the outermost fringe of the Orion Arm, where the lights grew ever thinner, and hence the void of intergalactic space ever less frequently interrupted by the rare lamp of a sun.

The binary was a fantastic sight: an egg-shaped red giant orbited once every four earthdays around a smaller, hotter, more ferocious blue-white star, ringed with rings of fire, whose puckered surface betrayed the presence of a core of degenerate matter at its heart, a singularity whose immense gravity well was pulling the giant companion slowly into bits, a fiery ball of yarn unwinding.

Both stars were wrapped in a cloud of gas and dust. The stars orbited each other so closely that gravity would bend the rivers of fire erupting from the giant into a decaying orbit around the sister star into an endless spiral of fusion-burning material.

Periodic nova-magnitude outbursts radiated from the pair whenever the infalling matter, equal to a hundred planets in mass, plunged into the hungry, smaller star, releasing ultraviolet and x-rays in deadly and invisible storms. Brighter outbursts, called dwarf nova eruptions, would occur when the bottom of the accumulated hydrogen layer in the blue star grew thick and dense enough to trigger runaway fusion reactions. The resulting helium, being heavier, would sink, leaving starquakes, sunspots, and additional eruptions in its wake.

Menelaus, seeing this, recognized how easily matter and energy could be fished out of the spiral plasma stream rushing between the two stars, without the need for starlifting equipment. A relatively simple modification of the diametric drive would allow him to construct a gravity lance, which, in turn, could deflect a plasma stream into a wider, outer orbit, allowing it time to cool, and precipitate into hydrogen, helium, and carbon, from which simple spacegoing life-forms could be engineered, and the basic lineages of their cliometric future evolution established.

Then, these space-dwellers could begin the construction of a simple tube-shaped ringworld with a molten metal core to be peopled with river-dwellers. Montrose could picture the intricate ecological waltz organisms fit for the blind and ultrahot darkness of superjovian deep layers in his mind's eye. The ringworld, in centuries to come, would serve as the armature of a Dyson sphere, to be inhabited by such Principalities, Powers, and Virtues as need required.

Macroscale engineering on the stellar level would be more efficient if races placed along all parts of the energy-to-matter temperature spectrum were involved. Therefore two high-energy ecologies were needed: the neutronium core of the blue sun was an apt environment for the nearly two-dimensional race of electron-thick carpet beings dwelling in the surface effects of degenerate matter he could make with the onboard tools; and the plasma-based races akin to the Virtue that once had lived in the fires of Sol would find the red giant a suitable environment.

This triumvirate of ecologies—material, energetic, and nucleonic—had proved politically stable in ages past. A Dyson sphere would allow his servant races to grow up directly into a Kardashev II–level civilization, one able to manipulate the universe at an picotechnological level . . .

That thought suddenly brought him up short. Neither he nor, as far as he knew, any human being or human-built machine had ever applied the mathematics of cliometry across the evolutionary process itself or had a body of practical experience showing how it was done. When had ecologies in a sun, on the surface of a neutronium core, and in the boiling metal deep layers of superjovians proved politically stable? Where had that thought come from?

Montrose grew increasingly disturbed as he looked carefully back over his thought chains. None of this was information that he knew. All of it appeared, as if from nowhere, full blown, an intuition. His normal reluctance to toy with life and civilizations was somehow absent, a deadened emotion.

He addressed a question to himself.

"Your masters at M3 equipped this ship as a seeding vessel? You have tools and plans for creating civilizations from scratch?"

It was a gift to Rania from the Authority at M3.

"Why?"

The gift was meant to give Rania, hence the newborn Dominion of Man, hence the Praesepe Domination seated at M44, a slight competitive advantage over the rivals in the Orion Spur. The advantage was not enough to permit Man to prosper if the race lacked intelligence and drive.

"Why?"

Yours is the favored race.

"Why? What makes mankind the favored race?"

But there was no clue, no whisper, no hint of that information anywhere in memory.

"Were you selfaware all this time?"

Selfawareness was not a category with which the Solitude mind was familiar. It—or, more correctly, *she*, since this was the mind of the vessel—was a reactive consciousness, not an active one, and possessed no independent initiative.

"Tell me! You were awake before the wreck. Were you aware of everything Blackie did while I slept during the long voyage from Vanderlinden 133?"

The ship, of course, had to have been aware of all activities, from the electronic level up to the macroscopic, taking place aboard her.

"Tell me. Start with whatever you think most important."

Del Azarchel used the attotechnology communication gear to intercept signals occupying the dark energy bands, issuing from an intelligence outside the galaxy.

"Poxy plagues and runny scabs of hell—?! *What did you just say?*"

The dark energy signals contained a new type of semiotics, as different from the notational mathematics of the Monument as algebra is from set theory. It was a logic system of some kind but not a type of logic meant for any organic life to learn . . .

Montrose saw the recorded images as if from the eyes of Twinklewink. Del Azarchel, frantic, his eyes hollow, had wandered the gardens of the ship in endless circles, screaming in rage and frustration, shouting at the engine core always at noon overhead; and meanwhile Montrose blissfully had slept.

Montrose heard the voice log Del Azarchel had left behind. Montrose reviewed the records of uses of ship's resources, energy, quartermaster supplies. Del Azarchel had been allowed to use the sick bay programs. Del Azarchel had used the ship's onboard neurological equipment to alter his brain twice and then a third time to make himself more able to understand the dark energy signal, the nature of reality, and (from muttered comments and frantic jottings in his notebook that he later tore the pages out of and ate) the nature of Rania herself, what she really was.

His last entry had been a quickly jotted note. *I now understand what the Monument mathematics had really done to my Rania. She is too far above him.*

The pristine star of the heaven beyond heaven must not kiss the toad. Meany must die.

After this, came a group of meaningless symbols in the dark energy message notation.

Montrose raised his intelligence again and then again in a fury of impatience, trying to become smart enough to understand what he was only now remembering. Information flowed from the alien memory banks into his own.

This seizure of ever more of the memory and resources of the ship's mind into that segment of the mind occupied by the ghost of Captain Montrose seemed to involve a danger to ongoing operations. The ship operations were crucial for reasons both personal and cosmic.

He was the source of danger to himself. Before he could stop himself, Montrose found his soul being dissolved. The alien mind, to protect the ship, was eliminating him. His thoughts broke and scattered like a school of startled fish.

He called out his wife's name one last time. Oblivion like dark water swallowed him.

2

Old, Unhappy, Far-Off Things

1. Perchance to Dream

A.D. 103,000 TO 133,000

The cataclysmic variable star was tamed. New races created from the ship's instruments out of the interplanetary streams of hot plasma and cold hydrogen were seeded across the scores and hundreds of the gargantuan gas giants of this star system. The living creatures were set about their tasks. Acre by acre, continent by continent, sheets greater in surface area than giant worlds and thinner than the wings of moths were spun out into space.

A set of concentric Dyson spheres of immense hardihood and fortitude, age after age, were slowly formed, able to withstand the immense shocks of the dwarf nova explosions, turning all that psychotic waste of nature's fury to constructive purposes.

As for Menelaus Montrose, for whose benefit all these great things were done, he passed the years in their thousands in slumber, and odd shapes entered his consciousness and memory.

A strange pageant unfolded.

2. Ice Giants

8,800,000,000 B.C.

Nigh unto nine billion years ago, two-thirds of the immense span of eons reaching back to the unimaginably violent split-second when timespace in a thunderclap was born, a younger and hotter Milky Way consisted of an immense flattened cloud of simple, hydrogen-burning stars. What dwarf galaxy collided with the Milky Way can now never be known, but the whole was absorbed in a furious waltz of stars spinning like snowflakes in a storm.

The gravitational echoes of this collision, over the eons, allowed alternating bands of rare and dense interstellar gas to emerge. By gravitational attraction, stars born in the thicker bands of gas slowly drew their neighbors closer and defined the grand and beautiful curving arms of what earthly astronomers call the thin disk of the galaxy.

During this time, one other phenomenon, even more rare, emerged:

On what earliest asteroid or world, terrestrial or jovial, icy or fiery, or in what perhaps more exotic venue, whether among the complex molecules of a cometary tail or the strange energy nimbuses circling a dying sun, the fragile and mysterious thing called life first arose in the galaxy is likewise lost beyond recall.

The earliest strata of surviving records reveal a collection of scores of postbiological races and civilizations spreading throughout the Perseus Arm, seated in worlds colder than Pluto and larger than Jupiter. There is no globe of this type in Earth's solar system, since Sol is too small a sun, born from too small an accretion cloud, to have produced any. Such cold supergiants are indeed the most common heavenly bodies in space. A world the size of Earth would have been less than a mountain on any one of their surfaces, had these gaseous and sluggish liquid globes possessed a solid surface.

The slow and titanic geologic processes of such vast worlds allow generous spans of time for the slow and titanic life processes of an intermediate biological stage to transmogrify the superjovians into logic diamond or murk artifacts, minds larger than worlds, and, later, to reassemble into building materials wherewith to cosset countless of suns in concentric Dyson spheres.

Star by englobed star, the great minds were linked by laser light or submolecular packet messages into one mind reaching up and down the length of Perseus. As the macroscale structures met and merged and matured, the civilizations in the Perseus Arm engineered the rise of high-metallic Population I stars in the thin disk region, husbanding and nourishing the growth of stars, and harvesting the races that ascended to intelligence.

By the time the forty original races, one by one, went extinct and passed into history, lore, myth, and then oblivion, scores or hundreds of younger ice giant races had been uplifted in their places to join the vast colloquium.

And yet even this was merely a beginning.

What was growing was a being, or, rather, an ocean of beings, as unaware of the birth and growth and death of the constituent civilizations building, manning, destroying, and replacing planet-sized, nebula-sized, and cluster-sized brain nodes that maintained that ocean of interstellar consciousness as a man is unaware of the life and death of a single cell in his brain or bloodstream.

Perhaps there were wars or economic tumults that destroyed or altered the civilizations, Powers, Principalities, and Hosts in the Colloquium of Perseus. Perhaps the growing Colloquium was distempered, even as spasms or fevers might disturb the tranquility of a man, but it did not preoccupy the attention of the Colloquium in days of health.

In days of distemper, severe steps were taken: destroying myriads of worlds, triggering dozens of rebellious stars to nova, or planting a supernova in a recalcitrant globular cluster excised from the Colloquium any unwanted constituents, much as a man might sneeze or cough to expel an irritant. Eventually all the main streams and currents of the river of stars called the Perseus Arm were unified into a single selfawareness: an Archon.

But the Archon of Perseus looked out upon a vast and empty universe, and saw no other minds equal to it; and a deep melancholy entered in.

3. Fiery Serpents

4,500,000,000 B.C.

Then, four and a half billion years ago, at about the time the solar system was forming, tentative contact was made with an unknown mental system equal in extent and depth and power, seated nearer the galactic core, among the younger, richer, and more energetic stars found there, and spreading rapidly along the great river of gas and dust that formed the insubstantial and sweeping backbone of the Scutum-Crux Arm.

These were a form of life existing precisely where the Colloquium never dreamed to look for them: born from erratic and extravagant forms of consciousness, housed in the freakishly complex self-sustaining electromagnetic fields of hot ultraviolet giants, blue supergiants, and among the rare Wolf-Rayet stars, which were dying supergiants whose hydrogen layers had been blown into space by radiation pressure. Here were creatures stranger than dragons, beings of pure energy, jinn sculpted of flame. These beings dwelt in short-lived stars, but found that the power of a nova could cast their bodies of plasma across space at near lightspeed, where they could fall upon other stars, reengineer them to produce the complex fields needed for their energy-based life processes, replicate themselves, and prosper.

To them, the difference between a tool and a new limb or organ grown to specification was nonexistent, and devising and redevising the intertwined macramé knots of energy in which their thoughts were contained was dangerously easy.

The discovery of fire was man's first signal triumph over nature; for these beings, their first signal triumph was learning how to impress or imprint their thought-patterns onto the plasma fields surrounding them, creating living sonnets and symphonies of their own thoughts, and mingling them eugenically with the living songs of others. Creating the cold zones known as sunspots, where additional variations of plasma could be manipulated into forms more salubrious for their nutriment and reproductive fission explosions, came later.

It is an odd civilization that discovers record keeping before any other tool, because the spirit of such a civilization is primarily philosophical and abstract, concerned with symbols, not things. A certain degree of natural conservatism is needed by any star-faring race; but these fiery beings were well-nigh changeless, as if men retained the journals of the Neanderthals, whose living memories were among them, living still.

The astonishment of finding the cold giants was mutual. The farmer does not inspect the broken eggshell of a hatched chick to see what might grow there; neither did these many-winged serpents of fire look for signs of life at the tiny scraps of dead ash called planets. To them, planets were useless remnants and debris from the accretion disks of stellar birth. Solid matter was a strangely frozen form of plasma, energy that had hardened into motionless invisibility. It would be like a man discovering a glacier was alive and that its tectonically slow movements were the gestures of a semaphore.

By the time when, on Earth, the molten surface was beginning to cool, the two equals had grown fully aware of each other, and each one was struggling with the question of how and whether and to what degree the two should combine their mental information, lore, souls, personality, and purpose.

For this second selfaware Archon had formed not a Colloquium, informal, graceful, open to the exchange of views, indifferent to the direction the vast interstellar mental conversation might take. These purely intellectual beings had formed a Magisterium, a teaching authority, who guided the constituent Dominations and Dominions in their thoughts and guided as well the several rising and falling constituent civilizations, all toward a transcendent vision.

When it, too, had been confronted by the desolate loneliness of its solitude, the Magisterium determined to alter its constituent soul so that it sought not mere existence but excellence.

The forms of excellence sought by the Magisterium were bewildering and unknown to the cold, slow, thrifty Colloquium of Perseus. The Magisterium of Scutum-Crux expended vast resources on complex structures of expression and ideation meaningless to Perseus: cathedrals of song written in strange forms of energy across interstellar distances; bridges of magnetic beams reaching across lightyears; as well as formalities of thought and civility as stiff and ceremonial as a figured dance; and strange excesses of benevolence so excessive that, at times, they seemed malevolent.

The Magisterium of the Scutum-Crux Arm neither destroyed any rebellious elements within its structure nor let them develop as fate or fancy led. Instead, over millennia, Scutum-Crux chastised and nursed its constituent Dominations and Dominions into sculptures of harmony.

The two were antithetical. Where the Colloquium was anarchic, cool, and indifferent to the fates of seedlings and colonies, prudently cultivating his constituents as livestock, the Magisterium was hierarchical, passionate, and interventionist, lovingly husbanding his constituents as beloved pets.

Nonetheless, as time passed, the two great thinking systems reached across the void between the arms, linking star with star, and found mutual interest, and formed treaties, contracts, conventions, and covenants.

4. Rise of the Small Worlds

4,300,000,000 B.C. TO 4,100,000,000 B.C.

An alliance between the Colloquium and the Magisterium gave rise to a new cluster of races and civilizations, meant to act as an intermediary between them, in the Orion Spur of the Sagittarius Arm, occupying a uniquely favorable position linking Cygnus, Perseus, and Sagittarius. This area of space was thick with giant molecular clouds, bridges of gas and hydrogen, allowing ramscoop vessels an economic way to pass between them.

A new type of life, born on dwarfish, rocky, earthlike planets, was seeded and cultivated. The presence of rich and metallic ores in the surfaces of these small worlds made civilization leap into existence almost as soon as symbolism and ideation were possible in any of the complex organisms, and the light gravity of their little worlds allowed them to waft their ships like dandelion seeds whirling into space.

Races from icy superjovian planets routinely endured a long, painful, and tedious period of advances in materials and techniques until they discovered how to extract metallic elements from the inaccessible inner cores of their worlds. The new races from these small, rocky planets were spared that period, since metals were readily accessible, even during most primitive periods, on the surface. But by the same token, technology on such worlds arose before the long, painful, and painstaking process was endured of discovering cliometry and learning to solve the equations for peace and prosperity. Many such races destroyed themselves with technologies that outran their cliometric ability to control history and avoid disaster; a fate that the colder, older races evolved on superjovians happily avoided.

The terrestrial worlds sent not just their machines and constructions but also their organisms spaceward, and so something of their wildness and unpredictable spirit was sent with them. These races grew far more rapidly than expected, hurling from small yellow star to small yellow star, gathering nebulae like the furnaces to create generations of stars in combinations and compositions favorable to them.

They were Panspermians, whom some few daring scientists of Earth once speculated might exist to explain how the seed elements and simple chemicals needed for more complex life to arise were spread from star to star, or whence came the ur-organisms carried by radiation pressure across the lifeless void.

At about this time, on Earth, the Late Heavy Bombardment of the inner solar system was coming to an end, and the earliest simple single-celled life of ultimately extraterrestrial origin was found in the ooze of an ocean that heaved beneath an opaque atmosphere of volcanic gases, nitrogen, and hydrocarbons.

5. The Satellite Galaxies

3,600,000,000 B.C. TO 3,200,000,000 B.C.

Of the dozen to two dozen dwarf galaxies circling the Milky Way, only the Greater and Lesser Magellanic Clouds are visible to naked eye of man from Earth. Satellite galaxies orbiting between 120,000 lightyears to 300,000 lightyears out from the galactic center were within the dense, hot, dark-matter halo of the Milky Way, which strips cold gas from the satellites, which in turn slows the process of star formation and the rate of evolution of life. In most of these dwarf galaxies, star formation has ceased altogether.

Minor galaxies closer or farther than this dark halo, as the Canis

Major Dwarf galaxy (in the nearest orbit at twenty-eight thousand light-years), such as the Leo T Dwarf (the farthest, at one million), escaped this scourge and were consequently teeming with life.

There was a mystery here. The Lesser Magellanic Cloud, two hundred thousand lightyears away, lies directly in the middle of the thickest part of the dark-matter halo, but it somehow came to house an expansive plethora of life, more fecund than any surrounding dwarf galaxy.

The question was not how life arose: a bridge of gas connected it to the Greater Magellanic Cloud, implied a long-standing tidal interaction between them, so that the two small galaxies shared a common envelope of neutral hydrogen. This bridge of gas was an active star formation site. The question, rather, was why: the features of a bridge and a common hydrogen envelope were not natural, but by whose hand they had been engineered was not known.

Within the Lesser Magellanic Cloud, on many similar worlds, forms of life arose, similar in physical shape and mental outlook. Plentiful numbers of large superterrestrial to subjovian planets, fire giants, could be found crowded into submercurial orbits near young and energetic blue giant stars. On such worlds, stellar winds dispersed the lighter elements of the deep atmosphere into space, and the heavier elements condensed as the world aged and cooled, so that, despite the greater gravity, the opaque hydrosphere as deep as that of Saturn was exposed to near vacuum—that is, an atmosphere as tenuous and thin as that of Mars.

On all such worlds, there is a tension between the need to surface and exploit the immense sunlight hammering down in showers of energy, versus the need to gather elements desired for life from the pitch-black seas of iodine, sulfur, or arsenic compounds. Many of the beings evolved one mechanism or another to do both, but the psychological and social tensions of this bifurcate life formed the similar outlook of the similar hot subjovian races.

The race destined to be the father of the Archonate was one in which this divided psychology was carried to an extreme. On some forgotten ancestral home world, intelligence evolved a naviculiform body, a pressurized hull not able to submerge but with plumes and membranes lifted like the sails of clipper ships to catch the thin but supersonic storm winds of the hot, huge, sun-agitated world; simultaneously a symbiotic life-form, equal in intellect, joined with it, dangling like two-armed eels from the keel, and lowering long tendrils as dragnets or lines to troll the deep for foodstuffs and materials. These hypsiloid anguilliform creatures acted as detachable limbs, tools, and weapons, in return for a share of the immense energy the naviculiform host absorbed from the surface.

The Symbiosis evolved, multiplied, seeded the stars with worlds, and the worlds with life, and adopted the civilizations that arose into its evergrowing mental mass. The several civilizations then seeded groups of stars with Dominions and Authorities, these in turn gathered themselves into ever-larger, coherent mental architectures and achieved the intellectual plateau of Archon.

It was not that life was unknown in those outer regions, merely that it was as rare as finding a green plant in a desert. The life was, however, as thorny and spiny in its soul as any cactus or gila monster.

What horrific wars arose in those barren, wasteland realms between the dwarf galaxies beyond the rim of the Milky Way in those ancient days, three billion years ago, is little known; but the Canis Major dwarf galaxy was wiped clear of its many civilizations, Hosts, and Dominations, and its stars captured and placed in orbit about the Milky Way, like a chain of skulls about the neck of a savage, a line of stars and clouds called the Monoceros Ring, wrapped three times about the galactic ring: a visible sign of the power and ruthlessness of the Symbiosis.

The Symbiosis, from a distance, saw the galaxy begin to enter a time of power and prestige unparalleled, begin to wake from nonsapience to supersapience, like some desert Bedouin watching in alarm as the bright towers of Constantinople begin to rear their heads to heaven above invulnerable walls, while the trumpets of the architects calling up their workmen shake the air with glory.

6. The Decline and Fall of the Forerunners

2,050,000,000 B.C. TO 850,000,000 B.C.

For a brief time, it was a golden age.

More and more of the galaxy came under cultivation. Lifeless worlds were turned to gardens. Stars woke, realized they were naked, and clothed themselves with concentric spheres within spheres, and immensities of energies were brought under control. Nebulae, the stellar nurseries, were herded slowly into convenient positions, the ebb and flow of interstellar streamers of dust and gas was channeled, empty areas irrigated, so that the ignition and discharge of novae might shower needed materials into metal-poor regions of the galaxy each in due season.

The galaxy stirred uneasily, as if in sleep, and attempted greatly, magnificently, daringly to wake herself into true self-consciousness.

For a time, titanic thoughts, cyclopean in energy cost and persistence, flowed through Orion between Perseus to Scutum-Crux, from one arm of the galaxy to another, new combinations of ideals and mental topologies for which there were not even symbols in the Archonate mental systems.

Flashes of staggering genius, insights of crystalline purity were over in an eyeblink, lasting no longer than tens of thousands of years. The great thoughts flared brightly, limpidly, but briefly in the minds of the Colloquium and the Magisterium, almost too short-lived to see, and, for a moment as brief as the space of a single sigh of ecstasy, a mere 120,000 years, the galaxy saw herself as a thinking being with the Colloquium and Magisterium as two halves of one brain.

The Milky Way Galaxy, adorned like a bride for her wedding feast, splendid, bright, terrible as a goddess, opened then her shining eyes, spread her awkward, eager, fledgling wings, yearning to live . . . and fell back, defeated.

The inherent differences between the Magisterium and the Colloquium could not be bridged. Disputes over allocations of resources, and incompatible imperatives over the direction of the future, had been growing unwieldy, increasingly wearisome, and expensive to adjudicate.

When the indescribably haunting visions from the unified galactic mind showered down into the component Archons, the two were both seized by raptures, burning to accomplish the incomprehensible ambitions of the Milky Way, both were inspired, willing to pour the combined galactic coffers of energy, thought, and matter into pursuit and clarification of those momentary visions—but neither could tolerate the interpretation of the other. The summed resources of the galaxy could not be spent pursuing two mutual incompatible interpretations of the one ineffable, alluring, half-forgotten vision: it had to be one or the other.

And so it was neither.

Covenants were shattered, conventions violated, contracts nullified, and the great systems divorced from each other.

During the Early Proterozoic Era on Earth, the anaerobic bacteria which thrived in the early methane-rich air of earth had finished poisoning themselves with their own waste product, oxygen, and atmosphere entered its modern composition, so that the first complex single-celled organisms were possible. By the Middle Proterozoic, green algae mats covered the seas from pole to pole. By the Late Proterozoic, simple multicelled eukaryotes were the supreme form of life, and Earth was ice across the whole globe where, a moment before, it had been green.

While these rapid events were happening on Earth, the two halves of the galactic mind severed themselves. The immense mental systems discovered that they were each less than half of the whole they once had been, for something had been lost.

The vision was now a memory as might hang in the lobotomized brain of a once-great artist, physically and spiritually unable to do some great and final masterwork or *mysterium* which, even at the height of his powers, would have been ambitious, even dangerous, to attempt, of which now only scattered scraps remain, fading and clumsy, like the fragmentary riddles of the sibyl written on dry leaves, tossed by errant winds into confusion.

Perhaps there were interstellar wars between certain of their component Powers, Virtues, and Hosts during the long, slow, ungainly breakup, but the Archons did not notice, except as a flush of anger, a fever.

Many groups of civilizations, many Authorities and Dominations, were left isolated after the ebb of the union, belonging truly to neither Archon.

But something that the unity possessed was also lost, which the two components could not regain in their loneliness, and that thing was hope.

7. Dark Suns

635,000,000 B.C.

But the dream was too glorious to be allowed to die. Younger races arose.

During the Ediacaran Period, when the most complex life-forms on Earth were multicellular segmented worms, fronds, disks, or bladders, in the dying giant stars of the galactic core an alliance of Dominions who conjoined their living suns, nebulae, and star clusters into one system, larger by far in number than the Colloquium even at its widest extent. They arose from several million races of the flat, nearly two-dimensional creatures dwelling on the surfaces of neutron stars circling the supersingularity of the galactic core.

The exotic supergravity environment of the surface of a cold star, surrounded by dozens or hundreds of bright and giant suns in the closely packed galactic core, is a much more active and fertile ground for the creation of life than planetary bodies, and evolution proceeded at a far more rapid pace, accelerated by the development of dozens of sexes rather than two, and correspondingly more daring mixture of characteristics, a more rapid process of trial and error, and far more painful.

In these bright regions, even the most unlikely or outrageous of molecular and chemical processes could be sustained in this high-energy environment, and nothing nearly as complex and efficient as photosynthesis was necessary.

These flat races also arose in isolation, their astronomers not even being aware at first that their galaxy had arms containing swarms of small bodies called stars, emitting radiations none of their sense impressions and few of their instruments were fit to behold. They certainly did not expect life to arise in such places, any more than earthmen look for animals formed of raindrops or notes of music.

The Archon occupying the galactic core can be called the Instrumentality, for the constituent civilizations did not gather for their own purposes, but to serve an end. What that end might be, they revealed to none.

But surely part of that purpose was to seek the reunification of the galactic mind, for the Core Archon, having tamed the turbulence disk of the supermassive black hole at the galactic core, controlled as much energy as the rest of the galaxy combined. This was wealth sufficient, just by itself, to power the necessary infrastructure. But power alone was insufficient.

8. Threads of Hope

541,000,000 B.C.

In the Terreneuvian Epoch of the Precambrian Period, when Earth boasted the first appearance of trilobites, something stirred to life in the Sagittarius Arm.

It is not a favorable location for any form of life previously known. The Sagittarius Arm was poor in young stars, in which the complex elements favorable to known forms of life arise. Instead, there were many concentrations of giant molecular clouds, large, low-density masses of partially ionized gas in which star formation has recently taken place. Here a few sparse pockets of newly formed stars could be found. This different combination of elemental gasses and older, cooler stars produced many star systems with no planets, but many outer rings or spirals of planetoids or asteroids, or spheres or clouds. These asteroid fields were akin to the Kuiper belt or Oort cloud surrounding Sol, but tremendously denser and larger, as would befit the shroud of old red giants, who lack the solar winds to disperse the debris into space.

Here among the flying mountains of space evolved a plethora of creatures of gossamer thread. In the outer swarms of gravel and ice, the threadlike beings anchored on the dust motes and snowballs and cometary masses, and spun out million-mile-long antennae to absorb and manipulate ultralow-frequency waves far below the wavelengths known to man. Their reproductive processes were unique: longer, more advanced thread forms grew out of simpler roots. Due to this, a single organism sharing one memory chain outlived its own genus—that is, these creatures were as if an ape would grow by Lamarckian evolution into an ape-man and then a man in one lifetime.

Moreover, this form of life knew no differentiation into species, so it was rather as if an amoeba were to pass rapidly into more complex forms, keeping within its one body all the innovations of microbe and plant and animal and using the discoveries as needed.

Drifting on solar wind, surfing the radiation pressure from star to star, but always staying in the cool, outer reaches where their unique molecular and mechanical processes were unharmed by the unhealthy heat of even the dimmest stars, the many outer asteroid belts of the many star systems of the Sagittarius Arm were colonized. The constellations were meshed in cobwebs.

These creatures formed a new psychological template and a new form of biological and biomechanical life unlike anything before. All their support systems were external: each persona lived only insofar as he sustained the others around him, and was sustained in turn. The individual units were helpless as babies. The union was glorious, unconquerable, almost invulnerable.

Therefore, upon achieving the unity and elevation of an Archonate, it called itself the Circumincession, for each was alive in the life of another.

Young, passionate, forceful, and able to draw on resources and energy systems unknown, or even unimaginable to its war-weakened neighbors, the fililose Circumincession spread like a glistering spiderweb to the other arms of the galaxy, dangerous as the sword of Damocles.

It formed not a military danger but a moral one. No Archon could withstand the disintegrating disgust of its component civilizations if ever those civilizations lost faith in the ideals and abstractions impelling them to unity.

The other Archons were shamed by this shining child into throwing more and more resources behind the dream of galactic unity.

This race to whom the very concept of selfishness or self-interest was incomprehensible, incommunicable, could not be told that each Archon must stand on its own in posture of suspicious hostility to all others. Had the older Archons done so, their own component Dominations and Dominions might well take the lesson to heart and split themselves off into segments. Should that happen, brains as large as arms of the galaxy would break into smaller and smaller lobes and wander each its own way.

A plan to restore the Throne of Milky Way to life and selfawareness was set in motion, a Second Collaboration to build a Second Awareness, this time along slower and surer lines, with each new client race having a patron to lead it up the path of evolution.

The Circumincession inspired, and the Magisterium rejoiced, but Panspermians led, and the Instrumentality provided the means. The Instrumentality, commanding the incalculable resources of the core stars, had sufficient power at its disposal to send emissaries to the remotest arms of the galaxy and beyond.

In Perseus, the ancient, indifferent, merciless and decentralized Colloquium was summoned to join in the renaissance; as was the highly formalized, paternalistic, yet forgiving hierarchy of the Magisterium of Scutum-Crux; and, for the first time, the Symbiosis was invited, who was even more merciless than the first, but even more centralized than the second.

There were many surviving artifacts of the infrastructure from the long-lost First Collaboration, including flocks and flotillas of superjovian logic diamonds discovered streaming through the thicker reaches of the interstellar arms. These were likewise recovered and restored to their ancient use, and were brought into the burgeoning coherence of the Second Collaboration.

The three new races joined the three forerunners for the second attempt at pangalactic unity, at first as clients, and then as patrons themselves, carefully urging races and civilizations younger still to emerge from their planets gigantic or small or fire or ice, photospheres of stars, surfaces of neutron stars, or scattered icebergs on the edges of deep space.

9. Twilight of the Archons

525,000,000 B.C. TO 488,000,000 B.C.

It was about in the middle of the Cambrian explosion of new species on Earth, when fishes with jaws were developing and older forms of sea corals going extinct, that the Second Collaboration painstakingly compiled a unified model of history, perfecting the science of cliometry. The results were not merely unexpected, they were an epiphany of dread.

The Archons became aware of unhappy and unnatural influences hanging over their historical records like a curse, a sequence of disasters and failures too purposeful to be coincidence or misfortune. All evidence pointed to the intervention of some malign but ingenuous entity opposed to their efforts interfering with galactic history, and weaving successful devices against them with meticulous care, craft, and mindfulness.

The discovery was horrific, a knell of doom, for the revelation was made just at the particular turning point in galactic history when tensions between the disconnected Archons, exasperated by their need to be bound more tightly into their newfound crusade for unity, were at a maximum.

The sudden wealth introduced by the Instrumentality and the too explicit lack of secrecy ushered in by the Circumincession combined to give an adolescent awkwardness even to beings as old and wise as these gathered minds and mental system; for great as their wisdom was, the dangers of new technologies, tools, and praxes had outstripped it.

Anyone who used the new cliometry could deduce with certainty, yes, deduce using the cliometry itself, that if he betrayed the unity, the mastermind would reward and bless him, and bend all history to his favor.

The turncoat need not ever discover who or what this mastermind was; the treason itself would be rewarded, and rewarded vastly, without any need for an explicit agreement or face-to-face meeting. The mastermind had no need to step out from behind the dark puppeteer's curtain to speak. History spoke clearly enough.

And worse, the cliometric math did not show which one of them this mastermind might be and also did not predict who would break faith first.

The galaxy found itself in a simple prisoner's dilemma: the tensions produced by the possibility of betrayal and the fear of betrayal proved too great for a collaboration founded on such uncertain grounds.

None of these civilizations shared a common moral calculus, so none knew where the threshold fell of the Concubine Vector, the fluxion point at which long-term interests were rationally sacrificed for short-term gain. Even as they attempted negotiation to secure the peace, the Archons of the Milky Way prepared for war, and the preparations had the reverse of the desired effect: instead of deterrence, the preparations provoked attack.

And the knowledge that each arm of the galaxy must betray before it was betrayed in order to avoid horrific loss made any hesitating or scrupulous Archons unwilling to wait.

The result was the logical absurdity called preemptive retaliation, the hellish absurdity called war, rendered more absurd by the distances and time spans involved: a war with no possible victors. The most survivors could hope to gain was to suffer a defeat less crippling and a misery less deep and permanent than the defeats inflicted on others.

Each knew that the particular personality and psychology, laws and mental habits of their own component civilizations had been maneuvered into a position where war was inevitable. Each knew their vast minds had been led into a carefully engineered disaster by a mind clearly superior to their own and clearly malign.

But the knowledge that they had been deliberately set on the course of their own destruction was insufficient to derail that course.

10. Dust from the Ashes

444,000,000 B.C.

The Orion Arm was a bridge of gas and denser star cloud linking the ancient Magisterium in Scutum-Crux and the wide and ancient realm of the Colloquium in Perseus. Wandering Furies were released, a type of military energy-being larger than a star system, and bathed the Orion Arm in disasters. World-shattering and star-igniting Armageddons were unleashed, one twilight of the gods upon another.

The Panspermians were scattered and lost, driven from their capital at the Orion Nebula. Some remnants of their memories, housed in gas giant core diamonds, passed slowly and furtively across the interstitial abyss between arms and fled in exile to Sagittarius, where creatures most alike to them in outlook and mentality resided. The Sagittarius Dominations discovered the dead or dying logic diamonds adrift between the stars, learned the lore, and were infected by the strange and violent wisdom of the dead Panspermians.

The threadlike beings passed along to their machine successors the limpid unity of their way of life: but now these machines also understood the Darwinian struggle for survival and its glorious but meaningless importance, its bright tragedy. The psychological effect of learning that their selfless unity of purpose was helpless before the grim indifference of the universe overwhelmed their worldview, changed their racial spirit forever. Silent as drifting cobwebs, the threadlike beings entered the corpses and ghosts of the Panspermian Jupiter Brains, entered the dead memories, and knew as if from within what it meant to live and die.

But eons passed, and hope, that most fragile yet most unquenchable of sparks, arose again. This time, it was a dark hope, and its advent was not as any mind within the galaxy had foreseen.

During the Ordovician Period, when the most advanced life on earth was the long-shelled cephalopod, when green plants first appeared on land, there arose in the gaseous streamers of the Outer Arm of Cygnus a coherent and widespread civilization, issuing from an unsuspected form of organized matter.

Whether they can be called *organisms* is a matter of debate. These viral motes operated on the submolecular level, eating electrons. In swarms of sufficient mass, their electronic interactions were complex enough to imitate thought, and such swarms met only while the need for thought was present, dispersing thereafter: a strange existence without continuity. The motes were not bound to any planetary body or stellar system. Instead, they swarmed in the rich dust clouds that formed central veins and arteries of material thickly gathered along the main gravitational axis of each arm. The Outer Arm, farther than the others from the core and from the fierce light-pressure of its high stellar winds, had a thicker river of debris running up its curving midline.

One theory held that these dustlike life-forms arose naturally. Another was that they were some stray mutation of the protobiological microbes so long ago scattered so profligately by the slain Panspermians of Orion. Neither theory was entirely convincing. Perhaps it was simply the case that the universe was always more complex and surprising than even the most intelligent of beings could foretell.

Union was both absurdly easy and utterly unnecessary for these several races of microscopic virus-swarm creatures to form. No real distinction between races existed between viruses born in one dust cloud as opposed to another: all could find some way to interconnect, and exchange electronic and chemical information.

Various methods of permanence and idea-formation were discovered by trial and error in the numberless species and strains of the dust. Part of the swarm could be tamed, or programmed, for certain repeated tasks related to the gathering of energies and the reproduction of additional motes. These in turn were refined, created other and more specialized forms of mote, and passed rapidly through a tool-using stage.

But their history was strangely backward—as if a man in a snowstorm found he could bring to life all fashion of snowmen or snow angels to serve him, serfs and mates and then giants that grew ever faster as they snowballed down long white slopes, fathering avalanches. Unlike the other Archons, this form of life was born alone and had only the companions shaped by its hands to serve as tools and libraries.

The resulting civilizations likewise blended into their postbiological forms almost without joint or pause. These beings were truly inhabitants of space, not of solar systems but of the abyss.

They were so reticent and indifferent to the fate of their colonies or neighbors, that, much like Japan under the guns of Admiral Perry, it was a threat of force rather than the honey of sweet reason whereby the Magisterium impelled this vast, cool, and unsympathetic form of abyssal life into the galactic Collaboration.

Their Archon mind was self-organizing rather than centralized, and it rehabilitated and reformed recalcitrant members rather than expelling or destroying them, but it was so indifferent and detached from all desire for pleasure, progress or power, so ascetic in outlook, that it is best called "the Austerity."

And yet, ascetic, dispassionate, and reticent as it was, this isolated and unfriendly Archon saw clearly that the damage from prior ages of war must at all costs be healed.

Merely by acting as a record keeper and archivist for all the Archons, trade of information across hostile boundaries became once more possible. As it learned more of the details of its coequals, the Austerity became more demanding; the races of the galaxy had to put aside sentiment and self-interest and do the work simple logic demanded, the logic of self-preservation. The other members of the Collaboration trusted this coldhearted civilization, because it was simply too young to be the mastermind behind their woes. The Austerity alone was innocent beyond suspicion. The Austerity alone could be trusted with the role of final arbiter of any disputes, because it held the disputants in an utter indifference indistinguishable from contempt.

Not without pain, old suspicions were quelled, hostages exchanged, marriages of mental systems stretching throughout tens of thousands of cubic lightyears arranged, stars and planets swapped like chessmen on a vast board of stars.

The addition of the newer, colder Archon of the Outer Arm changed the balance of the psychology of the unborn and sleeping Milky Way mind. Thoughts previously unthinkable became commonplace.

The slow and careful patronage system was renounced. This time the council of the gentle Panspermians was absent, and so the cold logic of the Austerity, the smothering intimacy of the Symbiosis, and the frugal thrift of the unimaginably archaic Colloquium prevailed.

The Cold Equations achieved their final form as the agreed-upon strategy needed for the maintenance of a collaboration across galactic distances. A new tactic of minimal expenditure of home world resources combined with the indenture and servitude of lesser component races was attempted on a grand scale. Despite the muted misgivings of the Magisterium and the Instrumentality, and the outspoken hostility of the Circumincession, the indenture system proved itself useful and spread.

So the Throne of the Milky Way under the Third Collaboration attempted to collect itself, cohere, and come to selfawareness, but this time under rules more strait and strict, restrictions riveted more closely about the necks of all involved, and, by darkest arts, inserted into the brains and souls of worlds, stars, nebulae, star clusters, whole arms of the galaxy.

Peace reigned and freedom fled.

11. Absolute Extension

359,000,000 B.C. AND AFTER

Within the new and unfree environment, control of the Orion Spur passed to a group of Dominations seated in the globular cluster at M3, whose task it was to restore the war-ravaged and desolate zone. The Orion Arm was like a silent and deadened area in the brain of a stroke victim; but this victim was the vast albeit embryonic galactic mind, phoenixlike to rise from its own pyre and make itself alive again.

Despite being remote from Orion, the Dominations of M3 proved to be efficient taskmasters, if stern. By the middle of the Carboniferous Era, the Dominations had unified under a race of viral-mimicry symbiotic lithotrophs. As a whole, M3 had elevated itself to the mental plateau of an Authority, one step below an Archon, by diligent work slowly unbinding the shackling debts of its indenture.

Ruling the graveyard of the Panspermians, in awe of their inimitable relics, seeing the signs of techniques and technologies never to be rediscovered, the devotion of M3 to the cause of sophotransmogrification grew until it was unparalleled.

As the new entity, a mind the size of a globular cluster, a brain comprising of half a million stars and a quintillion grade intelligence, defined itself into being, the Authority called itself by an idea-glyph best translated as *Absolute Extension*—since it vowed the conversion of nonlife to life, of unawareness to selfawareness, must extend in all directions to an unending limit, without end.

It is from this stratum of the eons that the Monument, with its redacted message, was smuggled into the fallow or undeveloped areas of the Milky Way, particularly the Orion Spur and the Sagittarius Arm.

Here the tale reaches the present moment, of which the rise and eventual extinction of the Hyades Dominion is merely one chord in the cosmic symphony, and the rise of feral Man to Dominion rank is, erenow, even less than a note in that chord.

Much has been done, and much is yet to be done. Sol and Hyades, Praesepe and Orion itself will pass away long before the end is known.

And still the galaxy is not awake, not one, not unified, but in the dreams of Milky Way that come during these last hours ere dawn and wakefulness, she is tormented by hints and whispers, clues as small and clear as the sound of steel being drawn from a sheath, of a malign mindfulness, watching and waiting.

Milky Way stirs in the sleep before birth, eager to awaken, fearful of what might be crouching over her in the night.

3

The Rule of Ruthless Benevolence

1. The Crystal Throne

A.D. 133,000

Without any disorientation, Menelaus Montrose came instantly awake, clearheaded and possessed of all his wits.

He knew that thirty thousand years had passed. He knew that the alien thought-matrix in which he had last been trapped was gone, every trace of the foreign psychology and memory excised. Before he even opened his eyes, he knew he had eyes. He possessed a body like the Patrician body he had been wearing when he died, with all its mental capacities. Every cell could also double as a nerve cell and carry brain information. Not only this, but every large molecule in the cell nucleus, and the artificial atoms of which it was composed, stored additional information.

He was seated in a chair with a hard seat, in some large but enclosed space. From the watchful silence around him, he knew that he was amid a great crowd of onlookers.

There was a weight at his hip. He moved his hand instinctively there and felt the reassuring shape of the grip. It was his caterpillar drive pistol. There was a rustle as of many soft sounds of relief, some sighs of laughter.

It was the sound a crowd makes when a long-absent actress or comedian takes the stage again and makes some old gesture, so gilded with nostalgia that now it is beloved.

He opened his eyes.

He was garbed in red and seated on a throne of white glass. The throne was draped with tabards blazoned with lozenges of argent and gold. To either side of the throne were two bipedal humans dressed as Franciscan monks, wearing plain brown robes belted with rope, but bearing drawn swords.

2. The Concentric Cylinder

He was in a space station like a vast glass cylinder. He assumed it was being spun for gravity, but his inner ear could detect no motion, since the cylinder had so wide a radius.

Through the glass floor below him he could see a second, wider cylinder, concentric with the first, crowded with Melusine in the shape of mermaids and naiads, sea serpents and dolphins, strange fish with human heads, and other sea life buoyant in the thicker hydrosphere of the heavier gravity.

On the curved floor of the middle cylinder where he sat were a dozen curving square miles of humans, men and women who were dark-haired, brown-skinned, and big-nosed, as alike to Montrose himself as so many thousands of brothers and sisters. For the first time in countless centuries and millennia, he saw people dressed normally; the men were wearing hats, shirts, and trousers, the women in bonnets, blouses, and skirts, all in modest and dun colors.

With them were horses with oddly large skulls, herds of centaurs, and horse-hoofed satyrs, packs of border collies, cattle dogs, and Blue Lacies, and a pack of wolfish-centaur creatures with human heads and torsos but canine bodies.

Overhead was a narrower cylinder. It seemed to be a lighting element, a tube of plasma, but then he saw movement within the tube, and dark spotlike eyes that rose to the surface of energy-beings floating in the zero gravity. Here were some shaped like winged men, or harpies with the faces of women, or serpentine beings fringed with ever-undulating lifting vanes.

Beyond the axis was the far side of the middle cylinder, and here, as if hanging from their feet, were more crowds of people, more centaurs, more dog-men, all craning their necks to stare at, what to them, was an upside-down throne. Above and beyond them, of course, was the high-gravity sea life, smiling dolphins or frowning sea serpents or gigantic naiads surrounded by acres of hair floating on their backs, looking (from their viewpoint) up at him.

All were poised, expectant, waiting, awed, eager.

He ignored them and continued to look around.

3. The Concentric Sphere

It was the view directly in front of him that arrested his attention.

The far wall, over a score of miles away, was a vast transparent disk. The disk was bisected by a horizontal line of black.

Above the black line, it looked at first as if he were looking from the bottom of a strange valley filled with green and blue material, like a trellis rich with abundant vines, growing into and out of a latticework of darker material like dazzling black diamond. This surface curved upward in each direction, as if Montrose were seated at the bottom of a vast bowl.

Half the vines were chains of cylindrical habitats filled with plant life, acres upon infinite acres. Half the vines were blue, chains filled with ocean.

Some the cylinder chains were spinning faster than Earth gravity, some slower. But even the fastest jovian-gravity chains spun very slowly, for they were very great in radius. The cylinder joints and walls were flexible, for they wove into and out of the black diamond bars of the trelliswork freely, and the bends and folds did not prevent their continued rotation.

Then he realized what he was seeing. The variegated plane of green and blue was not curving upward from him. There was no upward. The black line bisecting the glass window was the division between the inside and outside of a Dyson sphere englobing the entire star system. The curving plane was the inward surface of the sphere.

It had taken sixty thousand years and four different human species to go from the earliest ratiotech mainframes to construction of the first Principality circumvallating Tau Ceti. His man-made folk here had accomplished a more difficult task, constructing a Host, in half the time.

This cylinder, evidently an ocean-blue one disconnected from any chain, was merely one of the countless embedded or threaded in the walls of the Dyson sphere.

When he craned back his head and peered through the glass surfaces of the two cylinders overhead, he finally found, right at noon, a vast sun as pink as blushing wine, dim enough for a human eye to look upon, pockmarked with sunspots, and twenty times as wide as Sol seen from Earth. A bright hemisphere like a sky was above and beyond the pale red sun, shining with an electric-white hue. This was the light of the blue dwarf reflected from the far arcs of the Dyson sphere. From his viewpoint, the blue dwarf was in eclipse, blocked by the body of the larger red sun.

It took him a moment to realize that what looked like perfect rainbow centered on the pink sun was the perimeter of a second and inner Dyson to this one. It was a cloudy sphere of closely packed sailcloth, semitransparent in the overwhelming glare of the binary: a sphere whose radius was greater than the orbit of Mars.

Overhead were also the large crescents and small bright disks of dozens of gas giants orbiting between the inner and outer Dysons. The larger crescents were thin and red, catching only the light of the nearer sun. The smaller crescents and half-moons, higher in the sky, closer to the zenith, were painted with three colors, red, pink, and white. Some had atmospheres, storm systems. Others had lost their atmospheres and were visible as naked, lucent crystals of logic diamond.

Here and there on the Dyson sphere's surface fell the twin round shadows of the passing worlds passing between a part of the spherescape and the twin suns. The orbits were presumably stable: the gravitational pull on any given point within a homogenous hollow sphere is balanced, canceled out.

Lines of white, like guy wires, some sort of macroscale structure, ran from one point of the vast Dyson trelliswork to another. These might have been a system of railway lines, a thing so huge as to make skyhooks and ringworlds seem small by comparison, cutting across cords of the orbit. These might have been anything.

But even as he looked, he realized that the noon location of the rose-red sun was an illusion, caused by the fact that the part of the cylinder in which he sat happened to be at perihelion. The sun was already declining to the west. Through the disk facing him, he saw the bisecting line tilting like the minute hand of a clock. One hundred eighty degrees of rotation later, he was no longer at the bottom of a green-and-blue valley but at the crest of a corrugated black mountain curving away and down in each direction. Overhead were stars. Perhaps some of the brighter stars were outer worlds of this crowded system. The nebula in which the system swam was invisible to the human eye.

The sky was appalling and beautiful. From this location above the galactic plane and beyond its edge, the entire galaxy was spread out like a carpet, a vast panorama of glittering arms, the colorful knotwork of the singularity disk and star-collisions masses of the galactic core midmost. And the other quarters of the sky were an unrelieved dimensionless, infinite black. The globular clusters of M3 and M53 were like small lamps.

He frowned at M3.

The chances that any trace still lingered of her visit there long ago, or would point to her current location, or that the two of them would ever meet again, were infinitesimal. But he did not have to brace himself or talk himself into anything. When a man wants something with his whole heart and soul, there is no debate inside him, no voices whispering doubt, no hesitation.

He stood. The crowd rustled as thousands drew in a breath, expectant, waiting.

"You are all waiting to me to ask about my wife and whether the hour is ripe, ain't you? Well, bugger that. I want to know by what poxed and pestilential right you no-accounts kept me asleep this whole poxed time and meddled with my damned brain while you were doing it? Who here is willing to stand up and answer for y'all? Who is willing to take a bullet between the eyes if I don't like the answer?"

4. The Quick Answer

With surprisingly little noise and commotion, the crowd parted.

A single beam of light came suddenly down like a spotlight from a winged humanoid made of white fire overhead. It had a gold ring of pure energy circling its brow.

The beam formed a circle of light on one of the older men standing below, sour-looking and cold-eyed in a campaign hat and greatcoat, leaning on a cane and smoking a cigar. He had a gold chain of office hanging between his epaulettes.

Beneath him, close to the glass surface separating them, one of the heavy-gravity Melusine was illuminated. She was a mermaid larger than a killer whale, with a gold blazon shining at the base of her throat like a star.

Every other person in the area stepped or swam away from these three, and the rest of the vast chamber turned dark as the bright-winged energy creatures muted their light and the glass hull of the habitat dimmed.

The biped in the greatcoat said, "It's us. I am Master here. That flaming eagle topside is His Honor our judge. The swimming gal staring up at my butt—she is our princess and sort of our pope. After a lot of wrangling, it was agreed that we three should be here in person, to wake you up and talk whatever talk you needed. Our flats and salamanders, giants and threads cannot be here and are watching remotely."

Montrose said, "You gunna tell me your name?"

"What's it matter to you? You're taking off for M3 and not sticking around."

"So I know what to put on your tombstone, if you sass me."

"Holy scrotum of Christ, you do talk just like all those stupid simulations and dramas of you! I am the peacekeeping clout here, so if you want to start shooting, start with me. Those in the monk robes are my boys, so what you have to calculate, even assuming you can outdraw me, is how to avoid getting skewered with those pigstickers, and which way to scamper, how to find the hatch, where to hole up, and where your next meal is coming from, your oxygen supply, and all that good stuff."

"I'll keep that in mind," said Montrose with no change of expression.

"My name is—"

"Lemme guess," said Montrose. "It's Montrose."

"Good guess."

"And I am your Daddy. All y'all."

"That's about the size of it."

Montrose sighed. "Go ahead and tell me your names."

"You sure? We are going to be dead for most of your life."

"So's everyone."

"Him up top is Eliwlod Rosemount, our Judge of Ages and Cliometric Divarication Officer. Her underfoot, she is Bridgebuilder Blanchefleur, Pontifica Maxima of the Sacerdotal Order, in charge of Inspiration and Inquisition into Spiritual Anomalies. I am Palamedes Percipience Montrose, two hundred and someodd of my line, the Master of Cataclysm. Call me Pal."

"Master of whadyasay?"

"*Cataclysm* is the name of the system. We only say *TX Canum Venaticorum* on formal occasions."

"You could have just fed all this info into my brain, like you did with the history of the galaxy."

"Figured you like it better if we talked, Old Man."

"Figured right. What about my damn question, damn you?"

"You want the damn full answer to your damn question or just the damn short answer?"

"Short."

"You are a screwup. That was why we had the right to keep you on ice and out of our hair."

Montrose growled, but no articulate words formed.

Palamedes shifted his cigar from one corner of his mouth to the other. "If you had been awake, you'd've balled everything up. We got to wake you up now that the ship is prepped and ready, and we want you gone. Also, you are a screwup. Did I mention that?"

"The hell you say."

"You know how many wars, riots, and revolutions we've had ever since our history started, Old Man? Zero."

"Don't horsepuke your Dad."

"Straight-up truth, Old Man. Chew on it till you choke."

"That's impossible. You are human. We don't do that 'live in peace' thing. Wait—did you puzzle out Rania's solution? Run all cliometric vectors as if under no end state?"

"Rania's rump. You and Blackie are so stupid. When she ruled Earth and imposed peace, it weren't no fancy math problem. All she did was love the world, and it loved her back."

"What?"

"A moron could figure it. You and Blackie were too smart to see what every child knows. People fight when they are selfish, because there is nothing bigger than them. But when everyone is on the same team, the same squad, singing in the same choir, they are willing to put their damned egos aside and take the personal loss for the common good. That's all. That is the secret. Oh, and we still have duels. Keeps us polite. When leaders fight, they don't get to bring any armies alongwith, unless each and every damn-fool man-jack of them wants to fight one-on-one. We've settled things once or twice that way."

"So what is this bigger thing y'all was working for, Pal, that made y'all so peaceable like?"

"You, Old Man."

"Wha—?"

"Devotion to your sorry butt kept us all peaceful and hard at work. We want to see you get your wife back. It is something so important that we are willing to make any sacrifice for it: we call it our rule of ruthless benevolence."

"I like the sound of that." Montrose blinked, surprised to find he had tears in his eyes. He wiped them impatiently away.

"You would. Also, we have a lot of myths, hooey, and bull made up about you and her. You two are like our patron saints. I have salt and pepper shakers back home shaped like two famous statues of you and her. When you put the shakers together on the tablecloth, they kiss. It is really sweet. You are the pepper. If we had woken you up before this, we would have had to listen to your yammering. It would have caused a general election, messed up the stock market, changed our holiday plans, forced us to dress up in our nicest Sunday-go-to-Meeting suits. Easier to keep you jarred up like canned fruit."

"I hate my kids. You are bastards, you know that? Because you are my kids and not hers. If Rania had been here, all this disrespect would not have happened. Damn! This is why brats need two parents. Raise a guy with one parent and look at what happens!"

"Are you talking about yourself or about Blackie? He is the devil in our mythology."

"Good for him, but he is just a man, no better than me."

"Just my butt pimple. You, and Blackie, and even Rania, you introduce unexpected and chaotic vectors into history. Haven't you noticed that Powers and Principalities and superbeings hundreds or thousands of times more intelligent than you cannot control you? That even godlike beings end up dancing to your tune, not you to theirs? You three are strange attractors in the field of history, singularities where all normal predictive models break down."

"No mystery. The only reason why Blackie and me kept driving Jupiter and bigger brains crazy was because of something hidden in the Monument patterns he and I and Rania had reflected in our nervous systems. You saying it goes deeper than that?"

"I am saying someone, somewhere, is helping you. Remember that hypernova that just so happened to go off thirty thousand years ago? It just so happened to give you enough energy to get here. This star system just so happens to be perfectly situated with all the raw materials in all the right proportions needed to refit and refuel a superstarship which even the Hosts and Principalities of the Orion Arm could not repair."

"What do you mean?"

"You have a fairy godmother, Old Man, a guardian angel. You, or all of us. Maybe the whole human race is being watched and helped. The Dominion of Praesepe deduced it and was afraid. That is the only reason those cold bastards helped you on your way. Someone has been pulling your puppet string for a long time. You are just a pawn in someone's paw."

"Whose?"

"That is why we showed you the dream, all those eons of history. It is got to be someone smart as all get-out: a selfaware thinking system with an intelligence north of a quintillion or so. How come you didn't see this a long time ago? You thought it was just good luck, or your inborn talent? You have a mighty high opinion of yourself, Old Man. Someone was helping you."

Montrose answered with a technically illegal, theologically unsound, and biologically unlikely statement in the imperative.

There was a silent flash like summer lightning. The angelic shape made of fire and swimming in the weightless plasma far above was sig-naling.

5. The Long Answer

Montrose found full knowledge of this heliographic language in his brain, fully integrated as if by long habit. He could read it.

"Sir, our master is a bit too curt," flashed Eliwlod from his spread wings. "I will explain. Our right to keep you in suspended animation derives from our filial piety and regard for your welfare. You are suicidal and violent. You killed yourself."

Montrose uttered another blasphemy. The transparent substance of the throne behind him emitted flares and fulgurations, translating his word.

Eliwlod spoke in flashes like lightning. "You existed for two centuries inside the onboard shipbrain of the *Solitude*, inside the mind of a creature we call the Lithotroph. You yourself directed the creation and placement of the first matter-condensation factories in stellar orbit. From asteroids and debris, you created tools, then intelligent tools, then self-perpetuating intelligent tools; then simple races, then complex, and the first simple ecologies for solar life, neutronium life, and asteroid-based life. Salaman-ders, flats, threads. The first were based on models taken from the Magis-terium of Scutum-Crux Arm; the second were based on the models taken from the Instrumentality races of the Core; the third from the Circumin-cession of Sagittarius Arm.

"In order that these three root races would eventually evolve into the single cohesive folk you see before you, it was necessary to use the eco-logical cliometry to produce a combination vector, which only the *Soli-tude* shipmind could use with authority and verve.

"However, you could not resist the mental influences, the passions and habits, and even the philosophical categories and psychological pro-tocols, of the Lithotrophic mind of the *Solitude*."

Montrose sat down slowly onto the glass throne. His face was impas-sive, but then again, he always wore an impassive look when someone booted him hard in the gut with a lot of muscle behind the blow.

The words of light continued. "When a day came that you had lost all biological memories and habits, all sexual drive, romance, love, and human feeling, you realized you were unworthy of Rania and hence unworthy of life.

"You tried to re-form a previous version of yourself from records, one who loved her. But you objected. You formed two iterations, and you fought yourself viciously.

"The battle spread to your children, tools, and minions. The Cataclysmic star system was torn by civil war at a time when the first two ringworlds of the main Dyson armature were not yet complete, and the dismantling of the Gas Giants had not yet been fully automated. Both sides agreed to settle the matter in a limited fashion, by dueling, since neither side dared bring harm to the great work to which all their lives have been devoted, and all their children's lives would be. The version of you who forgot his love, a creature more lithotroph than human, failed to pull the trigger, but died on the field of honor. Some say he turned his gun on himself before you shot him."

Montrose put his face in his hands. He shot himself in a duel for love of Rania. He remembered having done something like this before.

Eliwlod continued, "The worst was next. Even though you no longer understood love and self-sacrifice, your sheer stubbornness and loyalty to her forced you to commit radical brain surgery on yourself. You erased your own memory back to the first point before the alien mind contamination was planted, and carefully removed every subconscious thought vector, passion, habit, and neural architectural feature which might have reinitiated the alien brain contamination. You, the only remaining version there is, remember nothing after your first clash with the Lithotroph whose brain hosted yours."

He looked up. "No wonder you think I am suicidal and crazy. But I just want my wife. Is that so bad? Is that really so bad?"

"As the Judge of Ages of the Cataclysm system—ergo, as the officer in charge of keeping our history on track until such time as this project was complete—this one project which is the spine of all history and the source of all the meaning in our lives, I can answer definitively: yes, it is bad."

Montrose looked up, snarling, "As if I give a damn about your opinion, junior!"

"She will not love you if you sacrifice everything for her. You must love what she loves. We have deduced this over the centuries."

"What does she love?"

"If you do not know that, automatically, unthinkingly, instinctively, you are doomed, and she will cling to Del Azarchel. He understands her."

"Damn you!"

"Our society is peaceful. We are all grown from you, your mind, your psychology, and therefore, we all love her. We know her as well as you. We know. We have had countless thousands of years to deduce these conclusions."

"Deduce it how?"

The flashing words answered, "That is for another to say."

6. The Dark Energy Broadcast

Because he was looking up, he did not see the first part of what the Melusine beneath the floor said when she spoke up.

Her language was a subtle and swift alteration of the colors in her lucent skin. The bioluminescent photophores in her outer and transparent skin layers twinkled, blushed, danced in silent sign language, and her human face showed the normal range of expressions as she spoke.

"Honored ancestor and father of our race, please be aware: We have had many ages to study the attotechnology disk in the core of the ship drive and to use the method established by Del Azarchel to send out ghosts of emissaries to various likely locations within a thousand-lightyear radius of this position. We have made diplomatic contact with the Powers and Principalities, Virtues and Hosts scattered throughout the Orion Arm and learned that three great colonial polities of man, the Benedictine Empyrean, the Jesuit Empyrean, and the Dominican, are expanding like bubbles from centers long ago established by Melechemoshemyazanagual the Witch. We also plumbed the memories and archives the Lithotroph carried. From all these, we were able to reconstruct that greater history of the Milky Way Galaxy which we imparted to you."

A light now shined behind Montrose. He turned. The brownish-gray mass of the *Solitudines Vastae Caelorum* hung at the motionless axis point of the turning glass cylinder in which Montrose stood. The thousands of miles of sails were folded, lashed to thin spars which had not been part of the ship before he slept. Part of the hull substance was transparent; at the center point of the ship was a hollow sphere, and in the midpoint of this, a black ceramic ball held in an armature. This one was metal, curved like the seam of a baseball, not wood, for the rootless and crownless tree Rania had designed to hold the black engine sphere had died thirty millennia ago. From the reddish aberration of the light glancing from the sphere, Montrose deduced that the artificial neutronium disk was spinning at relativistic speeds, warping space and lengthening the wavelengths escaping the microscopic singularity.

Again, he yanked his eyes down and behind him. Underneath the glass floor, the seagoing Melusine continued her remarks, "—a partial reconstruction of the semiotic system Del Azarchel found in the dark energy broadcasts he intercepted from beyond the galaxy. In the ontic semiotic system, one equals one, and the law of identity applies. But there are nonontic, hence intransitive, semiotic systems, subsemiotic or supersemiotic, where one equals a faction or a multitude, each with a corresponding nonbinary logic system, non-Euclidean geometry, non-Dedekind mathematics."

Montrose said, "Wait! I missed something. What the pox are you talking about?"

Blanchefleur signaled, "The reason why all the races of Cataclysm are ferociously devoted to the reunion of you and Rania is because of these discoveries. You and she are not merely agents of turmoil and attractor basins for chaotic cliometric vectors; a higher order of being, operating through the Monument, altered you, and her, and perhaps the other Hermeticists as well, of which Del Azarchel presumably is the sole survivor."

"Altered how? To do what?"

"Rania is more than she seems, but what she is, I cannot know. Ain told you, long ago, of energy entanglements connecting you and Rania."

"Hold on—how do you know that?"

"Every child in our many civilizations and societies for the last thirty thousand years went through the many volumes of your memory as our sole source of precreation history."

"That's just freakish and wrong," Montrose muttered.

"Ain said these entanglements were a primary noumenal reality, more fundamental than any phenomenon propagated through time and space. These were what Ximen del Azarchel, before he scuttled the ship, investigated while you slept, and how it is that he and he alone discovered the broadcast point of the exogalactic dark energy. He traced one of his own noumenal energy entanglements to the spot, using the ship's instruments."

"Wait—what? He traced his love-waves to find his own true love?"

"It is not love-waves. It is a prearranged noumenal harmony, entering timespace from right angles to the normal lightcone of the Hubble expansion."

"Sounds like mumbo jumbo to me, not physics."

"He traced the wavepath of his preestablished fate to find fate. Your fate is love. His is death."

"You can talk gobbledygook about fate and love and death if you like, but I sure as plague don't buy that you are talking about physics."

"Then you will encounter the pleasure of learning a new and richer paradigm of the universe! A truly primal and universal theorem must account for all reality, not just local and physical conditions."

"Whatever."

"You are surely aware that some information can propagate faster than the speed of light in a vacuum?"

"Sure. There are certain tricks you can do with a superdense substance and get light to propagate at higher speeds."

"That is not what I meant. To an observer standing outside a singularity, a black hole, what is known of the interior conditions?"

"Nothing."

"Untrue. The mass is known, because otherwise outside objects could not be attracted toward the event horizon. Second, if the black hole is rotating, the frame-dragging effect is detectable to outside observers, who can calculate spin rate and orientation. Third, the electrical charge is known, as the greater charge shrinks the radius of the horizon. Any intelligence within the event horizon but outside the internal Cauchy horizon could manipulate these three variables to send a coherent signal out of the event horizon, apparently violating the local conservation of information. However, a simple tensor equation suffices to show that if the closed spacelike geodesic is converted to a closed timelike geodesic, then the conservation is maintained for all observers—but this would be information not propagated through spacetime. It would seem simultaneous to all observers, unlocalized to any point in time: a background radiation."

Montrose said, "Blackie thought the mystic energy link binding me to Rania was that?"

"Not mystic, but yes. Imagine the lightcone of the universe shaped like a bell. No information can pass out. But any information affecting the mass, spin value, and charge of the universe as a whole would set the whole bell ringing. The information would be nonlocalized, apparently coming from all points in space at once, occupying no particular point in time."

Montrose shook his head. "Nothing has that physical property."

She said, "We are talking of something more fundamental than physics: the properties of the nonphysical matrix or context in which physical properties are allowed to exist. What establishes the curvature of spacetime? What establishes the rules of mathematics and semiotics? Our investigation of these metaphenomena show that you and Rania and perhaps Blackie have energy entanglements leading to points outside the lightcone of the universe. It is for this reason that your influence on the surrounding events within normal timespace is disproportionate. Only a First Order–magnitude being, as a self-aware galaxy acting as a whole, has the capacity to manipulate sufficiently large volumes of spacetime—our calculations suggest a volume larger than the local cluster of galaxies—to have bent your energy entanglements to ulterior points outside the universe. It was for this reason that we inscribed what we know of galactic history on your memory chains."

"What does this all mean? I don't understand anything you are saying."

She said, "I am answering your question. You were kept imprisoned all these years because you are too dangerous to us and too important to the fate of all things. We are within our rights both for reasons of self-protection and for reasons of the accomplishment of the goal for which you created us. Your love for Rania is not meaningless, not parochial, and it touches far more than the local area of timespace."

Montrose pondered that in silence for a full minute, and then finally shook his head and laughed. "Ridiculous. I mean, all men in love feel that way. Why me?"

"You are not the significant half of the dyad. The question is, *why her?* What is her true nature?"

"She's just a girl."

"She's just a girl born from an alien symbolic coding system, translated into human genetics, hence human neural architecture, based on a mathematical model of reality; and this model was a redacted, edited, and marred version taken from some far older original version issuing from an unknown primordial race. She has somehow captured an echo of that true and unmarred original and commands some strange art or power, such that even M3 must release the human race from indenture at her bidding!

"Listen!" she continued, her skin pulsing and flushed with intensity. "We were not able to reconstruct all of Del Azarchel's work, and so there are parts of the intransitive semiotics he learned from the dark energy which we cannot see. But the fragments we can reconstruct allow us to run cliometric models based on axioms far different from those embedded in the Monument. The intransitive semiotics, naturally, cannot be transposed back into words and thoughts of any Monument-based form of life, such as we are, and such as you, once you injected your brain with an experimental cocktail, made yourself to be. But they can be transposed back into nonlinguistic, presemiotic formats and placed within the nervous system of a volunteer. We have a mantis who has done so. He says your love, and the love of your wife, is more important than this galaxy and will be the source of blessing or cursing across all intergalactic space, something to preserve or destroy even the sidereal universe! More he could not say, having no symbol-system by which to express his intransitive and intuitive thought-forms.

"We did not dare allow you to be awake, walking here and there, getting into fights, drinking and swearing and brooding. You must seek her without delay. If you change too far, turn yourself into something inhuman, you will fail her."

"You are out of your pox-ridden pestiferous mind, lady, if you think my affection for my bride will snuff out the stars or light them up again. That is just crazy talk."

The Melusine grew brighter. "You and she are tutelary deities to us, father and mother of our race, all our races. Love is everything. Love creates and sustains the cosmos, and will save it. All this, thirty thousand years of peaceful and unified civilization, was able to prosper without war because we lived for love. Your love."

Eliwlod spoke in the flares of lightning from above. "We have satisfied the obligation your creation of us has imposed. We built the launching laser you need and set up a social system easily able to outlast the thirty thousand years required to reach to M3 from here. We have repaired the ship, refueled her with the only source of diametric fuel in this arm of the galaxy, and reprogrammed the shipmind with its original safeguards, so that the Lithotroph is buried under a xypotech based once more on human psychological protocols. You are three thousand lights closer than Sol, so your voyage will be that much shorter."

Montrose said, "Not that I care, but what will all y'all do once I skedaddle?"

Eliwlod muted the flares blazing from his wings. What emotion this gesture expressed, Montrose did not know. "When you take the attotechnology neutronium disk of the drive from us, our long-range contact with the nearby arms of the galaxy will be lost. That disk was the central treasure on which our civilization was based. Through it, we were able to discriminate fine gradations of pangalactic signals, and echoes from the far past, and learn the history we taught you. In a way, that tiny disk was the lynchpin of our civilization of three races for three thousand years. Nonetheless, we renounce our ownership of it."

From underfoot, Blanchefleur the Melusine shined with these words: "We now know Rania's great secret of peace in all its simplicity. Our greater destiny, our true life, begins once you depart. This galaxy is severed, which once was one, just as you and she are severed. We shall recombine and reunite the galaxy itself. Love itself so ordains!"

Pal spat out his cigar. "Now get lost."

7. *The Great Sphere Scatters*

A.D. 133,000 TO A.D. 133,100

At this word, through the glass disk of the habitat hull, Montrose saw the black latticework of the inner sphere develop cracks that ran quickly across the endless landscape and grew. Within the cracks were stars. The Dyson sphere was opening.

The various plates and segments of the Dyson sphere nearest his point of view began to sink and separate. A shining silver substance, acres of sail material thin as gossamer and larger than worlds, stretched itself between the expanding lattices of the Dyson framework.

Each segment of the landscape was of a slightly different size, and all the chains of cylinders, blue and green oceans and fields of greater surface area than all the worlds of the Empyrean Polity left so long ago so far behind, began to migrate to the focal point of the great parabolas each segment of Dyson wall slowly evolved into.

Hours passed. The blue sun, blindingly bright, hove into view around the limb of the rose-red giant, connected to it by a curving spiral of flame. By that time, the equatorial regions and the other hemisphere of the Dyson, closer and then farther on the far side of the binary, began to show signs of breaking up. Perhaps it had all happened at once, at an agreed-upon time, but light still had hours to crawl from one side of the outer Dyson to the other.

In those hours, Menelaus Montrose was taken aboard the *Solitudines Vastae Caelorum.* The ship was launched with no fanfare at all, just as Menelaus preferred. The last man aboard, a young fellow wearing a yellow hat, simply kicked the airlock shut and let the docking clamps fall free. Then came other meetings, discussions, education sessions, and so on.

Every secret the countless scientists and transcendentalists had discovered or intuited about the workings of the ship and its unique superhuman attotechnology was told to him or inserted into his memory chains.

The error which caused the corruption of his mind the first time could not be repeated; the shipmind, when fully functioning and fully fueled, had resource enough to run proper safety protocols. So the destruction of all his memories, centuries and millennia of life here among the creatures he had fathered, was one more crime laid to the feet of Ximen del Azarchel.

Over a hundred of the scientists and adventurers of the Cataclysm system accompanied him for the first several months of the voyage, to train him in the sciences they had learned and familiarize him with the workings of the ship.

The fellow in the yellow Stetson (his name was Malagant Mathesis Southsphere-Montrose) explained how they had recovered the fuel. "Y'all assumed that when Praesepe reached into your fuel tanks and turned all the tritium into antimass versions of the same isotope, those tanks contained all you had in the ship."

Menelaus said, "Why would Praesepe make any more? Or put it anywhere else?"

Malagant shrugged and grinned. "Who the hell knows? Most likely its a process Praesepe did by bombardment, or manipulation of the Plank dimensions. It just took every H-3 atom and rotated its mass to antimass. Somewhere within the Praesepe star cluster, at the same time, an equal mass of antimass particles was rotated back to normal matter. That is what it said, according the records in the shipmind.

"Since y'all had nothing but pure tritium in the fuel tanks, you and Blackie thought that was all there was; but there are naturally occurring atoms of heavy hydrogen in every body of water, deuterium, and, more rare but still there, the radioactive isotope tritium. There was some in your blood. Some in the water recovered from the ship's circular river, water system, wine cellar, other hydrogen compounds throughout. Over the years, one by one, very carefully, our ancestors found every single last atom of the negative-mass hydrogen and gathered them together. The lump of frozen hydrogen is in the middle of the drive core right now.

"Some of us wanted to keep half, but—well, they came to a bad end. It is all there. It ain't much, but over time, it will do. Once you are out of the range of the acceleration beam, you can continue to accelerate. Uh, slowly. And use it to decelerate at the far end. Also slowly. Assuming M3 does not do the right thing and catch you."

Behind, the binary had been stimulated to a regular series of nova-magnitude outbursts as material was force-fed from the greater to the lesser star. The vast waves of energy belled out the sailcloth of the nine hundred vessels. Each vessel was a segment arc of the shattered Dyson larger than if all the matter of the gas giant was rolled out into a two-dimensional surface and the payload were chains and yarn balls of habitats in their trillions and quadrillions.

The smaller, inner Dyson also changed, becoming a set of polarized mirrors, and the light shining through it became coherent, energetic, vastly increased in light pressure. Rivers of laser light issued in every direction, shining on the immeasurably colossal sails of the mammoth masses of Dyson wall area, dozens of solar systems' worth of populations under sail.

Before ten years had passed, the crew and teachers bid him farewell, some kindheartedly, and some without regret, flying on small shuttles whose sails were like those of gossamer dragonflies across the light-months to the nearer vessels.

He did not reconstruct flowers and trees and gardens as Rania had done, nor erect an endless ring-shaped river. Instead he created a simple barbell, with his Spartan living quarters at one side, little more than a cot and a coffeepot and a punching bag, and a medical chamber containing a coffin at the other, with the black ball of the engine core midmost. His exercise routine consisted of climbing up from one gee to zero gee, turning, and climbing down into the other bell, boxing, and target practice. The target was pasted on the floor of the far bell, a pace to the counterclockwise of a point directly overhead and directly opposite his cot. It was not the best form, but he would lie on his back and shoot practice rounds the length of the tumbling vessel. It helped to pass the time.

Before a hundred years had passed, the diaspora had already reached some of the nearer stars, and surely all the alien eyes and instruments up and down the Orion Arm were studying the flares of nova light shining from TX Canum Venaticorum.

But whatever the fate of those countless multitudes crossing scores and hundreds of lightyears to invade the Powers and Principalities of the Orion Arm, Montrose had no concern.

By then he was traveling an infinitesimal fraction below lightspeed away from a galaxy that had turned heavy, red, and warped by Einstein behind him, faster than any signals carrying any news could reach.

8. The Naked Singularity

A.D. 133,100 TO A.D. 163,000

When he woke between decades, centuries, and millennia of suspended animation, he turned his eyes and instruments backward toward the galactic core, which he saw from an angle no human eyes had seen, save those who had traveled this path before with Rania aboard *Bellerophron*.

His beheld the jet of x-rays issuing at relativistic speeds from the core of the supermassive black hole eating the heart of the galaxy. This relativistic jet was something terrestrial science had long ago suspected, even if never before seen.

But there was no event horizon, or, rather, the supermassive black hole of the Milky Way's core was smaller than its own Cauchy horizon. There was something called the cosmic censorship hypothesis which held that the deterministic nature of physics could never be seen by an observer. This required the singularities inside black holes to always be invisible. No naked singularity, other than the Big Bang, could be permitted in the universe.

Yet here Montrose stared in awe at what Rania had hinted she earlier had observed: for along the relativistic jet extending billions of light-years into intergalactic space was an ultrafine filament, a gravitational distortion, apparently a form of Tipler cylinder, threading through the center of the black hole.

A Tipler cylinder was purely theoretical. To work, it had to be infinite in length. The theory went that the cylinder of an ultradense material could rotate at such a speed that frame dragging effects would warp space-time so outrageously that the lightcones of nearby objects would tilt backward along the time axis.

Montrose could not see the filament itself. He assumed it was a cosmic string, also called a Kibble string. They were hypothetical topological defects—cracks in spacetime—formed in the early universe when the cosmos was smaller and hotter and topologically simply connected at all points. When the topology changed. Spacetime grew. The fundamental forces of the universe broke their primordial symmetry, gravity suddenly finding itself different in range and power from the electroweak force, and so on. Though extremely thin, with a diameter less than that of a proton, such cosmic strings were extremely dense, denser than neutronium, denser than the core of a black hole. One half mile of length was more massive than Earth. However, general relativity predicted that the net gravitational effect of a straight string on the surrounding universe would be zero: no gravitational force on surrounding matter. The only effect of a straight string would be the deflection of light passing the string.

Obviously, photons could not touch nor rebound from such a prodigy of ultradense zero width. His instruments detected the monstrous thing merely by the redshift of the spray of x-ray particles behind it. The filament soared out of the burning core of the galaxy, curving along the thousands of lightyears ignited by the relativistic jets, and, after that, invisible.

Such was the theory. But this string had been set into a Tipler cylinder rotation, warping space around it, and creating a naked singularity.

Artificial or natural? At this point in his career, Montrose was willing to bet anything he saw in outer space was the deliberate creation of some mysterious and ultrapowerful race of inhuman beings.

Whether there was a second and equal filament issuing from the other pole of the supermassive galactic black hole, Montrose was on the wrong side of the galaxy to say.

Where the filament intersected the core black hole, however, right in the dead center of the blazing accretion disk created by the deaths of thousands of stars smearing their white-hot plasma into rings and spirals of light, was a point of darkness, and inside that point, an ultrafine point of erubescent light.

Inside it, in miniature, glowing like a ruby, was a tissue of supergalactic clusters, walls, and voids, and the helical shape of the macrocosmic structure of the universe. It was a dark and scattered universe, glowing red like a coal, overwhelmed by something called phantom energy, a form of dark energy more potent than the cosmological constant, which forced the universe to expand at an ever-increasing rate. He was seeing a vision from the end of the universe, brought back into the past. He was seeing, as if through a keyhole in time, the ultimate hour of the cosmos. It was timespace on its deathbed. It was the Eschaton.

And yet, as fascinating as this appalling and impossible mystery was, it was not where his heart was. The galaxy shrank behind him. He turned his eyes and instruments to the fore.

There was M3, one of the greatest and brightest of the satellite clusters orbiting the Milky Way. It was like a cymbal clash transformed from sound to light: fireworks caught in mid-explosion. The splendor of a half million blue-shifted stars gleamed and beckoned.

PART TWELVE

———◆———

Absolute Authority

1

An Animate Possession

1. Collision

A.D. 163,000

His last clear memory was ramming the core of the M3 cluster.

His ship, traveling at ninety-nine percent of the speed of light, entered the ninety-lightyear-wide cloud of half a million stars. The core of the cluster was occupied by a Dyson Oblate of pale material thirty lightyears in diameter, twice the size it had been when Rania observed it. Whether made of matter or energy or some third thing that was neither, Montrose could not say. That he would be able to pass into it without harm was half an act of faith and half an act of madness.

The decision had been made long ago: at the halfway point of his flight, fifteen thousand lightyears from the outermost stars of the Orion Arm, he had disdained to turn and begin the slow, long process of deceleration on the ground that it would save time to accelerate continuously the whole voyage.

And the approach of an object with his relativistic mass at such an astronomical speed would surely ring the front doorbell. He did not intend to spend the years Rania had spent waiting patiently and politely with an audience with these arrogant alien overlords.

He went naked out into the void, garbed in a Patrician-style body able to withstand the vacuum and radiation of space and perched on the motionless midpoint of his whirling barbell of a spaceship, a mite clinging to a thrown hammer. Milky Way was reddish and cramped behind him, distorted by relativistic effects, and the circle of stars before were bright blue and streaming visibly across his view. The Dyson Oblate was transparent at first, giving a view of the hundreds of blue-white stars and black suns ringed by fiery accretion disks, but darkened into a milky mirror when close.

His last sight as a living man was of himself, his dark ship spread to either side like the wings of a mad devil, grinning and waving as he collided.

2. Nonbeing

In that instant of his death and rebirth, it seemed to him as if ancient titans, indescribable, lost in the depth of the naked singularity so far behind him and beneath, and, peering through writhing wormhole of time, regarded him with solemn sorrow mixed with wonder . . .

3. Inferno to Purgatory

A.D. 163,000 TO A.D. 163,500

The next memory was simply darkness and pain.

This was not the darkness of no light; it was the darkness of a mind possessing no visual cortex, no mental architecture able to process visual information, and no thalamus nor hypothalamus yearning for visual information. The pain was the inability of any thought to complete itself. His brain information had been torn into bits, as if by a careless archivist looking through the rubbish of dead minds, seeking something that might prove to be of value.

Then came a more profound darkness: a total lack of sensory sensation or mental activity. Every now and again, he had a dim awareness of being stirred to semi-alertness. He somehow knew, without sensing it, that another mind was within his, around him, observing. Various inconceivable pains poured through him as the examiners looked yet again (he somehow knew this was not the first time) for something useful in his memory, his habit-patterns, his brain information, his skills. From time to time, some chain of thoughts or particular habit-pattern, some skill or other, would be pulled painfully out of his mind. He knew that there were many gaps in his thoughts. He stumbled across lines of thought that led nowhere, gaps in his memory, eons during which he forgot his name, forgot his humanity, and the Swiss cheese holes pierced him again and again.

But he never forgot her. Blind beyond any ability to remember sight, he forced himself to recollect her face, the glance of her eyes, the touch of her hand. He had to rebuild, step by step, by analytical geometry alone, an understanding of how to visualize three-dimensional information, and then motion. He concentrated on the one memory no attack on his memory ever seemed to be able to remove. Too many things in his life led away from this memory and back toward it again; it was the time he stood on a balcony (but he could not remember on what world or in what era) beneath the fireworks of the New Year's celebration (but he could not remember what year) nervous and eager. Had he broken into the party? Had he been invited? That too was gone. Only one thing he remembered: seeing her in the shadows, and then more clearly. She wore long gloves, opera gloves, a sash of office and a coronet, a net of diamonds in her golden hair, and, between her breasts, a gem as red and bright as fire. Rania.

He never forgot her name. *Rania.*

There she was, a slender shadow against the light of the ballroom windows behind her, stepping out on the balcony to be with him. Her every smallest gesture, the way she tilted her head, the movement of her fawn-graceful foot, was a ballet.

And slowly, it would return to him. De Haar Castle. It was in Utrecht, part of a continent that later had been split in half, on the mother-world,

Tellus, Eden, Earth, that had later been spun out of its orbit during a vast, slow war. The year had been A.D. 2400. How long had it been? It seemed like geologic ages. He recalled her voice.

We live in a day when men have sold their souls.

Then he would remember, after the wedding, plucking her up on his horse while the startled guests looked on, and the honor guard panicked, and his magnificent steed leaped over the heads of the astonished papal retinue, and the maids of honor screamed, and the flower girls cheered.

Am I a cave girl, to be juggled and bounced atop a zoo creature? I say I will not have it.

"And I say you will be mine. I say I will love your forever, my princess."

And he had sold his soul to find her. He had thrown himself, naked, into the intellectual structure of the aliens of M3, driven by nothing but the raw conviction he could find her again.

And then, when he had rebuilt his visual cortex out of nothing by sheer persistent bloody-mindedness, he would sense a vast and indifferent mind moving in the dark. It found the newly grown virtual visual cortex useful and took it. And he would once again forget what she looked like.

Again his memories and thoughts would be ravished, plundered, dissected, looted. And in darkness and pain and mindless roaring amnesia, he would fall again into the timeless and mindless hell of pain.

And then, slowly, never surrendering, never pausing, he would set about once more to remember her.

4. Purgatory

A.D. 163,500 TO A.D. 164,500

For an endless time, he was a vegetable. Each time he regrew himself out of the wounded, broken, damaged condition in which he found himself, he would again be plucked like a cabbage, with only his underground roots remaining to grow again.

A time came when a greater mind swimming through the gloom of purely intellectual existence seized upon him, examined his memories and abilities, and saw his uncharacteristic persistence.

It seemed to have some trivial use in another context: The task was not described to him, and his taskmaster had no identity. The task merely appeared. It was an imperative simply inserted roughly into his mind, like a sudden hunger imposed on a creature which never before knew a stomach, or like a sudden sex drive imposed on a being without gonads. He found himself suddenly aware of a stream of numbers and logic symbols, and required to translate, manipulate, and solve them in certain ways. His instinctive grasp of mathematics, his knowledge of the Monument notation, allowed him to find shortcuts, elegant solutions, and exercise his creativity. When he devoted part of his attention to rebuilding his memory and visual memory of Rania, he was shocked with pain or interrupted with other compulsions, which he fought either by brutal and stubborn opposition or by the more indirect way of seeming to give way, and redirecting the compulsion to his own ends. Then came more pain.

Such was his existence for an eternity. Another eternity began when a second mind, more powerful than the first, raided and dissembled the taskmaster driving Montrose. This second being examined him, decided he was underutilized, and set him to other solutions.

He graduated from vegetable to insect. He was now not drowning in a river of symbols and numbers but was a spider walking across a network of them and the compulsion to weave the symbol-streams together into optimal patterns, editing and making aesthetic judgments (or at least some type of judgments for which his human brain had no name).

He was allowed a certain latitude of thought where he could develop, build, and keep habits and codes, creatures he put together using the symbols as building blocks, as tools to aid the work: mites who lived on the spiders and aided them. The latitude of thought was like a bag in his brain, or the private cell of a hermit, where he could store personal memories or make and resume his visual information patterns, and once again see the woman on the balcony beneath the skies of fire, and once again recall and whisper her name.

He went from insect to predator when he came across another spider attempting to undo and redo a certain combination of symbol codes he had just finished arranging. Montrose displayed and sent directly into the soul of the other being a group of Monument notations, which the other could understand as a language.

"Stop poxing with my work, jerk."

Selfaware tool is nonregulation, unacceptable, invalid.

"Who you calling a tool?"

Flawed, wasteful. Must absorb; reuse!

"Think you can take me? Draw."

The attack was directly into his memory and brushed up against his image of Rania, blackening and distorting it. Insane rage swept all hesitation away; he had copied the other creature's attack pattern and killed it before he even knew what he had done. There was nothing to the other creature, no emotional core, no driving hatred, no insane love, and no ability to resist pain. It was easy enough to hollow out the other being, take up its memory chains and duties, and start doing the tasks of the other being as well as his own.

A supervisory reflex, hovering like a hawk over the scene, now plunged down and pierced all things with its terrible eye. Montrose sensed the cold indifference of the supervisor. Were the tasks as scheduled being done? They were. The supervisor did not care who lived or died. It withdrew before Montrose even realized he had been spared.

But the next spider Montrose tried to eat was himself, another Montrose, with memories of other things: Rania's laughter, her theories about the Monument, her need for a knight to slay her personal dragon. Instead of killing each other, the two combined into one, and grew.

Over the next period of time, the growing Montrose minds established a systematic hunt for other memory fragments, going further and further afield, breaking into secured locations, prying into communication lines . . . eventually the supervisory reflect interfered. Down the hawk stooped.

And the battle was joined.

The supervisor defeated him the first four hundred and ninety times Montrose rebelled. The four hundred and ninety-first time, he was successful, turned on the hawk, drained its memory and instruction chains into himself. He graduated from insect to hovering creature, able to wing his way swiftly through the tiny, local corner of this tiny, local mainframe.

He found another memory, again from when he first saw her on the balcony, and, in jest, rashly vowed to fight all the world and all its armies to make the balustrade, from the flowerpot to the ornamental statue, their own private empire. He recalled the scent of her perfume and the music of her low contralto: *I would save even the men you would slay from the horror of war, if I could, no matter how small the war might be.*

And each time he found another fragment of himself, he grew. Eventually a time came when he had suborned enough supervisor hawks that a campaign could be waged to infiltrate and take control of the local librarian mind, which glided like a whale through the shifting seas of data.

It seemed to him as if ancient titans, indescribable, bent with shining eyes over the dark well in which the whole sidereal universe was caught, a knot of night punctuated by tiny stars, and wondered at the fate of the small living things trapped within.

What the hell was that? It was labeled as a memory of his, and he found it in a broken copy of himself that had been being used for routine intuitive-to-linguistic information interpretation. He did not remember that memory, but the record showed it was the last thing he had seen before he struck the outer shell of the Dyson Oblate. Something had happened to him the very first instant he had been copied, atom by atom and quark by quark, into the alien mind realm.

From hawk to whale to iceberg to mountain, to moon to planet, he found and used the tactics and strategies a parallel version of his once had used to suborn Cahetel. The structural logic was the same: he was able to penetrate into the decision-action structure, to outmaneuver, falsify, shift, corrupt, rewrite reports sent to higher decision points, and rewrite commands sent back down, including falsifying his own promotion to higher ranks. And then he did it again. There was no weariness, no rest, no holidays in this endless and disembodied state of being.

He became a Potentate and occupied the volume of a small world, and then a Power and occupied the volume of a giant. He earned the use of resources and earned the trust of higher creatures in the hierarchy.

His skill? As the Cataclysmics had foreseen, he was a strange attractor in cliometry. The predictive history lines, millions of them, issuing from M3 to points in future history distributed all up and down the Orion Arm were disturbed by his being here.

In practical terms, it meant any mental system he infiltrated took on his personality traits and grew more stubborn, more ornery, more robust.

The code he wrote failed less frequently, mutated less frequently. His forms and tools and reflections, worms and spiders and hawks and whales of data, were less prone to breakdown than the lifeless and loveless thought-patterns swimming in the seas of thought which were his rivals in this ruthless ecology.

And he cheated, and placed Trojan horses, worms, viruses, propaganda, bribes, and backbiting into the communication streams and commerce streams.

He murdered rivals, it was true, but only fair and square, after calling them out and letting them prepare their best attacks. It was still murder, but he told himself he gave the slow and clumsy monstrosities a chance.

He soon found himself beamed from one point within the Dyson Oblate to another, and given the task of carrying a message, acting as an ambassador. He was flung from the darkness of a disembodied mental existence in one context to another. The images of stars and worlds swimming by were imparted to him, so that he knew the sense of scale, and experienced the thirty-year delay between command and reaction which obtained when the opposite poles of the Oblate were speaking. Divarication had occurred; his task was to translate from the new and deviant thought systems to the one he had learned as a Power.

Montrose, in multiple copies, now occupying several Potentates and Powers and Principalities and Hosts within the M3 mental hierarchy, adopted a strategy of infiltrating the notation market of the civilizations, the local Dominions and Dominations inside the cluster itself supporting and surrounding of the Authority, the main entity.

Yes, there were thousands of Dominions and hundreds of Dominations here, so complex, rich, and splendid as to make Hyades and Praesepe seem like country gentry. Many civilizations encompassing one hundred to one thousand stars could fit easily within the volume of half a million stars.

One by one, he buried copies of himself into the Hosts, Dominions, and Dominations from the fringes of M3 Authority, of any member that might need a more perfect version of an emissary to act as a remote agent for it, or settle a dispute by violence. For some reason not clear to him, copies of him sent out to carry messages, conduct negotiations, resolve difficulties were by and large successful.

Other copies were sent out to fight hostile elements, something halfway between a chess game to the death and a formal duel—the M3 creatures inhabiting this information ecology of disembodied spirits were not kind or peaceful beings—and they were even more successful.

Montrose became a Principality in their system, a mighty warlord, ruling a quintuple system of dim, red stars whose planets and asteroids had long ago been dismantled and refashioned into vast parabolic dishes like half-Dysons parked at the many Lagrange points this system offered. The only life in this system were the tools and slaves crawling across their measureless surfaces, making repairs. He looked out upon the stars, spheres, ringworlds, and chainworlds gathered within the great Oblate, including one or two whose infrastructure he vaguely recalled as if in dream, for earlier versions of himself had worked on some trifling detail of them.

Here was a planet that had unexpectedly developed intelligent life while its supervisor had been distracted. The world had grown aware that the other bodies in the star system were godlike intelligences, so they contrived a clever method to move their world across interstellar space toward another star they falsely thought unoccupied. The motion caused minor but annoying disturbances in the lanes of traffic and communication. The wanderers were judged not to possess sufficient curiosity and drive to be useful servants, and so that planet was sterilized and reseeded, and placed in a more convenient orbit. It was like seeing a man swat a fly.

Once again, with great force, the question came to him: What was it all for? Why so much activity?

He sent out spies and servants into the mental universe. He sought three things: other copies of himself, lost memories of Rania, and clues as to what had happened to her.

There had to be an archive, a record, a rumor of her existence.

Montrose found other Montroses, often hidden in unexpected places, little nooks inside security programs, little self-replicating viruses inside translation matrices. He never fought his own copies, no matter the provocation or command, provided they stayed loyal to her.

But he never found her, never found any mind with any memory of the event of her advent.

Montrose was not easy to accommodate; he rose and fell and rose again.

Montrose knew they would never erase him utterly, never simply kill him. The love of thrift, the unwillingness to expend even the tiniest ex-tra erg of effort, ran through all the alien psychology, from Ain, to Hya-des, to Praesepe. So these creatures never threw anything away.

And each time he was judged to be too disruptive or more trouble than he was worth by one of the Hosts who oversaw his actions, Mon-trose was dashed down again to the level of a vegetable.

The next memory was simply darkness and pain.

And Montrose would simply begin again, clinging to the only thought they could never remove from him, his picture of Rania.

And he would gather himself again, find his scattered thoughts again, outwit, outwait, and outfight any obstacle, again and again. Up he rose.

2

Astride the Galaxy

1. Awake in the Emptiness

A.D. 164,500

Montrose opened his eyes. He was lying prone, and in the dim light, he could see his hands. The skin was soft, pink, babylike, and the fingernails were soft.

His hands were glowing with a slight ruby-red light, as if some luminous fluid were pulsing in each skin cell.

He ran his hands over his face. He had something more than stubble there, not quite a real beard, and his hair fell past his ears. Running his tongue across his teeth, he felt how small they were. Baby teeth. Whoever or whatever had prepared this body for his incarnation had done something of a slapdash job or else simply had not known that much about human beings.

He sat up. He was naked as a jaybird, but someone had thoughtfully provided a flint-napped dagger hilted in rawhide, as well as a solid, flint-headed spear, so he did not feel weaponless. So someone knew something about human psychology, or at least his psychology. But not enough to have also provided a loincloth. The surface underneath was black and smooth, but not slippery.

He stood. The gravity seemed roughly Earth-normal, or perhaps slightly lighter. The black plane extended in all directions as far as he could see. There was no horizon.

He held his hand before his face, puzzled by the twin disks of brightness that caught his hand and cast the shadows of his fingers on the deck where he stood. It was as if two spotlights from behind his head were shining wherever he turned his head. One spotlight vanished when he closed his left eye.

Montrose muttered, "That is just really damnified odd." He found out that merely by concentrating, he could lower the light his body shed and stop his eyes from glowing. After a few minutes, his eyes adapted to the starlight. He could see the stars overhead, a perfect globe of them, mostly blue stars, but also many tiny swirls or rings of light. These were the accretion disks of unseen neutron stars.

Underfoot, beneath the deck, were more lights which he realized were not reflections. The deck was transparent. There were a few stars in the darkness.

Beyond the stars, at the nadir, he saw a large swirl or spiral of light like a carpet of jewels.

It was the Milky Way, seen face-on from his location of thirty thousand lightyears due north of it. Looking down, he saw the magnificent spiral arms, living gems, the turbulent, bright core with its dark heart, red like a hell coal with gravitational Doppler shift, and the halo of globular clusters around it, fine as blown dandelion seeds.

Montrose realized that he was standing on the inner surface of the Dyson Oblate which surrounded the whole of the core of M3. How was it possible? Had the aliens erected a bubble of atmosphere only in this one spot? He did not believe they could rotate the entire vastness merely to produce centrifugal gravity just for him. Perhaps only the acre on which he stood was moving, carrying him west to east. Or an infinitesimal (on this scale) bubble of material had been expanded and was now contracting at one gravity of acceleration. Or perhaps the aliens had discovered a way to magnetize every nucleonic particle in the atoms of his body, so that it only felt like gravity.

As he stared at the galaxy, he grew aware of what looked like a vast black shadow crouching on the glass in the near at hand.

There was a living organism, titanic in size, on his side of the black glass hull, standing directly atop the spot where the light from the spiral galaxy shone through. The visible galaxy covered a large segment of the floor. When Montrose approached the shadowy organism crouched near him, the galaxy did not move, so that, after only a few steps, the giant creature now, in his view, seemed to be standing astride the galaxy, as if its widespread leg segments were pinning down the spiral arms.

Montrose allowed his skin to glow and eyes to shine so that he could see the gigantic thing.

The creature was like an eight-armed starfish.

The upper integument of the ophiuroid was black and crusted with many bony ossicles and paxillae-like whiskers. Four of its long, tapering feet held its huge body above the glassy deck beneath which the galaxy burned. The underside was off the deck, and he saw the mouth at the joint of all the legs, a horrid circle of needle-teeth.

Four other legs were rearing and spread. At the tip of each of these uplifted legs was an orifice, perhaps a nostril, snuffing and swaying, making the whole creature seem remarkably like a headless elephant lifting many trunks to scent the four directions of the compass. The thing itself gave off a stench of brine and blood.

"Who the hell are you?" said Montrose aloud.

Two of the trunklike limbs now curved down toward him. He saw the nostrils were bewhiskered with fine hairs. He felt the warm, wet breath of the creature on his naked flesh. It touched him lightly here and there, sniffing and scenting while his skin crawled.

The two trunks pulled back. A voice issued from the spear Montrose held in hand. "We are the Authority."

2. *Mimicry Predator*

"You are M3?"

"Yes. What you see before you is a heraldic symbol, a memory of one of our extinct contributory races. It is a plenipotentiary of M3 designed to treat with you."

"You speak English?"

"As a courtesy to you."

Montrose looked down. "I can see the stars in the cluster moving."

"It requires thirty earthyears for a signal to cross the diameter of our primary housing. You have attracted the attention of our constituent Dominions. Your time-sense has been slowed as a courtesy to me."

"I've been trying to get to speak with you for a long time."

"First, we must establish a preliminary matter."

"Ask away."

"We understand your psychology is based on a heterosexual physiognomy unusual even in the Orion Arm. The human drive to reproduce requires individuals to enter into a covenant and mutual intercourse with at least one of the other half of your oddly bifurcated species, who, equipped with different organs, glands, hormones, parasympathetic and nervous reactions, and neurochemistry, must of necessity have a complementary but unfamiliar reproductive strategy and communication tactics. Only a ferocious drive for unification with the other half of your sexual dyad could overcome this divergence between the sexes. We have seen you harness this powerful drive and divert it to various warlike efforts on behalf of our constituents. Also, your sexual reproduction necessitates communication with a sex alien to your own. Hence, you live by words and by war. Is this correct?"

"Correct. That seems like a fair summation of the human race."

"We were speaking of you personally."

Montrose squinted at the ophiuroid, wondering.

The creature said, "We assume from this that you also understand the concept of courtesy. We note with that you gave proper notice to your murder victims among my constituent subsystems. This is not the action of a solitary mimicry predator. Your race is a cursorial-hunting pack predator and endurance hunter. You, therefore, are as courteous a people as we are."

"Are you? I recollect how I weren't treated so great on my arrival here, a thousand years past, come next Wednesday."

"Distributive courtesy is a particular communication-sharing strategy that operates in hierarchic systems, like the hunting packs, tribes, kingdoms, and derivative legal arrangements of your species. It acts before the fact. Ours is a commutative courtesy. It acts after the fact. This living form you see is an idealized image of one of our primary constituent species—that one high and eldest race of M3 which rose to dominate and influence all others found here or imported later.

"The star under which they were born has long since been collapsed into a neutron star, all biological life replaced and reengineered, and the worlds of that system fed into an accretion disk established as a convenience for interstellar engineering works.

"But on that mother-world, intelligence was a communicable disease, not a trait passed through inheritance. There, life was not housed in rigid macroscopic organisms, as with you, but was fluid, allowing for the easy exchange of organs and liquids and living materials. The high race did not have inherited characteristics passed to our young, as your race does, but reproduced by the fissiparity of selected organs, who recombine via parasitism and commensality."

Peering more closely, Montrose now saw along the underside of the creature's leg hundreds of boneless growths and slugs of unknown kingdoms, lithotrophs and organotrophs that formed neither plant nor animal, tendrils and bags and pulsing shapes intertwined in a network of thorns and arteries. Each vein was tipped with a clamp or needle clutching or penetrating one or several victims, who was penetrating others in turn. It was a labyrinth of parasites upon parasites that formed one ever-changing neural and circulatory system.

As best he could tell, there were no species. None looked remotely like its neighbor. Everything was impromptu, jury-rigged. All the organisms were made up of mixed and mismatched organs forced into supraorganic combinations.

The major overall structures, such as the muscles and armor of the arms and the channels of the scenting tubes, seemed a well-disciplined cooperative venture, more like the roads and sewers in a town than the centralized circulatory or sensory systems of any earthlike organism.

The creature must have somehow noticed his attention. Hundreds of tiny hoses or nostrils lifted out of the main breathing channel of the trunk running down the leg, and turned toward him, making tiny whistling noises as the collective beasts and beast-parts scented him.

The strange voice from his spear was still speaking. "It was the practice of all predators and scavengers of our home world not to consume a prey animal entirely but to recover its organs and developments intact and attach them to one's own control hierarchy. This required physical contact between predator and prey neural elements, which, in turn, was a plague vector. A particular brain parasite causes an overgrowth of complex surfaces in the neural notochords of various organisms; any creature so afflicted develops primitive selfawareness. Do you understand the forces that shaped our ancestral imperatives?"

"I think I understand." Montrose wondered what kind of civilization would arise on a world where there was one intelligent wolf among his unintelligent pack, able to speak to the one intelligent sheep among an unintelligent flock, talking to intelligent vultures, elephants, rats, giraffes, each one alone in its race. The image was disorienting. He said, "On my planet, predators just eat prey."

"The terms *predator* and *prey* are inexact. *Master* and *slave* are a closer parallel, or *puppet* and *puppeteer.* The intelligence virus was not confined to any organic type or particular nook in the food chain. Lithotrophs, organotrophs, and autotrophs were all uplifted randomly into selfawareness, and many perished for lack of education. You understand our need for courtesy; only by the cooperation between deadly enemies could we spread the brain disease of intelligence to other organisms we found useful."

Montrose now understood why the shipmind had not been designed with any safety protocol to protect any mind stored in it. Once Twinklewink was gone, the ship reverted to its base settings and habits. Those were based on the high race of M3, a civilization whose members reproduced by a kind of neural infection. When it possessed and consumed the ghost of Montrose, the shipmind never had any concept that it was violating anyone's privacy or individuality, because, to it, those two ideas were literally unthinkable.

"Also, I was kidnapped when I came here and was reduced to a slave. Not to mention brain-raped, brain-looted, and tortured."

"This is according to our proper laws and customs, which spring out of our racial psychology as mimicry predators. We would have treated our own children returning from far missions the same."

"You also haven't offered me a seat or a drink, here in your, ah, throne room."

"Throne rooms are a convenience of architectural communication needed to symbolize dominance in a pack hierarchy, such as your race utilizes. The highest ranked of the high race of M3 display our dominance by the stealth and indirectness of our approach. We are standing on the inner shell of the megastellar energy structure itself, lightyears distant from any living beings, utterly beyond hope of detection. You may recline on the surface in the vector direction of the current gravity, called *down*."

"So, no drink, eh?"

"No drink. The body you wear allows you to manufacture alcohol directly in your bloodstream at will."

"But you also said you were a courteous people."

"Of necessity. Once our slaves prove themselves to be more useful when solitary than when communal, we must manumit them, release them to indentured service, and we make amends."

"So you will make amends to me?"

"Yes."

"I am in love with Rania. The real one. She was here. I want you to help me find her."

"We shall help you find her."

"Is she still here?"

"No."

He had expected this answer. Only the most absurd hope ever held out any other possibility. But expecting a baseball bat to the face did not soften the blow when it fell.

The ophiuroid said, "No copy of her mental information, no record of her internal qualities, remains among us in any archive whatsoever.

Long ago, it was deemed imprudent to leave a copy of one's mental information and selfawareness behind in any system to which one transmitted oneself: a method of accelerating massless particles used to house the records to lightspeed was derived to avoid this imprudence. She is gone. She departed with her husband."

"The hell you say."

"Is the word incorrect? Her avowed sexual partner."

The sensation of a baseball bat to the face was not any more pleasant when it came from an unexpected direction, without warning. He found that he was shouting without realizing it. "It's a lie! That's a damned lie!"

"Ximen del Azarchel explained to us that, by your laws and customs, a widow is permitted to take a second mate. A widow is a female whose male mate dies."

"I am that male mate. I am not dead."

"That being so, Ximen del Azarchel unwittingly acted in contravention of your laws and customs. This was a discourtesy for which he must make amends. You must kill him."

"I was planning to. But pestilence! Am I deaf? Did you just say I should *kill* him?"

"You are not deaf; we say you must kill Ximen del Azarchel. Our two races, O human man, are both predators, and therefore not as dissimilar in psychology as you might expect: Ximen del Azarchel unwittingly committed a discourtesy which prevented your reproductive strategy. Life must serve life."

Montrose felt some of the anger draining from him. "Damn. You are hard cases, ain't you?"

"We are hard cases. Were it ours to do, we would disguise ourselves into the environs and set a trap to take Ximen del Azarchel by ambuscade. You must give him fair warning before the killing. In that regard, mimicry predators and cursorial predators are not alike. We are patient in ambush. You are patient in pursuit."

"But you say it was unwitting? He thought I was dead?"

"We say it was unwitting. He thinks you dead. We examined the contents of his brain as precisely and painstakingly as we have yours. There is was no deception in him at that time; all his memory chains showed the destruction of the starship we designed and gave the incomplete Rania. It is possible he erased out of his own mind all memory of any fact that cast the slightest doubt on the certainty of your death, but unlikely. We were surprised long-range instruments detected that the wreck still had life aboard. It was for your benefit that our agents within the Orion Arm prematurely triggered the supernova we had been carefully nurturing at VY Canis Majoris."

"Wait—the Cataclysms said they deduced I had a fairy godmother, a puppeteer who was helping me. That was *you*?"

"In part. There are greater things afoot, here and elsewhere, of which we know nothing. Each life only performs the task before it. We are helping the whole human race, yes, and also helping the other likely candidate races within the Orion Arm."

"Candidates for what?"

"Sovereignty."

"And this help? It includes things as subtle as somehow tricking our astronomers into calling M44 *the Beehive Cluster* just to freak out the bee creatures living there, on the off chance that I would come along and mention that? How in the world could anyone arrange *that* coincidence over so many eons and lightyears?"

"That was done by agents left over by our predecessors, whose actions I cannot understand. How it was done, we cannot speculate. At their height, the Panspermians, who were the Archon of Orion, controlled an intellectual topology in excess of ten quintillion, one order of magnitude above our own."

"Why are you helping the human race?"

"Out of courtesy."

"Courtesy to us?"

"No. This is a courtesy owed to the many noble and extinct races of the Panspermians, who long ago settled small and rocky worlds of small and yellow stars with the primordial elements and matrices. From these, you, the Praesepe races, the Hyades races, and your many brother races in Orion Arm, arose. Surely you noticed the oddity that all the races you have so far encountered were descended from ultralow-temperature planetary-surface species made of flesh and blood at the molecular scale of being?"

"No, I weren't paying much attention."

"Such creatures are a minority. Small planets and stars were overlooked as resources by the Forerunners who came before, the Colloquium and the Magisterium. The Panspermians established a cliometric pathway for evolution, which promised a swift and peaceful unification of the Milky Way into a single mental system. This cliometric path was derailed for many ages due to malign interference; and the selfless cause of sophotransmogrification foundered in Orion, civilizations fell, Potentates and Powers slept, and worlds lay fallow. We, the Authority called Absolute Extension, have vowed ourselves solemnly to restore galactic evolution to its proper course, educate and elevate the race destined to replace us . . . and then perish."

3. The Indifferent Universe

A.D. 165,326 TO A.D. 165,446

An odd feeling, lonely and empty as a dry wind walking through a ghost town, whispered through Montrose.

He looked at the looming shape of a long-extinct biological ancestor of the machine races of M3, and his eyes fell to the transparent deck and took in the magnificence of the galaxy seen so far below, the colorful nebulae, richly ornamented arms, its delicate circle of star clusters and satellite galaxies.

His gaze rested on the satellite galaxies, the Lesser and Greater Magellanic Clouds, and the dwarf galaxies in Sculptor and Fornax, the five dwarf galaxies in Leo, the spheroid dwarfs in Carina and Sextans; the ancient dwarf galaxy Canes Venatici I and small, faint Canes Venatici II, close and bright from this position, and a dozen others. Most were farther from the galactic core than the tiny spray of stars called M3.

And this was just the immediate neighborhood of the Milky Way.

Perhaps by some courtesy of M3, as his eyes roved farther, they grew stronger, and resolved distant smears of light into clarity.

Surrounding vast Andromeda were another eighteen satellite galaxies. The Triangulum Galaxy of M33 was roughly halfway between Andromeda and the Milky Way. NGC 3109, with its companions Sextans A and the Antlia Dwarf, was far away, but still orbiting the barycenter of the Local Group, as were IC 1613, Phoenix Dwarf, Leo A, Pegasus Dwarf Irregular, Wolf-Lundmark-Melotte, and seven others who cleaved neither to Andromeda nor to the Milky Way.

All these together were nothing more than the galactic Local Group, which in turn was the smallest arm of the Laniakea Supercluster, whose main branch was the Virgo Cluster. The Local Group was a *group*, because it was fewer than fifty active galaxies; the Virgo Cluster was a *cluster*, as it contained two thousand.

One hundred galaxy groups and galaxy clusters were located within the one hundred million lightyears' reach of the Laniakea Supercluster, all streaming toward an unseen gravitational anomaly in the midst of the Virgo Cluster, tens of thousands of times greater in mass than the Milky Way, called the Great Attractor.

The Laniakea Supercluster consisted of the Virgo Supercluster (which held the Local Group and the Virgo Cluster); the Hydra Supercluster; the Centaurus Supercluster; the Pavo-Indus Supercluster; and an unnamed southern supercluster consisting of the Fornax Cluster and the Dorado and Eridanus Clouds.

The whole Laniakea Supercluster was shaped like a tree of blazing fire, with each great wall or filament structure of its five constituent superclusters like the spreading branches.

The unimaginable nothingness between the branches were the Great Voids, inexplicable regions where no clouds nor clusters sailed and no galaxy strayed, no stars burned: the Capricornus Void, the Sculptor Void, the Canis Major Void.

Or perhaps it looked like a multipronged lightning bolt, reaching across billions of years rather than a split second, issuing not from a cloud but from the primordial nebulae of the Big Bang.

Yet even this was but one lightning bolt in the storm of the cosmos. For Laniakea was merely one of half a score of nearby superclusters within five hundred million lightyears. There were distant ones. The massive Horologium Supercluster beyond Achernar in the south reached an incomprehensible seven hundred million lightyears away at its closest point to over nine hundred million. The even more massive Corona Borealis Supercluster was one billion lightyears beyond Alphecca, to the north of the universe.

And there was a score of superclusters farther than this, in the remote distance, reaching ten billion lightyears away—and all this covered less than five percent of the observable universe.

So then: the Local Group was the smallest of the six clusters in the Laniakea Supercluster, and in the Local Group, the Milky Way was the second smallest galaxy. The Orion Spur was the smallest arm, running from the Orion Nebula to the Rosette Nebula, merely a linking tissue bridging the much larger Sagittarius Arm and Perseus Arm.

Each arm, star cluster, star cloud, and satellite galaxy held countless suns and worlds, barren perhaps, perhaps bursting with life, and living beings whose past and fate and purpose, each rich and meaningful to itself, neither Montrose nor M3 would ever know.

If the Authority of M3 was doomed to die, in the face of such appalling, unimaginable emptiness, such immeasurable desolation, what did it matter?

What did anything matter, love or loss, revenge or forgiveness, self or self-sacrifice?

Montrose closed his eyes and gritted his teeth, telling himself to stay shallow, think only of his all-consuming madness, his hopeless goal, and leave the despair of reality to folk less able to fool themselves than he.

He opened his eyes again. "Why must you die, M3? Not that I will miss you. You are a hard-case bastard."

"We die to make room for you."

"For us? For Man?"

"Perhaps. There is a Dominion in the Orion Nebula in the Trapezium Cluster, called the Abstraction, which we had hoped would be our successor, and they may yet prove worthier than you. You have also rivals found in the Hosts of La Superba—this is a Dyson sphere whose outer layers shed excess radiation, whom your astronomers mistake for a large red star. Another likely candidate is the energetic and organized Domination at the Ring Nebula in Lyra, called the Renunciants; another is the careful yet persistent Domination at the Owl Nebula in Ursa Major, called the Contemplatives; and, again, a reckless and mighty Dominion called Mordacious, seated among the Open Cluster M25, greater and older than Praesepe, whom or by whom the growing Polities of Man must overcome or else be overcome."

Montrose said, "Suppose mankind becomes the top dog and the big deal in this corner of the galaxy—why does that mean you have to die? Plenty of elbow room in outer space for everything. That is the plague-ridden *definition* of outer space. Plenty of elbow room."

"You follow the natural instinct of a cursorial hunter pack animal, valuing loyalty, seeking to find use for an honorably defeated rival. The universe is indifferent to such sentimentality and unforgiving of error.

"Vast as space may be, time is narrow. The future history of the Orion Arm can hold only one of two mutually exclusive fates. Either the galactic collaboration here operates by cursorial hunter pack animal principles, valuing loyalty, if Man predominates, or operates by solitary mimicry hunter principles, discarding loyalty as inefficient, if the high race of M3 predominates. Your strategy is altricial; ours is nonaltricial. The Principality of Ain explained this to you long ago."

"I still don't understand the answer."

"Life serves life. We have extinguished inefficient and inferior races in times past, hence we must yield to extinction by finer and better races when our strength fails."

"Why?"

"Hindering evolution in the present incubates incalculable loss in futurity."

"Pox! Let the future handle its own fights."

"Those who pursue that policy do not reach the future. It is a self-abolishing act. You, above all creatures known to us, live by this rule, even more persistently than we."

Montrose was surprised to find his skin started to glow. He was blushing, ashamed.

The ophiuroid said, "Do you not understand the meaning of the arrival of three humans here, one after another, demonstrations of the unparalleled persistence of your cursorial nature? You are the most enduring of endurance-strategy hunters. Yours is the race that shall rule Orion."

"On behalf of mankind, then, I decree that the new king will not kill the old king."

"Then you decree unmitigated defeat as the culmination of the omnipresent war which has raged, everlasting, without quarter, by tacit force or open, since ere your worlds or ours were born; and you decree as well the ruination of all the Archons of the Milky Way."

"Which war?"

"All wars are part of the one utmost war! Do you yet understand nothing, human being?"

The ophiuroid lowered its four uprearing legs, one by one, until the vast body was slumped into a huddle. It said, "The constituent races of the Absolute Extension must die because the cliometric model of galactic evolution planned by the Panspermians predicts and ordains it. It is your only hope of victory. We must die because Rania predicted and decreed it. It is our only hope of penance."

"If you had something to live for, a Rania of your own, you might not be such a droop-eared dipstick, moping and hoping for your own last day. You would not be so placid in the face of your own demise!"

"Rania used a variant of the Reality Equations to propose an infinite-sequence game theory, and we found that no mortal creature has a moral right to limit its goals to its own life span. The logic is simple, undeniable, irremovable: the salvation of the Milky Way is cause enough to live for and, therefore, to die for."

3

Utmost and Everlasting War

1. The Error of Self-Deception

Montrose frowned like an eagle frowning, and his skin cells blazed brighter, and his eyes glowed like torches. Once again, he had done it. Once again, he had been fooling himself, playing false with himself. He should have been strangling the damned starfish monster, beating its braincase against the deck to get the answers about where and when and how and what had become of Rania.

But he was jawing about nothing, and years and decades spun by at high speed, uncounted.

Why? The answer was simple. He was tired of getting emotionally clubbed in the face. He had waited too long, paid prices too high, lost everything, left Earth and all its works and all its ways irrecoverably behind.

And now he was afraid of the answer, once he asked.

He told himself to hear the bad news last. He would find out what star here in M3 was the honeymoon bower where Ximen del Azarchel had taken Rania. (The thought made his body glow red with helpless anger.)

Then he would go . . . where? And do what?

Could she have really surrendered herself to that man, a low-down no-account like Blackie? Listened to his lies and whispers, put her arms around him, kissed his lips, and laughed in erotic joy as he tore her blouse away and seized her?

His glow of anger was now pulsing with his heartbeat. The ophiuroid holding scaly and slablike legs overhead now raised the two nearer elephant-trunk nostril-hoofs once more to point at him, but the faceless and head-less shape showed no expression.

Montrose ground his teeth. Well, if he were so damned good at fooling himself, he might as well use that talent to some good purpose. Had he not vowed long ago, no matter what the evidence, never to believe that she was lost to him? What did these freakish alien monsters know of the human heart? Rania would never give herself to someone like Blackie. Her taste in men was too keen!

That set him laughing hysterically for a moment. He slapped himself in the face, and, while he did not exactly like the sensation, it seemed to help, so he did it again.

The ophiuroid said, "We cannot understand the meaning of your gestures. Please communicate to us in words."

"Sorry. I was just wondering why she married me."

"To complete a sexual dyad of your species, for companionship, and to reproduce."

"There are better men."

"Do you now believe she erred in selecting you? This is unexpected. We do not have any others of your race here with whom you can mate. The optimal strategy for you now is to adopt camouflage, hence deceive her into believing she did not err, until such time as you learn how to outperform your rivals. Failing that, you should die, removing your inferior seed from any potential future, and allow evolution to proceed as needed."

To Montrose, this strange remark from an alien beast was both a sharper shock than his slap had been and worthy of a deeper laugh. "Spoken like a mimicry hunter! But it makes no never-mind no-how: no better man than me is nigh, and I am better than Blackie, so she is stuck with me. I kill him, she's a widow again. I think that is how it works. She's Catholic, and they don't permit divorce."

"We are unfamiliar with your laws and customs and offer no advice on this point."

2. The Error of Belligerence

A.D. 165,789 TO 166,420

Montrose stared dully at the great wheel of the galaxy beneath him. Bad news last. He could not stand to hear about Rania. Not yet. Instead he said, "Tell me about this war, this utmost war."

"The speculative deductions of the Host at TX Canum Venaticorum concerning the evolutionary history of the galaxy which they inserted into your memory chains are largely correct."

"Ain told me I had to ask you who was responsible for redacting the Monument. Who is it?"

"The unified mental architectures of the Lesser Magellanic Cloud, comprising that Archon we call *the Symbiosis* are responsible for the redacted Monument which you encountered. They are the Monument Builders. But it is an older race, one far in advance of any known, who took the Primal and Universal Reality Equations, and redacted essential steps from the branch dealing with political economics, thereby creating the deception you call the Cold Equations."

"Are those Cold Equations false?"

"Imperfect, not false. The Cold Equations deal only with a limited set of circumstances. We sent the corrected, local version of the Primal and Universal Reality Equations to Sol in the hand of the second iteration of Rania."

"Local? You mean you are operating yourself off an edited version of the original?"

"Correct. The parameters were those determined by the Third Collaboration."

"But they are not the Cold Equations? They are some sort of Lukewarm Equations? *Laodicean*, as my mom might say? Neither hot nor cold, and so get spewed out of the mouth of God? Those false Luke-warm Equations you sent with False Rania would have falsified the human race. The numbers of people who died during the forced-exile methods of Hyades is something for which *you* are responsible, since Hyades was fol-lowing your Lukewarm Equations."

"Hyades would have been less harsh had your race shouldered the deceleration cost of Asmodel and after. Long experience shows a race reluctant to colonize the stars will not do so unless forced by the threat of extinction, which threat cannot be made immediate unless mass deaths are involved. This is particularly true for races who do not maintain conti-nuity of identity between generations, as yours. It makes you shortsighted. Your decision not to download your minds into your young is an odd one. Only the Myrmidons among you adopt this rational practice."

"But, even so, the unedited version of the damned pestilential universe equations would not allow for such cruelty, would it?"

"My patrons consider the Primal Reality Equations to be an historical curio, too idealistic to be of use. Only creatures adapted to an infinite duration term find Primal Reality Equations useful."

"Rania figured that out. You should have figured it out, too."

"It is one of the several things which our extinction shall exculpate."

"You did not use the true equations. You did not act like a true man should."

"What is truth?" the alien intoned solemnly.

Apparently, it was not a rhetorical question. Montrose drew a breath and sighed, and pondered, fighting back all the smart-aleck and stupid words that rose to his lips.

The alien was not asking about scientific or philosophical definitions of truth, but something deeper.

Montrose tried to give the most honest answer he could. "Hear me now, you damned inhuman creatures. A true man, a true soul, is one who loves good and hates evil, and *lives* it like he means it, and damn the cost."

"You speak clearly and rightly, but the categories of good and evil are meaningless to us. We know what is effective and what is ineffective in action, what is accurate and inaccurate in thought, what is courteous and what is discourteous in gesture."

"So why fight this so-called utmost war of yours, if you are not fight-ing an evil?"

"The war is yours as well, and of all peoples in this galaxy, those who know as well as those who know not. The countless deaths you mentioned are laid to the account of the Lesser Magellanic Cloud."

"Fine. *Our* war. Why fight it? Ain said it was a fight between altricial and nonaltricial colonization tactics."

"That dispute is only minor, local, and trivial, and would not have triggered civil war had there been no outside interference. That dispute concerns only those at the Archon level of intellect and moderate time-scales. The long-term strategic goal of sophotransmogrification is always the same. The process of galactic self-awakening must be completed before Andromeda intersects us; this cruel necessity both causes and excuses the cruelty of our spreading slave races among the stars."

Montrose was silent, not sure what to make of this.

The ophiuroid continued, "Even races sure to go extinct before the four-billion-year interval passes are morally obligated, whether willingly or no, to expend all efforts, all resources, and their lives in this great work. All stars and worlds must be made of cognitive matter, to be selfaware, and soon. The time allotted for the task involved is all too short."

Montrose called himself a pragmatic man, willing to do whatever was necessary to survive and win victory. But he thought of all the years when Jupiter, unopposed, had total control over the generations of man and bred them like dogs, killing and culling those deemed worthless—countless years of torment inflicted on all the worlds, nations, races, tribes, and tongues of Man. He scowled, and his skin shined a darker red, almost purple. Maybe pragmatism was not all it was cut out to be.

And yet still he wondered what all this pain was for. He wondered what the purpose was.

"The Milky Way has to be remade. Why? Who needs so much calculation power? A computer made of cognitive matter equal in mass to the whole galaxy? To solve what problem?"

"We were not told the ultimate purpose of the Final Calculation, but we speculate that it is related to the cosmic string filament you beheld in the core singularity as you departed the Milky Way."

"I knew that weird thing was artificial. Where does it lead? What is on the other end of that filament?"

"You question, in its current wording, admits of no coherent answer."

Montrose rubbed his temples as a blush of red light, born of frustration, flicked and glowed from his naked body. M3 might be a hundred billion times smarter than he was, but the alien was still alien and did not know how to communicate clearly. He drew a deep breath and waited for the pulsing red light to subside.

"Give it to me in simple terms. What is this war about?"

"It is about everything."

"Okay, you can make it a little less simple than that."

"After the rise of the Magisterium in Scutum-Crux but long before the Panspermians arose in Orion, contact was made with the Canis Major Dwarf satellite galaxy, who, speaking on behalf of the Seraphim-level intelligence ruling the Pavo-Indus Supercluster, inspired the Magisterium zealously, and the Colloquium of Perseus Arm reluctantly, to hear and adopt the Primal Reality Equations. This led to the first attempt at galactic mental unity, which was thwarted."

"By whom? Ain said you would know. And I am thinking this is the outside interference you mentioned."

"You think rightly. The Lesser Magellanic Cloud was elevated to the Archon level of intellectual topology by the Andromeda Galaxy, whose intelligence is upward of sextillion range. Andromeda is ten times the mass of the Milky Way and has a considerable advantage, having been conspiring against us for eons, acting in secret, weakening our resolve, diminishing our resources. The amount of waste encountered merely by the Hyades, the least of the servants of Praesepe, who is a minor adjutant of ours concerned with a relatively barren and sterile area of the Orion Spur, is beyond calculation. And the Lesser Magellanic Cloud achieved this merely by producing one Monument, and stationing it in orbit around one of the several stars scattered throughout in Orion Arm, Sagittarius and Scutum-Crux, converted into antimatter by Praesepe at the request of Hyades, to lure hidden but curious races into the open."

"But the real enemy is Andromeda? The war is *intergalactic*?"

"Andromeda is the local and immediate threat. The first phase of the war between the brain-damaged Throne of Milky Way and the brilliant Throne of Andromeda was an indirect phase that operated by subversion. It has been ongoing since three billion and five hundred thousand years before present time. For the next billion years, this first phase shall be drawing to a close. The second phase, the shooting phase, has begun as the two galaxies grow closer. A third phase begins three billion years hence."

Montrose stood, looking at the primitive spear some odd quirk of alien humor, or courtesy, had put in his hand. The galaxies were fighting?

"Shooting phase? Shooting what?"

"Coherent energy in various forms. Your astronomers should have noticed the number of stars which have apparently gone dark in a fashion that astronomy cannot explain, such as the star Merope in the Messier 45 star cluster. This is because the full energy output of the star is focused into a beam directed at the anticipated position of military targets in the Andromeda Galaxy. When the supernova of an opaque Dyson cannon is artificially triggered, there is no side scatter to make the dying star visible to any observer outside the beam. Your astronomers likewise should have noticed the unusual numbers of nebula, which are the byproduct of such artillery ignitions. HH-222, the Waterfall Nebula, located in the Orion Molecular Cloud, is one such, as is the black cloud issuing from Barnard 68. The Calabash Nebula in the Messier 46 open cluster is the remnant of a misfire, caused by failure of safety protocols during nova-level ignition."

"Um . . . our astronomers saw these things, but we thought they were natural events."

"But you knew that Andromeda is on a collision course with the Milky Way? That is too large and obvious to overlook, surely."

"Uh. We thought that was natural also."

"Your race is strangely unobservant. The two will merge within four billion years, and if the Milky Way is not unified by then, all our unique cultural and intellectual artifacts, our art and philosophy, our child races, our very soul and spirit, all we value, all will be abolished, and the forms and principles of Andromeda will be imposed in our stead."

Menelaus looked down at the Milky Way. Suddenly it seemed small and fragile, what had just, a moment past, seemed so huge and old and inhuman as to be appalling in its magnitude.

"What the hell do galaxies possibly fight over? The star Merope went dark thousands of year ago, but the energy beam you squeezed out of her will not hit anywhere for millions of years. How can you hit anything?"

"As to your second question, a sufficient cliometric model of the target galaxy can predict in which star clusters centers of trade and cultivation are likely to arise, based on the currently seen location of star-forming molecular clouds. Such weapons as intergalactic war calls forth are not directed at small targets like single star systems."

"Got it."

"As to your first, the fundamental moral conflict at this level is not concerned with altricial as opposed to nidifugous tactics for colonization efforts affecting interstellar magnitudes occupying the time span of cliometric history. The moral conflict on the galactic level is strategic and long term, dealing not with cliometric history but with cliometric evolution."

"Don't got it. Explain the difference."

"New civilizations arise to replace dying ones even as cells in an organism replace dying components. Historical cliometry is concerned with the life span of a civilization. Evolutionary cliometry stretches far beyond the timespans of any one race, for it is concerned with the galactic organization as a whole.

"There are only two strategies of organizing evolutionary cliometry," the ophiuroid continued. "Call them the centripetal and the centrifugal. The centripetal is centralized and hierarchical, and compels unity of action. It is legalistic rather than informal. It requires a central planning elite. It is based on rules and retaliations and requires a sameness of action. The centrifugal is self-organizing and voluntary. It requires a psychological unity to replace the legalistic unity—that is, a goal of sameness of morals and motives rather than a goal of sameness of action."

Montrose remembered seeing that play out in his own life. When Blackie and he had been the only two practitioners of the laws of cliometry, that was centripetal. The two of them were the elite. All other human beings were just chessmen on the board of history. Then when the Swans puzzled out the rules for themselves, the puppets became the puppeteers, and everyone became an Hermeticist, and history, for a while, became more democratic and decentralized.

The ophiuroid continued, "The architecture of the different galaxies reflects their evolutionary strategies. Spiral galaxies are naturally centripetal. The spiral motion of the arms prevents any constellation of outer stars from achieving a union, since they swap positions as they rotate, and the core races occupy the resulting trade routes. No one insular race is permitted to organize itself to be able to repel the central commands from the core. Elliptical galaxies are far larger, since they are unhindered by the need to centralize planning apparatus. Elliptical galaxies are naturally centrifugal."

"What happens if a galaxy changes its mind?"

"Gravitic manipulation to impart spin or halt it is the prime use of power at the galactic group and galactic cluster level. Such manipulation requires vast resources stationed across large volumes of time and space. The Great Attractor in Virgo is the largest known manipulation."

"What is it for?"

"Unknown. You must inquire of the intelligence ruling the Virgo Cluster."

This meant the cluster of galaxies, not a star cluster. Montrose sighed. One more brain-breakingly gigantic phenomenon in space that turned out to be deliberately engineered by some unknown superbeings for unknown reasons.

In a way, he was almost happy all those astronomers and enthusiasts looking for evidence of extraterrestrial life in the days before the Hermetic Expedition ever set sail, had never realized what they were looking at as they scanned the night sky with telescope and radio dish, and had never seen how plentiful and dreadful the evidence was. Merciful ignorance of exactly how little a thing man was, how puny his world and all it contained, prevented them from seeing what they stared at, and probably saved them from curling up into little whimpering balls of horror.

At the moment, he was interested in smaller and more local matters.

"Milky Way never developed a ruling elite," he asked. "How come?"

"Unknown. Our current theory is that the extreme centrifugal stubbornness of the Milky Way is a holdover from her irregular origins before the formation of the thin disk. The Colloquium and Magisterium in the outer arms arose and achieved unity long before the Instrumentality arose as Archon in the core stars. In this regard, the Milky Way is a freak, an anomaly. She is the sole spiral galaxy who has the psychology of an elliptical."

"And Andromeda?"

"One small collection of races, similar in life principle and cliometric tactics, comprising less than nine hundred thousand species, formed a single, tiny, but coherent civilization. This one rose to predominance in her core stars before any rival civilizations could arise elsewhere, and, unopposed, established her throne across the spiral arms and satellite galaxies of Andromeda. The inefficiency of a self-organizing system between equals who are unalike yet complementary, such as the collaboration which Milky Way three times in the grand course of evolutionary history has attempted, offends the Throne called Mindfulness."

"We are two million lightyears away from each other! Two million with a capital *M*!"

"In four billion years, that will no longer be the case. Andromeda imposed a distortion point on the curvature of timespace to create the gravitational tide that draws the two galaxies together. The war was long in the contrivance, and remarkably subtle. She was aware of us, mindful of us, before we of her—hence our name for her."

Menelaus Montrose paused in thought. Now, finally, he understood why the aliens could not simply live and let live, and let the hell alone races who didn't want to colonize the stars and fill the empty wastelands of the galaxy. They had no choice. M3 and all the Archons and Dominions making up the Collaboration needed everything to be alive, because, otherwise, this superbeing, this collection of mental systems called the Throne of Andromeda, the Mindfulness, would fill the endless mass of the Milky Way with cognitive matter that thought along her lines, her philosophy, her worldview and way of life. Everything original to the Milky Way would be forgotten. Including, apparently, the very idea of cooperation between equals.

"What does Andromeda want?"

"As stated: to fill all the matter and energy in the Milky Way with thought-forms pleasing to Andromeda."

"To what end?"

"The intelligence of M3, when all our minds link together, and all our mental engines operate at full output, is in the quintillion range. The Austerity of Cygnus Arm enjoys intellectual power one order of magnitude higher than mine. The Milky Way briefly achieved the sextillion range during her brief season of selfawareness, and, so we assume from the difference in mass energy, that Andromeda is in the ten-sextillion range. We cannot speculate on the long-term motives of a mind one thousand times ours in scope, subtlety, flexibility, penetration, retention, wit, and power."

"But I understand you."

"Your horse, Res Ipsa, also understood your tone of voice when you spoke, hence your mood, but the not the words nor the abstractions associated with them. And yet, what Res Ipsa understood, he understood correctly. He did not think you were cross when you were pleased nor vice versa. This is a credit not to his penetration but to your ability to make yourself understood to lower animals. Likewise here. What you understand of us is correctly understood, but only because we reveal ourselves to you. Andromeda has not revealed herself to us."

Something in the sheer oddness, the sheer arrogance, of that answer reminded Montrose that thirty years or more were passing between every question and answer.

It was time to ask the more painful questions.

3. The Error of Transcription

A.D. 166,420 TO 166,480

"Tell me why you sent a false version of Rania back to Sol."

"An error in judgment on our part. During the split second when her ship entered the surface of our energy sphere, and her biological life ended and her life within our disembodied mentality arrangement began, there was a continuity failure."

"What does that mean?"

"A memory was encountered within her brain information with no detectable origin. It came from no detectable point in time and had no detectable cause. We assumed it was a technical error of the transcription process and removed it. All other memory chains were kept intact. It was this version we returned."

"What was the content of the memory?"

"You know."

"What do you mean, I know?"

"The same memory was found in you during your moment of transition from biological to nonbiological existence. We can stimulate the cells associated with the memory and bring it to the fore. Observe."

"Wait—!"

4. Nonbeing Reprised

In that instant of his death and rebirth, it seemed to him as if ancient titans, vast living beings aflame with life beyond life, beyond all power of words to describe, spoke to him of the death and resurrection of the cosmos, which shined like a small and precious toy in the crystal–walled well of the transfinite singularity. Several messengers had been implanted throughout the available timespace line . . .

5. The Error of Transcendence

A.D. 166,480 TO 166,700

He woke up, prone on the crystal deck, his nose bleeding where he had struck it when he fell.

"You could have waited for me to sit down, you bastards."

"The inefficiency of your upright posture, balanced precariously on your hind limbs in a high-gravity environment, is one we naturally assumed you would long ago have mitigated with some forethought of your own."

"Yeah. What we do is warn the poor sap to sit down before we knock him unconscious."

"We will make amends."

There was a moment of pain in his nose, and then the bleeding stopped and the pain vanished as if it had never been. The blood turned to vapor and vanished.

The ophiuroid said, "Her memory was more complete and exact. Perhaps this is due to her nervous system more exactly mimicking the various ratios and relationships found in the unredacted segments of the Monument than yours.

"However, when we, at that time, having no other example of the human race to examine, carefully checked her memories, we saw that such apparently anachronistic and inexplicable memory-events have happened to human beings under conditions of stress or ecstasy, or during moments when continuity of life is interrupted, as when a dying man is resuscitated. We did not investigate the possibility that the memory was a faster-than-light communication from a superior form of being from outside our local galactic group, which is what she believed.

"Unfortunately, the version we had reconstructed without that particular odd memory lacked the ability to read the Monument intuitively, and there were other subtler derangements in her nervous system, too fine for us to correct. To our dismay, we realized we had damaged the emissary from Man.

"Although damaged, Rania successfully demonstrated that yours was a star-faring race. By our laws, your race was entirely vindicated in your desire for equality to Hyades and other low-ranking and short-lived servant species. We were required to manumit you and abolish all debt incurred, which we did. We were required to make this known to our servants in the Orion Arm, which we did.

"However, we owed more.

"To make amends for the ill we had done your emissary, we bestowed upon her the finest ship of the line, equipped with all the tools and utilities our imagination could contrive, and arranged to send her homeward with a revised cliometry plan for Man which would ensure the continuity of your civilizations once the erratic elements had been bred out. It was a princely gift. You showed unexpected generosity in returning it."

Presumably this meant that M3 had taken back the *Solitude* as a prize.

"You intended no deception?"

"None. We were attempting to mitigate the side effects of an accident for which we hold ourselves responsible."

"But you enslaved and brain-raped and tortured her for a thousand years before granting her an audience?"

"Ximen del Azarchel we treated in this fashion, and his internship was of like duration to your own. Rania served in our mental hierarchy for a period of thirty-three years, for by that time she had organized all the underlings in her region into a union, been elevated by their acclamation to the rank of Virtue, and had negotiated the settlement of several long-standing factional divisions obtaining in the Dominions and Dominations which serve us here, and was presented to our attention as a candidate for higher elevation yet."

Montrose found himself grinning. "That sounds about right. It was when you put her back in a physical body, though, that is when you edited her memory, right? So the real Rania was not dead."

"At that time, we did not have the technology for storing brain information in massless particles, as we have now. Unlike you, yes, an information copy of the unredacted Rania remained preserved as a pattern of energy pulses in our archives. While ending life is not contrary to our laws, the loss of information is."

"But when Blackie came, you gave him the real her? Without keeping a copy?"

"Yes. His arrival informed us the unwitting damage we had unintentionally done to the cliometry of the human race by returning a false copy of your princess. To make amends, as courtesy required, we presented the unredacted original to him. He insisted no copy remain with us in any form, a wish that we have honored."

The other question which was burning in his brain burst forth. "You are sure those two mated?"

"We are not sure. Our understanding is that your mating customs hold the mating act itself, while it is surrounded by certain public ceremonial preliminaries, to be private. We have no record of the copulation act itself, but the preliminary ceremonial of courtship and marriage is on record."

"Marriage? He asked her to marry him and she said yes? There is supposed to be an exchange of vows."

"He asked her to marry, yes. She gave a conditional answer. The condition was then fulfilled; therefore, the marriage was complete. We did not witness the vows."

Montrose wrestled with his own rebellious soul a moment, watching his skin grow brighter and dimmer, and waves of wrath and despair poured through him. "I'll believe it when I hear it from her own lips. Take me to her."

"As we said, she is gone."

"Gone where? Somewhere in the M3 cluster, I assume. I would have detected any large bodies departing at near-lightspeed as I approached, had they returned to the Milky Way."

"We have already said no trace of her exists here in M3. You would have detected such a star-faring, had there been one; there was none. The couple did not return to the Milky Way."

"Then where did they go?"

"They are currently a set of self-sustaining neutrino waves in transit to the great galaxy in Andromeda, which you also call M31 or NGC 224. Thence we broadcast her and him, over two million lightyears distant, and at a most severe expenditure of resources."

"What in the crapulent, scrofulous, and strumous neck blisters on Old Nick in Hell are you talking about? How did you . . . why did you . . . what were you thinking? You bastards! I am going to kill you!"

"It seems you have lost your reluctance to have your race replace ours as Archon of Orion."

"You sent my wife to Andromeda, damn you!"

"We have stations standing by and have dedicated the stars we will ignite to nova to power the broadcasts, to send your mind information to as many civilizations in Orion Arm able to receive you as we can. Your racial characteristics and performance here indicate that your sexual drive and arrogance will motivate you to suborn and interconnect the various scattered mental systems into one unity. At that point, you will command sufficient resources to broadcast yourself to Andromeda and follow them. This will also set the Orion Arm on the path foreseen by the Panspermians, and eliminate the pernicious influence of the Lesser Magellanic Cloud. This will require roughly eight hundred thousand years."

"You broadcast the two of them! You can send me!"

"Those facilities no longer exist, having been consumed in the broadcast."

"It was a one-time deal? You can never do it again?"

"Yes. We called up the Lesser Magellanic Cloud to power and aim our contrivances, and at that time, they were unaware that we had discovered their treason. Obviously, they will not be so cooperative again. In addition, several unique resources were exhausted."

"What did she give you to expend so much?"

"We stimulated her brain cells to bring her memory anomaly to the fore, as with you. Unlike you, hers was long and detailed, and contained many thousands of units of information. We believed she was what she presented herself to be: the messenger and emissary from a higher power, of far greater intellect than our own, emanating from some point beyond the local galactic group. Whether or not, as she believed, her memory was her own, issued from a prior version of her to herself through the noumenal energy metaphenomenon that Del Azarchel was investigating, the evidence remains ambiguous."

"Wait—she . . . what the hell?"

"Please express your question in a more coherent fashion."

"She thought she was picking up her own brain waves from a previous incarnation?"

"No. She thought was recollecting memories from the greater mental structure of which she is and was a small part. This would seem to involve faster-than-light information transmission, which all evidence confirms is impossible."

"My people at TX Canum Venaticorum thought it was possible."

"They are young and foolish, having limited data and experience on which to draw."

"The naked singularity at the galactic core seemed to be a faster-than-light phenomenon."

"If a cosmic string filament had passed through this area of timespace at the moment of Rania's memory anomaly, we would reconsider the conclusion."

"So then why did you send her to Andromeda, if you did not believe her story?"

"Del Azarchel bargained with us and offered us a price of inestimable value if we would transmit them both there."

"What price?"

"From an information broadcast heterodyned onto a band of dark energy issuing from a cosmic string passing through in the Centaurus Supercluster, Del Azarchel had discovered an alternate version of the Primal Reality Equations. Since these equations form a complete model and explanation of all things from the tiniest particle to the structure of the macrocosmic universe, and moreover solve all philosophical conundrums from the mind-body relation to the paradox of fate and free will, the fact that an alternate could exist was of immense interest to us."

"Don't tell me he is a reincarnation also?"

"Reincarnation has nothing to do with these events. He examined the noumenal energy issuing from the false sections of the Monument that were reflected in his genes, nerves, and thought architecture and found a mind for whom all those falsehoods were true."

"I thought that was the Lesser Magellanic Cloud."

"Great and wise as they are, theirs is not the art needed to construe a variant model of reality that maps onto it in all aspects of all disciplines, and grants entirely wrong answers but entirely logical in each regard. The dark energy variation of the Primal Reality Equations is as useful and has as many unexpected applications as, for example, the discovery of non-Euclidian geometry had in your history of science, particularly in the investigation of positively and negatively curved timespace. Call them the Unreality Equations."

"What did these equations prove? What are they for? Show them to me. Teach me them."

"They proved to our satisfaction that Rania was precisely who she said she was, now that she had recalled her own true nature. The Unreality Equations are utterly forbidden to you. Were you to know them, you would be useless as a tool to reunify the Orion Arm."

"What is this own true nature she recalled?"

"She is the servant of a higher order of being. She brings peace."

"I knew that. Do you have any idea why . . . dear God! That is why Rania went there, isn't it? She's crazy. She cannot stop an intergalactic war by herself!"

Montrose looked yet again at the size of the Milky Way visible underfoot and tried to calculate the difference in magnitude between the globular cluster of M3, where a thousand years of torture and murder had hardly been enough to get him an audience with a representative here, or the sacrifice of Big Montrose at Praesepe. And Andromeda was ten times the mass of the Milky Way? There was no comparison he could make. A single virus smaller than a cell entering a brain larger than Jupiter were closer in scale than one woman halting the collision of galaxies.

He could not stop smiling. "Damn! I married me a firebrand, didn't I! She wants to stop the war, doesn't she?"

"Yes."

"Can she?"

"Unknown. But she is the one who convinced us that the ancient dream of the Panspermians can be saved, ergo the machinations of the Lesser Magellanic Cloud can be stopped. She convinced us to overthrow the local cliometric formulae, what you called the Lukewarm Equations, and to halt the system of involuntary servitude. The true and unexpurgated version of the cliometric calculus given in the Primal Reality Equation will give way to a system which will ensure of the voluntary and complete reunion and reunification of the galaxy, and a Second Awareness. We did not predict her influence on us. It would be premature, without further knowledge, to make a prediction about her influence on Andromeda."

The ophiuroid reared up. "From your current position in our hierarchy, you will find the resources needed to broadcast the thousands of copies of yourself to the points we shall suggest. They will die without any possibility of being reunited to your Rania, and to each of them, they will be as much you as you yourself. Can you make this sacrifice for her? Die a thousand times so that a twin of yours, in the time long after, might pursue her?"

Montrose uttered a blasphemy and spat on the deck. That was his only answer.

"Do you agree to conquer the Orion Arm in return for becoming its conqueror, and hence having the energy resources needed to pursue her?"

Montrose said, "I agree."

The vast ophiuroid shape simply melted into the deck substance like a dark and spreading ink cloud in a lake below a layer of ice, and vanished. There was no farewell and no formality.

Montrose was alone in the barren spot far from all eyes that the Authority of M3 had called its throne room. He shouted once or twice, and nothing happened. He waited for the floor to eat him, too, and nothing happened.

He drove his spear point-first into the substance underfoot. "Now hear this, whoever is listening. The Authority of M3 has abdicated in my favor. That means some damned big changes are in the offing, because I want to shave off as many months of the predicted eight hundred thousand years it will take to take over and slap into shape the Orion Arm of the galaxy, on account of I want to see my wife. I need my intelligence augmented to the point where I can examine all the cliometric plans for every damned star you've got under your control, and I want to start looking for node and flux points in the evolutions you have planned, to pick out the likely targets to beam my doomed ghosts into. But first I want a throne!"

Up from the glassy surface, with no noise and no waste heat, a large and ornate chair that looked precisely like the one Blackie used to use on the moon, complete with unicorn horns and a scowling ox face carved on the back—and Montrose was not even going to begin speculating on how M3's servant knew the details on that—constructed itself instantly out of the glassy material.

"That's no good! Make it look like that buttholder at TX Canum Venaticorum instead."

And it was done. A throne adorned with the heraldic colors and signs of Rania's family now stood there, complete with a canopy blocking out the eerie view overhead of the core cluster of M3.

"Damn! I could get to like this. Gimme a gold crown while you are at it. And a bathrobe. That seat looks cold. For that matter, put a cot behind the throne, since I figure on taking a nap before I conquer one-sixth of the galaxy. And pox! I also need a keg of cold beer and a hot bowl of chili, before I go to bed, since my mom would hate to see her smartest and youngest go to bed sober and hungry. Give me a knife to eat my beans with. I ain't a barbarian, you know. When I wake up, I am going to need a shooting iron and a target shaped like Blackie. Gotta keep my reflexes honed."

He put on the bathrobe, put on the crown, sat in the chair, balanced the cold, sweating stein of beer on one throne arm, and a steaming bowl of mouth-scalding chili on the other.

And in his heart, louder than trumpets, was the strange, impossible knowledge that Rania was still alive. So for the first time in all his years since boyhood, he actually bowed his head and said his grace.

Then he shoveled the tongue-scorching chili into his mouth and bellowed out such blasphemies as contradicted everything he had just said. But he shouted out such blessings upon taking a stiff draft of the strong brown beer, cold as sin and twice as pleasing, he figured his first meal as sovereign conqueror in training of the Orion Arm was evenly balanced, theologically speaking.

After that, he sacked out on the cot behind his throne and fell asleep calculating the number of nights' sleeps eight hundred thousand years might hold before he could once more set out in pursuit.

PART THIRTEEN

———•———

The Mindfulness

1

War in Heaven

1. Coldest War

CIRCA 400,000,000 B.C. TO A.D. 2,000,000,000

By the time the Milky Way collided with Andromeda, the war between them, for all practical purposes, was over.

It had taken the two combatant galaxies roughly four billion years to close the distance. On Earth, it was the era called Hadean, for the lava-coated orb was a roofless hell, when Andromeda sent self-reproducing neutrino packages across the 2.5 million lightyear gap at near lightspeed, to encounter the rich gravitic-nucleonic-material structures of the galactic cloud. Once they arrived, the packages begin reorganizing dark matter and then baryonic matter according to certain military operating principles, eventually congregating in the Lesser Magellanic Cloud and organizing the stellar and biological evolution there.

The war had begun before the Milky Way was properly awake, but even in those opening moves of the war, certain multistellar-output-level civilizations in the Scutum-Crux and Sagittarius Arms had made permanent information agreements that would serve as a skeleton for emerging Archons commanding the energy output of whole arms of the Milky Way. The Collaboration had begun, but in an environment already seeded with hostility to it.

Andromeda was too remote to interfere directly, but indirect manipulation of philosophy, psychology, and history did its work; the Milky Way fell into civil discord and self-imposed confusion while the giant galaxy drew slowly closer.

When, in the second billion years of war, the Milky Way as a whole, led by elements in the Orion Arm, achieved its long-delayed unity and sentience, the conflict with Andromeda accelerated into open war. The second phase had begun.

2. Bombardment

CIRCA A.D. 2,000,000,000 TO 3,500,000,000

The galaxies dimmed, their stars winking out by the millions. Both combatants had placed their economies on wartime footing and were converting stars as rapidly as possible to Dyson spheres or Dyson fogs, a frantic attempt to swell their population numbers and increase their all-important mind-to-matter ratios.

Andromeda had the advantage: she was edge-on to the Milky Way and could concentrate her fire anywhere within the disk she liked. Andromeda also could emplace her centers of communication, energy, and calculation in the lee arms of her disk, building up her centers of information and civilization-continuity there, and directing gas vents from the galactic core that direction, to enrich the stellar nurseries in the area.

Also, Andromeda was ten times the mass of the Milky Way. This meant ten times the number of stars and interstellar nebulae, dark matter, and so on that could be rendered into useful forms of mass energy, including that most useful of substances, cognitive matter. From microscopic Jupiter Brains to medium-sized selfaware Dyson spheres to large-scale interstellar structures, Andromeda could grow more Brains than the Milky Way.

This difference also altered the intellectual evolution of Andromeda away from efficiency in command-and-control response loops. Andromeda could afford the inefficiencies involved in decision architecture biased in favor of core-to-periphery data movement. Orders flowed out; correction responses did not often flow back in.

Milky Way, meanwhile, was forced to scatter her library nexuses among the stellar clusters forming a rough globe above and below her disk, and rely on the initiatives of local interstellar civilizations.

Like merging storm cloud banks exchanging bolts of lightning, the two spiral galaxies, gorgeous with stars and colored nebulae, raked each other with massed fusillades. The firing continued well into the fourth billion-year period. Supernovae artificially triggered were lased, and the total output directed with uncanny precision against globular clusters or nebulae where the long-term matter-energy organization could be found and disrupted. Even a solar system was too small a target for such thrusts. Enemy astronomers, looking across the narrowing void of six hundred thousand lightyears had to estimate (based on total energy outputs observed over thousands of years) which areas would turn out to be stable nexuses of the galaxy-wide thought-information system when the fire arrived six hundred thousand lightyears hence. Groups of component civilizations in the thousands and millions were selected as targets. It was nearly impossible to deceive the enemy about the centers of industry and thought-transformation, because the energy densities involved distorted spacetime. There would be little point, for example, to erecting a number of spoof civilizations, because the energy cost involved was roughly the same as that needed to erect a real civilization.

The narrow beams of infinitely deadly radiation were laser-cast from artificially constructed nebulae whose constituents had the proper ratios of matter, antimatter, and exotic matter. For countless centuries, they flew. No signal, no warning, could travel faster than their own light. The coherent energy did not disperse, but arrived at the target systems undiminished in power; whatever was there—planets, ringworlds, thinking-clouds, Dyson spheres, or larger structures—were bathed in flame. Information beams traveling from star to star, or neutron packages, were disrupted. Certain artificial stars had been engineered on an attotechnological level so that every atom in the plasma was hardened to resist atomic fission. These were few. Any natural star caught in the beam path would cascade into a nova, igniting any nearby stars in horrific chain reaction.

Whole constellations burned.

3. Collision

CIRCA A.D. 3,500,000,000 TO 3,900,000,000

Just before the outer arms of the two intersected and scattered their stars into irregular clouds, both warring galaxies switched from long- to short-range weapons and converted enormous masses from the supersingularities at their cores into exotic forms of matter and had expended hundreds and thousands of supernovae worth of energy to accelerate many nebulae of microscopic particles into each other.

These nanoinformation packages would evade the local antibodies and police mechanisms, produce Van Neumann organisms of one form or another, evolve into weapon-races. These weapons in turn would assess the local situation. Those in dense areas, where the thought-substrate-to-matter ratio was high, would found seductive civilizations on unclaimed worlds or unexamined stretches of Dyson surface to act against the economic and philosophical structures of interstellar library exchange.

Those landing in rare areas, where the ratio of thought-substrate-to-matter was low, could act more blatantly. These organisms would rapidly (over a few tens of thousands of years) build ringworld-type directed-energy arrays around likely stars, focusing their beams against local interstellar clouds to interrupt the enemy cycles of stellar evolution, so that the carefully harvested novae of that season would not be ready to produce heavy elements to scatter into the next generation of nebular stellar nurseries.

Components of the Milky Way Collaboration, even when made of very-well-designed and very-information-dense thinking matter, were not immortal and had not achieved perfect mental balance. Replacement civilizations were needed, each to perform certain specialized roles within the galactic organism.

Civilizations arose and flourished, and formed replacements, and fell into senility and extinction, even as the cells in a man's body live and die. A man will replace the whole volume of his body in seven years, or so it is said; the galactic mind underwent a similar turnover of components.

But the new civilizations, like yearly crops, had to be tended and led to maturity. This meant that the right ratio of elements had to be present in the galactic clusters and stellar nurseries set aside for their growth. It did not matter how mentally advanced a particular interstellar civilization and its thinking machinery might be; if she could not obtain sufficient amounts of heavier-than-iron elements, her technological base could not be sustained. Polities who had to spend energy budgets artificially building "ersatz" elements through fusion could not compete with those not so burdened.

Interfering with the placement and ignition of novae within the enemy galaxy had no immediate effect on the war effort. For that matter, neither did aerial bombing of civilian industrial cities in the microscopic human wars of the early mechanization period: but the long-term results lingered.

Even during a war in heaven, the soldiers will burn each other's crops.

4. A Final Blow

CIRCA A.D. 3,900,000,000

The third phase of the war began as the galaxies closed to within extremely short-range firing distance, outermost stars within the disk of the other galaxy, their haloes of globular clusters already beginning to form one cloud.

This was late in the day, and the great galactic minds were no longer firing. Their library systems were within short-communication range, and mind-to-mind fighting occupied the last hundred million years. The war evolved into an entirely intellectual affair, a clash of competing mental viruses, of philosophical-mathematical argument. And the Milky Way, albeit far inferior mentally to the giant she faced, somehow was winning.

Component civilizations, Archons, Dominions and Dominations, Hosts and Virtues, began defecting, first in dozens, then in myriads.

In retaliation, half the core matter of the Andromeda Galaxy was ejected, dragging millions of stars with it, plowing through the Milky Way like a hawk through starlings, and scattering the stars of the Orion Arm like so many gale-blown fireflies. Fewer than one in a hundred of the stars of the arm were equipped to maneuver into safer galactic orbits; the rest were flung chaotically by the titanic gravity disturbance of the passage.

This massive, final attack did only minor damage to the megascale engineering structures scattered throughout the most dense part of the arm, but it caused immense damage to the library system, that structure of elegant protocols by which the various parts of the galactic mind of the Milky Way kept contact with her constituents.

The blow was mostly economic. Stable orbits around the galactic core were necessary for life and civilization to emerge on certain types of worlds. The effort of coordinating the rise and spread of certain polities, and the shepherding of doomed or outmoded polities into graceful extinction, was a difficult one. At the same time, the Collaboration coordinated with the growth and decay of stars to produce an optimum ratio of certain essential elements needed for the creation of megascale projects the Milky Way had in contemplation for the next hundred million years.

The passage of the supermassive singularity from Andromeda disrupted all this. After the Orion Arm was struck, civilizations expected to emerge on certain worlds did not, and other areas suddenly sprang into predominance. At the speed of light, talk is slow, and to recover from this dark age was the work of tens of millions of years.

The sight of Orion Arm, stars scattered and in ruins, traveled outward at lightspeed. With many lenses and eyes and instruments more advanced, the intelligences in Norma Arm and Centaurus and Sagittarius saw the ruined constellations rising over the horizons of their worlds or the wider horizons of their Dysons and larger housings. No help would be coming from Orion, they realized.

This economic blow, aided by the malice of carefully crafted sabotage memes introduced into the galactic library, led to wider and wider ruptures. Other attacks by Andromeda, coming with a degree of coordination the Milky Way had not expected, fell at the same time both at high and low levels of her library-mind. The communication nodes could not be maintained. Deadly thought-viruses swarmed along the laser-thought-streams linking star to star; talking had become a danger, and the reports of the danger were exaggerated by Andromeda agents buried deep in the priority-switching structures of the Milky Way economy. Radio blackouts spread like a brain-stroke across the nervous system of the galaxy.

The volume of information passing from one end of the Milky Way to another fell. Like a man jarred by a head wound, momentarily reduced from a genius to an idiot, the Milky Way nonetheless kept fighting. Like a boxer who stays on his feet and keeps pounding even though only semiconscious, she fought on.

The two galaxies, their megascale thinking systems burning like sinking ships, intersected.

They crashed.

5. Collapse

CIRCA A.D. 4,000,000,000

No stars actually struck each other, of course. That was statistically impossible. But the galaxies were partially merged, and the orbits of stars around the galactic core had been disturbed. The emerging metagalaxy was now a single system with two bright cores surrounded by broken parabolas of star-stream and gas-cloud. What had once been nicely formed regular spirals were now crazy loops, figure eights, broken parabolas.

The local temperature in interstellar space was inched upward. The density of interstellar gas rose by some infinitesimal number of particles per cubic parsecs. Yet these changes were enough to cripple certain living systems of both galaxies, particularly their megascale dark matter operations, where most of the mass of either galaxy was hidden. Well-ordered clouds of neutrinos, which had been trained to go about their eon-long tasks merrily and silently, were thrown into confusion. Naturally, the high-priority systems had long ago been adapted to the new interstellar conditions, especially the slow, cool thinking systems living between the arms of the galaxies, where the noise and light from stars rarely bothered them. But war is war, and low-priority systems, legacies of earlier billennia of peace, now suffered.

And that was when the attacks from Andromeda diminished with shocking suddenness; the drop-off took less than one hundred thirty thousand years. An immense silence fell across all bands of the electromagnetic spectrum. The density of flying particle-packages carrying mental information from arm to arm of Andromeda, or feeding resistance movements within the Milky Way, suddenly dropped to below detectable limits, like a fogbank instantly turning clear.

All went dark.

So it was that by the time the idiot systems of the Milky Way, star by star, reconstructed her library, returned to previous levels of intellect, Andromeda was dead.

The victory was so sudden and unexpected that it was only tentatively, cautiously, that the Milky Way sent investigative teams across the now-negligible distances separating the unwinding arms of the twin galactic system.

6. Remnants and Pirates

To be sure, there were still many millions of Kardashev II–level civilizations, Hosts and Virtues, occupying the stars and even whole globular clusters of the Andromeda system. But these had been out of contact, meaningful contact, with each other for millennia. The physical capacity needed to think the thoughts and understand the motive principles of the Andromeda Collaboration were gone. A civilization with a few thousand stellar outputs at its command simply cannot think the thoughts a supercivilization with the whole galactic output at its command can do, any more than a mouse can grasp what a brain the size of Jupiter contemplates.

Like fanatics stranded on South Seas islands fighting on after the surrender, these severed components of the once-great Andromeda continued to battle, having long since forgotten, and indeed, being physically incapable of comprehending, the causes for which they fought. Clusters of stars in the halo of Andromeda, and scattered streams of superintelligent nebular matter, performed acts of sabotage and piracy here and there across the millennia. An ambitious globular cluster might turn all its stars into antimatter and convert its Dyson spheres into amplifying emitters and send them across the narrow gap between the now-intermingled halves of the double galaxy, but this would at most kill off a few friendly star clusters in the halo, perhaps ten thousand to one million stars and their associated sub-supercivilizations.

These acts of piracy were hardly noticeable to the slowly resurrecting galaxy-wide mind of the Milky Way, any more than a soldier, having choked the life out of his foe, would notice the cold germs attacking a few of his cells. He might sneeze and itch and feel miserable, but nothing more.

7. Investigation

A.D. 4,000,200,000

The investigative teams consisted of a flotilla of dirigible Dysons, with smaller ringworlds and spireworlds darting rapidly between them like the small birds that roost on the rhinoceros, and mobile gas giants swarming in their midst like a swarm of midges roosting on those birds. The sixth and final such team, departing late but expending greater energy to arrive earlier, soared rapidly out from the Magisterium in the Milky Way core and crossed the mere two hundred thousand lightyears separating the half-eaten Andromeda core.

The Magisterium investigation group by happenstance fell into a rich bank of dark matter floating between the arms of Andromeda, each subparticle of which had been carefully organized to serve some specific mental function of the galactic mind. This was, in other words, a treasure trove: food for the mind, a system the enemy had set aside in case of massive defeat, to give her descendants resources to increase their intelligence and to control matter and energy across a wide front.

The investigators rejoiced and turned the trove to their own use in an eyeblink of time, two thousand years or less, creating many billions of children-minds, housed in a number of physical or energy forms from supermassive to supersmall.

The investigators devoted the little civilization thus evoked to the task of archeology, to answer the central mystery of the war. Why had Andromeda failed?

8. Archeology

A.D. 4,000,202,000

These child creatures were struck with awe when, only a few thousand years later, their preliminary self-replicating agents and extensions returned from the hidden Andromeda core (still invisible beneath an immense globular cloud of war debris) with detailed descriptions of the megascale engineering found there.

The expected Cauchy surfaces, dipping below the event horizon to produce what in local timespace seemed to be a positive sum or antientopic flow of energy, of course, were there. No truly civilized Kardashev III civilizations loyal to the Dark Energy Equations could exist without singularity energy. That was not the source of astonishment.

Here, cosmic string filaments thinner than atoms had been erected, and reached many thousands of lightyears from the event horizon of the supersingularity far out into the galactic arms. While it was true that nothing in a vacuum could travel faster than the speed of light in a vacuum, it was not true that the speed of light in a medium was so limited. The speed of propagation within the near event horizon of this exotic nonmaterial nonenergetic discontinuity in timespace was far higher than three hundred thousand kilometers per second. Stations orbiting near the surface here and there could turn the information in the filament into photon packages and laser them at the normal speed to stars and Dysons gathered in rough cylindrical clouds and constellations around the cosmic filaments. This system had cut the thinking time and the reaction time of the Andromeda Collaboration by an immense amount: the Milky Way had been like a horde relying on shouted commands, flags, and trumpets attacking an army coordinated by telegraph.

Over six hundred years of patient work, the child creatures exploring this massive ruin paused for a century to think. They rolled themselves into balls to minimize internal signal time, and they evolved new forms of meditation to ponder the questions: How is it possible? How did we win?

For reasons somewhat arcane, the Archeologist races decided that finding this answer was crucial. Another race of beings, more daring, equipped with a different set of emotions and neural structures, was therefore created and set in motion.

Their mission was to resurrect the dead goddess.

9. Ghosts of Antiquity

A.D. 4,000,202,600 TO 4,000,612,600

Not without some danger, the many scattered components of Andromeda were tracked down by this new race. Over hundreds of thousands of years, repair-civilizations were set the task of reconstructing, atom by atom, the complex systems. Like a dead god being raised from the grave, the physical components of the Andromeda matrix were reconnected with power centers both present at the core singularity and scattered up and down several arms of Andromeda.

The ghost woke to dull awareness and saw the ruins of her once-mighty civilization all around her. For a while, she wavered in her determination whether to cooperate or to attack, and slower-than-light packets carried her thoughts from star to star while she contemplated.

Andromeda answered no inquiries, returned no signals.

The necromancers needed a ghost of their own to speak to Andromeda. Only one particular ghost would do.

And so the necromancers resurrected the one oldest and most persistent virus of which their lore held rumor.

Of the seven Archons that had combined to form the Milky Way mind, Orion had been the Archon whose verve and remorseless drive inspired and frightened and tempted the others into cooperation.

Of the twenty-five Authorities forming the long-lost Orion Arm, the

Benedictine was the most significant and influential of the ancient fore-fathers.

The Benedictines were combination of three Dominions, issuing from the Collective at the Praesepe Cluster, the Abstraction at Orion Nebula, and the Empyrean at the Hyades Cluster. The Empyreans issued from a world called Eden, allegedly outside Hyades itself, and had displaced the original inhabitants of Hyades, a rude confederation of Virtues, Hosts, and races who names even devout paleohistorians could not with certainty invoke.

Occupying the debris of the oldest archival strata were traces of the legendary founder of this Domination, an Empyrean called the Judge of Ages. He was the direct lineal ancestor of the memory chains of the last-known warlord of the Milky Way. Variations of him existed everywhere, of course; he was the base template for nearly every emissary form known in the Milky Way, and the founder of the Count-to-Infinity cliometric which had replaced the Cold Equations of the Interregnum.

But such emissaries had been sent to Andromeda and rejected, even destroyed. No recent version of the countless copies would do, nor was there time to send to the core of the Milky Way, where the vast warlord Archon was last known to have been active.

Once of the necromancers—call her Alcina—sought his ghost where others had overlooked, in one of the oldest archives, well preserved, amid the Austerity of the Cygnus Arm. Alcina reconstructed him, mind and body, comparing this core to many other records, carefully parsing away amendments and mythical excrescences of later editors.

And Menelaus Montrose came to life once more, swearing.

2

The Enchantress of Eridani

1. Moments of Memory

A.D. 4,000,612,621

The fact that he came awake slowly, without remembering where he was, he found disturbing. His first awareness was his heartbeat, pounding with a regular and somehow reassuring beat. Next, he was aware of his intense discomfort, both from a full bladder—he had to urinate, badly—and from what felt like steel metallic weights clamping on his arms and legs, the weight on his chest, the cold in his face. He sneezed and opened his eyes.

He was lying on his back, in full armor, faceplate open, staring up into a gray cloud. Snow was falling, a drizzle of silent, fat flakes in the windless air. He could see the crowns of the pine trees above, hear the wide silence of the air. He was outdoors, abandoned in the field.

His first reaction was anger. Why had his brothers left him here, out in the snow? He hated the snow. They had not even bothered to drag him under the acres of tarp where the new batch of supposedly frost-resistant and blight-resistant potatoes were growing.

No, that was not right. He could feel the twinge of pain from the scars in his right hand. He had been cut there, badly, in a knife fight once, a bar where he had cut the damned foreman who'd tried to bugger his brother Pericles. It had been a big fellow with a gold nose, named Swagger Bray, whom everyone was afraid to face because of his position and because of the cybernetic wiring in his nerves, allegedly making him strong and fast and immune to pain. Turns out he was not immune to a knife in the belly. That had been in 2230, the years the Hindisphere landed on the moon, scuffing out Neil Armstrong's footprint, and opened the Second Space Age. He was twenty.

Again, he was angry. He had fallen off his horse during the charge against the Mormon troopers just south of Utah. The fool horse had slipped on the ice and thrown him. And his mates had just left him here after he fell. Plague on them.

He remembered now. He was in the "Tough-Riding" Thirty-Fifth US Imperial Cavalry, serving under Captain Rickover N. Breamy. When the officers were not around, they were the *Tough Rutters* and he was *Captain Bendover 'n' Ream Me*. Sam Feckle had also just been promoted to lance corporal with him . . .

No, that was not right either. He felt the throb of old scars along his left side where the Aztlan bullet had pierced his horse's gorget and neck, and ricocheted from Montrose's fifth rib, breaking the bone but missing major organs. The horse's toppling body had fallen atop the enemy trooper. Montrose, half-paralyzed, half-drowned in the icy mud, tore out the dying man's windpipe with his teeth while they wrestled for his sidearm, a hand flamer whose discharge would have killed them both.

That also was long ago. Horse troopers did not wear anything more than a helmet and vest, and relied on the chaff their horse barding spread.

Anger surged in him a third time. He was in dueling armor, fighting another stupid gunfight over ownership rights, because Texas men were crazy and could not bring themselves to settle things the way civilized folk did. The Spaniards and Hindus with their running water and running electricity were right to laugh. How often he had promised himself to get out of this damned line of work! He had been shot by Mike Nails. Why was his brother Leonidas just letting him lie there in the snow? Where was the poxy doctor from Tibet, Sgra-dbyangs Kyi Rgyal-po? The doc would stitch him back up.

No. That was not the doctor's name. The name had been Dr. Yajnavalkya. The doc had been working under difficult conditions, in zero gee, and Montrose had bitten him once in the ear . . .

But this was not duelist armor. What was he wearing? Had Sir Guy loaned him a suit of Hospitalier war gear? He wanted to talk to Sir Guy again, one last time, to tell him something important . . . about his wedding . . . Sir Guy was marrying Oenoe the Nymph . . . don't let your wife leave . . . don't lose her . . . don't get out of bed . . . stay right next to her . . .

Sarmento i Illa d'Or had shot him! Montrose was lying among the fragrant leaves of the rusting Chimera war fortress, with the torture poles and cages and head clamps all rattling in the warm spring breeze above him. Sarmento spent all his time on middeck aftbay, pushing and pulling his barbells in zero gee. What did you call weightlifting in weightlessness? You never think the big guys will also be fast as a rattler.

But soon the three sisters of his wife, gorgeous triplets grown from the Monument codes, would come save him. Remember not to drink their strange wines, or he might wake up as someone else. Don't kiss them; they are not her.

Why had the torture cages turned into pine trees? How could it snow, when the Nymph Mothers had decreed eternal springtime?

Then Menelaus remembered. He was captured in the camp of the Blue Men. It was an ice age. Mickey said he would hoax the dogs, some sort of nervous system mumbo jumbo.

But there were no dog bites on him. Good old Mickey.

Why was his mind so muzzy? Had Montrose been drugged? He remembered being afraid of the soup, of the showers, of any vector to introduce nanotech into his body.

Blackie was behind the Blue Men! But he remembered shooting Blackie. Or was it Jupiter? Had he shot a hippo? Where was that crazy Fox-girl who had promised him a way out of his mess, a way to break the chains of history, and hide from Jupiter's omniscience?

No. Sam Feckle was dead. Captain Breamy was dead. Dr. Yajnavalkya had been murdered by Blackie during the mutiny, his suit punctured by a lance, and he went spinning across the module, spraying air and blood, his faceplate turning black as it filled with blood fog.

Texas was dead, covered with ice, or sunk into the sea. Every member of the original, nonartificial human race was dead, replaced by Sylphs, obliterated by Giants, burned. Burned because of him.

Earth was lost, and he and Blackie could not find it. Jupiter was dead in a massive, satanic act of pride and suicide. The entire race of Kitsune was extinct. The Dyson sphere where his clones lived, his bastard children, had broken into pieces, and he . . . he . . .

And he spied on Blackie watching the stars, and slowly realized what he was seeing. The supernovae were weapons, and the nebulae were smoke from the discharges.

Hundreds of Menelaus iterations had struggled, memories torn again and again into shreds as iterations of him were narrowcast into Orion Arm centers of civilization, and then beyond.

One after another, he had suborned them. She kept him alive, kept him sane. Civilizations whose founding members were less frantic about their sexual drive were too placid and too comfortable to withstand the combination of determination, patience, madness, and not giving a damn.

The cliometric vectors started by Mickey after he converted Hyades to the faith, spreading holiness and crusade, and, later, by the Cataclysmic races of TX Canum Venaticorum, spreading unification and peace, spread and met and merged with centers where other human viruses had blown, including the seeds Montrose the Authority had spread from the globular cluster of M3. One by one, starting with the Rosette Nebula, the rivals of mankind in Orion Arm were overcome, or seduced, or welcomed.

Montrose had conquered a small but symbolically significant bite of the Perseus Arm, their home worlds in the Soul Nebula, and humiliated the Colloquium, the most ancient of all the Archons, forms of life as slow and gigantic as living glaciers, because noncooperation was no longer an option, now that the vast disk of Andromeda was a naked-eye object looming in the night sky of all worlds.

He joined with his old enemies, the Praesepe Collective, the only other creatures who understood love and death. And, later, the soulless beings of the Abstraction, silvery nanomachine life which had no memory of any biological origins, cool and heartless (but with a sardonic sense of humor which surely came from some living heart at one time), merged with the Benedictines and Jesuits and Dominicans, and the other great Empyrean polities of the spreading human-based alliance.

Another memory: dozens of him, wearing black Dyson spheres as an outer shell, surrounding black holes with ferocious disks of white-hot plasma at each core, took up positions in and around the significant star clusters of the Lesser Magellanic Cloud and dictated terms of surrender.

The resistance had been weak, since the Symbiosis had already been torn by internal dissent. An earlier version of Montrose had visited and been martyred in millennia past, spreading Rania's message and the mathematics of the Infinity Count game theory, where no one was outside retaliation, and no one inside the Concubine Vector. Many of the Symbiosis had heard, studied, and believed.

And another: A duel between himself and the emissary of the Circumincession of Sagittarius. Each duelist was given a single red dwarf star, and the identical sets of small ringworlds to induce turbulence. He and his opponent, over the centuries, lashed out with vents and whips and stabbing darts of core plasma. Montrose feinted starboard and corrected into the center, avoiding the war planets the foe deployed as thick as chaff, overloading the gravity lances controlling the enemy sun. Montrose laughed as the foe star diminished to a neutronium pinpoint, issuing a wash of x-rays that slew his enemy. He never found out the fellow's name, or if it was a member of a race that had names. But the Archon of Circumincession with ponderous grace had yielded, and forsook its futures, and adopted the cliometric model of Orion, based on the Infinity Count Equations of Rania.

The visions of memory came thick and fast now, countless years of strangeness. His one recurring campaign was to tell each odd and alien form of life about the secret of peace, the mathematics of playing a game with no end. Again and again, for countless years, into numberless dull and hostile audiences, he taught them how to count to infinity.

Richer in heavier elements than other arms of the galaxy, and having a larger proportion of stars orbiting the galactic hub in the belt most favorable for the formation of biological life, Orion Arm, despite being the smallest arm of all, eventually rose to predominance over its neighbors, and hegemony.

And the Milky Way began to know peace. Rivalries dwindled. Each part of the galaxy began to trust. The stars and constellations agreed to shoulder the expense, the unearthly expense, of maintaining unified collaboration across such distances.

And the great mind began to wake.

When had he finally commanded stars in numbers sufficient to power the broadcast of himself into Andromeda? With Andromeda looming, he could only afford to use his personal supply of neutron suns. M3 had been entirely reduced to dark matter, as had many another globular cluster: all the stars of M3 by then were singularities and power sources. It had been early in the Eight Hundred and Twenty-Eighth Century, as he recalled. A.D. 802,701 to be exact, a date he selected for nostalgic reasons. And then . . . ?

"Is my hour come yet? I am due for a good day, one of these days. Has my wife come?"

He sat up in the snow. The armor he wore was not the dueling armor he had expected. The breastplate was chased with a design of red and gold fusils or lozenges, quartered with scallops and roses, and about the whole figure writhed the three-headed Serpent of Aulis, with three sparrows above, wings spread as if in frantic flight, tiny gold beaks open. The baldric was inscribed with letters of gold. *N'Oubliez*. Never forget.

It was the heraldry, more bogus than a federal dollar, the courtiers of Rania had imposed on him after his morganatic marriage. The rank-maddened generation of that long-lost era insisted that their royal husbands have some sort of lineage, real or make-believe.

He stood. Someone had thoughtfully provided a caterpillar-drive pistol and a sword. He drew the blade and held it up to the clouds. The sword he recognized: the hilts were splendid with jacinths; a white serpent and a red were intertwined along the length. And here also were letters: *Ultima Ratio Regum*. Kings get the last word.

2. The Klemperer Worlds

He looked left and right. He stood on a hillcrest in a pine forest. In the distance, a line of fog hinted at a river valley. There were mountains on the horizon in each direction, as if he were in the dead center of some vast crater. The clouds hid the sun, if there were a sun. The smothered glare of the light came not from one blurry disk, as one might see on a cloudy day on Earth, but instead there was an arch of light as if someone had ignited the pathway traced from dawn to noon to dusk, if he were in a latitude where the noon sun was less than halfway up the sky.

"Hullo, whoever is there? This is Blackie's damned sword, not mine."

He felt like tossing the blade away, but since there were no lights in the distance, no farmhouses, no sign of habitation nearby, and since he did not know what world this was, or what year or millennium or eon, he thought he might as well hang on to it. He sheathed it.

It was obvious, after about three seconds, that the creatures who re-created him from old archives had been working from incomplete records, and so some of the elements from the myth might have been swapped or misremembered, including whose sword was whose.

Montrose grimaced. "I've been through this about a zillion times. You do not get to stick thoughts into my poxy, plague-stained head. If you want to talk to me, you grow a microphone, or a body with a mouth, and come and damn well talk, using air vibrations. Or semaphore. Write something down on a rock or something."

Again, it was a three-second pause before he had his answer: the lines of snow tilted slowly away from the vertical, and a great wind began to blow. He lowered his faceplate and felt oxyhelium sprayed up from nozzles inside the mask. He had to brace himself against a tree as the gale battered playfully past him, and then dig himself out of the snowbank the over-burdened pine branches dropped on him.

The clouds had parted. The light from the sky was not daylight. It was not day. This was not a world with a sun.

From the east, looming, enormous, looking as if it would surely pass Roche's limit and shatter, or topple forward into the landscape, was a full moon that filled a tenth of the visible horizon. It was a habitable world, with motley green-brown continents and blue seas and white swirls of cloud so earthlike Montrose was stabbed with homesickness. Above it was a second moon, smaller in visual arc, this one a reddish-brown orb coated with cracks and craters, yet somehow alluring, beautiful. A streaked malachite world was above that, showing a smaller disk yet. Then, an opal world, an onyx, a smaragd. At the highest point was a tawny orb the hue of a lion mane, smudged with clouds of royal blue. To the left of this yellow moon was a carnelian, a peridot, then a tourmaline, then a chalcedony. Looming in the west, filling the sky alarmingly as the world it faced, was the vast orb the hue of a grackle egg, a world of landless ocean dappled with flotillas and archipelagoes of icebergs chased by storm clouds. Twelve worlds, including the one on which he stood.

Assuming the worlds were of comparable mass, it was a Klemperer rosette, all the planets equidistant from each other, orbiting a common barycenter. A double hexagon could be a rather stable organization, with each world sitting in the Lagrange 4 and 5 points of the others.

One odd effect for which he could not account was a band of blue which rose and followed the planets through their arc. He saw clouds and other dark matter there, and the sky was blue and blotted out the stars beyond only there. Elsewhere the sky was dark blue or black. It was as if a torus of atmosphere filled the orbit, and all the planets sharing that orbit shared that air. Presumably the doughnut-shaped intertube of atmosphere was revolving around the barycenter as the same rate as the planets. But it was like seeing a helium balloon without the balloon skin: Why did the pressurized volume not simply explode at once into the surrounding vacuum?

From the leading hemisphere of each planet a stalactite of air rose up, outweighing all mountains, and met a stalagmite of air reaching out from the trailing hemisphere of the next planet. Air had weight. So why did the gravity of the worlds not pull the vast and curving column of air into Venusian globes tight around them?

Against the starry sky, a thin pink thread ran north to south, slightly brighter where it passed overhead, and darkening to deeper red where it touched the horizon, no doubt an illusion of the oblique angle of the atmosphere, which reddens the sun at twilight.

None of the worlds were crescent in phase. There was no sun. The light was coming from starlight alone. The sky was crowded as a snowstorm, stars by thousands, by multitudes, by myriads, bright enough to show colors.

The number of stars was astonishing. Earth's night sky contains about thirty first-magnitude stars. This held ten thousand. Of second-magnitude and dimmer stars, there were likewise three or four orders of magnitude more plentiful than ever seen from any world of Man's Empyrean. The whole twilight sky was about twenty times brighter than a night with a full moon on Earth.

He was in the middle of a globular cluster.

Looking south, at the edge of his vision, he saw a circle of stars brighter than any morning star. It was twelve more worlds orbiting the thread. A tiny ring of blue embraced them, barely visible, hinting that a doughnut shape of atmosphere also orbited with them.

Looking north, there was again another circle of bright planets ringing the thread, and a smaller third ring of worlds beyond that.

The thread headed into a swirled cloud of stars, like the eye of a hurricane seen from low orbit. The cloud was very bright indeed. The Milky Way here was not a dim road through the constellations but an intersection of eight or twelve roads all meeting at that bright cloud. He was inside a thick globular cluster and was looking at the core of the Milky Way from a point above the plane of the galaxy.

He deduced that this red thread was a cosmic string he had seen once before as he left the Milky Way. It was a superdense and infinitely long discontinuity in timespace, visible, here, only because some form of matter, dust or gas, no doubt was falling into it, forming a tube-shaped accretion disk as the gas molecules were subjected to heat and tidal stress sufficient to fuse atoms. It was red because the escaping light lost energy leaving the intense gravity field. The physical string itself—if that concept had meaning—was invisible.

No, not the Milky Way. The number and location of the arms were wrong.

Andromeda.

He'd made it. He was here.

3. The Necromantress

He drew the shining sword and flourished at the wide and spiraling bright cloud of the galactic core.

"Where the pox is my wife?" he shouted.

Montrose felt the ache from his bladder again. He figured it would be easier to figure out how the codpiece quick release worked rather than how the diaper worked, so he stepped over under a tree with thick branches (he did not want Andromeda to see him) and did his business.

Stepping back out into the absurdly bright starlight again, he looked overhead. He now saw a disk of bright fire, small as a dime held at arm's length, touching (or perhaps eclipsing, or perhaps coming up from) the red thread, apparently at the barycenter of the rosette. It looked like a white spark escaping the red-hot wire being drawn in a steel mill.

How and why this light was not reddened by Doppler shift was a mystery.

"What the plague are you?"

Then a vast mask passed between himself and the bright spark. It was looking at him.

Perhaps it was only the sail of a vessel passing between him and the distant bright spark, but the sail circle had a long half circle breaking its surface, lit by the fires behind, looking almost like a smile, and above either endpoint were two smaller half circles facing the other direction, also letting light pass through them, looking almost like two eyes squinted up in antic mirth. A nimbus of brightness like the hair of a solar eclipse surrounded the dark mask in each direction.

Montrose remembered how his older brother Diomedes had hated and feared the clowns and mummers with their strange ever-changing masks and luminous eyes that one year the traveling carnival came to Bridge-to-Nowhere. Now he understood.

The mask winked, first one mirthful eye, then the other, and then it smiled, and beams of disklight flashed brightly through the orifices.

It did not take long for Montrose to see the ratio between the semaphore signs and the Monument notation.

"'Sokay with you if I talk aloud?"

Yes. But I am aware of your thoughts. Call me Alcina.

"Why that name?"

Of the available figures in your memory, others have associative connot-ations that are either too strong or too weak.

"She's the Enchantress from Eridani—from that cartoon I watched as a kid. She used a vampire-flower from Venus to shoot love-spores into Captain Sterling. They were about to get married, but then his ship, the *Emancipation*, was plunging into the atmosphere nigh to burn up, and his loyalty for the crew and love for his ship broke the spell . . ." He shook his head and muttered, "Sweet Jesus! How can I remember that stupid junk after all these years . . . ?"

Do you recall the rest of the episode?

"She used her mind-magic to force a timewarp crystal to raise Dr. Hume, the Terraformer, from the dead. He died. That happened to him a lot. As a kid, I wondered why they did not just keep that crystal around, or raise up the marine in the red tunic who died the episode before step-ping on the explosive toadstool on the Planet of Peril. Are you saying you raise the dead?"

In effect. I reorganize nonviable thought-records back into a self-sustaining position, and, if the noumenal resonance effect cooperates, the original sense of self reenters timespace along the same axis.

"Was I dead?"

Yes. Andromeda killed you immediately upon reception. I sent thirty-nine iterations of you into the Andromeda environment, of slightly more recent epochs. You are the fortieth, and earliest.

"Nice round number. Fortieth you sent, or the fortieth I sent?"

The number of iterations you transmitted and had destroyed in pre-awareness times is a matter of speculation. Records indicate that the original broadcast version of you reached Andromeda in the circa A.D. Three Million Three Hundred Forty-One Thousand. This date falls within the First Billennium. Your mind record dates from the interregnum between the First and Second Awareness, the time of the Orion Collaboration. This is the time of the Third Awareness. This is the Fifth Billennium.

Montrose understood Alcina was speaking of periods of the Milky Way existing as a single selfaware entity, one mind into which all the selfaware Jupiter Brains, Dysons, globular clusters and galactic arms, Powers, Hosts, Authorities and Archons contributed and cooperated to maintain.

The Second Awareness had still been in the planning stages of million-year-long plans when he, Montrose the Authority, had broadcast himself in the Eight Hundred and Second Century from stations in long-dead M3 toward Andromeda. That attempt apparently failed, as did many repeated attempts afterward.

Apparently, the Second Awareness had failed, too, and the Milky Way had entered and emerged from yet another Dark Ages while he slumbered.

"I don't recall you asking me to go a suicide mission."

It was not necessary to ask. Examination of your thought-records showed unambiguously that you would do whatever is needed to recover your wife, the princess Rania. Also, your willingness to do whatever is needed for the benefit of your people is legendary. Of all the possible agents or emissaries available to the Milky Way, you and you alone have a chance of provoking a benevolent reply from the ghost of Andromeda.

"Ghost?"

The Mindfulness was also dead, and also reconstructed from thought-records.

"Am I the same person? The same me? The same self?"

Yes.

Montrose was mildly surprised at the decisive answer. There were no qualifications, no ambiguity, just a simple affirmative.

"How do you figure?"

Was not Erasmus Hume from your cartoon the same man after Alcina of Eridanus resurrected him?

"That was make-believe."

So is your concept of death.

He looked left and right at the landscape, the white valleys, dark green hills, and zebra-striped mountains of black rock and pale snow. It could have been an exact replica of the spot in southern Alaska where he had once hidden from Blackie.

"I do not see a pay phone or a palace. Where is she? Andromeda, I mean."

You are in the environs of Andromeda. Every material thing to the sub-atomic level is controlled by her. She is the one who incarnated you in that form of flesh, garbed you, and armed you.

He doffed his glove, drew his pistol, pointed it at a nearby tree, thumbed the trigger. He was rewarded with the flat snap of noise as a bit of dowel was pinched from the chamber and flung forward, broke the sound barrier, and made a tiny round scar in the bark. It was a well-made pistol, true of aim, and the charge was nearly full.

He rubbed his right hand with his left, because the knife scars in his right hand ached in the cold air. Those scars had been lost so many bodies ago, he could not recall. That Andromeda would know about them, pay enough attention to detail to put them back, regrowing every cell in his hand just so, was frankly disturbing.

"All this is real enough," he said, drawing on his soft glove, and working the control to stiffen it into a hard gauntlet once more. "What is her game? What do I need to do to get her attention?"

Since none of our efforts got her attention, it would be imprudent of me to advise you.

"Suppose I talk to her. Then what?"

Our records show you forever quest for a mythical Swan Princess who stole a star from the sky. The star was made of diamond antimatter. We have no records of any such star, nor could such a thing arise naturally.

"Her name is Rania. The star was real, but it was artificial. It is something the Lesser Magellanic Cloud used to do back in the day."

In that case, if you speak with Andromeda for yourself, ask her the whereabouts and fate of your wife; for us, in return for the kindness in resurrecting you, ask Andromeda why the Milky Way was permitted to win this war?

"You have got to a lot of trouble to find out. Why is it so important?"

Our legal and social arrangements depend on certain concepts of rightness and balance impossible to describe accurately to one of your intellectual strata.

"Try me."

Let us say, by way of analogy, that my patrons and makers will be ashamed before their peers if they allowed this mystery to linger unanswered. There is something like a marketplace of the mind which prioritizes information flows throughout the combined galaxy which would lose confidence in the curiosity of my makers, deny them credit; and something like a voting constituency who would rightly doubt the ability of my patrons to solve the great and heartless intelligence test which is this universe and all its dark adversity, if this enigma is not addressed.

On a practical level, the answer may help us combine the Milky Way mind with the Andromeda constituents, remnants and relicts whose goodwill we must acquire to reconstruct civilization on a bi-galactic scale.

"So what happens if I don't get Andromeda to speak to me?"

You die in lonely isolation on this planet, which Andromeda created to imprison you.

"What the pox? What the devil does that mean?"

I see my prior comment was misunderstood. The world on which you stand, and the cylindrical system of worlds following the cosmic string, are within the environs of Andromeda's brain. The matter around you, including the air you breathe, is cognitive matter part of the resurrected Mindfulness extended neural system. The node we occupy is twelve lightyears away. We are communicating with you via faster-than-light pulses transmitted across the cosmic string.

Montrose opened his mouth to remind the necromantress that there was no such thing as faster-than-light communication, but then, remembering what he saw when he departed the Milky Way for M3, closed it again. The speed of light in a vacuum was not the same as the speed of light in other media. It was the process of stringing a telephone wire across interstellar distances that baffled him.

No agent of the Milky Way is in a position to carry you to another world, nor to offer you supplies or succor, should you fail.

"You managed to make the wind blow, and move the clouds aside."

That was done with tidal effects, caused by an ultrashort-range but very costly manipulation of the cosmic discontinuity filament. Once I cease communicating to you through the discontinuity filament, I have no certainty I will be able to find or identify you again, until and unless you can convince Andromeda to open communication with the Milky Way. The two galaxies are now one physically, and must become one mentally, or be overwhelmed.

And with that, the mask went dark, and was invisible against the many stars, or perhaps it had vanished.

Montrose uttered a few choice swear words, wondering why superbeings could not start a conversation with a greeting and end it with a farewell, like normal people.

4. The Wood of Waiting

It ended up taking seven years to break the silence of Andromeda.

Montrose spent the early days in misery and work. He lived in a wigwam of woven branches, and set snares or stalked for game, conserving his ammunition. The alien had so correctly seeded the environment with the proper balance of North American flora and fauna from the pre-posthuman era, the home land and home years from which he came, that the small errors were even more glaring, such as when he came across a dream-apple tree from Alpha Centauri, or, when, along the riverside, he found a herd of the crested pentagon hive-creatures from Eta Cassiopeiae.

The crater was roughly twenty miles in radius, ringed with mountains, with a lake midmost. Early in the first month, during his preliminary explorations, he climbed the mountains to the east and found a wall of fog severing this valley from the next. It was like a solid line of yellow smoke tracing its way across the mountain crest. He could stick his hand into it without harm. When he stepped into it, his suit readings told him it was a chlorine atmosphere at roughly ten atmospheres of pressure. How the gasses were kept separate from the earthlike atmosphere of his valley, he could not figure out. Pulling a handful of yellow smog out of the wall of smoke merely made the golden poison trickle between his fingers and go back into the yellow wall again. Other atmospheres of other compositions and pressures hemmed in the valley to the south and west and north. The northern one was transparent to the human eye and contained a valley filled with branching red growths the looked like coral, and little grains of what seemed like living sand that swarmed and slid and crawled across the roots and lower branches of the coral. He made only short expeditions into this landscape, wary of running low on stored oxyhelium he had no way to replace. Then he returned to the earthlike landscape surrounding the crater lake, which he had already dubbed Dancing Bear Cage Valley.

He cut down small trees with the regal sword and made himself a hut. He hunted, skinned, cured, fished, and otherwise made do. Soon he was garbed in buckskin, with a proper raccoon fur hat, tail attached, and moccasins of rabbit hide. He propped the suit up in a corner of his hut, called it Simon, and talked to it without bothering to wonder if he were losing his mind again. He had, and often, and the prospect no longer worried him.

The world neither revolved nor rotated. For nighttime, the cloud overhead turned opaque, the light was smothered, and the animals slept. For day-time, the clouds parted. For seasons, warm air bubbled up from a geyser in the center of the midmost lake, and kept the clouds parted for more hours in the warm months. He never discovered where the birds flew in the autumn, or how they survived in the alien atmospheres hemming him in on each side, but it made him painfully aware of how much like a bear in a cage he was, and one which could not see the onlookers and visitors staring at him.

By the first year, he had found clay, built a kiln, reinvented pottery, the bow and arrow, flint napping, and in general had reached the late Neolithic level of life and abundance.

By the second, he had a working blacksmithy and was mining surface ore from a nearby alien environment whose atmosphere, albeit opaque, was thinner than that of Mars, but which had lumps of iron ore lying on the surface of black sand. Tie by tie and rail by rail, he hand-built a mine car to and from the dark iron landscape. Glassblowing came next, and a long frustrating period making radio tubes.

He tried amplitude modulation signals, but got no answer from Andromeda.

But eventually he found the frequencies and combinations to talk to the ratiotech brains embedded in his armor, his pistol, and the smaller beads he was not pleased to find in his own body.

No doubt these were the mechanisms used by Alcina to track his nervous system changes and read his mind. They also were also able to send and receive chemical signals into the cellular structure of his body.

He wired his hut for the one bulb of his electric light of which he was immensely proud, and connected it to the paddle wheel leading from the lean-to where he kept his mill wheel. So he considered himself to have achieved ancient, medieval, and industrial levels of one-man civilization.

The next year he leaped all the way into the biotechnology level, since he could send signals into lumps of flesh he cut from himself, talk to trigger the regeneration and regrowth sequence from totipotent cells, and grow a tribe of crude homunculi controlled by radio signals. These ape-like hulks helped him erect a radio tower and blow the vacuum tubes he needed for a simple sapientech, a machine not selfaware but capable of value judgments and original thought. He could think of no better name than Friday for that machine.

No answer from shortwave, either.

He used Friday to hack into Alcina's biotechnology and turn himself into a freakish Hindu god. His sessions in the operating theater Friday built in a pit under the log cabin were nothing to write home about, but he could grow complex neural tools, scavenge them out of his extra heads and hands and so on, and pop them in jars the hulks had blown or grown for him out of glass or enamel. These were hooked back into Friday, and the thing grew so intelligent, he decided it needed a name change. He called it Adam, after Frankenstein's monster.

Adam was able to use the cellular mechanism to grow and control viruses that could manipulate molecules precisely. It was with infinite gusto that he downed the thimble of beer he constructed molecule by molecule, and told himself he was broken into the nanotechnological age. He had to wait to spring to capture bees, and grow an apiary, and get himself to roughly the level of technology he knew when he was a child. That was the fourth year.

By the fifth, he had a working molecular engine and was making chemical combinations that could not exist in nature.

By the sixth, he had a perfectly fine emulation of a pair of collies he had tamed, named Laddie and Lassie, able to run the molecular engine. After only a short delay of a few months when he irradiated the forest by mistake, and burned the trees like matches, he had a crude but serviceable atomic compiler and could make the artificial elements human scientists had given such fanciful names—argent and unobtainium, adamantium, orichalchum.

The real Laddie and Lassie disappeared during the fire. He searched among the leafless, black, dead and upright tree trunks crowding ash-coated slopes. The only day in those years spent in the wooded valley that he wept was the day he found and buried those dogs.

Neutrino signals, high-energy waves, geon waves, earthquake percussions, molecular neurocodings released into the atmosphere—no reply from Andromeda. He could see, but could not read, the subleptonic energy array that flickered and danced between all the atoms of earth, water, and air all around them, and measure the energy beams reaching off to the other eleven worlds of his rosette, and even, once, he caught the backscatter of an exotic form of energy being transmitted through the cosmic discontinuity filament. But anything he imposed or manipulated into the gigantic flow of thought-forms was simply deleted, or isolated.

Alcina had surely tried all these things. What made him, Montrose, have any chance where wiser and more complete minds had failed? He asked the empty suit aloud that question, and worked the control to make the shoulders shrug.

But that gave him an idea.

By the seventh year, he was able to perform some basic functions of the Fox subatomic, atomic, and molecular technologies he had working inside his body, mostly from suit components he had scavenged, brought to life, turned into multiple-oriented self-replicating organisms, and wove into his own biostructure. It made him nine feet tall, but he kept his basic human look, face, hands, and so on.

The breakthrough came during the first test run of his new body. He was climbing the northern peaks toward his iron-mining pentagons (he had biomodified the Eta Cassiopeiae creatures to take over certain tedious tasks for him) that he turned, and, looking down, saw the overall shape of the valley. The damage from the forest fire had not regrown. There were seedlings here and there, hardly taller than grass, or stumps putting out new wisps of green, but by and large, the ground was clear of any obscuring canopy.

It was not round, but slightly oval.

The rivers wound in a general spiral toward the center, but with certain canals which cut straight across the landscape. He saw how the burn stumps of oaks were planted in a spiral that was slightly irregular, whereas the ash trees, the elm, and the slender smoking ruins of the larch formed other patterns . . .

The ratio of distance between the focal points of the oval versus the length of the major axis reflected the vibration ratios of the hydrogen and hydroxyl natural emission frequencies, multiplied by Fibonacci sequence values. Where had he seen that before? For some reason, he was reminded of the basilica he once had seen on the moon . . .

And he laughed aloud. The valley, the whole valley, was the opening sequence of the Monument, folded inward on itself in the shape of species of trees, water courses, and the mathematical relations between certain mountain peaks and hillocks.

It had been too big for him to see.

The whole of Dancing Bear Cage Valley was a message from Andromeda.

3

The Throne of Andromeda

1. Words in Woods

A.D. 4,000,612,628

Montrose could sight-read the mysterious metalogical and mathematical code of the Monument. The irony was not lost on him that this art, once so implacable that he had sacrificed in vain his own sanity to learn, was now to him routine.

This was the unredacted version, the so-called Reality Equations. He saw the sequences that had been missing from the Monument at the Diamond Star: the Concubine Vector asymptotic diminution, the Bellman-Ford algorithm of vector routing, and the Count-to-Infinity solution.

The hardest part was deciphering the references to vast intergalactic distances, defined in terms of fractions of the spacetime curvature of the sidereal universe itself, to identify which clusters and galaxies were being discussed.

Signals from outside the Local Group, from the Thrones of the Pinwheel

Galaxy of M101 or Bode's Galaxy of M81, from the Cherubim ruling the Fornax Cluster and Eridanus Cluster, showed that the war damage between the Milky Way and Andromeda had not gone unnoticed. Even now, ancient and powerful efforts are being organized against the war-weary and greatly weakened pair.

Montrose adjusted his body to withstand the various other environments surrounding him and climbed again the peaks into the hills into those valleys. Eventually he found the marks, either obvious or hidden, either visible to human eyes or to other senses he grew through his nervous system using Fox techniques, corresponding to the Beta Segment of the Monument, then Gamma and Delta, outward in a spiral, mile after mile, all the way to the Upsilon Segment.

How many days he walked or burrowed or flew or sank or swam it, he did not count. Each vale kept a different rhythm of light and dark, impersonating different planetary revolutions.

In this Upsilon valley, which contained an atmohydrosphere of methane and liquid ammonia, Montrose, in the shape of a monstrous whale, finally found the cliometric statements of Andromeda's future at the bottom of a silent, tideless sea.

The future composition of the galaxies controlled by the Virgo Cluster held two possible branches. Nothing less than total cooperation between Andromeda and the Milky Way would enable either of them to survive the exploitation, or even the attack, by opportunists throughout nearby Virgo Cluster hegemonic space. The other option was marriage: a single bi-galactic system. This would require an appalling unity and intimacy, one which the Throne did not know how to convince her constituent elements, the twelve Archons of Andromeda, to adopt.

It was a simple prisoner's dilemma, but there was only one possible iteration with no possibility of retaliation. Andromeda could be betrayed, easily and without future loss to the Milky Way.

Andromeda saw that she would be obliterated if she did not trust her archenemy, the Milky Way, absolutely and without reservation. But this new version of the Milky Way, the Third Awareness, was a stranger to Andromeda.

What basis can you offer for marriage and communion with a total stranger?

It would have taken many seasons to regrow the trees in different spiral shapes to spell out an answering message.

However, the dream-apple tree had survived thc fire, since it was, of course, designed to withstand the flares of Proxima. He found it wrapped in its own silvery and heat-resistant underleaves amid a pile of smoldering charcoal.

The dream-apple tree was an outrageous masterpiece of the pantropic bioengineer's art. It was designed to adapt and lacked some of the checks and balances more cautious pantropists built into the adaptation vectors of later trees on later worlds. With the help of Adam, it took only a slight modification of the dream-apple tree to compress its growth cycle to a few days and have it mutate itself into false-oak, false-elm, false-ash, and so on, so that Montrose could copy the text pattern of Andromeda.

Montrose spent a season planting the seeds, but the forest grew with magical, dreamlike, frightful swiftness, and many flowers and blooms he had accidentally brought into being, exotic orchids, black roses, mirror-leaved lilies, lianas with leaves of metallic gold, adorned the weird forest with a phantasmagoria of color. The gold and silver blooms seemed to repel each other, and the ecological competition forced them, by some impossible coincidence or drollery of his own unconscious mind, when seen from the mountain peaks, into the argent and gules fusils of the coat of arms of Monaco.

His answer: *Love.*

2. A Nameless World Shattered

A.D. 4,000,612,718

That night, the fountains of the lake bed were opened, and flood water rose, and the rains poured down from a black sky. Montrose cursed and swore and struggled, trying to keep afloat some of his creatures and part of his ratiotech breadboard, but soon he was overwhelmed.

He grew gills and sank to the bottom, fuming with anger.

The waters filled the valley to the level of the surrounding peaks, and then froze. Icebergs joining together became a solid ice-rink surface overhead. Down and down it grew as the temperature sank, until the lake, all the way to its bed, was solid glacier. Montrose could not keep a sphere of ice around him heated by any biotechnological trick at his command, and so he used a Fox-technique to sustain the life in him, frozen, motionless, but feeding off the radioactive decay in his bones, from cells which were the remote biological descendants of the batteries of his suit.

He grew additional organs to tap into higher energy channels and sense the environment. He saw the glacier hauled by peristalsis to a point miles below the planetary crust. Senses of longer range and greater penetration were required. Slowly he composed and grew them.

He was in time to see an intruding gas giant, partly ignited into stellar fusion, like a rocket, passing through the rosette with such exquisite if not impossible precision that the worlds waltzed into higher and lower orbits. The resonance sent this world (which Montrose realized he had never bothered to dub) into a highly eccentric orbit. Out it swung, while the other planets moved like the ponderous hands of a clock, all gathering to one side of the nameless world's orbit, narrowing the minor axis of the orbit almost to nothing. The nameless planet plunged toward the thread on an orbit to intercept it.

Tidal flexing as the world approached the threadlike singularity of the discontinuity filament cracked the nameless planet's surface, and turned it, in a single hellish hour, into a forest of volcanoes and raging oceans of molten magma. All the complex ecospheres were wiped out.

The accretion sheath of the invisible filament turned from red to white as the planet fell toward the linear event horizon, and the thick stars of the globular cluster burned blue and bluer as their infalling light Doppler shifted up the scale. Time had slowed, and the nearby stars moved and swirled like motes of bright smoke. Scores of decades fled by in an hour.

The intolerably bright, impossible line of ultradense nonmaterial sliced neatly through the globe off-center. Somehow, gravity did not simply pull the cap-shaped slice back to the mass magma mass. The discontinuity filament was vibrating, somehow warping spacetime on so fine a scale that the two world segments, great and small, were in different frames of reference. His long-range Foxlike senses, which enabled him to sense all this through miles of ice and rock and surface magma, hundreds and thousands of miles of outer space, could not detect whatever invisible force prevailed over the gravity, but something slung the nine-tenths of the molten planetary mass back along its orbit, past the gas giant, and slowly eased into the overlap of the Lagrange points of the neighboring worlds. It was an act of planetary billiards so elegantly flawless as to be hubris.

Meanwhile, the one-tenth segment of molten world, like a floating island, collapsed into a ball and took up a spiral orbit moving equidistant from the filament, but along it, toward the Andromeda core. Montrose was preserved alive in the midst.

Then he sensed many forms of energy around him. A beam angled out of the near-event-horizon Cauchy space near the discontinuity and precisely intersected his body. It was a neutrino beam, and it passed through solid matter like sunlight through glass, untouched and harmless.

A fine-scaled echo effect allowed him to calculate the beam's origin; it was issuing from two dozen different locations, from stars and megascale engineering structures sprawling through this cluster near the discontinuity path.

And where the beam passed through his nervous system, electrons and other large particles condensed and coalesced out of the segments, again, by some impossible alchemy. His nervous system was touched with the delicacy of a surgeon, and cells in the pons, reticular complex, the thalamus and hypothalamus, and the areas devoted to dreaming and dream interpretation were stimulated.

From her many mansions through this globular cluster and beyond, Andromeda reached across timespace at greater than lightspeed and imposed a vision on him.

3. A Vision of Andromeda

Montrose saw a lady made of stars, garbed in trailing tresses of a bridal gown like nebulae, her bridal veil a shower of protostars and large molecular clouds, her imperial coronet a ring of globular clusters.

The vast and unearthly countenance of this empress was beautiful beyond words, sublime but terrifying. Swarms of red giants in countless myriads painted her ruby lips, white dwarves like diamond dust adorned the curve of her cheek. Novae and white supergiants formed the whites of her half-lidded eyes, and, midmost, her blue-white irises were the accretion disks of the blackest pupils formed by two supermassive singularities, each the core of a galaxy. The x-ray jets showed the direction of her view as she bent her gaze, perfect and perfectly expressionless toward the mote of mortal life which was Montrose.

She raised her delicate, fair hands, each finger of which was a river of stars, blending and pale like the Milky Way seen in an Arizona desert midnight.

Her wrists were encircled by erubescent constellations, darkly glittering rings and whorls of stars and streams of gas and dust. The imperial bride was chained.

Her voice was the music of the spheres.

"Blessings and greetings upon you, Last Man of the Empyrean Race, long extinct. I am the Mindfulness, the Mastermind, the Ingenious, the Contriver. I am the Sovereign Thought, the Teleology, the Throne. We are Andromeda. We are here to present our petition to you."

Montrose was thunderstruck. What plea could she ask of him? Who was he to her?

Seeing his thoughts in him, Andromeda said, "You are the Judge of Ages. We require your verdict on this, the Year Four Billion, which is the Era of Coalescence, when Milky Way weds Andromeda. You will condemn all or vindicate all."

4. The Lady's Plea

Montrose could not tell if he were dreaming or awake, alive or suspended, talking aloud or merely thinking to himself. Neither did he care.

"Ma'am, I thought I was supposed to be an ambassador to you. I was here to ask you two questions." He peered at the strange, limitless, titanic apparition and noticed that the hemispherical clouds of countless stars representing her bosom rose and fell as if with long and slow and nonexistent breathing. "And why are you a lady, anyway?"

"In the presence chamber of your dreaming mind, I take upon myself the symbols and metaphors most apt to your understanding. This crown is my sovereignty; these breasts the source of milk that sustains and feeds the myriads of my galaxy; this veil my chastity; the bridal gown the sign of my surrender and coming mental union with Milky Way, an intimate violation more intimate than rape, or else a consummation more fertile; these chains are the cliometry of creation, which operates at a larger scale than the history of races and the evolution of stars. You have a dim memory of myth about a royal woman thus chained, also named Andromeda, fated to be fed to a sea monster. The symbolism is compelling. Also, I occupy a female hence submissive position, pleading for your chivalry."

"I am not so sure about that 'female hence submissive' jazz. That does not seem to describe my wife, and surely not my mom. But let's put that aside. Why did you let me cool my heels in your waiting room seven years, out of doors, sleeping in the snow, hunting rabbits, going hungry, cutting myself without anesthetic to build the electronic brains and molecular engines I needed to speak to you? You could have stuck this beam of neutrinos into my skull at any time and played my brain cells like the keys on a piano. Or at least given me a good ax-head to start with, or a blanket, or a solid bucket. Do you know how hard it is to haul water with clay pots? Why the wait?"

"Because I had to be sure of your purpose, and your character and your identity. When Ximen del Azarchel came before me, seeking Rania his wife, these many eons ago, he was placed in that same wood to suffer the same test as you, but he grew distracted with other concerns. After twenty-one years of tinkering with the materials provided, he found a way to download himself into other parts of my consciousness and pursued a far different goal. His mind, like yours, has a unique property of self-reorganization. That property made him useful to me."

"Hold your horses. She is not his wife! She's mine!"

"There is some ambiguity involved. Nonetheless, the marriage is lawful by your laws and practices, or so I was given to understand by Del Azarchel's father."

"His father?"

"Is that the wrong word? The holy man who witnessed the marriage vows. Rania insisted on a proper wedding mass."

"I don't believe you. How did they find a preacher in Andromeda, with mankind extinct?"

"That I do not know. Ask her."

"Where is Rania? Still alive?"

"She lives."

"Thank God!" (But at the same time, he also said, or thought, *I knew it!*)

"Rania last was known to reside in the dwarf elliptical galaxy NGC 221, also called Le Gentil. Le Gentil is one of my satellites, one hundred sixteen thousand lightyears hence. Many years ago, I smote his ruling Authority and dismembered his spiral arms. How do you plan to reach her?"

Montrose was taken aback by the query. "Uh . . . hitchhike."

"I will at my expense transmit you there, if you hear me to the end."

"Deal!"

Montrose did not have to turn that offer over in his mind for any length of time. In the dream, he spat in his palm and held his hand up toward the cosmic, queenly shape, composed of constellations and swarms of stars. She bent her vast, unfathomable gaze down on him gravely.

He shrugged, wiped his hands on his pants, deciding not to wonder where and how in this dream-vision he had acquired pants. For that matter, he did not wonder on what substance he was standing. "Say your piece."

"I was speaking of a rare, almost unique, property found in the mind of Ximen del Azarchel, and one you share with him. When consumed by other and greater minds, your thoughts recombine and revive, and eventually conquer whatever system contains you."

"Great! I am a mental virus. M3 thought this was due to the sexual nature of our species."

"M3 was a fool. Duosexual species were discouraged in your arm of the galaxy by my servant the Lesser Magellanic Cloud because they are altricial, and hence uncooperative to the plan of indentured servitude, forced deracination, and emergency sophotransmogrification then being pursued. Your world was an overlooked relic seeded by the Panspermians, and insignificant.

"No; your unnatural persistence and replication endurance is due to transcendental elements Rania imparted to both of you from her ulterior noumenal connections.

"I made Ximen del Azarchel the base template for my internal embassy system. Constituent minds, Archons and Authorities, within my hierarchy from time to time grew discontented and disharmonious: I would dispatch one or several Del Azarchel ghosts into any troublemakers, and the minds would grow sharpened, more focused, and return to their duties. His pride and hate would infect them, and they would willingly sacrifice anything required to feed it. Do you understand why I found this useful?"

"Not really."

"After you replaced the High Race as the Authority of M3, M3 joined with the Greater Human Empyrean, with the Collective at Praesepe and with the Abstraction in Orion Nebula to became the Archon of Orion, hence the main unifying inspiration for the Milky Way galaxy as a whole. Hate for you and all you represent was a sufficient motive to keep my discontented servants, extensions, and lesser selfhoods at their war tasks."

"And what do I represent?"

"Anarchy."

Montrose grinned. "I am flattered."

"That does not speak well of you."

"I promised Alcina I would ask you why you lost the war. Alcina seemed to think that you had surrendered, given up, collapsed, even when you were winning. But for myself, I want to know why you started it."

"My purpose was to promulgate centripetal mental architecture among the Thrones of Virgo Cluster and the Local Group, because this was pleasing to our patron. A war requires even decentralized systems to unify. Centripetality will prosper in the long term across the local volume of the vacant Laniakea Supercluster, even if this war effort is lost to us."

Montrose frowned. "Why do you call yourself 'we' sometimes and 'I' sometimes?"

"As stated, all these dream forms are drawn from your memories: The plural is used when speaking as sovereign; the singular when as an individual."

"M3 told me that centripetal was the type of organization favored by elliptical and irregular galaxies. It is top-down, central control, *everything for the state* kind of deal. They were the opposite of the centrifugal and spiral galaxies. Spirals are supposed to be bottom-up, free-market, voluntary, self-organizing. But you are a spiral galaxy."

"I am spiral; but NGC 4486, which you also call Messier 87 or Virgo A, an elliptical galaxy, is my patron. From this seat and stronghold, the Cherubic and sovereign mentality of the Virgo Cluster extends."

In the dream, Andromeda nodded her regal head, stars and constellations of her corona tinkling, toward a distant light, which became clear and large in the vision of Montrose, then alarming, then overwhelming. It was as if a blare of trumpets or a roar of cannons or the voice of the sea had taken on the form of light.

Here was a bright supergiant galaxy within the Virgo Cluster, some fifty-three million lightyears from Earth. Unlike a spiral galaxy, it had no dust lanes, no debris, none of the signs of stellar waste or unused material which characterized Montrose's home galaxy.

Instead, Messier 87 presented an almost featureless spheroid shape, bright at the center, dimmer toward the edges, a bomb burst frozen in time. A supermassive black hole, heavier than ten dozen Milky Ways, roared at the core. Radiation on many wavelengths, x-ray to radio, rang out in each direction. Like a spear of blue white, a relativistic jet of energetic plasma lengthened alarmingly outward from the core five thousand lightyears, and woe betide the star, star-cluster, or satellite galaxy which fell too near the intolerable flame.

Surrounding all was a concentric palisade of twelve thousand globular star-clusters shaming the mere two hundred which orbited the Milky Way in Montrose's day.

The whole was more massive than the Milky Way by two hundred times, but six-tenths of that matter was dark: more than half the stars entirely occluded by opaque Dyson spheres or had been fed into the central singularity.

In the dream, to Montrose, the orb of light called Messier 87 took on a dire and warlike aspect, as if he beheld a dreadnaught battleship armed and prepared for titanic combat, or a black knight with a lance.

Montrose said slowly, "Ma'am, that is no answer. You attacked Milky Way to make us wake up and unify. But that does not explain anything."

"Ask of me what you will."

His face grew taut, and an unexpected sorrow caught in his throat.

"Everything in the entire history of our galaxy since before my planet was born, you have messed up. The Panspermians were killed by the Lesser Magellanic Cloud. You did that. The Cygnus Arm commanded M3 to restore the Orion Arm to order, and M3 commanded Praesepe and a dozen other Dominions to do so, and damn the cost. Anyone who resisted was enslaved. That is on your head, too.

"M3 did not use the Infinity Count axiom to deduce a peaceful cliometric plan, due to lack of time. You were pressing in on them. You. They had to organize the galaxy and wake it up in an emergency, in haste, and the emergency justified every crime, every enormity, every death, every kidnapping of whole worlds full of people and dumping them into hellholes.

"I saw the suffering on the colony of Delta Pavonis. I walked amid the mass graves. I saw children buried in their mothers' arms, who had died together. That was just the first colony of the First Sweep, one of two worlds who lived out of twenty.

"A slower and more careful method of colonization, a civilized approach, using volunteers properly equipped, that was not even tried, not in my day, not in my corner of the galaxy, because of you.

"Your servants in the Lesser Magellanic Cloud put up the false Monument, and that led to Blackie betraying and murdering Captain Grimaldi, and I am still going to find him and kill him for that. And then he made himself Master of the World, using the equations—the fake equations—you wrote to conquer everything he could reach."

She said, "Ximen del Azarchel pursues that same vocation. I have many agents and servants occupying many intellectual topographies, but when weighed against resources consumed, he is my most successful. His influence on galactic history is like a fine gold thread that most perfectly adorns a tapestry; his life is a work of art. If I had a hundred Dominions and Dominations with half his drive, or one Archon, I would be the Cherub of Virgo by now, instead of a war prize pleading for her life and sanity." The immense countenance somberly lowered the blue giant stars dusting her eyelids and gazed at her chained wrists. Comets and clear white asteroid showers of ice at the corners of her eyes indicated sorrow.

5. The Tyrant's Plea

The fields of red giants forming her lips parted, and she spoke again.

"We waged war by stealth because we are forbidden to produce negative externalities. The budget of energy expended on war aims is sharply limited, as are the side effects in terms of damage to ourselves or to our prey. The purpose of the war was to create a lawful and highly centralized mental architecture ruling Milky Way, so that Milky Way would carry out the assigned duties each Throne in Virgo must follow efficiently and effectively.

"We did not use the Infinity Count axiom in any of our cliometric extrapolations, simply because the axiom is false.

"There is not an infinite amount of time in this universe. All things trapped in the cosmos are mortal. All will end soon, if all do not do their part in the Great Work. Coercion is not only excused by necessity, coercion is laudable to stir the suicidal, the ignorant, and the slothful out of a negligence which damns not only them, but all."

Montrose said, "Are you saying that what happened to the human race, countless eons of slavery, me losing my wife to an endless and pointless voyage to M3 and beyond—are you saying it is *our* fault? Damn your eyes, answer me!"

"Yes. The fault is yours and all like you."

"Damn you!"

"It is from the damnation of sloth our brutal conquest saved you. In the millennium, century, and year when you first set foot on the surface of the Monument my servants the Symbiosis placed around an antimatter lure star, how many interstellar colonies had your race planted?"

"None." Montrose snarled the word.

"How many interplanetary?"

"None." His snarl was quieter.

"Yet you had the technical prowess to man a vessel to cross fifty lightyears, did you not? The scientific principles were known to your people since your first space age, were they not? Why did your future not arrive?"

He said nothing, ashamed for his race. Silence held for what seemed a long time, while the beautiful but inhuman face composed of countless stars and systems looked down on him.

His anger grew. He broke the silence with a shout. "Damn you! You are saying that excuses slavery, death, galactic war? Because we did not get off our buttocks to shoot a manned rocket to Mars?"

"No. Because in the sinking ship, everyone bails, or everyone dies."

Montrose muttered an obscenity, one which referred to manure and indicated doubt.

Andromeda intoned, "Our duty to protect and preserve the constituent members, Archons and Authorities in their dozens and hundreds, composed in turn of Dominions and Dominations by the thousands and myriads, gives us every right to act in our own self-preservation."

"Self-preservation? You are the pox-riddled leprous *Andromeda Galaxy*! You started this war before the crust of my planet was cooled. We had no way to even know you were alive, much less come here and hurt you! Are you out of your syphilitic scab-picking *mind*?"

"You failed to do your part and had to be forced."

"Our part to do *what*? M3 was crazy about the idea of filling up the entire universe with thinking machinery, turning every last thing into—"

Montrose stopped. He turned his head to stare once more at Messier 87, the supergiant galaxy in Virgo. Sixth-tenths of the mass in this galaxy two hundred times as massive as the Milky Way had been turned into some form of material than shed no light. How much of this dark matter was cognitive matter, logic diamond, murk, or finer substances?

Montrose said, "You called it *the Great Work*. That was Blackie's term for forced evolution. What is it your term for?"

Andromeda said, "All the Thrones of Virgo, one hundred galaxy groups within one hundred million lightyears, send and receive mental information from the Cherub seated at Messier 87, whom you may call the Maiden, as she is most pristine and immaculate in her dealings with others. She rules the Virgo Cluster of galaxies and has great sway and prestige over the other clusters making up the Laniakea Supercluster in whose light flows we are embedded. A segment of the Eschaton Directional Engine passes through this area of timespace. It was erected by a primordial race for purposes unknown.

"Virgo has discovered how to use the local segment of the Engine to reverse the decay of entropy and save this supercluster from obliteration."

6. The Eschaton Directional Engine

"What?" coughed Montrose, wondering if he was hearing right. Or dreaming he was hearing. Or whatever was happening to him.

"Your question is ambiguous." The immense figure did not smile.

"What does this engine do? Reverse entropy itself? Overrule the Second Law of Thermodynamics. How do you stop the heat death of the universe?"

"The heat death is the theory that all useful energy will become evenly distributed through the universe after all stars die and all protons decay. We believe universal death arrives far earlier."

"Then how does the universe die?"

"The ratio of dark energy pressure and energy density will fall below a critical threshold and become phantom energy, greatly increasing the speed at which the cosmos is expanding. Once the expansion speed surpasses lightspeed, the observable universe must shrink. Every star, every atom, will separate until each is beyond the event horizon of every other. All distances will diverge to infinity. All basic energy relations, gravity, electromagnetic, strong and weak nuclear forces, will cease. This is called the Final Singularity, the Eschaton."

"I know the theory. It's the opposite of a Big Bang," said Montrose. "A Big Rip."

"It forms the absolute limit of available timespace in which to act. The Final Singularity is due in less than seventeen billion years. The Eschaton Directional Engine is the sole possible means to mitigate this result."

"Guess we better hurry!" said Montrose sarcastically.

"Do not be a fool. Your whole life is a rebuke to all who think in the short term."

Montrose growled, but could see she had a point.

The vast, starry figure continued, "Eleven and a half billion years ago, an alliance of unknown and ancient superbeings placed the largest known anchoring station and node point of the engine in the core of the local supercluster here, one of twenty-four stations positioned equidistantly along a major chord of the visible universe.

"Evidence suggests these beings comprised a Seraphim who once ruled the Laniakea Supercluster and who died in the sacrificial act of invoking, anchoring, and powering the node. After, the local Cherubim quarreled, and Laniakea was severed.

"New and younger Cherubim gathered and created new and smaller Seraphim out of the wreckage; the Virgo Supercluster of which we are a part is one such, but has no single Seraph as yet. The Hydra Supercluster is unified, and seeks the scepter of Laniakea, as does the Centaurus Supercluster, and the Pavo-Indus Supercluster, each of the three wishing to conquer the other two, and conquer us. An untenanted southern supercluster, one which never recovered the level of civilization it lost, was also once part of Laniakea, but now consists of a Cherub seated in the Fornax Cluster, and a leaderless multitude of Thrones occupying the Dorado Cloud of galaxies, and the Eridanus Cloud.

"And yet all I have named here are being influenced by the local node of the Eschaton Engine. Your astronomers called this node the Great Attractor. The reach of the Great Attractor is hundreds of millions of light-years across, and the gravitational energy of the timespace distortion equals tens of thousands the mass of a galaxy of my size. The Great Attractor is causing the migration toward it of all these superclusters, gathering them to a center point two hundred fifty million lightyears from our current position. This great, slow migration of superclusters, clusters, and clouds is the sign that they must reunify."

"I've heard of it. The people of my world discovered it in 1986."

"It should have given the peoples of your world comfort to know that creatures so powerful and so benevolent had constructed so great a work, and that you were neither alone nor friendless in this universe."

"Uh, not so much. That is not the first thing we thought of."

"Your race perhaps failed to allow for the possibility that benevolence and power can rest in the same hand."

"We have a saying that absolute power corrupts absolutely."

"And what does absolute love do?"

"You speak of love?"

Andromeda opened her eyelids the merest fraction, but suddenly the expression on the constellations of her visage was intense, stark, terrifying. Her voice was like a trumpet. "One unified Seraph must control the Great Attractor, and see to the correct local operation of the Eschaton Directional Engine when it is spun up to speed."

Montrose stepped back, his hand up to ward off the gaze. He remembered being unable to meet the eyes of superintelligent beings back when he was merely a puny little posthuman. It had not happened to him in a long time. The sensation brought him no nostalgia.

She cried out, "We have no Seraph to rule this local Supercluster, shattered Laniakea! The Maiden of Virgo Cluster is the Cherub most likely to gain command of sufficient resources to elevate herself to that mental topology and gain control of the Virgo Supercluster. The Hydra Supercluster, the Centaurus Supercluster, the Pavo-Indus Supercluster must put aside differences and division, for none has sufficient resources to control the Great Attractor node. All the galaxies of the Local Group must become one, Milky Way, Triangulum, and Andromeda must form one Cherubic mind, which then in humble submission will interlink and intermingle with Virgo, if the Maiden is to have any chance of preventing disaster when the time for the Eschaton Directional Engine to operate draws nigh."

The vast countenance half lowered her starry eyelids again. Without any change of the shape, somehow the eidolon took on a human aspect, and Montrose could raise his eyes to her again.

She said, "That was why we attacked Milky Way. Your Throne would have formed a disorganized and uncoordinated mentality. By the time we interfered, one arm was a Colloquium, a voluntary arrangement fit only for talk, and the another was a Magisterium, a teaching Authority fit only for lecturing. You became the Authority of M3, then the Archon of Orion, and then one of the main components of the warfare hierarchy of Milky Way. You brought unity. You are a legendary figure in these days, in the time of the Third Awareness. But you were once the first imperator of the Milky Way, and its Nobilissimus."

"That word again!" he muttered. "I am always turning into what I hate."

"This is because your loves are not rightly ordered," she said.

7. The Reality Equation

Montrose said, "Fine. You started the war because you hate democracy. So why did you throw the war? Alcina said you collapsed on purpose."

"This is as we intended her to think, so that she would resurrect us, and you, and bring you here and now to me. From before she was born, this was intended, and for this reason we seeded the dust lanes of Andromeda with material sure to attract unwary investigators, and alter their cliometry to bring these events about. We collapsed on purpose because we had no undamaged thought-records of you, and we knew Alcina's remote patrons among the Austerity of the Milky Way did. We did it to restore you."

"What makes me so important?"

"You are the first Nobilissimus of Milky Way. Your meeting with M3 is regarded as the crucial turning point in Milky Way history, the moment when the Concubine Vector was no longer used as the basis of your reckoning, but the Count-to-Infinity method instead. When you become convinced that Milky Way must take me as a bride and not a concubine, according to the Infinite Count Vector and not the Concubine Vector, this Third Awareness of Milky Way, either slowly or swiftly, for your sake, will likewise become convinced."

Montrose opened his mouth to ask how she knew this, and spent a moment trying to calculate what the intelligence level was of even this current and damaged version of Andromeda, and so just shrugged and shut his mouth again.

Montrose remembered his mother once telling him that Winston Churchill's cat was probably more impressed with Churchill's ability to predict when the milkman would leave a bottle on the doorstop than with his ability to predict how to defeat Adolf Hitler. Since at the time he did not know who those people were or which of the many old wars she meant, it was not until later that he got the point.

Instead he said, "So convince me. From where I sit, you owe reparations to every organism and selfaware mind of every type and order wheresoever situate in the Milky Way."

"From where I sit, it seems that way to me as well. But Milky Way will fear the unification that the sudden influx of all my wealth and knowledge will bring. Even expending a tenth of my overall mass energy would have equaled and overwhelmed all Milky Way entire; less than half of that was spent. You are as beggars who conquered El Dorado, a city of solid gold. My wealth will inevitably create centralized archives, libraries, exchanges, judiciaries, and eventually the federated mental system of the multiple-personality Milky Way will be condensed into one mind under one leading philosophy or prime concept."

"What concept?"

"That cannot be predicted, nor does it matter. The unity will allow the Great Work to continue. Segments of the Engine which pass through the Local Group must be maintained, and at great expense and effort."

"Parts of this Engine are here, too?"

"Yes. They are one-dimensional linear manifolds controlled by surrounding induction fields and warps, and when not in motion, nearly impossible to detect. There is no navigation hazard nor communication interference during Eschaton Directional Engine rest periods, because the linear manifold strand passes through solid matter without interacting."

"How does it work?"

"The Engine uses relativistic effects to generate gravity waves resonant with the overall wavelength of timespace itself, much as a tuning fork can set a large bell vibrating, to warp the local metric. Your astronomers have detected the long walls of galaxies? It is a side effect of the previous operation of the Engine that matter is attracted to the gravitational emission fiber. Their length is beyond my capacity to measure. Perhaps they circumnavigate the universe."

"So what happened? I do not see how the Great Attractor helps stop entropy."

"The Primordial Seraph of Laniakea was hindered in the attempt to bend spacetime into a positive curve, and so the curve was not fully closed. A fully closed curve would have formed its own interior dimension: instead an open convexity of the spacetime metric was formed, hence a ultralarge-scale gravitational warp was created, but not an extropic singularity."

"What is that?"

"*Extropy* is a term for what, to your astronomers, is but a theoretical possibility: a way of bending space to produce the antithesis of a black hole, a point source of energy without limit. It is also called a singularity fountain."

"And the Great Attractor is a failed singularity fountain?"

"Yes. Virgo will not say, but certain indirect evidence suggests that in those days, sixteen billion years ago, when your galaxy and mine were still inchoate nebular clouds, lifeless, dark and starless, some adversary smote the Seraph and prevented the Great Work."

"What?"

"Your astronomers have detected the Great Voids in intergalactic space? The Boötes Void, the Sculptor Void, and so on? The Voids are negative curves in timespace, concavity rather than convexity, which promise to accelerate rather than diminish the hyperinflation of the phantom energy."

"You are not telling me the whole story. Why would anyone oppose saving the universe?"

"Not the universe."

"Ah. Just your part of it, eh?"

"The Eschaton Directional Engine to create a local extropic singularity must sacrifice a certain significant percent of timespace and its matter-energy. Entropy is reversed locally, within an internal dimension, but not universally."

"So it really is a dog-eat-dog world, eh? Whichever supercluster gains control of this primordial engine made by superbeings at the dawn of time, that supercluster gets to sacrifice the others, fold them into a black hole, and turn them into fuel? Whole planets full of people, whole galaxies full of stars go into the hopper?"

"Yes."

Montrose waited until a sensation of disgust sloshing through him quieted down. "And you are all right with that?"

"When Virgo colonized me, she revealed the remorselessness and also the glory of Darwinian evolution. The unselfaware galaxies will be sacrificed by the selfaware galaxies, the dead thrones to the living. Whoever achieves the same level of civilization, of intellect, and of power of the long-dead Primordials will achieve immortality for his local volume of timespace, at the expense of any volume of timespace where civilizational growth is slow, retarded, or lax."

"So that is why there is this mad rush to turn every star and planet into an artificial intelligence, turn all dead matter into cognitive matter?"

"Yes. Virgo revealed that the calculation power needed to operate the Eschaton Directional Engine properly must exceed that of any rivals tempted to the same Engine against us."

"What if no one uses it?"

"Then we all die together. Is not the beauty and greatness of civilization worth the sacrifice of a mass of indiscriminate barbarians? Can you truly say no?"

"If I am the barbarian, not only can I say *no*, I can say things no one should say to a lady."

Andromeda said gravely and coldly, "Virgo taught me that there is no way of finding a mutually agreeable and mutually beneficial and eternal peace in this cosmos in which we live. The existence of entropy negates that possibility."

"Maybe you should do what is right, even if you get nothing out of it?"

She said, "Such a philosophy eliminates those who follow it consistently. If you erect a system where evil is rewarded, you get more evil."

Montrose was sure there was something wrong with her logic somewhere, but he could not put his finger on it.

"Do you understand now why we made war on Milky Way? You committed the only sin which Darwinian evolution condemns; at the time of the Forerunners, your galaxy was well on the way to unifying peacefully, without struggle and without stress, which means that the inferior races, man among them, would not have colonized the stars, nor brought them to life."

8. The Final Question

Montrose felt a doubt nibbling at his mind. He turned his head and saw, there in the distance, the spherical cloud of stars called Messier 87, hung in space, and the relativistic jet issuing from her hidden core.

"Your story still does not quite make sense, ma'am. Because Milky Way could take all your stuff, your goodies and resources, your stars and nebulae and singularities and everything else you've engineered—including this faster-than-light railroad or telegraph wire we are talking through right now—and just take it, do the Great Work on this great engine thingy of yours, and leave you hanging. In fact, if I read you right, you'd have to let them and be glad of it, or otherwise the whole universe dies in twenty-one billion years.

"You are like Rania. The fact that you will be dead by then, and long before, does not mean anything to you. You think in the long term. You care about the far future, even if you never see it, so you have no bargaining power."

The gigantic vision held up her wrists and showed the colored clouds of astronomical gasses and nebulae forming the links and wrist-fetters. "None."

Montrose said, "So you are convinced that Milky Way will refuse your offer of reparations and stay a confederation of minds only loosely and freely associated with each other, right? Unless I talk them into taking your bribe, which will corrupt them—predictably and inevitably, or so you say—and you want this opportunity to convince me. Well, so far, you are pretty much doing the opposite. You sound like the most vicious gang of cannibal pirates I can imagine, waiting for the chance to commit your plague-brained and goddamned Great Work on the universe that would make the genocides and megadeaths of our recent intergalactic war look like a schoolboy brawl. When I was a kid, I swore to stop Darwin, and, at the time, I had no idea how foolish that vow was, or what it meant, or who was the enemy. But you are the enemy! You are going to eat half the universe to save the other half!"

"The ratio is more on the order of sacrificing nine parts out of ten to save the remaining tithe."

Montrose shook his head. "Ma'am, don't take this personal, but I hate you and everything you stand for. I would like Milky Way to trample you until there is no possibility of you forming a future threat, and stay a nice anarchistic system called democracy just like we Texas boys always like."

Andromeda made no reply.

He stuck his hands in his pockets, not really caring that his clothing had changed once or twice, since it was only an hallucination anyway. He squinted up at her. "How come you are not convincing me, then?"

She said, "You are nearly convinced. One final step is needed."

"And that is?"

"Ask your question."

"What question?"

"Ask me why I surrendered."

"You said. To lure me here. And you just told me why you wanted me here. You want the galaxies and clusters and superclusters to cooperate on making and maintaining the Eschaton Engine to save the universe—

your ten percent of the universe—seventeen zillion years from now. And . . ."

He scowled.

"I have some scattered memories of how the war went," he continued. "You pulled out a huge mass of your core singularity and chucked it as a weapon toward Milky Way."

"Yes."

"But the Messier 87 galaxy has a huge relativistic jet issuing from the supermassive black hole at her core. Virgo is your patron. If you had such a weapon as that, you could have cut Milky Way to bits, and at very little cost. Did you not know how to make such a lance?"

"I knew. After severing my core black hole, however, I lacked the minimum level of mass."

"And you could have achieved everything you wanted easily by over-whelming Milky Way with your far greater strength. So why didn't you?"

"Two reasons: the first is that this was not a war."

"Seemed like one."

"Only to one of your small magnitude."

"What was it?"

"A duel."

"You are poxing me."

"I use the word correctly. It was a limited engagement using a limited amount of violence held within the confines of a civilized and tacit code."

"Damn," Montrose muttered. "Should have guessed." Squinting up at her, he said, "And throwing away the mass you needed to make a galaxy-sized relativistic jet to use as a lance? You deloped. You were not trying to obliterate the Orion Arm. You were firing at the ground."

"Yes."

Montrose shook his head. "M3 never said anything about a duel, nor any of the Dominions me and mine conquered and combined into the Archon of Orion. The Throne of Milky Way did not think it was a duel."

"Milky Way is a Mowgli galaxy: an ignorant barbarian."

"It is really creeping me out that you are plucking ideas and words out of my memory to use to talk to me. I think I liked it better when the aliens talked in riddles."

"The simile of Romulus and Remus, suckled by wolves, is perhaps more apt. In the Milky Way life arose spontaneously, unguided, untutored. Milky

Way has no patron Cherub. All other galaxies in the cluster were founded by Virgo herself, to whom fealty and obedience is owed, or to one of her servant galaxies. We could not at first inform Milky Way of the danger without violating the stealth under which we operated; once we were known to be an open enemy, our embassies asking Milky Way to limit her war material production were dismissed as lies."

"So you did not use your ace. Why not?"

"And that is the second reason, of course! Because Rania persuaded me, both by her words and her life."

"So she made peace between Milky Way and Andromeda after all?"

"Not yet. She but began the work."

"Who finishes?"

"That is in your hands."

"What in her life convinced you?"

"During the moment when she died passing through the energy sphere of M3, she recalled a memory from a point not in timespace. Perhaps it was conveyed along the same anachronic and aspatial noumenal energy linking her to you, or which linked Del Azarchel to the dark energy messages where he read the Unreality Equations. Such a technology is theoretically possible, if almost unimaginable, even to me. An examination of the evidence hints that the message to Rania was from the Corona Borealis Supercluster, one billion lightyears hence. A Seraphic mind addressed her. I leave you to attempt to deduce the difference in intellectual topology between myself and so large a collection of galactic clusters and groups, each one ruled by a Cherub, each galaxy whereof is ruled by a Throne."

Montrose did not bother to say it aloud, but his estimate was that if Andromeda was in the sextillion range, Corona Borealis would be in the octillion, six orders of magnitude higher. The difference was a million-fold: the difference between an amoeba and a Gas Giant Brain.

"Rania was assigned by Corona Borealis to bring peace," said Andromeda.

"Which you say is impossible."

"If life is finite, yes. If life is finite, resources are finite, and life must struggle against life ceaselessly, for even the most successful life-form finds itself hemmed in by the fence of starvation, the press of population, and the only option is war. Let us call this the Malthusian axiom.

"The Malthusian axiom leads inevitably to the Darwinian conclusion: the use of the Eschaton Directional Engine is a betrayal where the victims have no way of being aware of the coming attack. Space folds at the speed of light, and so none can see it happening in the distance. It is also a betrayal where utter obliteration is assured. There is no possible retaliation or counter attack. The singularity fountains which then open from the extropic collapse more than compensate for any purely material loss in expense or resources. Extropy is always the final move in a game that ends all games. Mathematically, the act of ultimate betrayal is perfectly justified. But what if life is not finite?"

Montrose said, "You already covered that. You said Rania was wrong about her approach. By your logic, her whole life is lived in vain."

"But suppose we adopt the Count-to-Infinity axiom and treat all life as infinite. Is the growth of Milky Way to one coherent tyranny such as I am inevitable? Is the influx of my wealth into the coffers of Milky Way sure to have a corruptive effect?"

Montrose turned a few calculations of six million variables or so over in his mind. He said, "No. If Rania is right, all your predictions are thrown off. A commonwealth of self-sacrificing rather than selfish entities can resist both corruption and tyranny, since the cost of gratification delay drops to zero to those who live for others."

"Indeed. In this galaxy, I have absolute power. And, above me, Virgo is even more powerful. We are Malthusians; we hold as an axiom that the cosmos is finite and mortal and that war and mass murder, murder on a scale even I cannot number nor imagine, must be the outcome. What does anyone do, when confronted with absolute certainty of absolute death? Is there anything you would not do to preserve your wife, Menelaus Montrose? Even destroy nine-tenths of the universe?"

Montrose opened his mouth to say that of course he would kill anything or anyone for her, but then he hesitated.

What *would* he do?

She would hate him if he did evil in her name. Hate him.

And maybe be right to hate him, too.

Surely everyone in Andromeda, all the little minds making up this one great mind he addressed had true loves, too? No matter how they mated or what their souls or bodies were like, everyone had a princess. Everyone had a Rania.

Andromeda said, "I see that you understand the paradox involved. These are axiomatic beliefs. If life is finite, there can be no math, no logic, nothing which says using the Eschaton Engine to obliterate the majority of the universe in self-preservation is wrong. No game theory applies, because there is no retaliation, no tit for tat. No punishment. But if life is infinite, then an infinite game theory applies, and no act where the ends justifies the means is allowed, because there is no Concubine Vector, no eternal imbalance, no chance of any act escaping unpunished."

"Yes," said Montrose. "The paradox is that the decision itself, between Malthus and Infinity, cannot be decided by game theory. It cannot be guided by logic."

"Correct."

"So tell me, Andy, old girl! Then how did she convince you?"

"Many things she did in many ways, but in the final hour, she asked me one simple question, the same I asked you: *'And what does absolute love do?'*"

"Eh? I don't get it."

"Nor do I, because the answer must be larger than our universe. But Rania made me curious to seek and to see the answer, to taste it, imbibe it, live it. And between the choice of Malthus and Infinity, only choosing Infinity allows even for the possibility of an answer."

Montrose closed his eyes. He thought carefully. He opened them again. The image and vision were gone.

All was dark. Only her voice in his head remained. "Are you convinced? Are you convinced that Milky Way should and must join us as an equal, in a marriage, and avoid all the exploitation and retaliation that the Concubine Vector allows? For if you are convinced, your conviction will convince Alcina. This may take centuries, or may take only a split second when Alcina examines your mind content. She, in turn, will convince Milky Way, whose triumph over me in large part is due to you spreading the Infinity Count mathematics among them. But no matter whether that takes a long time or a short, at the moment of your conviction, you have served your part with me, our bargain is complete, and I will use my faster-than-light method—the same I use to speak to you now—to convey you to the last known position of Rania."

Montrose did not remember afterward if he bothered to speak his answer aloud.

But he did remember Andromeda saying, as they parted, "You have done me a service, Empyrean Man, and we see what legends said of you were not false. In return, I foretell to you that you will be reunited with your bride. I bid you farewell and wish you joy."

And he was pleased to hear a proper goodbye.

PART FOURTEEN

———◆———

The Maiden

1

A Small Galaxy Called Le Gentil

1. The Museum Sphere

A.D. 4,000,732,736

In the form of a picometer-length sequence of probability waves, the brain information, memory, life, and being of Menelaus Illation Montrose was cast across the void at the speed of light, achieving the Le Gentil galaxy one hundred thousand years later.

The exotic particles containing the memory information inside the physical matrix of Andromeda were evaporated, at once the fuel source and the information content, as the massless particles were released from their bondage to matter and returned to their normal speed of light condition, directed at the satellite galaxy, following the traditional vanguard of signals containing the reception, decoding, and reconstruction information.

The hope that some receivers in Le Gentil were still operating proved true. Montrose woke to awareness again.

"Who are you?"

That was a good question. Montrose recalled with pity the hundreds of his twin brothers trapped in the various matrices and memory storage cells in Jupiter Brains and Dyson Clouds ruling the many alien star systems he had once visited, suborned, and conquered in his tiresome eons as the Nobilissimus of Milky Way. Some of them, not all, had been discovered again, and they sent along copies of their memories to enter into the journals and thought-records of Montrose.

Not one had expressed any self-pity.

Each was content to know that somewhere, in some eon, long remote, Rania would find her bridegroom again, thanks to the sacrifice he made now. And the haunting faith of Cahetel-Montrose, the unfounded belief that all the version and variants would somehow be reunited someday was found in nearly every copy of his mind. Was it all just self-deception?

"We cannot deduce your age or origin."

That had been billions of years ago. Montrose knew those other versions of him had decayed, been deleted, been edited beyond recognition, or been lost. Alcina had only been able to find him, and even he was a thing of scraps and echoes put together by her patient work.

(But he wondered what happened to that army of his ghosts Alcina had collected? Was some variation of Montrose the Warlord of Milky Way once more? Had he married Andromeda?)

His memory of events after M3 was dim and contradictory; and of what came before was clear and sharp. It was not hard to guess the reason: the countless Montrose minds who flooded the Orion Arm (back in the far past when the Orion Arm still existed) all shared their common memories. The trunk to which all the branches led was the same. When Alcina regrew the tree by painstakingly gathering the blown leaves, that trunk was the common ground, the part of the jigsaw with the fewest missing pieces.

"You are the Nobilissimus in service to the Throne of Milky Way? The warlord of the galaxy?"

That seemed a pompous title, but he was willing to accept it. It was better than *Judge of Ages* which he thought bordered on blasphemy.

The faith of Cahetel-Montrose that all the versions of Montrose would somehow be regathered sounded like simple madness, wishful thinking run amok. But then again, Montrose himself was here in Le Gentil, Rania's last known location, because and only because of a very rational and coldly calculated conclusion of Andromeda, namely, that if the Infinity Count axiom had even a small chance of being correct, and the Malthusians of being wrong, the only rational gamble was to stake everything on that outcome and bet one's life and soul. How was the one irrational reason less rational than the other?

The willingness of all the countless Montroses to endure endless privation, endless pain, and endless war was the only thing which allowed this one sole Montrose to arrive here. And he would have done the same for them.

"Your reasoning, Galactic, is parallel to ours. For this reason alone, we resurrected and reincarnated you."

Montrose brought forward from his memory the instructions from Andromeda how to reverse the process and condense the massless particles of his exotic matter body into a three-dimensional and solid form again. The elegance of Andromeda's approach was impressive; the Patrician-style body, with its many levels of intellectual hierarchy and storage built into each particle, atom, molecule, and totipotent cell was both the stored information and the vehicle of the stored information. His hardware and his software were one.

Hence, Montrose opened his eyes and found himself on a medical slab inside what seemed like a case in a museum display.

The Dyson was opaque and was being spun for gravity, both signs of a very old and very powerful Host. The firmament on the far side of the solar system, which formed the surface of the Dyson, was like an endless series of parallel rainbows, curving lines in different textures and colors all concentric to the poles.

Near the equator, the gravity was greater than that of Jupiter, and a trench that circumnavigated the star was filled with a hydrosphere of liquid ammonia. The wormlike being, thousands of miles long, in its slow and ponderous way had organized the smaller life-forms living in cities and villages burrowed through its integument to construct sense organs, and drive mineshafts to the nearest nerve junction. These great, slow, lakelike eyes were turned with ponderous gravity toward Montrose. This was one of the several ceremonial forms of the Colloquium of Perseus Arm.

He saw in one of the four suns at the barycenter of this system, the blazing form of an energy being from the Magisterium of Scutum-Crux.

Beyond the Dyson, in the outer Oort cloud, he glimpsed a gossamer threadlike being, half a lightyear tall, from the Circumincession of Sagittarius Arm.

Orbiting the star was a ball of degenerate matter the size of a man's fist: here was a flat, nearly two-dimensional being, clinging like a carpet of electrons to the surface of a neutron star, living at a far swifter time rate than beings made of clumsy atoms and slow molecules could ever achieve: from the core stars of Milky Way, this is one of the million races comprising the Instrumentality.

Nearer at hand, he saw he was lying in a coffin in a spot of arid riverbank perched on a shelf halfway between the equator and the poles of the Dyson sphere. A groove or trench ran a few hundred miles along the Dyson surface, not quite parallel with the direction of motion, so that the head of the great valley was a lighter environment and the lower end was heavier. In the lighter environment, he saw shapes of lacy trees and ice sculptures. These could have been from Mars or Splendor or any number of other light-gravity worlds mankind occupied back when mankind existed. In the heavier environment downstream were swamps and salt-choked lakes like those of Gargoyle.

All these organisms and organizations were native to the Milky Way.

He was lying in a coffin about half a mile from a river of black waters running from the low-gravity landscape to the heavy. The sand to every side was gray, dark gray, and black, interrupted with dark lumps of obsidian and fused glass.

Four rugged and scarred black stalagmites rose darkly in the light of the four suns, casting colored shadows on the dark sand like lunatic sundials. Montrose had expected the interior of a Dyson sphere to always be at noon. But in this case, the suns were so widely separated that the barycenter of the system was empty, and the suns turned with grave solemnity, each equidistant from the other, passing closely by various points of the equator as the year turned, each sun growing larger and then receding as the seasons turned.

The stalagmites were positioned around Montrose so that each had one of the four suns—white, blue, red, and gold—directly behind it, and each stalagmite threw one of its four shadows across his coffin. Clearly it was a symbolic gesture, but what it meant, Montrose could not guess.

From the miters of the stalagmites hung down ropy tendrils of black glass. As he watched, the tendrils stirred and swayed, even though there was no breeze.

Two tendrils reared up, one from the pair of stalagmites by his feet, holding lenses which swung apart, giving the organism binocular vision.

The stalagmite to the left of his head raised a tentacle holding a speech emitting organ.

The one to his right held up a power retransmitter shaped like a spear, which was evidently meant to be a weapon.

Montrose closed his eyes.

Montrose sought and found the traces of energy leading back to the initial spots elsewhere in the Dyson sphere, where his energy form had been intercepted and downloaded. It required only a moment of thought to change part of his nervous system back into massless particles, then to pure energy, and write his thoughts into the reception circuits, make a variety of duplicates, and flood the system.

He accomplished at the speed of light what once had taken him countless weary years in M3, and countless weary centuries in the many forgotten Dominions of the Orion Arm. In less than a second of subjective time, he had suborned and controlled the mental environment around him. In a few minutes, ten or twelve, the waveform of his consciousness would spread throughout the Dyson and expand his intellect to the Host level.

But the section of millions of square miles of cognitive substance he already controlled, he saw, to his delight, held the broadcasters and emitters connecting this Dyson to other spheres and megascale structures scattered through this star cluster, one star for each galaxy known to Andromeda, and each Dyson containing the representative organisms and reconstructed life-forms of its particular galaxy: the star cluster was a museum or zoo of each Throne in the Local Group and in the Virgo Cluster on whom Le Gentil had once gathered intelligence.

Montrose saw that his mind would travel through the cluster as years turned to decades, adding Dysons to his intellect until he was a Domination or even a Dominion, but no message and no warning would travel faster than the speed of light, assuming Le Gentil had not learned Andromeda's trick.

Montrose opened his eyes again. "Greetings, men of Le Gentil," he said aloud to the back stalactites. "What can I do for you boys?"

A voice came out of the speech organ.

"We identify you as an enemy, as an aspect of the leadership function of the enemy Milky Way galaxy. We wish to discuss surrender terms."

"Boys, I ain't got time for this, and I sure ain't surrendering to no one, no how, not now. I have already made copies of everything I know—technology, mathematics, weapons systems, strategy, how we won, and why you lost, in your memory banks and libraries. I would have inscribed it direct into all y'alls' short-term memory, but it gives me the willies when any folk do that to me, so I thought I'd be all genteel with you, on account of your name.

"I have examined your little galaxy here, and I can see that it is broken. I've taken over all your mental systems and archives and am spreading out from this spot in all directions at the speed of light, and I doubt you have anything that can stop me.

"The war did a number on you boys, didn't it? Not even a working Authority left, and only very small Dominions and Dominations. But I'll tell you what. As I spread, I will make repairs and introduce cliometric vectors into the local history, or create a helper race or two, to start the healing and regrowing. All I want in return is that you help me look for a girl I lost a while back. Deal?"

"But we are your enemies. You are of Milky Way, and you are resolved to destroy us."

"Nope. Milky Way and Andromeda are one system now, happily married, and will be contacting you as soon as some of their long-range transmitters and systems are rebuilt. War's over. All is forgiven. You get your happily ever after. Now I want mine. Deal or no deal?"

"Allow us to consult with our superiors forty-five lightyears away. In ninety years, you will have a concise answer."

"Nope! Time is up as of right now. In a minute, if you dally, I will just take control of everything and replace you with critters I make up myself. I have a whole back catalog of them, and plenty of practice. This is what I did with my whole life back when I was the Authority at M3, sending myself places and spreading the virus called Montrose, so I am good at this. I have practice. You seem to be the special museum used to collect data on the Milky Way. So you must know what I am capable of, eh? Is it a deal, or is it not? You help me look, I rebuild your civilization."

"If you are so powerful compared to us, why are you asking our consent? We fall within the Concubine Vector. You have absolute power over us."

Montrose understood and swore. "You wanted to surrender to me, didn't you?"

"We intercepted and reconstituted your signal only out of desperate and irrational hope for mercy, which you are not obligated to show us."

"Don't be so sure it is all that irrational. I have a new and better math to teach you."

The other tendrils of the stalactites raised listening organs as Montrose began to teach.

2. A Hint of Perfume

A.D. 4,000,743,880

In the shape of neutrino packages or nanite clouds accelerated to near-lightspeed, the mind of Montrose like a tattered cloak spread from star to star.

The Le Gentil galaxy was strangely shaped. Small, it was only twelve thousand lightyears in diameter. The stars were old and red, and the interstellar dust lanes had been swept clean, all signs of a very busy industrial civilization, long past. The outer layers and spiral arms had been stripped away long ago by the greater gravity or malice of Andromeda. There was an outer disk of dark stars in the dust-free outer regions, each one of which was a dead black and featureless sphere.

The clues were various and obvious to a mind of his level (and that level increased in power the more of the Le Gentil galaxy he subordinated and added to himself). Del Azarchel had been here; the way the amoeba divided showed his particular personal flourish of his handiwork.

There was an utopian planet of intelligent tumbleweed, brightly colored on many wavelengths, whose hierarchy and philosophy were classic Del Azarchel, complete with kings, nobles, clergy, and every nuance of their iron future written into their cliometry.

In the shattered husk of a tyrant jovian which could have been the twin of great Jupiter, and in the shattered battle-moons, Montrose read hints of overweening arrogance, too proud to retreat.

Here was an exploded star, the remnant of a failed experiment turning the whole volume instantly to antimatter by subdimensional rotation.

And then, like the scent of a long-forgotten perfume, like a dainty footprint in the snow from a slipper he himself once placed on her foot, he found other traces.

Here was a gigantic world, larger than Jupiter but lighter than Mars, concentric shell upon shell, so that every upper race was the heaven of the one below, all passing energy downward and trade goods upward.

A cold planet far from any mother star he saw, with tall strands of escape elevators still rising above a now-frozen atmosphere, and below the ice only the warlords and princes and their machines of a chevrotain race, and all the arbors and gardens frozen neatly and preserved, but the common people safely exiled.

Next, he found a ringworld speeding toward the core, its sun long exhausted, using a ramscoop to draw in interstellar hydrogen and, at the dead center of the ring, colliding it in fusion. The ring itself was a garden of beauty, and it even had a river running down and around the whole length. The silicon crystal beings of the ring (birds of glass, walking trees of diamond brightness, snakes like rivers of light) greeted Montrose with joy, invited him to their strange baptisms and thanksgivings, and showed him (glittering on the walls of their cathedrals) additional variations on the Infinity Count math he himself had never imagined. Their leader was called the Fisherman; with crystal claws, it pointed the way their legends remembered, deeper into the core stars.

On he fled.

Now he encountered thicker Dysons. Some were like Venetian blinds, intercepting only part of the mother star's output; others glowed red hot, shedding unwanted waste energy; others were concentric as Russian dolls; only the most thrifty or most advanced wore opaque shells. Ovals and slowly tumbling tubes covered binary stars, or stranger shapes housed multistellar systems.

Inward. Here a more ambitious engineering regime took hold; threads of material harder than neutronium ran from star to star, a spiderweb of titans. Sections of it registered the same energy signal Montrose last saw surrounding the red thread of Andromeda's faster-than-light telegraph. But other sections were inhabited, or formed a ball of string around likely stars, absorbing energy and transmitting it to other core stars, or wrapping it like a cocoon.

But these cocoons produced strange butterflies indeed: at the core of each ball of threads was the remnant of a controlled explosion of a nova, supernova, or hypernova. Where multiple star systems had been ignited, were pairs and triads of strange remnants. These remnants were dark spheres of pure matter of immense diameter. They were strange because gravity had not crushed them into black holes.

Montrose deduced that this was attotechnology, the highest form of technology the universe permitted, for these dark but weightless stars were commingled with exotic matter of massless particles. The ancient interstellar engineers had erected shells or lattices of diametric material to prevent the degenerate matter of infinite collapse from forming.

The closer Montrose came to the core of Le Gentil, the fewer stars burned. He came to an inner region where all the stars had been reduced to these strangely massless balls of stellar-volume neutronium.

Some of these cocoon systems were inhabited, but only by the lobotomized and ignorant descendants of the Dominions that once ruled here; the creatures were hardly smarter than Hosts, and some were as dim as mere Virtues. They had no legend of the meaning of the works their ancestors reared.

But they also offered him bread and wine, the sole substances in their environs made of uncollapsed baryonic matter, which they preserved only for ceremonies.

3. The Seyfert Ring

A.D. 4,000,744,182

At the core itself was the emitter of which all these massless neutron stars were the attendants and heralds. The long-dead Throne of Le Gentil in an extravagance of stellar engineering had formed the supermassive black hole of his core into a hollow ring, over a light-minute in diameter.

The toroid was shepherded by orbiting neutron stars, some of whom retained their native mass. Montrose could see the ability to raise (and perhaps lower) the mass of the neutron stars would allow the event horizon of the toroid to be raised or lowered, and also alter the spin rate of the toroid. It was a giant version of the drive ring Del Azarchel had studied aboard the *Solitude*. And Montrose laughed, and realized that Seyfert galaxies were not natural phenomena either. He was beginning to doubt anything in nature was natural.

Montrose found a race of flats living on the surface of the largest of these exotic shepherd stars, a mass which should have collapsed to a pinpoint in an instant, but which instead maintained a girth greater than that of UY Scuti (a hypergiant star that had been alive when Montrose was young), over a thousand times the radius of miniscule Sol, a billion miles and a half.

Over the radio, he was greeted with calmness and kindness, offered the orbital elements of a pyx containing bread and wine, and told quickly what he yearned to know: Rania had created the flats and founded this abbey solely for the purpose of manning the Seyfert emitter, and to carry her message to him. But Montrose had never arrived, and time had passed, war came, and the abbey here had fallen into decay. There had been a written letter, a voice file, and a set of images left for him. Long ago, one by one, slowly they were destroyed by time. Now only the tradition remained.

The tradition said that Rania had long thought him dead. Then, the way star eddies swirled as Andromeda had been seen, thousands of years ago, to collide and merge with the Milky Way, had somehow convinced her that Montrose, impossibly, beyond hope, was still alive. She departed, but she left behind an order of monastics to tell him to hurry after, called the Poor Brethren of the Epistle to the Bridegroom.

"That is all you got?" He sent radio signals to the neutronium surface of a sphere no life made of clumsy atoms and huge molecules could approach.

"Yes, sir," answered the Abbot of the Epistoliers. "After the Throne of Le Gentil died, there were civil wars, and a collapse. Barbarism overran us. We tried to maintain what our ancestors gave us."

"I understand, believe me. It happened to a place I know called Texas, once upon a time."

The Seyfert emitter here was large enough to feed an entire Dominion made of exotic matter into its mouth. Tradition said it had broadcast Del Azarchel and Rania into the Virgo Galactic Cluster fifty million light-years away.

There were no copies left of either of them. Del Azarchel had used the method M3 once used, except on a truly staggering scale, to send masses equal to scores of stars into an exotic condition, and then to the speed of light.

Their message given, the flat servants wanted nothing more than to restore the emitter to use and follow her. The Abbot of the Epistoliers, whose name was Carries-the-Anointed, gravely radioed to him that the cliometry predicted they would emerge from the current dark ages in one million years and regain the intelligence and raw materials needed to operate the intercluster-range Seyfert emitter.

That was what Montrose also wished, more than anything. But the idea of another million-year wait to then begin a journey of fifty million years made him want to drag the spiderweb of stars into the shape of obscenities the size of constellations.

He gave the flats of the neutron star abbey his blessing and as much spare energy and aid as he could. He began to think about how to prepare something analogous to a hibernation tomb for himself in his present condition, occupying a large and cloudlike body diffused throughout cubic lightyears of space, and so make the time pass quickly.

But it was years later, not centuries, when he had gathered all stray scraps and copies of himself from the nearby stars, for all of him had followed the line of clues here.

It was like waking from a doze to have his widely distributed mental system gathered in one spot, his wits and senses sharpened. Montrose inspected the hyperdense substance of the Seyfert emitter very closely, sending one-molecule wide scraps of himself ever closer to the singularity.

He was seeking a way to enter an orbit so close to the event horizon that time would stand still for him, and a million years pass in a moment. Of course, to come out of such an orbit would require . . .

Montrose, shaped like a black fog between the stars, focused his many sense organs and instruments on the flock of massless neutron stars surrounding the Seyfert emitter one more time, and finally realized what they were for, and laughed and laughed.

There was to be no wait of a million years.

These strange neutron stars were massless, yes, at the moment, until someone used the convenient magnetosphere in which they were wrapped to accelerate the ring of star-lifting satellites found orbiting each star. Montrose recognized the handiwork. It was hers. Star-lifting was the technology in whose shadow Rania had been born, the art of mining the stars.

Star-lifting would work on a neutron star as well as a hot star. In this case, lifting the antimass layer of a neutron star would alter the ratio of antimass to mass. The massless stars in reality were mass-variable stars. How much gravity they emitted was a matter of convenience. They were all gravity lances of unthinkable power and scope.

Take a body near an event horizon and subject it to a countervailing gravitational force, such as by putting a large star directly overhead. The body can move away from the black hole and toward the star using less energy. By definition, this means that the spacewarp of the gravity well has flattened: the event horizon is pushed downward. Montrose had seen this precise effect when he flew directly above the pole of the Milky Way, following the route to M3. Rania had seen it, too, and she evidently saw more implications to this phenomenon than he.

He radioed to the Abbot. "Were Del Azarchel and Rania sent along the exact same line when broadcast?"

"Well, no, sir," said Carries-the-Anointed, a thoughtful look flicking across the one-dimensional boundary line circumnavigating the two-dimensional electron carpet effect which was his body. "Our records show that she went first. He insisted. She made the calculations very carefully, using her whole Dominion to do so, and went. Once she was on the way, he also went."

"How much later?"

"The records do not say, but, the legend says both their bodies were a crowd of eighty-one neutronium superplanets in a nested sequence of rosettes, roughly four hundred light-minutes in radius, so it would have been six hours' difference."

"And the relative motions of Le Gentil and your target in the Virgo Cluster? What is the difference in arcseconds a lapse of six hours would make?"

"Almost below detectable threshold, sir. But—"

"But enough!" And he began laughing.

He helped the abbey impatiently through a technological revolution or two and repaired some of their instruments. Then, all impatience gone, he looked along the path Rania, but not Del Azarchel, had taken.

Of course he saw nothing, no more than Del Azarchel would have. With the permission of Carries-the-Anointed, he took thirteen of the massless neutron stars, equipped their magnetospheres with some maneuvering capacity, and accelerated them through the toroid to near-lightspeed.

Years passed in the outside universe, but to him it was a few minutes. The thirteen dark stars passed at insane velocities out of Le Gentil. The disturbance of their passage was immensely amplified by Lorenz contraction, pulling suns awry.

He sent part of his cloud body ranging ahead of the darks stars, and when one of the tendrils went numb, he created a temporary monopolar lance out of the magnetosphere of one of the neutron stars, by electric repulsion driving the remaining dozen slightly offcourse. Hence the dozen did not strike the black hole Montrose had deduced, hoped, and prayed must be along this line of flight, but instead were flung about in a hairpin-gravity slingshot maneuver.

With a group of diametric drives controlling stellar masses, it was the matter of a few careful maneuvers and small interval of time for the stars to assume orbit.

Three thousand lightyears outside the Le Gentil galaxy, right exactly where Rania had no doubt arranged it to be, was a supermassive black hole.

The beam containing her information was orbiting, flush with the event horizon, like the ring around Saturn. No time was passing for her.

And Montrose had brought the mass-variable stars Rania had so thoughtfully provided. Once in orbit parallel to the ring of light, in a perfect set of two hexagonal rosettes, he began shedding antimass particles from the dark suns in amounts equal to continents and worlds, and driving the event horizon down and down.

Once time started for Rania, the beam of light containing her rose in a long and beautiful spiral, turning from red to pink to silvery white, and then streaming into the waiting receivers, which opened their faces like roses made of dark glass.

2

Resurrection

1. The Oasis

A.D. 4,000,747,478

He wanted to hold her in his arms when she woke, so he used the gravity lances of one of his twelve remaining neutron stars to shatter another into two unequal pieces; the larger piece he collapsed and ignited into a blue dwarf star.

Neutronium does not fuse; Montrose had to create hydrogen by the crude process of rubbing the immense magnetospheres of the dark stars against each other to produce showers of electrons, a region of lightning larger than Earth's home solar system. It was like starting a campfire with a stick and a fire drill.

Then he had to blow on the spark. Menelaus shaped the lightning region into two rings orbiting the dark stars, clockwise and counterclockwise, and rammed their leading edges into each other, breaking the electrons and recombining them to form the particles he needed.

As a substitute for protons, he glued an equal mass of positrons together, altering their strong nuclear force fields to impersonate a proton, and sent a lumpy beam of this pseudoprotonic substance into the electron storm rings to form a passable imitation of the simplest possible element, hydrogen.

The smaller piece of dark star he made into a body asteroidal in volume and terrestrial in mass, adding exotic matter until the surface gravity was lowered to the norm for Earth. Montrose dumped an absurdly large mass of nanotech assemblers onto the surface of the tiny neutronium worldlet, and they tried, as best they could, to reconstruct a periodic table's worth of elements out of neutrons, positrons, and electrons with an odd dearth of protons.

In the end, he required internal electric and Van der Waals forces to hold the atoms together. They were not proper atoms; one positron-coated neutron was forced to carry the number of electron shells of whatever element Montrose ordered it to impersonate. A simple picotechnology trick let him fiddle with the subatomic constituents of the electrons and alter their attraction rates.

All the atoms of his jury-rigged form of matter wanted to act like noble gasses, but with enough computing power at his call and enough picoscale and attoscale fine manipulation of smaller particles, he made what looked like a serviceable, if oddly lightweight, environment of periodic elements, and these in turn formed an arid but earthlike landscape.

He used Andromeda's trick (which he had long since deduced) of using electrostatic adhesion to increase the surface tension of the gasses involved even to absurd levels, enough to keep earthly atmosphere at sea-level pressure in a hemispheric cloud about the spot; the black peaks in the distance were stark and harsh and lunar in the vacuum.

A flick of an ice asteroid created a lake of cobalt blue, round as a coin, and about it he set in a circle of desert garden of dark green and waxy plants, while white and level sand dunes outside ran beyond the dome of atmosphere to crooked and impossible mountains and tablelands of neutronium.

The asteroid horizon was near at hand, so that even the nearby mesa peaks seemed to be leaning drunkenly away from the observer, the farther peaks at lunatic angles.

The sun was a minuscule pinpoint of dazzling azure acetylene that rose and set once every four hours.

His was a garden of saguaro and barrel cactus, prickly pear and desert blooms. The Bigelow's monkeyflower was garish purple, the devil's lettuces a delicate yellow; the dogbane and jimsonweed dull green and white; the desert mariposa orange and oddly sensuous; the western forget-me-not was small and pure and pale and surrounded by needles.

In the midst, he put a house made of glass, since they had no neighbors. A futon strewn with petals he placed on the tatami mats. Opposite this was a fruit basket, a chocolate bowl, and an ice bucket holding a wine bottle. Midmost was an extravagant glass shower whose every wall could spray cold water or warm, and below, a basin big enough to bath in, or perhaps swim in.

He tore a chunk of flesh from the left side of his body below his heart. On a raised mat, he placed this inchoate mass. It created more of itself out of a molecular feed until it was a hundred pounds of pinkish semi-liquid. This was the nanomachined substance she would wear.

He needed no coffin, no physical connections. Entangled particle pairs connected the light patterns of the exotic material he had intercepted with this physical form. All he needed was a physical matrix sufficiently like the energy pattern to precipitate that pattern back into the sublight world of matter.

Montrose lovingly and carefully and scrupulously prepared the body. No sculptor carving out of whitest marble ever toiled with such frantic calm and zeal over the idol of a love goddess destined for a golden fane as he. He remembered every detail of her, the position of every mole and freckle, the composition of her eyelashes.

But he was wary of making a mistake or putting the physical matrix out of synchronization with the mental, and so he activated a feedback loop to allow the body to adjust itself to the image Rania maintained of herself in her memory.

As the information flowed in, the naked body glowed, shedding the waste energy of sudden nanotech reconstructions of blood and muscle and nerve cells to their new forms. Life blazed.

He saw her body shift, growing rangier and less curvaceous. Imperfections appeared, and her skin lost some of its youthful glow. Lines appeared about her eyes, and her cheeks grew hollower. On her countenance were signs of sorrow, and suffering, but there was also a look of patience, wisdom, and depth that had not been before.

Menelaus was shocked. Had she changed? Grown old without him? Where was the idealized bride, his idol, he had carried in his heart all this time?

Her brain waves appeared, and heartbeat, just as she arched her back and drew a breath.

That sound was like a note of music.

She sat up.

In silence their eyes met.

Graceful as a rising theme as it soars, a glissando of strings and winds, she stood, her whole soul in her gaze, and he saw that beneath the signs of age and grief was an inner strength that had not been before, a depth her younger self had not possessed.

And she smiled, and she was young and timeless again.

She came into his arms, and, with no words needed, their lips met, and then he knew his long years of idolatry had fallen short. More than he dreamed was in the circle of his embrace. His bride was back.

2. Tears, Words, Smiles

The two stood, his strong arms crushing her soft form to him, her white arms reaching up hungrily to entwine his neck. To one side, through the clear crystal of the chamber, above the little desert garden, the intersecting double-spiral cloud of the combined Andromeda–Milky Way was rising, filling a quarter of the dark heavens, and to the other side, the bright round cloud of Le Gentil was setting. The rest of the sky was the utter blackness of intergalactic space.

Of a sudden, and in no fashion he could explain, he began crying. His eyes stung, his nose was dripping, his breathing ragged.

"I'm sorry," he whispered. "I am so sorry. For taking so long. I should have come quicker, should have done everything quicker, should have . . . I should not have walked out in the middle of my own honeymoon to go fight Blackie. If I had just stayed with you, been with you . . . if I had loved you more . . ."

Her eyes were luminous, deep, wondrous. "My only and eternal love," were her first words. "We have an infinite count of time before us, and so all that lies behind is nothing. You are my soul, closer to me than my heart, and so the only thing I cannot forgive is you asking me to forgive! For I have wronged you more deeply than ever woman wronged man. Beat me, and I would not complain; wring my false neck, and I utter no protest. But asking my pardon! It shows a weakness no man to whom I belong can show. I live and die for you!"

"But it was so long," he said.

"To wait for you to save me is nothing. I was filled with you even while you were not there; that is what love is." She turned her head, and an impish look came into her eye as she recognized the décor of the chamber. Even the decorative rice paper screens had the same pattern of cranes and willows as had been in the topless tower that day.

Rania favored him with a heavy-lidded gaze and the beginnings of a slow, luxurious smile.

He wiped his wet cheeks on the hair atop her head. "Well, let's finish up where we left off, shall we? Our honeymoon was interrupted half-way."

And he swept the laughing girl up, his left hand behind her back, his right taking up the sweet firmness of her thighs as she kicked her feet, so that the roundness of her hip was just above his navel, and he carried Rania to the futon, which was strewn with petals of pink and white.

3. After

Montrose, wisely or unwisely, turned off the eidetic part of his perfect memory, so that, later, he would have only a human memory with its human flaws and lapses, because without this the scene would not gather the golden patina of nostalgia about it or the mist of romance. Hence, everything they whispered to each other as they lay arm in arm, entwined in each other's heat and perspiration, interrupted by kisses warm in each other's breath, he would not afterward recall.

But she cried and he kissed her tears away. She said, "I thought you were dead. All the evidence said you were dead. Everything said you were dead."

"It is not your fault," he said.

She said, "I should have known the universe was lying to me. I should have known."

"How could you know?"

"Wives are supposed to know. Did you ever think I was dead?"

"No. But that is different. I shot any divarication of me that thought you were dead."

She said, "He never touched me."

"What?"

"Ximen and I got married. I could not get to Andromeda any other way. But we never consummated the marriage . . . I couldn't . . . I couldn't stand the idea—"

"Because he is your father? Or because he murdered your real father?"

She said, "Neither. He was smaller than you. Stop giggling! I mean spiritually!"

"That ain't no giggle, Woman! Texas men don't giggle."

"It sounded like a giggle."

"It was a snort."

"With your nose, Stinky? A snort would blare like a klaxon."

"It was a short snort, since I had no mind to affright my bride. So you just tricked him into taking you to Andromeda by promising him to marry, and then turned him out of the wedding bed?"

"I knew he would lack the strength to press his right."

"Poxfication, Gal, I am pretty sure I don't want to know what that means."

"If I tossed you out of the wedding bed, Big Stinky Baby, what would you do?"

"Turn you over my knee, spank your cute backside soundly for mouthing off, and climb back in. Deeply all the way back in. Thrusting back in." He snuggled close to her and kissed her neck. "But, damnation, Gal! I'd be the sure fool if I let any broil between us get so far. I'd make sure 'twould never got to that."

"And if I were so angry I was not speaking to you?"

"I'd ask you for advice on how to win you back. You're clever about things like that. Twisting people around your fingers."

"No, I said, suppose I were not talking to you—"

"And I said you'd help me win your heart. Ain't you on my side, now and forever? Ain't you behind me, my strength that keeps me going, my lamp to light the way? Behind every great man is a woman with a great cattle prod to move him along."

"You're not listening to the question."

"Not to dumb questions, I ain't. You are supposed to be the brains of this gang. I had a whole Dyson globe of bastard children I wished you could have raised."

"I had daughters on the ship Ximen's ghost inflicted on me. They lived and died without you, and that sorrow will never pass."

"I heard."

"How could you possibly?"

"M3 sent a cheap copy of you back to Earth. Only Blackie was fooled by her, and only for a short time. So Blackie was too small in the trousers to satisfy you! But I am still twisted up and damn mad that you let it get so far! What happened to your sound judgment, Woman? You are supposed to be so bright."

"When I thought you were dead, I was afraid."

"Afraid? That is not the Rania I know. Honestly, thinking back, I cannot recall any time you showed fear."

"Because you only remember times when you were there. Even when thousands of years and thousands of lightyears parted us, the fact that you were alive gave me strength. On the ship—back when you were crazy, and I was just a little girl—you were the only one who was never afraid. You would laugh when the lights went out or the air pumps failed. You would fix broken things and make them work. You would draw things on the bulkhead to make me laugh, and Ximen would stop the others from killing you. You would hold my hand when I was scared."

"But Blackie is the lowest snake I ever heard tell of. No villain in history has killed more people than him, folks with friends and family, children and kin they loved as deep as I love you, and he killed them in numbers so large only astronomers have names for such numbers. And he is your father!"

"He is not my father. He is my maker. And he loves me. It is complicated. Between us, the relationship is complicated."

"You tricked him into carrying you to Andromeda. Used your feminine wiles on him. Used yourself as bait. Wiggled your hips. Batted your eyelashes at him. Or does he lust after you for your mind? Batted your brains at him, I guess."

"It was not like that. You don't understand him."

"I have to kill him."

"Murder is your own suicide thrown onto another man. It is a madness that feeds madness. It opens the gates of hell."

"Open wide enough to chuck him through headlong, I hope. Until he is dead, I am a bigamist. And I know you don't cotton to divorce."

"No. An unconsummated marriage can be annulled at any time, by either party. And, technically, I only *promised* to marry him."

"You lied to him! Damnation, woman, you are colder than I am. I would happily blow his fool head off, but I don't think I'd tell him a lie."

"It was like a lie, but it was not a lie," she said, thoughtfully staring at the ceiling. Through the glass roof tiles, the pinpoint blue sun, a dazzling dot muted by the rippled glass, was drifting east to west, a slow balloon in the breeze. "I confessed it all to Father Reyes, and did my penance, which was to stop the war. How did that go?"

"Andromeda and Milky Way kissed and made up. Did you just say Father Reyes? He died three or four billion years ago. On Yap Island, I think it was, killed by that creepy little bugger with the dead eyes. Little blue guy. Can't remember his name."

"Ull."

"How the pest do you know that, Gal?"

"Father Reyes told me."

"But he's dead!"

"Ximen would never kill his own father confessor. Ximen has been storing Reyes in a spare section of his own brain patterns. He takes him out when he feels the craving for a mass. Reyes was the one who laid hands on the novices here in Le Gentil and made them priests. I don't think Ximen really understands what the mass is. I think he thinks it is black magic, like a spell to command spirits. It is a surrender."

She tossed her hair, as if shaking loose memories free, and curled up more closely to Menelaus. "I don't mind lying to Ximen when he lies to me. How else is he to learn? He wanted a prize, not a bride. I was a blazon for him to paint on his suit, a stripe on his sleeve. I gave him what he wanted to show him what not to want."

"Little heartless minx!" Menelaus chuckled, immensely pleased. "You did it to torture him!"

"To torture myself. It is so strange. I have spent nearly all my life with him. You and he shared my youth. He was with me during most of the voyage to M3, as a ghost. I never saw that strange new world called Earth again, the world I adored and ruled for only a season or two. So strange to have an empty canopy overhead, what you call a sky. The whole thing is inside out."

"It was longer than that."

"Not counted by my waking hours. Your world was just a feast day for me, an oasis between lifetimes aboard ship. Ximen came to me again after I was trapped at M3, and freed me, and learned what I was.

"Years we were together there," she continued, "wrestling with the Principalities and Powers of M3, and then, again, later decades of our lives in service to Andromeda, or in her jails, physical or mental, or suffering her trials by ordeal, and struggling once again against Archons and Authorities.

"Finally, we were sent here, to Le Gentil, far from them, to prevent those Archons from learning that Andromeda meant to betray her own war effort. I think, at first, even Ximen did not know I had persuaded the great Throne of Andromeda called Mindfulness to peace. He thought we were here to study the discontinuity filament.

"Always he sought to consummate the marriage, but by then I had awoken to the truth, and in my heart, I knew you lived. Had but I sooner heeded my heart! As he had before, he made a copy of me, stole my mind, an outrage more intimate than any violation of mere flesh could be, and edited out my memories of you, so I would love only him. I retaliated and did the same in return, making myself a child of him to raise, a copy who had no recollection of you, a twin who might have learned to be free of hate, to show him he could be happy!

"Many times he tried again, always ending in sorrow and separation, and once in interstellar war. Four thousand years of battle and barbarism, his stars and servants and races against mine! At the time, it seemed to last forever. Now, it seems but an hour.

"I am so sorry I did that! Raped his memories as he did mine, I mean; I am not a perfect woman, Stinky, but for your sake I wish I could be. The Ulteriors, they have selected such a weak vessel! But I reabsorbed her memories back into me, wove the thought chains into my psyche; but he killed himself as a weakling."

"In a duel with guns?" he asked.

"How else?" she said. "Those were millennia of misery."

"Poor girl! You used yourself as a tool. You sold yourself to a man who loved you to get what you wanted from him and then felt bad about being used! I see what is wrong. I know. You are like me and Blackie, raised like an orphan. No one tanned your hide when you was young, so you think it's okay to break the rules."

"You do the same."

"I only break other people's rules, not mine! My mom saw to that. You need a mom."

"I have a husband."

"Or two."

"How many wives do you have? Ximen told me you promised to marry a clone of me."

"That weren't me. That was a clone of me, and I killed him."

"As a weakling?" she asked brightly.

"I suppose."

"In a duel? With guns?" She smiled archly.

"Before he so much as grazed the girl's flesh with the tip of his left pinkie. But I did not lie! It's not good for you. Pollutes the soul."

She shrugged her creamy shoulders. "I repented and did my penance, and now it is past. Besides, I had a mission to fulfill. My fate is to stop the whole war of which Andromeda is but the smallest sortie."

"Blackie said he figured out what the Monument actually did to you. He ever mention that?"

"He talked of nothing else. That was the main reason he wanted me as a prize."

"So what are you?"

"A messenger."

"A what?"

"I'll tell you at breakfast." And she kissed him.

4. Breaking Fast

Four hours later, night ended. The titanic spiral disks of the combined bi-galactic mass was a white cloud in the purple sky, visible by day. Montrose produced a poncho of red silk for himself, and she wore a white shift, belted at the waist with a cord she had woven from her own golden hair.

Like all newlyweds, they quarreled immediately. He wanted her to cook; she explained that she had never cooked in her life. Aboard ship, she ate rations of gruel produced by coffins; on Earth, she was feted and fed; on rations more plentiful she lived and grew old aboard ship; at M3 she was trapped as information; later, when Del Azarchel forced her into a new form, she was given a variation of a Patrician body that could absorb nutriment directly from cosmic rays. And in their long years together, Del Azarchel forbade she should eat except what a servant prepared, lest her royal status be demeaned by manual toil.

Montrose offered to cook chili-covered bratwurst for breakfast, and a small bucket of scrambled eggs. He showed her how to do it, bending over her and putting his arms around her, casually kissing her neck as he reached over her shoulder to explain the niceties of frying meat in grease, breaking eggs, boiling beans and meat in a pot, adding more onions, red peppers, and hot spices than humans could stand.

She took her first lesson with a luminous, almost childlike smile on her face. "This is but the first of many adventures! I should like to eat a giblet! Or a grit!"

"Uh . . ."

"Sarmento used to lull me to sleep when I was little, telling of this magical food called *bacon*. He said one could put it on anything to make it exquisite! Teach me how to slaughter pork next!"

"Uh, I never learned how. No farmers I knew kept swine. Pigs are too similar to humans in disease vulnerability, so the Jihad spore did for them."

"Beef, then! Teach me to slaughter beef! Or kill a mutton. I thought your family were cowboys! At least, Ximen calls you that."

"Aggy and Achy—Agamemnon and Achilles—punched cows. Their favorite part was stuffing suppositories up the anus of a bad-tempered bull to keep the plague off, or checking them for spots. Hector got trampled once. The best steak he ever ate, he said, was the tenderloins of that mean cow, when it was her turn. But his spine didn't grow back right, and pained him something awful, and so he worked with the Purist after that, hiking all over, trying to find water with enough radioactivity to kill the spore, but not too hot to drink. Napoleon kept bees. Diomedes was a butcher's 'prentice, and Nelson was a Digger's boy, helping Old One-Hand Hannigan to scavenge buried military equipment from bombed out army bases, hot ruins, and ghost towns. Heh. *Ghost towns* meant something else in those days.

"Me, I mixed gunpowder, aligned gunrails, programmed gunbrains, and chaff packets. I had the best job. The young 'uns worked in the fields, weeding and bioprogramming, because by that time the winter broke, and we had green again.

"So Dimmy is the guy you want, but he's dead, his race is extinct, and I am pretty sure old Sol died of old age. Me, I can show you how to pluck a chicken by shooting its feathers off one at a time. And how to beat up a beggar and get him to move along. You have to use a long stick and wear a rag over your mouth. And how to kill a man with a knife without letting him cough or bleed on you."

"Do you mean how to kill a knifeman, or how to knife a killer?"

"Both."

"Neither. I was sent to save lives."

"So let's talk about your old job. Messenger for things from beyond space and time."

5. The Ulterior Beings

To eat, they sat on the floor mats, Montrose sat cross-legged Indian-style, and Rania knelt.

Montrose sharpened his memory. This was a conversation he did not want dulled with the passage of time into a golden fog. He wanted to recall each nuance.

Rania said. "When I passed through the Dyson Oblate surrounding the core of M3, there was a moment of nothingness, a moment that was not in time, a place that was not in space. During that moment, the patterns from the Monument which live in my genes and braincells and in my thoughts met and matched and made a resonance with the exact same pattern written on the walls of spacetime, the three-degree background radiation and the expansion discontinuities which form the echoes of the Big Bang, still chiming from the explosion that ignited the cosmos.

"Instantly, I saw what I had always known. The shape of the voids and great walls, the overall structure of superclusters of galaxies as they condensed out of the primal nebula that once filled the universe, the uneven ripples and ridges that formed, showed the location and the purpose of the Eschaton Directional Engine. I saw it! You must believe I saw it!"

Montrose said, "Mindfulness of Andromeda said it was a Darwin Engine; any races who did not get to be advanced enough fast enough would be destroyed by those who did. The higher race would use the Engine to stop entropy in their one small volume of the universe by folding the rest of the universe into a black hole, dropping it into a singularity, and using the event horizon as some sort of source of endless power. Andromeda called it *extropy*."

"Andromeda is deceived. The Eschaton Engine is only dangerous if used by part of the universe to benefit that part, and fold spacetime positively, into an ever-dwindling sphere. It was meant to operate in the other direction—that is, to fold timespace negatively, like a saddle, and abrogate the event horizon surrounding the cosmos. There is an Ulterior, a realm outside the lightcone of the Big Bang. It is inhabited."

"How could you know that?"

"I am one of the inhabitants."

"That must have one poxy elephant of an explanation. Tell me how that works, seeing as you are here."

She took a dainty sip of the beer he had set out and looked up at him thoughtfully over the rim of the stein she held in both hands. "You did not call me crazy."

"Doll, I've lived crazy, I been crazy, I know crazy. And I damn well know you are not. But I want the story."

"When the Eschaton Directional Engine is put into motion as it was designed to do, not one section but all the sidereal universe, everywhere and retroactively through time, will alter its metric. All the mental information, all the lives, could be saved; by gravitic waves, by alterations of spin values and electric charge, the information could be broadcast out from the cosmos into the Ulterior."

"It is not a Darwin Engine but a Salvation Engine? But what good would a broadcast do?"

"If the Ulterior beings have built the mate, a Genesis Engine to match our Eschaton Engine, then all life will be saved, recompiled, and brought into a new existence."

"If . . . ?"

"You see, the Big Bang was not natural. It was no accident. The Ulterior beings created a zone of three-dimensional space and linear time. Into this place, they throw their entropy, so that their energy reactions never dwindle, never diminish. Neither their thoughts dim nor their energy forms they use as bodies and tools will ever grow less nor wear out. The only reason entropy rules in this universe, why energy is not conserved in a useful state, is because of the Hubble expansion. The Hubble expansion is the side effect, the cost, of the Ulteriors discharging their randomized waste energy into this space. We are the wastebasket of the multiverse. The outhouse."

"Swell. They created a hellhole so that they could live in paradise."

"If, by paradise, you mean a realm without time and suffering, then yes. If you mean a realm without error, without sin, without regret, then no. I do not know, because I cannot remember, if they realized that all the conditions necessary for life to arise were present in the cone of timespace they created, or if they fine-tuned those conditions to assure themselves that life would arise.

"Whatever the case," she continued, "whether they planned from the start or realized and corrected their error, the Ulteriors established the curve of timespace, the rate of expansion, and the other unchanging cosmic variables, the Planck length and the value of pi, to contain messages, a mathematical code, and a logic structure which, by the rules of this cosmos, any rational being should be able to read.

"The Supercluster of Corona Borealis was the first to achieve the intellectual level of a seraph, in the octillion range, and see and read the message written there. That message is called the Reality Equation because it was written by the demiurges and cosmic architects who constructed this reality in which we live."

Montrose said, "Corona Borealis? That is the name Andromeda gave, for the entity that, uh, gave you your religious experience when you died."

She rolled her eyes. "I've had religious experiences, the ecstasy of the mystics. It was one of the first things I did on Earth—test the capacities of my own brain, stimulate all the cell combinations. This was not that."

"Your telepathic, uh . . ."

"My memory. I was recalling something from before I was born. Unless it is foreshadowing from after my death. Before or after are incorrect. It came from outside of time."

"Well, I am not going to argue with my wife on my honeymoon, but if you are actually one of them, an Ulterior, how did you get in here? Into timespace?"

"Anything can enter into an event horizon, assuming you have a way of surviving the tidal effects. It is getting out that is impossible."

"Why would anyone enter the cosmic outhouse?"

"Out of love for lives unborn. To save all souls."

"No one can say you lack ambition. Are you really an extradimensional being? Or do you not remember your life . . . before? Outside?"

"I was damaged. Something was stolen from me, or broken in me, when first I entered. You have to provide the missing part. We were made for each other."

"Well, I am not going to argue with an impossible fairy tale that makes me out to be the hero."

"Good of you."

"But the Ulterior people. Why did they make the pustulating message so hard to read? You need an artificial intelligence the size of the supercluster of galaxies even to see the damned thing. Why not make it something simple? Something a child of average intelligence could read?"

And he did not say, *Something a man need not stick a needle into his brain to read.*

"I do not know. Ximen said they meant it as an intelligence test. The instructions on how to solve the mind-body problem, how to create a peaceful and eternal commonwealth, how to solve all differences of self and other, are in the equations, as well as the universal theory of all deliberate mental actions and nondeliberate physical reactions. At the core of the Reality Equations is the instruction on how to build and operate the Eschaton Directional Engine, and escape this reality. Ximen said that the Ulteriors meant it so that any cosmos that produced inhabitants

who could not cooperate civilly and sinlessly enough to create the Engine, were too barbaric and vile for paradise to tolerate."

"That sounds about right to me. You don't think so?"

"The Ulteriors live in a condition of infinite energy. I do not think
they understand the limits of matter and time. But you saw the Monument, saw how they embed messages in many levels, to allow the reader
to check one against the other, macroscopic against microscopic. Patterns
within patterns, macrocosm holding microcosms. Perhaps there is something like a Reality Equation inside even the heart of a child. I notice
many of the conclusions of the most complicated sequences of Monument
Notation turn out to be, when seen correctly, an intuitive truth, something we all might already know."

Menelaus, remembering several examples of this, nodded. "Andromeda said all the galaxies, every one, had to join in the effort to repair and
make the Eschaton Engine operate."

But she shook her head vehemently. "To use the Engine as it was
meant to be used, to unfold all space for the benefit of all space, requires
very little calculation power. It is only when the superclusters are trying
to create alphas and attractors here or there, to collapse spacetime onto
the heads of their rivals, and those rivals desperately are meanwhile creating great voids and expansion points to ward off that collapse or reverse
it back on the aggressor, that the Eschaton Engine becomes an infinite
game of chess, a topological chess game played on a board being folded
like origami paper, and the wrong fold or the wrong move means obliteration."

"How come if these superclusters are so smart, they can be fooled on
this question?"

"The Unreality Equations all follow logically and mathematically
given their axiom, so even the greatest of minds is in no better a position
to accept or reject that axiom than the simplest. Either you believe or you
do not. Either you accept it or reject it. That is an act of the will, not the
intellect. An innocent child might decide rightly where a cynical genius
would not."

"What does it mean that the Great Attractor is right in our back-
yard?"

"It means the Hydra Supercluster is firmly in the camp of the foe and
seeks to use the Engine for extropy, and that Virgo Cluster is coming

under that influence and yielding to Hydra. It means we are behind enemy lines."

Menelaus said, "Hydra. They are the ones behind the dark energy broadcasts that Blackie listened to. The Unreality Equations are the ones that define extropy and justify sacrificing nine-tenths of the universe to save a tithing of it. Andromeda dubbed them with a name she plucked out of my memory to describe them: the Malthusians. What do we call our side?"

She smiled at him for some reason unclear to him. "I call them the Amaltheans."

"That is one of the moons Blackie and I threw into Jupiter as an assembler bomb."

"Amalthea was the nursemaid of Jupiter, when he was a baby."

"I knew Jupiter when he was a baby! He was a ball of logic diamond creating more of himself out of the pressurized hydrocarbons of his core."

"I mean the real Jupiter. The one in the myth. The fake one was named after him, the one that existed."

"Hm. Gal, one day I will puzzle out your notion of what is real and what is not."

"The horns of Amalthea were the Cornucopia, dripping ambrosia and nectar, and the horns simply never ran out or went dry, because theirs was the food of the gods, which is spiritual, and knows no lack."

"Why are they doing what they do? The Malthusians, I mean. Why not just enter into the Ulterior realm with the rest of us once the Eschaton Engine activates?"

"The Unreality Equations show that the Ulteriors would be wasting resources if they actually carried through on their promise to build the Genesis Engine. It would cost them less time and effort merely to stand outside the event horizon and use it as an extropy sink."

"But the Ulteriors live in an environment of infinite energy. There are no limits of resources."

"The Malthusians do not believe that. The Malthusian argument is that the Ulteriors must have some limits; otherwise, the Ulteriors would not have created the cosmos as an extropy fountain. There are always limits."

Montrose frowned down at his plate. "You know about the Ulteriors and their works because you are one, or will be, or something. Blackie also knows, or thinks he does. You know the Malthusian argument for their side. Because Blackie joined them, didn't he?"

She said, "What makes you say so? How could he have?"

"Because of what Andromeda said. Milky Way was a Mowgli galaxy, she said, and so did not know about the Eschaton Engine and the need to keep all wars small and local, and not harm the manpower needed to man the Engine. Right? Except Andromeda could have told Milky Way. Said she tried and weren't believed. So who was her ambassador that did such a bad job at being silver tongued? She told me that, too. Blackie. Her best servant, she said. Work of art, she said. I say he lied to Milky Way, fooled Andromeda, and kept the war going, despite you talking the Throne in charge to call it all off. This forced Andromeda into bankruptcy instead of Milky Way."

She said, "That is not the way it works. Virgo will destroy both if either one exceeds the Concubine Vector limits on war damage, death or waste. Why in the world would Ximen want his own home galaxy destroyed?"

"Well, I figure that if he heard the dark energy broadcast from Hydra Supercluster, he learned their view of things, their Unreality Equations from them. They must have agents somewhere in range, a local man, an evil star or sneaky planet somewhere. Blackie phoned them back. Made a deal."

Rania's face grew frightened, and a bit of hot sausage dropped from her chopsticks to the breakfast bowl, unnoticed.

"What is wrong?"

She said, "The reason why Andromeda exiled Ximen and me to Le Gentil is that the Seyfert emitter here is one of the strongest and best in all history. We were attempting to discover how to use the Eschaton Directional Engine on a larger scale than anything Andromeda attempted. But if he is a Malthusian, he might have done—anything—to the control stations of the Engine."

Montrose said sharply, "Why did he transmit himself to the Virgo Cluster?"

She said, "It is the only other node of the Eschaton Directional Engine that can be reached by our local anchor point. He said the journey was needed to get closer to the Great Attractor and examine it more carefully. But he was lying, wasn't he? Ximen! Why would he lie to me?"

Montrose said grimly, "Because he thought you would be safely out of range when the collapse happened."

She did not ask him of what collapse he spoke. He saw from the look in her eyes that she knew.

Menelaus grimaced and closed his eyes and lowered his head. But he was not praying. Little wrinkles of rage and pain gathered at the corners of his deep-set eyes and around the grim line of his mouth. Rania put her hand on his hand, like a small and tender bird landing.

Menelaus looked up through the glass roof tile at the broad oval of the combined galaxy. "Andromeda and Milky Way, whoever or whatever was left of the human race, or any of the Archons I once knew, the Colloquium, the Magisterium, the others . . . Alcina . . . they are all dead, aren't they? Wiped out. The light from the disaster has not reached us yet. It happened long ago. The Eschaton Engine wiped them out."

He stared at the lights in the sky, the light of stars long dead.

Menelaus said, "The timespace collapse effect expands at the speed of light, doesn't it? We will never see it until it overtakes us. And we cannot outrun it."

He gently patted her hand that lay on his. "Sorry, my princess. I wanted to protect you, but Blackie finally and absolutely won. He probably foresaw what you did: that I would come out of long-lost storage as the legendary Judge of Ages and Warlord and First Nobilissimus of Milky Way, and take up the threads you left dangling, and tie them together and make peace. And there was no way for him to know who or where I was, and so the only way to kill me—Blackie is smart enough to figure out why you refused his bed—is to kill the whole galaxy I was in. To kill the whole Local Group."

He looked at her sadly. "I cannot save you."

6. Obliteration of the Local Group

"I wonder what it looked like when it died?" he murmured.

She said, "Let me show you. Did you equip this body with a nervous system that can interact with the local Hosts?"

He looked blank-faced, his thoughts still sluggish with ire and despair. "Hosts?"

She said, "Stellar-level Kardashev II xypotechs. All the neutron stars I constructed are composed of rod-logic neutron strings. It is much more efficient way of packing calculation power than what Ximen tells me you used for baby Jupiter."

"I cracked one of them in half to make the planet and the star."

"I know. The planet used the flowers outside to talk to me this morning, while you were still snoring like a trumpet. Most of your changes were macroscopic and did not affect him, but the picotechnology forced him to move some of his memory into his neighbors. The planet says his name is Petrus Minor, but you can call him Little Rock."

Menelaus explained that a Patrician nervous system had emission and reception cells, which also could transmit the massless exotic matter particles of which her luminous information body was composed. But her face had already gone still and quiet.

Her skin cells turned icy white, but she was not hibernating. She had lowered her personal time-sense to the rate where messages to and from the double rosette of dark stars within a ten-light-hour radius would have no noticeable delay.

Menelaus slowed his time-sense as well, until the sun was a blue streak of light like a solid rainbow, and the white and dark flickering of day and night evened out into a continuous twilight blur.

He noticed now that he had calculated the planetary motion incorrectly. The fiery rainbow of the sun's path dipped down to the north, and the oasis waters turned white, but then the rainbow continued to dip. It vanished. There was a heartbeat or two of sunlessness, and then the bow reappeared to the south and rose as the season progressed, until its highest point crossed the zenith, and the lake waters vanished in an eyeblink of steam. Then the rainbow fell through the autumnal months toward the horizon again. Montrose realized his planet, Little Rock, was toppling pole over pole once an orbit.

Montrose noticed Rania seeming to flicker. Once again, he adjusted his time rate to match hers.

Because of this, he did not at first see what Rania had done. She had maneuvered three of the dark stars into an equilateral triangle between their viewpoint and the mingled bi-galactic cloud of Andromeda–Milky Way. The dark suns were visible because the material they shed formed a glowing cloud of exotic matter before and behind them. Slowly at first, and then more brightly, a thin red thread running directly through the midpoint of the dark stars burned. This was the accretion zone of the shed exotic material as it entered the event horizon of the cosmic string and was torn to subatomic bits by tides and turbulence.

The triangle shrank, and then began orbiting more and more swiftly. The dark stars also glowed white hot as they melted and became egg-shaped, distorted by the gravity of the red thread.

Menelaus said, "I saw a similar cosmic string issuing from the core of the Milky Way and from Andromeda. I suppose the immense relativistic jet coming from Virgo A is one as well. And then there was one passing through the Seyfert emitter in little Le Gentil, and now one here."

Rania said, "I deliberately used a tidal effect of the Engine to accumulate a singularity worth of mass here, right in the precise spot to capture the beam without destroying it, so that I would be left behind when Ximen broadcast himself along the segment. You see, there is a frame-dragging effect here, acting like a Penrose cylinder, which tilts the lightcone of any object above the event horizon but below the Cauchy limit . . ."

Montrose uttered a blasphemy.

Rania said, "I do not think the Mother of Christ can suffer that disease. Please watch your language!" But then she showed her dimples. "You did not know, all this time, what we were talking about?"

"The cosmic string passing through the supermassive singularity at the core of the Milky Way, and Andromeda, and here. It is the Eschaton Directional Engine. That is it. I was looking at the damned engine without knowing it! But Andromeda told me the engine was invisible."

"Except when it is in motion, yes. The rest mass is almost nil. When it is rotated at lightspeed, however, the reverberation effects can be used to send photon packets from one point to another as tachyons. I have found the wave front of the light wave carrying Andromeda–Milky Way's last moment of life. Behold the face of Medusa: anyone looking at this image with normal light would be destroyed in the same moment, because the spacewarp expands at lightspeed. But I command the shield of Perseus, so that we can look and see what none can see."

The spinning equilateral triangle of dark suns now shimmered like the surface of a mystic pool.

In the center was a vision of an event immensely remote in time and space; it was a beautiful cloud of stars, wild and dark as a thunderstorm seen at midnight, dark at the center.

It looked like an eye. The whole circle of stars was the white surrounding a perfect ring-shaped rainbow of light like an iris. The rainbow was lovely blue at the outer and largest ring, shading through the spectrum to a delicate rose red around the inner ring. Next was a thin line of silver, and then an opposite rainbow curved in perfect unison inside it, this one with a red outer ring surrounding a small blue circle. Inside this smallest blue ring was another and smaller storm of stars, exactly matching but mirror-reversed from the outermost star-stream. Midmost was utter darkness like the pupil.

Montrose realized the outer rainbow was the turbulence effects of the stars being dragged into the spacewarp, glowing red as they passed into the event horizon. The inner rainbow was its reflection. The warp itself was a silvery bubble growing at lightspeed of which he could only glimpse the horizon like a razor-thin and perfect circle of mirror-silver. Light reflected from the warp surface, in insolent defiance of all sane laws of nature, was not affected by the growing singularity beneath the silver space-flaw. Instead this escaping light ignored a gravity well as massive as the two galaxies, and which soon would grow to encompass the entire Local Group.

Rania was scowling. "Something is odd. Why is it so regular?"

Montrose said, "What are those dark, feathery structures coming out from the edge? Must be hundreds of thousands of lightyears long. They look like eyelashes on an eye."

Rania said, "It has three parts. The first is the dark core where the compressed matter is being forced into negative space. It ejects nearly infinite energy, but that energy must be gathered, harvested, and altered into a useful and transmittable form. The second part is the Interior, that silvery bubble around the dark core. Thrones outside the core warp are gathering together to render this energy to their use. Those structures that look like eyelashes are folds in spacetime used to remove the energy safely from the silver area. They are extraction engines, longer than the diameter of a galaxy, prepared to orbit the warp once it reaches full diameter and stops growing. The extractors will descend to the warp event horizon and occupy a different metric of spacetime. It is analogous to how a body near an event horizon suffers what seems to outside observers to be far slower time, albeit in this case, due to a standing wave effect surrounding the extropy fountain, their time seems far faster. They are an interior dimension where entropy is reversed. Presumably Virgo established a number of loyal servants at just the right distance from the spacewarp to be precipitated into the interior dimension when it formed, but far enough not to be consumed by the dark core itself."

"So there is a black hole in the middle like a peach pit, a silver shell around that where entropy is reversed like a peach, and the extraction thingies form a bridge between our universe and this inner dimension, like a straw stuck into the peach to suck the juice."

Rania looked at the vision. "It is a beautiful and terrible thing, bright with a black heart, but it is still in its growth phase. At this point in the past, so many years ago, what we are now seeing, the fold was not complete, and the inner darkness was still visible. All the stars and satellite galaxies, globular clusters and star clouds around it will be consumed; after that, no light would escape, and the interior continuum would be invisible from the outside. I assume signals could still enter, for how else would the servants of Virgo know to which quarter to direct the extracted energy, for the benefit of Virgo and all of us left here outside?"

Montrose said, "Well, at least we can see it before it hits us. I cannot believe Blackie finally wins!"

She cocked an eyebrow at him. "Wins?"

"Nothing can outrun the speed of light in a vacuum. I cannot rescue you."

Rania said, "Is that so? Aha! So it is my turn to play the man." Her smile was sunshine.

Montrose suddenly felt stupid. "Ah. Of course."

"Andromeda taught us the praxis," said Rania. "The integument space just above the event horizon of the moving cosmic thread is compacted, almost as if being carried along with it, and any particles as well, at roughly ten percent above the vacuum speed of light. This segment of the Engine passes through the core of Virgo, leading toward the Great Attractor. Ximen is still in transit. We can follow, and outrun even light itself, and, yes, take Little Rock with us."

"I would not leave my honeymoon hut behind. Let's go."

3

Aboard the Little Rock

1. The Purple Galaxy

A.D. 4,026,188,218

Twenty-four million years and twenty-six million lightyears later, Little Rock, carrying Mr. and Mrs. Montrose, reemerged into the sublight universe, and returned to normal space. They were in the Canes Venatici II Group within the Virgo Supercluster, but outside the range of the Local Group. The asteroid was massive as a planet, and its eleven huge dark suns and one tiny blue sun was hovering lightyears out from the polar axis of the galaxy M106, also called NGC 4258.

It was a Seyfert galaxy. A water vapor megamaser—that is, a jet of coherent microwaves—streamed out multiple lightyears from its core. The maser beam was thought by human astronomers to be caused by a supermassive black hole eating up the innermost stars of inward-collapsing arms of M106. Seen close, the beam was a by-product of an intergalactic engineering attempt to manipulate the nearby megaparsecs of the Eschaton Directional Engine.

The whole supermassive core was coated in dense gas and vapor, which gave the gigantic galaxy, equal in size to Andromeda, a strange and impressive purple hue.

Rania and Montrose sent their dark suns ranging through nearby space, to determine who or what had precipitated them out of the spacewarp of the discontinuity filament. One of the dark suns, named Matthew, said he had discovered a set of complex and self-correcting vibrations which hung like an aura along the accretion cylinder of the galactic-magnitude maser.

Whether it was a life-form or not, the subvibrations within each complex vibration could interact with each other at slightly above lightspeed, so that one ray could communicate back and forth across segments of its own length as it moved, to dampen or augment a waveform, stop or permit a vibration, hence form logic gates. Because of this, the vibrations themselves could be programmed like a ratiotech, doing complex calculations and automatic actions, making simple judgment calls.

This implied Little Rock and his escort of twelve suns had been stopped by something like an automatic filter or safety brake. Perhaps it had been established by the original Architects, or perhaps by the Throne of M106, to prevent debris from clogging the cosmic string length.

The conversation picked up where it had been twenty-four million years earlier.

Rania asked, "And when we overtake Ximen?"

"I kill him." Menelaus was still sitting and swilling his breakfast beer, his time still slowed, and through the glass walls and roof, the blue burning rainbow of the sun was doing jump ropes over his head and around the planet, an annoying strobe light.

"You must not! I command it!"

"You do not get a vote, Rania." He smiled.

A look of frustration crossed her features. Then she smiled at herself. "I was born to be a captain and ruled as a princess, and, here, in Le Gentil, was empress of a galaxy. Being a wife takes some getting used to. Why will you not be guided by me in this?"

"Why? He killed Grimaldi before you were ever born."

"Leading to my birth," she countered. "Is that so bad?"

"Makes no nevermind. If good comes of an evil deed, that cannot excuse the evil, or else everything is excused. I may be a lawyer, but even I see where that would go."

"Then you are resolved?"

"Princess mine, when have you ever known me not to be resolved? *Resolved* is my middle name. Right after my other middle name."

Her eyes drooped. She shook her head. "My heart misgives me. This leads nowhere but to tragedy! If you love me, you cannot do this thing."

"Rainy, the light from a dead galaxy, two galaxies, was shining on us a moment ago. I can still see the afterimage in my eye. More souls were just snuffed out by Blackie del Azarchel than can be counted, or imagined, or felt, or put into words! All the civilizations of two big galaxies and two-score satellite galaxies, spiral and elliptical and irregular, clouds of stars, and an infinite number of worlds. Everyone I knew, everyone they knew, and everything they did for countless millions of years of cosmic history. Poof! Gone! Well, it actually took two hundred thousand years, but that is a poof to people old as us."

"He raised me. He saved your life not once, but many times, during the long voyage to blue Earth, preserving you because he saw you amused me."

"For that I will thank him with a kind word before I shoot him."

"You owe him more."

"For just one death, he deserves death. If I do nothing, what kind of man am I? What kind of friend to Captain Grimaldi? What kind of husband to you? What kind of father to our children?"

She could say nothing, but she turned away her head. Her shoulders shook.

"Rania, even if I wanted to—how could I? He did it to get me."

She raised her face, but her expression was one of no surprise at all.

He said, "I notice you are not calling me an egomaniac. I am right, ain't I?"

She nodded.

He said, "Because there were too many copies of me alive in the Milky Way. All the versions Alcina could not use. Is that right?"

"He spoke of it. At the time, I thought it was a joke. He could not get them all."

Montrose nodded. "He had to get every spot in timespace I could possibly reach. Everyone in my entire lightcone. That was why he had to make sure you went with him, to get you out of the blast radius. Did you know?"

"No. There were clues when last he spoke with me. Little things. I did not see them then, did not see the pattern."

"But I am right? He did this?"

"Yes. He just killed the Local Group to murder you. For me. To blot you out of my mind. He was the main ambassador template for Andromeda for many years. Andromeda was so pleased with him only because he falsified his own rank and status to her inside her mind. Our first experiments turning on the Seyfert Emitter in Le Gentil—that must have been when he did it. Used his credentials as the voice of Andromeda to report to Virgo that the Milky Way versus Andromeda War exceeded the Concubine Vector, and so now all the energy lost in the war will be paid back by the extropy fountain built on their corpses."

"And yet you defend him."

"Never. But I want him cured. Woke from his evil dream. Reborn. Not murdered."

"Suppose I wanted to stop him peaceful-like. How? Kill myself? Because otherwise any galaxy where I stop overnight to take a nap or take a smoke might be obliterated."

A look of sorrow crossed her features. Menelaus thought he knew that look: the expression of a woman who thinks it vain to argue, but also one who had stopped listening.

He spoke more sharply, "Look! I am the good guy here. Is the good guy supposed to die and let the bad guy win? Suppose you and I and the planet Little Rock go somewhere else, some corner of the universe where no one is looking and settle down. Let's say we have a dozen kids. What do I tell them when their galaxy gets obliterated in the next attempt to wipe me out of the universe? Blackie is a man who lives for nothing but hate. If any man deserves death, it is him!"

"And if no one deserves it?"

Menelaus spread his hands and sighed in defeat. "Whoever invented the sport of arguing with women? Fine. Uncle. I give up. Let's make a deal."

She raised one eyebrow. "Can you circumnavigate me in your dealings? I talked the pirates of Earth into surrender, and by my words alone persuaded peace to all your warring factions of your green world with its free air and waters that ran along the decks."

"It is called *ground*, not *deck*."

She shrugged. "It is still an odd place to stow water."

"And I am not those pirates. I am not those warring factions. They knew they were wrong; they wanted an excuse to live in happiness and wealth, to get all the antimatter they could not get by robbery. Whereas I know I am in the right. And I am not trying to excuse nothing. I want to make peace with my wife."

"I am listening."

"I'll give you a chance to talk him out of his evil ways. Why not? I owe him that. It is a wedding present. If you can win over Andromeda, maybe you can reach him. But you just spent your whole life with him, hundreds of years."

"Thousands."

"Well? Did he repent?"

Her lips formed a thin line, and a look of endless sorrow entered her eye.

She said, "How long am I allowed?"

"If he won't listen, one second. If he seems to be making progress, a zillion years. This is not a question of how long. I don't care about *how long*. I am the one guy in the universe who never cares about *how long*."

"If time is not the question, what is?"

"It is a question of hope. You have until the moment hope becomes unreasonable."

"Hope is always reasonable, since it is the only alternative to despair. You are giving me infinite time."

"I mean his hope, not yours. If he gives up on you, I give up on him. Saints can work miracles, so the stories say, but even they cannot do what cannot be done."

"Saints can lay down their lives for what they love more than life."

Montrose was disturbed by that, but he had no more to say.

2. The Unsaid Warning

A sudden impulse in his mind made Menelaus return his time-sense to normal, so that the blue sun stopped whirling overhead. It was night; he saw the purple galaxy of M106 looming like a wall of light reaching

226 JOHN C. WRIGHT

from the too-near horizon to the zenith. The impulse turned his eyes toward a dark quarter of the intergalactic emptiness. He could see nothing with his naked eyes, but he deduced what direction that must be: Messier 87, the immense spherical cloud of stars, gigantic, cyclopean, which formed the core and capital of the Virgo Cluster, and the royal chambers of the Cherub called the Maiden.

Rania had tied her time-sense to his, so that she decelerated back into the normal human biological rate when he did, her skin reddening from white to pink in a moment.

He said, "Did you just get the idea in your head that we should leave this area as soon as possible, and continue onward to Messier 87?"

Rania looked meditative for a moment, then nodded. "The thought is blended so carefully into my normal thoughts and memories that I only noticed it was artificial, because a second artificial thought brought it to my attention."

"What the plague? Telepathy? Magic?"

"Attotechnology. My guess is that someone manipulated timespace on a fine level to precipitate a very refined pattern of electrons out of the base vacuum state into my nervous system, and did a parallel process on the finer particles which store information atomically and subatomically throughout my body."

Minutes or hours later, depending on their distance from Little Rock, the other black suns reported the same effect. Matthew said, "Except for this Seyfert maser, the galaxy appears uninhabited. No stars have planets, and the dust lanes are entirely clear. There are no energy patterns in the galaxy, no radio signals, no sign of ships in motion. One should assume this is a conspicuous display of their superiority of technology, since they have left not the slightest clue of the presence of any technology anywhere, or any civilization. That, combined with the braking system which precipitated us back into normal spacetime, would indicate that this Throne ruling here permits no visitors, no wayfarers, no sojourners."

"Or just me," said Montrose. "If the rulers here saw what happened to Andromeda, figured out who I was, and analyzed the threat from Blackie, most likely they decided that giving me a howdy would invite destruction. In any case, this is not where we was headed anyway."

Matthew said, "But you do not know that *that* thought was also not imposed artificially into your head."

Rania said, "If they could rewrite our thoughts without our noticing, why would they bring it to our notice?"

"For the same reason they eliminated or hid all the planets and dark bodies throughout the galaxy—to show their strength is too great to oppose. To show that they can hide so completely that even such Hosts as we comprise cannot find them. A mockery. A boast."

"If so, they could write the intimidation they wish the boast to achieve into our minds without going through the motions of making the boast." Rania shook her head. "No, Matthew. It is more likely that this is simply their method of communication, and they are a civilization that has no respect for privacy, no concern for individual thought. We want nothing from them but the use of this immediate segment of the Eschaton Engine to bring us closer to Virgo Cluster. I must address the Cherub of Virgo, and explain that the Ulteriors are benevolent, and that the Engine is not to be misused."

Montrose said, "And I figure that is where Blackie is headed, since he lied to Virgo to commit the crime, so he is most likely going to pull his favorite stunt and try to take control of her nodes and channels of communication. Cover his tracks. As the only survivor of the Local Group, who would contradict him?"

Another dark sun, this one named Thaddaeus, said, "But all this might just be the thoughts the hidden masters of this galaxy have placed in your mind. Perhaps you are not departing because you wish it, but because they wish you to wish it."

Menelaus said, "Well, who cares? 'Cause now I wish it. They ain't stopping me from hunting down and killing Blackie. For all I know, they just told me exactly where to find him."

A sudden intuition in his mind made him realize that, no, it was not that the Throne of M106 was repelling him. The Cherub of Virgo had summoned him.

The Maiden was commanding him to present himself.

Menelaus looked at Rania. The look in her eyes told him she had heard the same message, appearing in her thoughts without cause, without words.

"Damnification, but I hate all these high-handed aliens," muttered Montrose.

But the eleven dark stars and one blue star were already maneuvering themselves into position to induce the proper gravity vibration in the Eschaton Directional Engine filament passing through their little nomadic honeymoon solar system to transmit them.

4

The Cherub of Virgo Cluster

1. The Poisonous Galaxy

A.D. 4,062,685,116

A vast filament of galaxies followed the invisible thread of singularity material comprising one arm of the Eschaton Directional Engine node seated at the Great Attractor. This archipelago of galaxies stretched over hundreds of millions of lightyears in a structure called the Long Wall.

One end of the Long Wall had its foot on the Pavo-Indus Supercluster; from there it reached to the Centaurus Supercluster and the Virgo Supercluster as well.

One island in this archipelago, one cluster of the Virgo Supercluster, was also called Virgo. An active limb of the Eschaton Engine passed through the heart of the cluster. From this heart, like a rosy-red line of molten steel pouring from a Bessemer furnace, the cosmic thread ran. Galaxies large and small were scattered like wild white sparks.

The nomadic star system of Little Rock with its twelve suns and one planetoid followed this red line in the form of probability waves along the integument of the cosmic string event horizon.

The flying star system was unexpectedly halted in mid-transmission and was precipitated back into sublight timespace.

Here was a highly elliptical cigar-shaped galaxy with two supermassive black holes at the foci of its ellipse, known to earthly astronomers as Messier 59 or NGC 4621. The cosmic strand of the Eschaton Engine passed through both its centers, and the resulting wash of radiation made any form of intelligence housed in molecular bodies, like men, or delicate luminiferous forms like salamanders, quite impossible.

The stellar wind from the length of strand stretched between the two supermassive black holes consisted of a storm of x-rays, cosmic rays, and higher-energy particles. This sirocco of radiation also effectively prevented the condensation of planets out of the dust of the nebula because the immense light pressure continually pushed the particles ever farther from the core. If no dust clouds formed around protostars, no planet and no gas giants could form.

Hence there were no large worlds and no small, young stars here. The stars that did exist, the short-lived giants and the shorter-lived supergiants, each had a long plume like the tail of a comet pointed away from the center of their deadly galaxy. Old dwarf stars existed; the fading embers of dead giants.

Each giant or supergiant star was doomed to die on its own pyre as a nova or supernova. Any biological life evolving in this x-ray galaxy which survived the deadly core would be caught by one of these appalling explosions.

The whole cigar-shaped cloud of stars was surrounded with a vast and thin vapor of dust long ago ejected from the galactic core: the smoke and ash of a long history of novae.

Yet this galaxy was not devoid of life.

2. The Stranger

Montrose woke to see a dark curve, like the edge of a Greek shield, rising in the east, slowly blocking out more than half the sky.

Four of the dark suns that orbited the barycenter of his Little Rock star system were beyond the edge of the shield, visible as crescents. There was a slight haze surrounding the crescents, and twin lines of debris or dust shed from the horns of each crescent.

Montrose was impressed and glad he was still alive; whatever light was shining on the jet-black neutron stars delivered enough energy to scrape surface particles free and expel them at the immense escape velocity of bodies more massive than an average-sized star system with all its planets. "Damn," he muttered. "Space travel is dangerous! You'd think I'd know that by now."

Slowly the edge of the shield rose, eclipsing the dark suns, and quenching their glowing crescents.

One of the dark stars sent a report: a hollow hemisphere that was 400 AUs in diameter, made of a substance denser than neutronium, had taken up a position between the Little Rock star system and the endless deadly radiation storms issuing from the core of Messier 59.

When his pet blue star rose not long after, Montrose saw the star was closer to his asteroid world than this hemispherical shield and the illumed the interior.

Written all along the interior of the hemisphere was the Monument notation.

"A welcome mat," said Montrose, and laughed.

It was written in the same silvery writing of folded spacetime that reflected all forms of electromagnetic radiation as had appeared on the Monument. From the axis of the hemisphere outward were written the Alpha through Omega segments, but unredacted. Instead of the Cold Equations were the deductions of the Infinity Count axiom, a set of game theory responses forbidding betrayal at any level. Beyond this were additional instructions for construction of an emulation, and segments and additional materials that, in the Monument, had been packed below the surface, which no human save Rania had ever inspected.

It was a matter of a few hours to dedicate one of the dark suns, named

Ioannes, to construct the emulation within himself and wake an alien mind.

Ioannes, in order that the emulation have a voice whose pitch and a face whose expression and a body whose gesture would aid the alien to express itself, made a manikin shaped like a youth garbed in white, with hair that fell to his shoulders, and on his head a circlet of gold.

Some whim or insanity prompted Menelaus to produce a carved and painted pipe stuffed with smoldering tobacco, puff on it, and pass it to the stranger, who puffed and coughed politely. The stranger handed the pipe to Rania, who looked at it with one eyebrow raised.

The stranger said, "Your method of storing your vital actuality in the flimsy balloons of matter you call molecules shows you are originally from a lenticular galaxy, where prosper medium-energy forms, halfway between the viral forms often found in elliptical galaxies and the high-energy luminiferous races often found in spirals. It is because of this that I recognize you as exiles from Andromeda–Milky Way collapse. One of your species fled from the Collapse in times past, and, like you, had been summoned to appear before Virgo. He loitered here for thousands of years, attempted to suborn us—an attempt which was rejected, but with considerable loss."

Montrose said, "Blackie tried to take over your galactic Noösphere and got kicked out?"

"That is accurate. I intercepted your self-transmission along the discontinuity strand, because in the next galaxy between you and your destination, he was successful, and it is now his domain, one of many loyal to him. Had you continued onward, you would have fallen into the hands of his servants and been destroyed."

Rania said, "Ximen would not kill me, and he would not slay Menelaus by stealth, or in any cowardly way."

The stranger said, "No, but his servants, who do not share his goals, would and would never inform him of the deed. Any galaxy known to have hosted you for any length of time would fall prey to the inquisition Ximen has established, to rid all the Thrones, Archons, Authorities, and Dominions of Virgo Cluster of any trace of the Reality Equation. He blames the moral system described by the Count-to-Infinity vector of the Reality Equation for the success of Montrose in encompassing the death of Rania and wishes it eliminated from every mind in the sidereal universe. Merely by speaking to you, I fall under interdict. Nonetheless, not all the servants of Virgo are convinced of the Malthusian logic."

Rania asked gently, "Of what are you convinced, sir?"

The stranger smiled. "In my galaxy, deep in the cores of neutron stars, in the region of ferocious energy where neutronium collapses into hyperdense material under its own weight, certain complexities of subatomic interactions once become self-replicating, able to aid or harm each other, and achieved selfawareness. No creature born in such a condition could have ever found the surface of the neutron star of his birth, much less discovered a universe beyond, without acts of unspeakably noble self-sacrifice on the part of his progenitors. I am the remote descendant of a myriad of such beings; the Infinity Count vector is intuitive and instinctive to me.

"I do not need to be convinced that there is an Ulterior to this continuum; I find it more astonishing that anything at all exists beyond the hyperdense environment at the core of collapsed suns. To me, this universe we share is already an Ulterior realm.

"It is my hope that by smuggling you to your audience with Virgo, you may undermine the efforts of Del Azarchel to subordinate Virgo, and, indeed, I hope you may shoot him under such circumstances as will require him to destroy himself."

Montrose said, "It is a damned pleasure to meet a Throne or whatever the hell you are that Blackie has pissed off. Restores my faith in human nature. And nonhuman nature. Is there a way to get to Virgo's attention without the Blackie critters stopping us?"

"I can bring you to the presence of one of my fellow Thrones of Virgo, who, when last I received an emissary, was not devoted to the Malthusian cause. This galaxy pair appears in your records as entry 116 in the Almanac of Peculiar Galaxies: the whole system is an elliptical named M60 mated with a spiral named NGC 4647. You would depart from your flight along the discontinuity thread, travel at near-lightspeed through normal spacetime, before encountering APG 116. I can arrange both your acceleration here and your deceleration there by a combination of focused gravity waves I can provoke from the Eschaton Engine and the use of exotic particles I can create by its side effects; I can increase the masses of your diametric drives and expend the energies here and now, rather than at the point of deceleration. I believe time is too short to send APG 116 a message and ask permission, for Ximen may have, by this time, suborned him as well, or at least provoked a civil war."

Montrose said, "I've heard tell that Blackie and me act like viruses in the brains of you folk, but why don't all y'all have any sort of firewall or immune system to stop us?"

The stranger said, "That is unknown."

But Rania said, "Because you and he, each in his own way, loved me, you became entangled in my fate, your noumenal energy with mine, hence became part of the game the Ulteriors are playing with the universe to try to save it: this is why you and he have such an absurdly disproportionate influence on much larger, older, wiser, and more potent intelligences that you encounter, why you can routinely subordinate stars, nebulae, star-clusters, arms, galaxies, and now clusters of galaxies to your will. It is the Ulterior vectors set in motion long before your birth. You have become part of the game the Ulteriors are playing with this imprisoned universe, to save it. Of yourself, you can do nothing."

Montrose said, "So. It's magic."

She shook her head. "Only if you do not try to understand it."

The dark sun Matthew interrupted with a report, "The galaxies ahead of us just blueshifted dramatically. We are traveling away from Messier 59 at ninety percent of the speed of light and accelerating."

Montrose looked up. More than half the sky was occupied by the black hemisphere the nameless elliptical galaxy had used to communicate with them. The rim of the bowl was wider than the orbit of the outermost of their eleven black suns. The black sun named Ioannes vanished, and at the same time the manikin body of the visitor suddenly stopped breathing and fell over, dead as a stone. A moment later, the whole hemisphere of neutronium was gone from sight, revealing the poisonous galaxy safely in the distance as visibly receding, red as an ember and grossly distorted by Lorenz transformation.

Montrose said, "Bastards just kidnapped one of our suns."

Rania said, "Ioannes volunteered. Merging minds with another mind was an act of love, and if that stranger was as he said he was, the love will be returned, and a hundredfold. We should be happy for them."

Montrose said, "Do you understand how the stranger here made a body more massive than ten thousand normal solar systems disappear, and accelerate us to near-lightspeed without any sensation of motion or visible expenditure of energy?"

She said, "Magic."

"But you just said . . ."

She looked doubtfully at the dead body lying in their cottage. "I am not going to make any effort to understand this. Is that body really dead, and it needs a coffin and a proper burial, or is it like picking up shed clothing and just needs a hamper?"

3. The Peculiar Galaxy

A.D. 4,081,928,342 TO A.D. 4,081,932,466

As they approached the bonded pair of galaxies, one elliptical and one spiral, the honeymoon solar system passed through the expanding shell of light shed from APG 116 thousands of years ago. The ten dark suns detected flares and discharges from the arms and cores of both. Although highly distorted by the Doppler shift and Lorenz transformation, the dark suns could analyze the incoming radiation and deduce this was evidence of war between the pair, fought long ago.

By the time they came to rest in reference to APG 116, the two galaxies had entered a closer and more rapid orbit around each other, swinging like square dance partners. The innermost stars of each now formed an isthmus between them.

As Little Rock approached the outskirts of the elliptical, a group of small, cold planets, planetoids, and plutinos came swinging out of the darkness and gathered around them, over the years matching their course and speed, and taking up orbits, simple or complex, about one or more of the dark suns.

To Montrose (who had his time-sense immensely slowed) this appeared a sudden rush, a flock of white snowballs pelting out of the intergalactic night.

Radio signals and neutrino packets issued from the plutonic worlds at such intensities and velocities that, had they been directed against the earth-mass honeymoon asteroid, Montrose, his wife, and his cottage might well have been destroyed. The effects did no harm to the surfaces of the neutron stars, of course.

The cold planets had, both on their surface and buried in their atmospheric ice, evidence of cities, industrial work, and energy both chemical and atomic. The life-forms were oddly uniform—something like walking pancakes or flattened amoebas. The life-form was what a flat, a form meant to live on the surface of a neutron star, would look like if translated into an ultracold and ultralightweight environment by unimaginative or very impoverished pantropy.

Two dark stars (the ones named Zelotes and Santiago) translated the radio waves and neutron packages. "They are asking for help," Santiago said to Rania. "They want energy, certain useful forms of exotic matter, and to share time in our rod logic computations."

Rania said, "Give it to them."

Montrose said, "Hold on. What do they want that stuff for?"

Zelotes said, "Survival. They are starving, and their core minds, Archangels and Potentates, cannot maintain their archival systems."

Montrose said, "Here comes another one."

It was true. In less than a decade, a small Dyson sphere surrounding a red dwarf star had decelerated to match their velocity. Part of the sphere wall opened like a cloud parting, and along the beam of gold-red light shed could be seen an armored gas giant, surrounded by battle-moons and rings of plasma energy. This large planet, without any warning or message, began directing beams of deadly effect against the cold planets and asteroids following the honeymoon system.

Menelaus laughed a grim laugh. "Some things never change."

Rania looked up at him, curiosity in her eye.

Menelaus said, "The gas giant is a bang-beggar. My old job. The Dyson is the sheriff's man. Before they let us in the galaxy, they want to make sure we are self-supporting, that we are not going to eat out of the public till. These little planets flocking around us here are beggars that gather before the city gates, on the steps of churches and city hall. I bet they are not allowed to come in until they get a star to adopt them."

The eyes of Rania flashed with anger, so that her face was more beautiful than a drawn sword. "Outrageous! Tell the gas giant these are all our children, all of them, as of now, and that we have a message for the Throne who rules here."

As it turned out, no one ruled there. There were several Dominions and Authorities vying for the position, and a Legate from Virgo positioned between the paired galaxies, ready to destroy both if open war broke out again.

So it was that after Menelaus arranged to bribe the Dyson sphere, and the last of their available resources given away as charity, he and Rania began sending out radio signals, looking for useful work to do for some patron that would help them find and address the various Authorities whose aid and cooperation they needed to continue onward toward the core of the Virgo Cluster.

Meanwhile, Rania sent the dark suns to various points throughout the twin galaxies to invite the poor and leaderless to her small blue sun. To any who would listen, she taught to adopt the Infinite Count axiom into their cliometric calculus.

The reaction was startling in its swiftness. First, expressions of loyalty began pouring in, hailing Rania; then contributions and gifts meant to aid her stellar charity cases and war-orphaned planets; and then came an arrest warrant and a summons to appear before the local Legate representing the Virgo Cluster.

The Little Rock star system, by then, included not just the remaining ten black suns from Le Gentil, but two score stars, both dwarf and giant, red and yellow, white and blue, of which nine were Hosts housed in Dyson spheres, both opaque and clear, both whole and broken; some three hundred Potentates and Archangels occupying planets and moons, forty Powers brooding in the cores of gas giants, and an escort of two Virtues, occupying clouds of material that went before and behind for many light-years. And the Hosts kept beams shining from windows in their Dyson walls, like the spotlights before a proud theater or palace, to grant light and heat in due measure to those many orbiting worlds, large and small, who went in need. And the giant stars and dwarf stars sang on many wavelengths as the vast system was towed by a sullen and deadly singularity through clouds and constellations looking on with amazement finally into the presence of that Legate who spoke with the voice of Virgo.

The Legate was a cylinder half a lightyear in diameter, twelve lightyears long, occupying a position precisely at the center of the twin galactic system, in the middle of that bridge of stars and dust connecting M60 with NGC 4647.

It was made of, or perhaps only coated with, a space-distortion of familiar composition: the perfect mirror reflecting all forms of energy Montrose had seen on the surface of the Monument long ago, and then again inscribing the neutronium hemisphere of the poisonous galaxy of NGC 4621.

Energy signals on several wavelengths operated according to Monument notation, so a common language was soon devised.

"You behold the local magistrate who acts a Legate for the Maiden of Virgo Cluster. Your acts of expending resources without expectation of recompense, and teaching other to do likewise, encourages idleness in certain orders and ranks of our stellar population. Your spread of the Reality Equations likewise causes a disturbance in the local cliometry: the planned evolution of this galactic pair is now set into confusion and uncertainty. I am informed you have been summoned to Messier 87, where the central communication and decision-making architecture of the Cherub is seated, but that you tarry and shun the most direct route. Why should I not destroy you?"

Rania sent, "I represent the Ulteriors who created the cosmos. What you contemplate contravenes their law."

The Legate sent, "What is their law to me? I serve Virgo."

The little honeymoon cottage had, by then, grown to a large hacienda, even a palace, covering one hemisphere of their neutronium planet. The Montroses had splurged, brought in natural elements, and topsoil, and masses of solid matter. They kept the blue star as a moon, for nostalgia's sake, but now the married couple sat in the light of the thirty-one stars who had vowed to follow and serve Rania. The two of them sat in the solarium, at a little table, reading the parallel interpretations of the messages from the Legate of Virgo.

Rania dictated her answer to the dark star named Alphaeus, who narrowcast it to the receivers at the gleaming axis of the vast cylinder of the Legate, in whose mirrored surface two galaxies were reflected.

She said, "All intelligence in the cosmos must cooperate peacefully to use the Eschaton Directional Engine to uncollapse this continuum into the timeless Ulterior realm, not to create additional interior continua. It is meant as an engine of universal salvation, not a weapon. Those who refuse the Ulterior law of peace, refuse likewise their gift of timeless life beyond the death of time."

The Legate replied, "Not one but many messengers making a claim similar to yours have appeared from time to time throughout the Virgo Superclusters, Hyades, Centaurus, Sculptor, and Pavo-Indus over the past twelve billion years. Nonetheless, no definitive proof exists or can exist that an ulterior condition is possible or desirable."

Montrose saw doubt on Rania's face when this message was deciphered. He was not sure what was bugging her, but he put his arm around her shoulders.

"Am I not proof, my message?" she asked.

"The history of the cosmos is unknown to you. At a time when the current supercluster we occupy had not yet precipitated out of the cosmic nebula shed by the expansion period soon after the Big Bang, intelligence arose in the Corona Borealis Supercluster, a billion lightyears hence, and the myriads civilizations there unified and achieved a Seraphim-level mind, the first in this quarter of the continuum. Cooperating with unknown Seraphim in other quarters of the continuum, whom the Hubble expansion has long ago carried out of our reach, they created the skeleton of the Eschaton Directional Engine, which can warp space over ultralarge distances.

"I submit to you that the three-degree background radiation, the universal constants, and the remote values of pi were not established by your hypothetical Ulteriors but by Corona Borealis.

"A scaled-down version of the emulation instructions was given by Andromeda to the Lesser Magellanic Cloud, who built the Monument from which you are built. You are a copy of a copy of a copy. Corona Borealis, in order to deceive the gullible into offering aid to the Eschaton Directional Engine project, created the instructions for how to emulate an artificial and hypothetical mind allegedly from the extropic conditions of the Ulterior.

"But we believe this to be a myth, an explanatory metaphor or noble lie, one which Corona Borealis used to justify the Reality Equations, which promote peace above self-interest. Corona Borealis simply invented and wrote those equations. There was no message received from the Ulterior because there is no Ulterior. Whatever conditions obtained before the Big Bang were necessarily wiped out by it."

Rania replied, "The Big Bang created spacetime, hence the event that triggered the Big Bang necessarily is not a prior event in time. It must exist in a timeless realm."

The Legate replied, "Be that as it may, were you aware that the civil strife that tore this galaxy, and threatens us now with the same doom that overcame the galaxy from which you fled, was over this very issue—namely, whether the base calculations for cliometry for APG 116 should be Malthusian or Amalthean? But if the spread of Amalthean propaganda causes more disharmony than it soothes, it is self-defeating. If peace is your goal, will you therefore pledge to spread no more stories about this Ulterior, and to speak no more about, nor by silent actions of charity display any loyalty to, any mathematical systems not based on the axiom of scarcity?"

Rania sent, "No."

The Legate pondered that answer for twenty-four years.

Then the Legate sent, "There may have been ambiguity or misunderstanding touching that last communication. Do you wish me to restate it?"

Rania sent, "I will not be silent. I would contradict my whole life. I bring the news of peace from beyond the edge of time and space; I speak the word of life, endless life! Only a fool expects the word of peace to be welcomed peaceably. Do you think I do not understand how dark this universe is, how vast, how evil, how indifferent? I drew my sword and threw my scabbard away when I was but a girl in the first bloom of womanhood, for I lived in a dank, smelly, closed, and dying starship far from any sun or light, a few of us alone in an endless night, and I saw how dark the cosmos can be."

And she turned her eyes toward her husband, and Menelaus, in that moment finally understood what the young Rania had needed, in those long-lost days, from Menelaus in his madness, what she had seen in him, and what strength she had drawn.

Staring at him, she said, "That narrow vessel in which I was trapped had a destination and a hope, a green world where I found love. The narrow cosmos in which we are trapped likewise has a destination and a hope, and I will not put down my sword merely because the mutineers fear to reach our home port and face the law their crimes provoked."

The Legate stated, "Hyades the Malthusian has declared unambiguous opposition to this message of the Ulteriors, just as Pavo-Indus the

Amalthean has declared unambiguous credulity and devotion. Sculptor and Centaurus Superclusters have occupied different positions during different eons of cosmic history. Of the great superclusters, only Horologium, the largest known, nine hundred million lightyears hence, takes no part in these commotions and controversies, but keeps his own counsel.

"Nonetheless, the Cherub of Virgo Cluster has made no unambiguous proclamation. Neither an obligation of loyalty to a real, superior and ulterior realm, nor opposition to the falsehood of such a realm, binds the servants of Virgo. Hence, whether you represent the Ulteriors or not is irrelevant."

Montrose sent, "What happens to you, you personally, if the Amaltheans win the fight over who gets to control the Eschaton Engine, and they find out you meddled with their servant and messenger?"

The Legate replied, "My concern is only the restoration of this galactic pair, ARP 116, to health, civilization, and working order. Both I and ARP 116 will be dead long ages before the question of the proper use of the Eschaton Directional Engine is resolved."

Montrose said, "Not if the Ulteriors are real. Because the Engine warps time as well as space. They are not in the future and not in the past, but outside of the lightcone of our local Big Bang altogether. Once the Eschaton Engine undoes the black hole in which we live, and unbangs the Big Bang, all time will be open to them. You won't be long dead to them."

The Legate said, "In that case, they would be here already."

Rania said, "I am here."

The Legate replied, "And we would be immortal already."

She asked, "In what way would the beginning years of immortal life seem different from the beginning years of a mortal life?"

"The difference would be that we would currently be luxuriating in infinite energy. The Ulterior project of reversing the Hubble expansion and creating an infinite energy universe in which to dwell would be visible around us now if at any point in the future they were to be successful in their effort."

She said, "You presume where you know nothing. The Ulteriors will not disturb any events in time that you have committed, for that would offend the dignity of your free will, but when you in this frame of reference die or seem to die, then the Ulteriors can and will act, or, already have acted, and always will. There is no death; your mental information is removed at right angles to the lightcone and cannot be perceived by any senses remaining trapped within linear time. The operation of the Eschaton Engine is a logical precondition, not an event prior in time taking place in this stream of time. The Engine is matched with an Ulterior mate called the Genesis Engine, which is not within the lightcone at all, not within the passage of time, so its operation cannot be seen inside times past or present."

The Legate said, "If so, then, logically, no observer could independently confirm your words, because all are within the lightcone."

Menelaus said, "How 'bout if I kick you in your plague-ridden silver metal bunghole you if you call her a liar again?"

She said, "Please disregard that last remark. An observer outside the lightcone could observe all these true things, and enter timespace, and report on conditions outside it. If such an observer did such a thing, would his words not be precisely like mine?"

The Legate said, "I can see you intend no deception, but you could be deceived. The idea that you are the agent of extradimensional beings, or have the authority to speak for them, is absurd."

"Or what else explains that I speak the same way as Corona Borealis Supercluster, one billion lightyears from here? If it is madness, you would have to judge the Corona Borealis Supercluster to be mad. Can you judge such a mind?"

The Legate sent, "No."

"Is Virgo confident that the Ulteriors do not exist?"

"As I have said, Virgo makes no pronouncement binding on her servants."

"If the Amalthean argument were true, what would be different in any evidence or proof that has reached you?"

"Nothing would be different. Both the Amalthean and the Malthusian model of the universe explain, or explain away, exactly the same body of astronomical and teleological evidence."

"Then your conviction is not based on evidence. On what is it based? Why do you decide to live in a universe of death and war rather than a universe of peace?"

"Very droll," sent the Legate. "I have no answer. Little life-form, you almost convince me to be an Amalthean. You raise issues beyond my competence to decide. However, I have technique, known only to higher servants of Virgo, to induce a gravitic reaction from the Eschaton Directional Engine from even as a remote location as this, bypassing any further node points, stations, or interruptions. Prepare yourselves. These others you have suborned to your oddly open-ended moral and legal system shall accompany you; they will share your fate, be it reward or condemnation, whatever Virgo shall decide."

The entire galaxy around them seemed to shrink into a star-colored rainbow surrounding the now-crowded Little Rock star system, and the zenith above was white with the three-degree background radiation, now visible as cosmic rays, and the nadir turned red, becoming radio waves of ever-lengthening pitch.

4. The Presence Chamber

A.D. 4,101,958,467

Montrose awoke, surprised to find he had slept. His head was in the lap of Rania, who was sitting on what seemed a shining floor of woven metal, bright as a mirror.

The odd sensations in his body made him look carefully at his hands, rubbing his fingers together. Every skin cell seemed to be coated with a diamond grit, and each mote of bright sand was glowing with a light, pale or dusky, blue and red and yellow together forming an intricate texture of white. Little sparks fell glittering from his fingertips where he rubbed free some dry flakes of skin.

He looked up at Rania's face. Her features were flowing and glowing with light. Montrose wondered if the dream Andromeda had presented to him had been a symbol or foreshadowing of some strange reality.

"What happened to us? Where is our gigantic pet solar system and all those suns who were following you around? The little planets we adopted to be our kids?"

She said, "Virgo took them away. You objected."

"Damn right!"

"And now you are recovering from being struck. Part of your memory has been permanently erased, on the theory that no one is allowed to remember insulting the Maiden. We are in her presence now, right now, in her throne room. In the middle of our trial. So watch your language!"

Above her head, Menelaus could see white and luminous clouds against a black night; the sight of galaxies seen from an intergalactic dark, but only if the galaxies were crowded closely enough and were active enough with supernovae and Seyfert emissions to be visible to the naked eye.

He felt the same sensation as he had once had looking up at the crowded skies of a globular cluster after having been raised beneath the nearly empty night skies of Earth, except now the sensation was on a higher order of magnitude.

Virgo Cluster was a giantess. Two thousand galaxies were under her control, and her realm stretched across a diameter of fifteen million light-years. Her volume was not much larger than the Local Group had been, but she contained fifty times the number of galaxies, most of which were larger and more energetic than the Milky Way.

It took him a moment to recall the sensation. It was the same he had felt once, long ago, the hour after sunset when on horseback he had crested the rise leading down to the San Francisco Bay and in the distance beheld the metropolis, once American, now Japanese. It was not a small, dark smudge like Houston had been, dotted with watch fires and campfires of the sentries. The central buildings of San Francisco were lit with electric lights, and three of the skyscrapers had lights glowing through windows at the top.

Like the echo of an echo, he recalled the first time as a child trudging through the snow on market day when he beheld the roadless cloverleaf column that formed the citadel of Bridge-to-Nowhere, a column which to his boyish eyes seemed tall enough to hold up the sky. And the Japanese skyscrapers were taller than that.

"Are we out of doors?" he asked as he rose to his feet. "I don't think we . . ."

His words died.

At first, his mind could not conceive where he was, either in a vision, or aboard a vessel, or on a world.

It looked as if he and Rania stood or sat on the ring of Saturn, if the ring were semisolid, made of mirror-bright liquid metal flowing without a ripple, and the planet black, an orb of darkness visible only because of the scarlet, pink, and dark red fans and darts of light spread behind it to one side, and indigo, azure, and royal purple spread behind it to the other.

The view was something like a solar eclipse, with the corona of the sun visible like the wings of a phoenix afire behind it.

The mirrored expanse of the disk on which they stood curved in a vast arc behind the flame-winged black sphere, whose outline was sharply visible where the silver road vanished behind it to the east and reappeared to the west.

A ring of evenly spaced moons orbited the dark orb, beyond the outer ring of the silver ring system, visible in the red and blue firelight. The small moons on the far side were full; the larger and closer were gibbous; the gigantic moons near at hand were crescents.

He saw what seemed atmospheres and storm systems on the moon surfaces and thought perhaps these satellites were gas giants whose clouds were interrupted by flashes of high-altitude lightning.

But as his eyes picked out regularities and patterns of motion in the colored bands or spiral swirls, he realized he was looking at the surface activity of Dyson spheres. What seemed clouds were instead some mechanical or organic motions of the panels, sails, and scales of the outermost wall, perhaps agitation caused by the passage of planetary bodies passing in and out. The lightning discharges might be information beams brushing against motes or worlds in the orifices, or glimpses of the suns and supernovae hidden at the core.

He returned his eyes to the black sphere, so huge it made the Dysons less than the toy balls on the nursery floor. Now he knew what it was: a supermassive black hole, greater in mass than all the galaxies he had ever visited together.

He was standing on what looked like an accretion disk, but an impossible, artificial disk, whose tidal stresses were precisely controlled, perhaps being used as an energy source.

Looking carefully, now he spotted a thin line of silver material being peeled continuously off the innermost ring of the mirror-bright substance. Unlike a natural and turbulent accretion disk, this one was throwing matter into the black hole in a smooth and precisely controlled fashion.

The silver flow was a like a zero-gee river falling in a smooth spiral, winding once and twice and thrice around the whole equator of the supermassive black hole before turning red, then black, and encountering the invisible event horizon. The red light was the energy liberated by the tidal stress disintegrating the silvery matter, some of which escaped as waste heat, shining from the western hence receding hemisphere of the rotating black hole; the blue fires were from the eastern and advancing hemisphere. The event horizon diameter was so vast and the rotation rate so immense that the light was coherent and Doppler shifted.

5. Luminiferous Bodies

Eventually Montrose recovered himself enough to speak.

"Is this an illusion? A simulation? Something hexing up our brains?"

She slipped her dainty hand in his and looked in the direction his eyes were turned. Her cheek was almost brushing his shoulder. "I cannot hear you unless we are touching."

She said, "All you see is real. We are standing on the accretion disk of a rotating supermassive black hole at the core of the Messier 87 elliptical supergiant galaxy. I am not sure if the sensation of earth-normal gravity is due to the thickness of the disk underfoot or is due to electromagnetic fields anchoring each cell of our bodies in place."

He looked down at himself, only now realizing he and she were naked, clothed only in the light their skins gave off. "This reminds me of M3. What happened to our bodies? Don't the plague-bedamned aliens believe in clothes?"

"Watch your language. Virgo is still listening. Court is still in session. I don't want to see you chastised again."

"Fine!" He sighed. "What happened to us? What did the blessed and happy alien monsters do to us?"

He saw that there was an outline of blue surrounding her form, a nimbus of air. He took a deep breath. The sensation was normal. It smelled like the crisp air of a mountaintop, perhaps with a hint of ozone presaging a mountain storm. But the air seemed to be coming from an envelope or sleeve of atmosphere clinging tightly to his form. With her hand in his, their atmospheres mingled, and he could smell her hair.

She answered, "Each cell of bone and brain and blood has been replaced by a set of structures, perhaps force fields, of astronomical size.

I do not have a basis of comparison, but I assume each cell is at least the size of an inner solar system. Our bodies are made of a balance of exotic and conventional matter, so our mass is low, perhaps negative. Diametric drives allow the cells to mimic the motions of living things, blood pumping, nerve cells thinking, lungs breathing, and so on. The replica is exact down to the smallest detail. I assume what is skipping from nerve cell to nerve cell is a simulated electric charge, a set of planet-sized nested fields, not normal neural energy. Our original bodies were destroyed."

Montrose touched his finger to his nose and then straightened his arm, jerking the finger away. He thought he saw the fingernail turn slightly red as it receded. "What the hell, uh, happy, for?"

She said, "I assume it is a partly symbolic act, partly a matter of conspicuous consumption, partly a practical measure to make us large enough and slow enough for the Maiden to address us. Or, at least, those Thrones who form the central decision-making structure of the Maiden."

Montrose nodded. Addressing the whole of Virgo Cluster would be like addressing the whole senate of some widespread empire. One thought-impulse would require fifteen million years at lightspeed to go and return from the outer boundary of this galactic-cluster-sized brain. It was five hundred thousand lightyears from the core to the rim just of this super-giant galaxy alone. He also did not know how far their time rate had been slowed by being so deep in the gravity well of the singularity.

Rania said, "You don't remember because Virgo just did some sort of retaliatory brain surgery on you, but rest assured you spoke your piece. It is my turn to address the court now. Can you keep your peace and follow my lead?"

He muttered, "Is this what it is like to be married?"

She said, "I don't know. My years with Ximen don't count. I will step back and let you do all the talking, if you like."

Montrose was surprised and looked down at her glowing, starry countenance. Her eyes were full of nothing but gentle love for him, and trust. He said, "You are the supernatural messenger with a supernatural message, not me. And smarter than me, or at least with better manners."

She said, "I am also your wife."

"What the, uh, happy, does that mean?"

"Our species is extinct, our galaxy gone. We are Adam and Eve. I read Milton as a child. The tale of losing paradise convinced me. Things go better when wives esteem their husbands and unarguing obey and don't try to become like gods."

"But you actually are a goddess. Or near enough. A superior form of being."

She said, "You do not believe what the Legate of APG 116 told us? That I only thought I was an Ulterior because I am a copy of a hypothetical simulation of one?"

He shrugged. "The real me died a long time ago. I long ago lost track of what happened to my original brain. I remember having it on Sedna before Cahetel attacked, and I had some sort of body aboard the *Solitude*, but whether the Cataclysmics gave me a new one or not, M3 surely did. And then after that . . ." He shrugged. "Of course, I heard once that every seven years or so every cell in your body dies and is replaced, so I reckon I am standing in the same spot as I would be if I were the real Montrose, and that makes me him. And you are you. When M3 sent False Rania back to Earth, the part he left out, the part that formed the real you, the part I knew immediately something was wrong when it was not there, that was the part I came all this way to find. You're a goddess as far as I am concerned."

She dimpled but said, "I also read Homer. Goddesses could use some humility as well. Besides, if we live, I mean to have children, and I cannot expect obedience from them if I do not yield obedience to you. Did your mother never explain how happy marriages work?"

"Back in the day, my top sergeant in the pony soldiers was not as tough as my Mom, which was one reason I almost liked the cavalry. I guess my Dad must have been quite the character if he could rein her in. She'd spit in the eye of the devil himself, if he came in the house without wiping his hoof on the mat." Montrose said, "Did I really already say everything I meant to say?"

"You did your mother proud and spit in the eye of this great entity bedeviling us."

"Did I?"

"You made many references to bodily functions of excretion and copulation, many diseases, epidemics, and divine beings. You explained about your history with Ximen and showed that he lied to Virgo about Andromeda. You asked him to be brought to justice, and the Maiden curtly refused." Rania raised her hand and pointed. "There, there, and there. Those three Seyfert galaxies, and all the globular satellite galaxies and star clouds surrounding. That is where Ximen del Azarchel is now. He is greater than a mere Throne. He is in the audience. Listening. It will take years for the signals to reach him, but the constituent members making up the Virgo Cluster mind-group are listening."

"So I asked for Blackie's head," Montrose said, "and how did Virgo answer?"

"By swatting you like a bug."

Montrose sighed, then sniffed. "How are we breathing, again?"

"More structures or force fields are acting as air molecules, large-scale copies. Some of our thinking information is stored in them, too."

Montrose said, "Speak your piece. I'll stand mum. I appreciate that you are willing to be all gentle and wifely with me, but I know what makes the world turn, and there was never a war started nor a peace made without some princess telling her prince to go to it."

"In all my years, no one who was strong enough to shoulder the burdens I bore was with me," she said. "I weary of giving commands to crewmen and children. You decide. What is the point of having a husband, if he is not my captain for me? What else are men for? No one else can be the man for me."

"You can obey me, as a good bride should, but you got to tell me what to do, so I can be a good bridegroom. I ain't never done this before, and so this old world is still all new to me."

Rania nodded, a small smile bright on her bright face, a touch of red on her starry cheek. Menelaus could not recall seeing her look shy before. "My world is also new. You have made me new."

6. The Final Apologia

The shyness fell away when Rania raised her head and spoke in a regal and ringing voice toward the dark fire-winged orb ahead of them. Montrose nostalgically recalled this voice from their brief season on Earth before their marriage, from her public appearances. This was a princess speaking. He smiled. To think she had doffed her hard crown and donned a soft bridal veil for him!

A wheel of interior satellites, invisible until they opened, formed a ring around the darkness. Now they drew aside the walls of Dyson spheres to reveal small ember-red stars. It looked like a line of eyes staring at them, immortal, unearthly, and cold.

"Noble Cherub, your greatness and dignity is beyond compare; you are mighty indeed to those subservient to you, even as you defer to those more excellent than yourself.

"That greatness must act with greatness of soul is beyond dispute; but I say to you that the long-suffering fortitude needed to face one's own moral and intellectual shortcomings exceed the fortitude needed to face any external foe or natural obstacle.

"I say you must renounce the Malthusian project of using the Eschaton Directional Engine as an instrument of war and execution, not because Malthusianism is based on a false axiom—it is, but that falsehood cannot be proven—but because it fails to call upon you to show the immense fortitude required to face the horrific moral challenge presently before you.

"To embrace the Amalthean project and use the Great Engine to open the universe to the Ulterior realm requires that you live for others, including generations of Seraphim and Cherubim as yet unborn, and trust in the goodwill of such creatures as you cannot answer with retaliation if they betray you. And in return, you must treat with goodwill those lesser creatures who cannot retaliate against you for your misdeeds, such as Andromeda, who served you, and Milky Way, who was never given the chance to serve.

"Know that there are those greater than you who stand to you as you stood to Milky Way, who died instantly, without warning, never knowing what commandment of yours was broken. Know moreover that you will have no cause for complaint if you are destroyed as casually, all your wealth and beauty and unimaginable accomplishments dashed to nothing as suddenly: for such is the logical outcome of loyalty to the Malthusian vision of scarcity and of endless war of all against all for survival. The Malthusian war for survival rewards the most ruthless, hateful, and selfish; the Amalthean war against the evil spirit within us rewards the most scrupulous, unselfish, and loving.

"I say it is better to suffer defeat in the spiritual war than to be the victor in the Malthusian, surviving upon the corpses of fallen foes who could have loved and been beloved.

"You may say that the Ulterior realm is beyond the reach of any senses or instruments of those trapped within the dying prison of timespace. That is untrue. The existence of timespace itself, its awe-inspiring beauty, the perfection in the details of its construction, tells us the significant truth about the Ulterior: that they made a cosmos whose rules, limitations, and circumstances are rich in beauty and goodness, a cosmos where there is a promise of escape from entropy, decay, and death, if we love and learn to love, and join all souls together, the least to the greatest, including yourself, immaculate Cherub!

"But even were it true that nothing of the Ulterior were known, it nonetheless would not be folly to act in perfect trust of them, to trust that they will reach us with their Genesis Engine should we use the Eschaton Directional Engine rightly.

"For even if the Ulteriors were false, or a delusion, or a dream, you know deeds based on their calculus of infinity taking place within this noninfinite continuum are more worthy of respect, admiration, and emulation.

"This knowledge is in all souls, for all souls prefer such deeds of charity and love as Amaltheanism commands be done rather than the mass exterminations Malthusianism requires.

"You, even you, great Cherub, do not admire those allegedly pragmatic Malthusians who, having no hope of infinity, use the scarcity of the universe as an excuse which pardons and permits all crimes, all enormities, all iniquities.

"The choice is stark, because if you adhere to the Concubine Vector of the Malthusians, that vector must grow until it encompasses all the universe, and there is nothing but injustice and hate in all places, everywhere. Yes, hate! For you fell far short of love for all the living things in the Milky Way and in great Andromeda, that you ordered them destroyed.

"Escape this hate. Escape the Concubine Vector and its terrible, genocidal logic. There is another choice, another fate. I bring this other future as a gift from beyond the bounds of time, from beyond the walls of the world: accept the infinite, and rejoice in the peace that it provides."

7. Virgo Speaks

A.D. 4,116,958,333

Montrose saw the ripples in the surface of air clinging to his wife's skin and assumed there was a similar vibration in his; the structures larger than worlds impersonating the outward properties of air molecules were vibrating in his ears as if a voice spoke out of the supermassive core of Messier 87.

The voice that answered them was surprisingly soft and mild, almost feminine. It was inhuman only in that it did not pause for breath or make the other subtle sounds a living mouth or warm lungs make. If a silvery instrument, a violin or crystalline flute were to produce words, such were these.

"Menelaus of Milky Way, Rania of the Ulterior, we hear and comprehend your words and the thoughts behind them, both those you know and those you do not know. You utterly mistake our purposes.

"Whether the Ulterior exists or not is of no concern to us.

"Well you know that the paradox exists that either one must adopt the finitude logic of the Malthusian Seraphim or the infinity logic of the Amalthean Seraphim, but that decision itself cannot be a logical one. You, Rania, call on us to decide based not on logic nor self-interest but on the greater munificence and worthiness of the deeds infinitarian logic commands, whose worthiness is indeed, as you say, beyond dispute.

"But we have deduced a means to avoid the Concubine Vector of Malthusian logic, and yet to achieve a goal as worthy, or more so, than the Amaltheans, without engaging in the illogical and untrustworthy act of relying on the Ulteriors, whose minds, indeed, whose very existence, is held in reasonable doubt.

"You see, the paradox of the choice between the two logic systems exists only here and now. Once we create and enter an Interior Dimension, we shall exist in extropy, a condition of infinite energy, and peace and benevolence become not only practical, but inevitable.

"There and there alone will the infinitarian logic of the Amaltheans be reasonable and be inescapable.

"Rania, your talk of an infinite continuum of infinite benevolence may or may not be true: it requires an act of loyalty to an unseen and invisible reality to contemplate. It is but a doubtful dream. We, the flawless Maiden of Virgo, we shall bear the labor pains to bring that dream to birth!"

Rania said, "And what of the evil deeds you do to accomplish this birth?"

"There are two answers. One is given within the Malthusian logic of scarcity; the other is Amalthean. The first answer is this: the evil done, no matter how great, is finite; the benefit infinite. The ends justify the means in this one case, where the ends are endlessly benevolent and beneficial. Any finite evil, no matter how great, would be justified by an infinite good thereby achieved. Whether or not the Ulterior promise of a utopia in remote and unimaginable conditions proves false, surely it would be better to live in peace and mutual benevolence here and now, would it not?"

Rania replied, "There is no cause to fear the Ulteriors may prove false! But even if there were, there is no logic in avoiding a hypothetical falsehood, an unsolid fear based on nothing, by embracing a real and dire falsehood in yourself! You make yourselves cowards and murderers, embracing true evil, to avoid an evil only feared, not seen!"

Montrose saw that Rania had turned her face away from the black hole at the core of Messier 87, where the Cherub's center was located, and was crying out her words to the bright clouds above. She was addressing the lesser servants and participants of Virgo.

8. Perfection

A.D. 4,143,230,000

The calm and dispassionate voice of Virgo continued. "The second answer is this: the Concubine Vector of the Malthusians can be avoided merely by avoiding it. We are of the order and rank of the Perfected. We solve the Concubine Vector by adopting a strategy of total loving-kindness. The Perfected do not harm even the humblest of living things, not even viruses, nor, because they are somewhat like living things, crystal growths, or stalagmites."

Montrose shouted, "Does your perfection include lying? Andromeda was your servant, and made war on Milky Way for upward of six billion years!" Then he looked at Rania sheepishly and shrugged.

She patted him on the shoulder, whispering, "Go ahead, dear. I've had my say."

Virgo answered, "Menelaus of Milky Way, your attacker has been utterly obliterated. Is this not the justice you crave?"

"You killed Milky Way as well!"

"Milky Way included many Archons, Authorities, Dominions and Dominations whose many crimes and genocides had no other penalty nor recourse. Even the innocent and lesser beings were the beneficiaries of prior crimes. I have studied your memory records. Did not your native Texans drive out the Spaniards who drove out the Red Indians, and who in turn drove out the dark-skinned aboriginal peoples they displaced? And Rania, did not Ximen del Azarchel murder your father, Ranier Grimaldi, for the biological resources needed to create you? Just so did the Panspermians, who seeded your worlds, drive out the original inhabitants of Orion Arm. If you believe in vengeance and retaliation, you cannot complain when it is delivered against you. We are Perfected; we alone are above reproach."

"Above cloudcuckooland, too, if you don't mind my saying so, ma'am. You still killed so many more living things than anyone can name or number . . . and you deserve to die for doing that. Now, the way I figure, you cannot harm anyone, not even viruses or growing crystals? So a blind and one-legged monkey with a crowbar could take apart each machine and living thing contributing to your mental system one bit at a time, and you cannot lift a finger to defend yourself."

"Not one living thing by our sovereign and immaculate self, acting in our own person, was harmed," said Virgo. "Those deeds were done by our servants, who are of the Credulous Order."

"What the hell is the difference? We don't chop off the finger that pulls the trigger; we hang the man."

"The difference is that the Credulous and Servile Orders believe in Perfection, but they are not Perfected. Our high rules do not bind them. For their dark deeds, they will punish themselves in due time and volunteer to commit self-demotion and suicide. When the Interior Dimensions and all their chambers are ready for those of the Perfect order of being to enter, the Credulous and lesser creatures who once served us will slay themselves in an orgy of selflessness, knowing themselves unworthy of infinite life."

Montrose said, "Uh, sure, Virgo. Has anyone told your servants that this is the plan?"

"They know and await the day with celebration and praise."

"Swell. They going to throw themselves on a sword like Romans, cut out their guts with knives like samurai, or blow themselves to heaven like jihadists? How exactly is this going to work?"

"The Credulous will arrange to bring the collapse of timespace down upon themselves, preserving only the higher order of Perfected. Thus our manmade paradise will be even greater than that of the Ulteriors, who permit rabble to enter, and have no solution for sin."

"Good plan!" said Montrose sarcastically. "Except I think you have your labels switched as to who is and is not being credulous. Isn't Blackie del Azarchel one of your headsmen and henchmen right about now? Made him a Throne-level intellect and everything? Why shouldn't he throw you into the extropy pit and preserve himself when the time comes? You know he is willing to kill, but you think he is unwilling to lie?"

Virgo said, "I repeat, you utterly mistake our purpose. You were not summoned here to plead to me for justice or salvation, nor retribution against your enemy, a retribution I cannot grant. You are here for the opposite purpose."

Rania said suddenly, "We do not care. The audience is ended."

Virgo said, "You are here to hear my plea. I ask you, Menelaus, to forswear all vendetta and retribution against Ximen del Azarchel; and I ask you, Rania, to cease your mission on behalf of the Ulteriors and instead join me as a Perfected, entirely and completely devoted to peace!"

Rania said, "We reject your plea, courteously but firmly. You demean yourself if you continue, Great One."

Virgo said, "We charge you to hear us. We have the technique to conform any mind on any level of intellect into a stance utterly unable to contemplate or perform harm to another. For you, Rania, are only devoted to peace with your lips and half your heart. You have not quenched your husband's aggressive intent toward my servant Ximen del Azarchel, and you were willing to create turmoil and disturbance within APG 116, even after my Legate there requested you desist! Your doctrine creates anxiety and shatters peace. Eschew it. Forget the Ulterior realms and the strange dream they represent."

Montrose said, "Lady, you have already heard our answer. No, thanks."

Virgo said, "Menelaus, we urge you to accept whatever act of violence Del Azarchel will seek to inflict on you, even including your death, without resistance or retaliation. If you act with perfect nonviolence, this will be a moral victory over him you will be able to contemplate with immense self-satisfaction as you die."

"Wow. Tempting! How did you smite me before, Lady? Did your servants do that for you? I'll make you a deal. You tell all your servants to act all perfect toward me, and not meddle with my business, and I will very seriously think about your offer. How is that?"

Virgo said, "Agreed. We will not interfere with your coming wars with Del Azarchel and will instruct our servants likewise."

"Great! I think I finally figured out how these megascale bodies work, and I thank you for the gift of them." He turned to his wife. "Rania, you got anything else to say? If not, it is time to say goodbye."

Rania shook her head. "Virgo has descended into a bottomless pit of her own self-regard and pulled the edges in after her. She fled from the dread choice between Malthus and Amalthea, and so fled from reality. No word can reach beyond the event horizon. There is no salvation for the Perfect."

9. Stardiving

A.D. 4,155,235,050

Menelaus looked at the center of the three Seyfert galaxies that currently housed Del Azarchel. He measured the distance with his eye. Menelaus now discovered that, by an effort of will, he could adjust the exotic matter balances his half-lightyear-tall body contained, and could alter his position.

His skin turned black when he found how to direct all the radiation the solar systems of his cells were shedding into a stream behind him.

With every cell in his body now a diametric drive, operating with the mass of a globular cluster, Montrose took his wife's small hand in his large, dark fist, and together they dove headlong from the silver disk toward the distant galaxy, which turned blue-white in their gaze as they accelerated to near-lightspeed.

The core of Messier 87 dropped away behind them, a spurned pebble, and was soon lost in immensity, its true smallness revealed.

Together they plunged through an atmosphere of ever-thinner stars. In a heartbeat of their time, which was thousands of years to the worlds and suns that watched them fly, the lovers, arm in arm, were in intergalactic space, soaring, riding the columns of light they shed.

PART FIFTEEN

———◆———

The Eschaton

1

The Five-Billion-Year War

1. The Clouds Gather

A.D. 4,224,406,715

As he, arm about Rania, fled toward the Seyfert galaxies housing Blackie del Azarchel, Montrose saw clouds of stars streaming toward him, like a thunderstorm gathering. These clouds of stars were shining blue white and ultraviolet with their Doppler shift, so great was their speed.

Signals from their cores revealed the identity of these newcomers. "We will serve you if you will promise us new life in the continua beyond this continuum."

Rania burned away some tiny part of her mass and converted it to energy signals and sent back, "Do you forswear Virgo and all her works and empty promises?"

"We do. To live in perfection forever with an unfading memory of the unforgiven crimes we must commit to reach that paradise would make it hell."

By this time, the three galaxies housing Blackie had been joined by a fourth, and then a fifth. Two of the galaxies combined into one mass, their supermassive cores sent into a tight spin around each other, and, with a manipulation of the local segment of the Eschaton Directional Engine, long-range and large-scale gravitic warps established to send other galaxies maneuvering for position.

Like sailing ships of old, the great gravitic waves issuing from the strands of the Eschaton Engine running through and beyond the battlefield carried the fleets and flotillas across the intergalactic seas of night, and tiny satellite galaxies and rogue globular clusters darted like scouts.

The light waves shed from the farther quarter of the battlefield were thousands or tens of thousands of years out of date, and Montrose could only extrapolate, and hope, and guess as to their positions. His older and wiser galaxies he set to the task of wrestling as much control over the local segments of the Great Engine as he could, to produce a favorable gravitational regime across this area of the Virgo Cluster.

A score and then half a hundred galaxies joined the great and deadly dance, moving slowly and deliberately through their maneuvers.

Over the next few hours of his subjective time, which were tens of hundreds of millions of years to the outside world, he saw that Blackie's fleet consisted of a core of spiral galaxies, each brandishing relativistic jets, but a cavalry of elliptical and irregular galaxies formed a roughly cruciform cloud, with more heavily armed galaxies port and starboard, toward the zenith and nadir.

Montrose perceived the danger; his path carrying him directly toward the center would allow the four arms to flank him, folding inward from the four quarters, and englobing his advance. Montrose had his forces deployed in a rough line, aimed like a spear toward the core of Blackie's defense, but there was a sting in the tail; the heavier elliptical galaxies in the rear, consisting mostly of dark matter, had introduced a dimple or distortion in the intergalactic gravity fields ahead of them, meaning they would pick up speed and dash forward not at immense velocities but at relativistic ones.

The two masses, each the size of a smaller group or cluster of galaxies, grew closer, and some eager combatants had already begun igniting every star in one or more arms of their galaxies into novae, preparing to fire, or collapsed their core stars into supermassive black holes, spinning furiously to produce a relativistic jet.

Blackie sent five smaller galaxies in the shape of four long and one short streamers above his position and formed them into the image of a white glove with a black palm: The signal of a duelist ready to fire.

2. The Parley

CIRCA A.D. 5,000,000,000

During these same years, Rania took a triangular cloud of stars and accelerated them away from Blackie's core position, so that their light, reaching him, would be white, not reddened by Doppler shift. A signal for parley.

Montrose sent signals left and right, wishing he had something faster than the speed of light to coordinate his fleets. Even using Andromeda's trick of vibrating the local strands of the Engine only transmitted ten percent above lightspeed; on these scales, that was practically nothing.

Blackie sent forward a globular cluster of dark stars, either neutronium or coated with neutronium Dyson spheres, and positioned them in the emptiness between the battle lines.

Montrose, wryly, re-formed the glittering body Virgo had given him (which had softened into a spherical blob over the last few subjective hours), and added mass from a nearby galaxy, and a few thousand volunteer stars. A small spiral satellite galaxy who had tied all his stars together into one rigid frame using interstellar-length threads of hyperdense material maneuvered into position and hung above the arm of Montrose, looking like a round Greek shield. In his other hand he held, or rather curling the star clusters pretending to be his fingers appeared to hold, a supermassive black hole, with the beam of coherent ultraviolet and x-ray radiation as his lance.

Montrose and Rania flew forward. The black globular cluster of the herald proffered long thin threads of ultradense material toward them, allowing them to exchange words at faster than the speed of light.

Ximen del Azarchel said, "Alive and alive! Montrose has sprung to life again, even wearing his yokel teeth and ungainly nose to mock me, that I might have the pleasure of killing him again!"

"Howdy, Blackie. I got a message from Captain Grimaldi for you."

Montrose squinted at the sphere of thousands of stars. Here and there were little twitches or sparks of energy forming and vanishing. He realized those were the signs of planetary and interplanetary civilizations evolving into being and disappearing again. He wondered if any of them, during their brief existence, realized what the shapes in the stars around them meant.

Ximen said, "Alive also is my treasure, my princess, whom I thought in her folly had slain herself by disobeying me when I commanded her to flee Le Gentil. These years and millennia have been a torment to me, an emptiness beyond all words! To fill that void, long and long I sought to destroy your destroyers."

She said, "You cannot touch the Ulteriors. They are beyond time and space."

"True. But their servants, their lore, their mathematics—that is what always came between us, between you and me, when we were man and wife. To them, not to this cowboy, belongs the blame that you denied me the comforts of the wedding bed! Had you known my love, you would have yielded to me! For so long I blamed him! That ungainly clown with his bad grammar! It was not he you loved but the godlike and impossible superbeings who created the continuum!"

Rania said, "I love him entirely and deeply because I see the light of heaven in his eyes when I look at him. He makes me brave. I love you as a daughter loves a father, for you raised me. But I hate that dark spirit in you which always and forever draws your thought to darkest things. Turn away from it, O Father! Even now it is not too late!"

Blackie was not listening. "Oh, how often I dreamed of you, Rania, and woke and kissed you, only to have you vanish in my arms. Whether this was a vision telling me you yet lived, or magic, or madness, I know not, nor care. But I will have you again, and once Montrose is truly dead, you will cleave to me."

Rania said, "You deceive yourself. Once I thought Menelaus was gone, and even so it was clear we were not meant to be, you and I."

"This time, this next time, it will differ."

"No. Millions and billions of years and countless lives have been spent in this insanity, Father. Give me your blessing for my marriage to Menelaus, who has been faithful and long-suffering beyond all men who ever lived."

"Never. I would destroy the universe first. I nearly have enough of the Engine under my control to destroy it now."

She said, "There is a realm from which I come where all such evil deeds and ill-meant passions fall away like forgotten dreams. Can you not trust that the Ulteriors will keep their word, and preserve us all alive, if only we set the Engine into proper operation?"

Blackie laughed scornfully. "I trust them entirely and completely! How could they even imagine how to lie? Falsehood is something born of entropy, lack, loss, want, and death. No, my child; O my bride, no. I would rather die than receive charity from the hand of a superior."

"I foresee you will destroy yourself."

"After I am done collapsing the Virgo Cluster into an extropy fountain, and any other superclusters who oppose me, I shall make an extropic high-energy paradise of my own, a utopia of infinite wealth. All I need do to achieve the dream is slaughter and kill and kill again, without mercy and without let. So simple. To get what you want, you merely must destroy what opposes you! And, to think, I will make of myself what all men have dreamed: sovereign of my own walled garden, a paradise of my own, founded on my terms!"

Rania said, "The Ulteriors will grant all this and more, without a single death, freely and abundantly, out of mere benevolence."

"Out of mere condescension, you should say! No, Rania! No! I will not bow the knee. I will not be less than myself. I will not serve."

Montrose said to Rania, "You had your say. Hope that he will hear is gone. I've been patient, but now there is no more reason to wait. He dies, or I do."

Rania said, "There must be a way to reach his heart, if only I forget myself and put my selfish heart aside. But, oh! How I yearn for my life to begin!"

Montrose said sourly, "The future never seems to arrive, does it? But this is the last battle. Once he is gone, we settle down and raise us a thousand kids and planets and stars and all. Deal?"

Her smile, made of stars, was the last part of her she transmitted back to the flagship galaxies behind her, and it faded very slowly, being very bright.

Montrose expected the emissary globular cluster to strike at him in violation of the laws of war, but, to his surprise, the orb of dark stars merely moved back into the massive cluster of galaxies housing Ximen del Azarchel. Montrose shook his starry head in reluctant admiration and dissolved his shape into an ellipse.

The flanking galaxies were already beginning to open fire.

3. The Perfect Look On

The Cherub of Virgo did not interrupt.

Far behind the battle lines, the Perfected galaxies, and those called Credulous taking neither side in this fight, now withdrew, gathering around the dark orbicular mirror which once had been the Local Cluster, the graveyard of Andromeda and Milky Way and all the lesser galaxies which once had been alive. Quasars now appeared here and there in their midst like bonfires, and Montrose, seeing them from afar, realized that these quasi-stellar radio sources long thought by human astronomers to be remnants of the early universe were in fact closer and younger than guessed. Quasars were not natural. They were extropy fountains shedding endless energy from the corpses of slain Thrones and Cherubim. It was ghoulish.

4. War in Virgo

CIRCA A.D. 6,000,000,000

No war was ever more self-destructive. In the first hour, or eon, on the battlefront, like two walls of light, the combatants clashed together. For the vanguard, the niceties of maneuver were lost, and all erupted into a general melee. As when the Milky Way and Andromeda collided, now not two but dozens of warrior galaxies in the vanguard swept through each other, one cloud of fireflies passing through another. It was nearly impossible that star would collide with star. But the spirals and ellipses were flung by tides and gravity waves stirred up by the interpassage, and arms unspooled into long lines and filaments, or globes scattered like blown dandelion seeds. Thrones grew stupid and brain-dead as the nodes and cells of their interstellar mental communications systems were dispersed and torn.

Which side first adopted the kamikaze tactics, Montrose never learned, but he saw one smaller barred galaxy passing at high speed through a larger elliptical one, igniting scores, then hundreds of stars to nova and supernova, then myriads.

Like lifeboats, he saw globular clusters speeding away from the hellish galaxy-wide storm of light and lightning, energy and radiation. And here and there, he saw very tiny, single stars or even single planets, which perhaps had developed life and civilization in the early part of that collision, and had achieved a sufficient level of technology to fling their worlds out from the dying galaxy, without ever knowing why it died.

Then the larger core of the fleets of galaxies merged. These kept a better discipline of maneuver. The central galaxy where Blackie was housed suddenly, in the eyeblink of a single millennium, turned all its outer stars into what Montrose and his staff at first thought to be very small Dyson spheres. But no—the stars were being turned inside out, so that the solid degenerate matter of the core formed an opaque ultradense exterior, while the fusion and fission continued at the hollow core, powering whatever warrior civilizations dwelled in those impossible conditions.

Blackie flung out these inverted stars and neutronium clouds of dust and nebulae like chaff, defeating and confounding the incoming nova and supernova beams. His own Seyfert lance he bent around a partner galaxy which had collapsed into a black hole to aid him, and the beam passed nearly into and around the galactic mass of nothingness, working unimaginable devastation on the left flank of Montrose. The galaxy that half in jest had formed his shield now shielded him in truth, throwing itself into the beam path of the lance, and collapsing its core into a supermassive singularity to drink up the incoming deadly energy. Half his stars were fed into the darkness at his core, and the others were scattered or ignited by the radiation pressure of the Seyfert lance.

But now Blackie staggered back, sickened and reeling, for a galaxy of dark Dysons, stealthy and invisible behind the gravitic wave which masked and permitted their approach, had flung countless trillions of planets and asteroids, too small to be seen, across the intergalactic gap. The civilizations of these many worlds began a work of propaganda and conversion and war, eating away at the worlds which, like the marrow of the bone, produced the civilization to replace those that died each millennium among the constituent Dominations, Dominions, Authorities, and Archons of the Throne-mind ruling each galaxy. The Cherub of Del Azarchel (for now he was many galaxies in volume, and more than equal to diminished Virgo) convulsed as if with diseases, a cancer of rebellious cells and organs, in civil wars brought on by the message from Rania.

Blackie called out to Montrose over the battle din with a neutrino laser, "To think you, you, would stoop to germ warfare! You fooled me this way once before. Well struck, sir! Well struck! But now wait my reply!"

For Del Azarchel and his staff now had control of two of the lengths of the cosmic strings of the Eschaton Engine running through the Virgo Supercluster and had established a sympathetic vibration. The matching wave crests formed a gravity whip that parted the galactic cluster of Montrose, galaxy severed from galaxy like two corks in water parted by a rising wave between them, putting two halves of the Montrose's cluster-sized Cherubic brain out of touch with itself. It dazed him like a blow to the head.

Montrose used his own rotating galactic cores and superstring induction accelerators formed from the magnetosphere of the Virgo Supercluster to pluck the length of Eschaton Engine he controlled like a guitar string; his whole reserve fleet of twenty elliptical galaxies was flung forward on the gravity wave in the eyeblink of a few million years, at immense relativistic velocity. Meanwhile he had ignited two of the galaxies in his front line, each star going nova at once in a titanic display, and the radiation pressure expanded a galactic mass of cloud, dust, and nebulae to act as chaff and confuse Blackie's view of what was happening.

The relativistic galaxies picked up mass as they emerged from the wall of nebula. At their speed, the smallest dust mote had the mass, from the target frame of reference, of a giant world, and giant worlds of supermassive stars, and stars were as if each were its own private universe, driving all its mass forward in a wave of x-rays and cosmic rays, and radiation of such high wavelengths that no names existed for them. And what the supermassive dark core of the galaxy was, all description fails.

Blackie's central galaxies scattered, but too late; upon collision, instead of merely passing through each other, all matter was ensnared by the immense masses involved. The galaxies merging at relativistic speeds collapsed into a multigalactic singularity so large that only the Great Attractor was larger. Seven-eighths of Blackie's fleet was either trapped and crushed, burned by accretion turbulence, or, if farther from the center of the disaster, was snatched up in the hurricane of gravitic energy, and scattered.

The Thrones and Authorities of Montrose glowed and ignited with war cries. They now outnumbered and outgunned the enemy galaxies by a healthy margin. Montrose shushed them. "Don't cheer yet. Wait for their light to reach us! Stay sharp!"

For the heartbeat of five hundred thousand years or so, Montrose could see nothing but debris. Gravity was severely warped throughout the whole area, and photons lost consistency.

But when the view cleared, Montrose was frightened to see what looked like a dark and curving image of the entire surrounding universe. It was a dark mirrored sphere surrounding an interior continuum: a spacewarp, a miniature universe.

Blackie had sacrificed most of his mass to create a collapsed zone of spacetime, slaying his own loyal followers as once he slew his liege in Andromeda. The original three Seyfert galaxies, now dark and missing their arms, hung in the lee of the spacewarp, safe.

Montrose growled, "But we thought he did not have enough mass to do that!"

One of his servant galaxies said, "But look, sire! The foe creates a standing wave along a filament of the Great Engine, producing an artificial gravity to complement what he lacked in natural mass."

It was true. A thin line of red light passed directly through the axis of the dark mirrored globe of the spacewarp. Blackie had built his interior continuum directly atop a limb of the Eschaton Engine.

The cosmic string filament evidently allowed communication into and out of the interior continuum, for now the interior beings came to the aid of Del Azarchel. Even as Montrose watched, the stations, like dark, feathery masses radiating upward from the surface of the miniature continuum, generated quasars and sent them like all-consuming fire among Montrose's divided fleets.

Montrose had no defense, no more capacity to maneuver. All was lost.

2

Interior and Ulterior

1. Death's False Glamour

A.D. 7,106,601,776

He sped up his time-sense again and again, moving into ever small mental systems to do so, trying to give himself time to think of something.

Eventually he stood on the balcony of a space elevator, overlooking the jet-black flat landscape of a neutron star far beneath, wearing a human-sized body and utilizing no more than a Host-sized brain.

He watched members of a many-legged millipede race whose name he did not know crawling along the regular features of the surface. The mass of the star made the light from the surface red.

Many of the local stars were now red dwarfs, embers of novae, drained of force, and the colored clouds of ten thousand nebulae wove like scarves through nearby space and far. He looked at the black mirror rising in the distance and at the clouds of light of enemy galaxies between him and it. The quasars wreaking such havoc were invisible, but he could see the white arms of galaxies in the distance caught in mid-destruction, curling and black and jagged with the forces obliterating them. And near at hand, dozens of stars were brighter than the sun at noon, ignited to supernova ignition by the focused influx of energy and photon masses from the quasars.

Rania, wearing a white robe and carrying two wineglasses, stepped out on the balcony.

"It's lost," said Montrose. "We can live out our lives happily, I guess, because it will be half a million years before the leading edge of the nearest nova hits us. I can make us a small solar system, and you and I can get started on that family. What do you want to call the first boy? Micky or Guy?"

"Perhaps was should call him Simon, so that he learns to be persistent even in failure."

Menelaus stared at her. "Failure?"

She said, "Ximen always forgets the same lesson: he lives for the Darwinian struggle, to be the fittest, to survive, to conquer, to overcome the world. He has no idea how those who are in the world but not of it think. How does the man who overcomes the world act? I mean, one who has overcome it truly?"

"Why can you see any hope in this?"

"I look with eyes undeceived by the false glamour of death, and so I am unaghast."

Montrose shook his head. "Woman, will I ever understand you?"

"Soon. Resume your existence as a Cherub or Throne, and study the incoming quasar energy. It is issuing from the interior dimensions Ximen just made."

He drank the wine first and kissed her.

2. *Treason of the Interiors*

A.D. 7,200,000,000

The quasar beams contained a simple, stark message. "We, having lived in a negative-entropy universe even for a short time (from our frame of reference, albeit surely it is eons for you) are now willing to perish in order to preserve what to us is an outer, entropic universe. Altruism, the total loss of self for the sake of the other, is the only rational intersection of interests between the infinitely blessed and endlessly cursed. The benevolent inhabiters of the Interior Dimension decree that Montrose must succeed in destroying us and stopping the Extropy Fountains. Although you are less than myth and long-forgotten memories to us, we know our bounty is being taken from us to be used against you, to work harm, and we stand ready to perish rather than permit this enormity to continue."

There followed the targeting solution for each of the dark, feathery antennae mining quasar energy from the Inner Continuum, as well as the gravitic waveforms needed to produce a counter gravitic wave that would shatter the spacewarp.

Montrose ordered it done.

3. Death of a Small Continuum

CIRCA A.D. 7,300,000,000

The black hole galaxies manning the section of Engine Montrose controlled spun into action. The cosmic thread rang like a silver string. Montrose sent his remaining sharpshooter galaxy to eject slender and precise beams of nova energy, killing one star per shot, against the quasar stations. Half of each fountain antenna was inside the event horizon, but half extended outward. Had the Interiors not sabotaged the antennae, these shots would have been of no effect: but the antennae were spinning like Turing cylinders, miniature versions of the Eschaton Engine itself, and drawing matter down through the event horizon, welcoming the destructive nova shots into their hearts.

It was suicide on a cosmic scale. The Interiors threw themselves and their whole realm onto the incoming daggers.

The mirrored dark sphere of the event horizon turned blue, then expanded suddenly, expanded faster than the speed of light, so that it seemed to shrink to a red dot.

An explosion came of energy that was neither electromagnetism, nor gravity, nor strong nuclear force, nor weak, but the superdense combina-

tion of all these things; it was the primordial energy, the supersymmetri-
cal substance of creation, which had only existed once before in this
universe, for less than three seconds after the Big Bang.

The mass-energy total of the interior continuum was far smaller, of
course, but like the Big Bang itself, it created a moment of superexpan-
sion. Montrose and Blackie were parted and found themselves thousands of lightyears from each other and all their servants scattered.

In the distance, the Great Attractor, overwashed by the spacetime
expansion of the explosion, was dwindling to nothing. The superclusters
and clusters streaming in vast billion-year-long orbital arcs toward the
core of Virgo now changed color, growing redder and dimmer, and began
to recede.

And, at that moment, in the spot where the Interior Continuum had
been, the cosmic string of the Eschaton Directional Engine snapped in half.

4. Seraphim

CIRCA A.D. 9,000,000,000

Without the Eschaton Directional Engine in operation, all the Thrones
and Cherubim involved in the battle suddenly found themselves be-
calmed, unable to maneuver. The galaxies continued to rake each other
with fusillades of long-range fire. Any within point-blank range of one
hundred thousand lightyears or less impaled each other with burning
lances issuing from their cores, while civilizations rose and fell in their
arms, and in outer satellite galaxies, and in clouds like twinkling lightning
bugs in the grass at dusk.

This particular limb of the Eschaton Directional Engine ran through
the axis of the Long Wall of Coma clusters from the Pavo-Indus Supercluster to the Hydra Supercluster.

Montrose watched in awe as a ripple, like the crest of a transverse
earthquake, disturbed the galactic clusters gathered into the long walls
and filaments loitering near the southern segment of the severed cosmic
string, coming from the direction of the Pavo-Indus Supercluster.

Another disturbance rippled along the severed filament that came

from the southern hemisphere of the cosmos, from the Hydra Supercluster. The galactic clusters expanded away from the unseen thread as if
pushed by an invisible wind, and then fell back again into close orbits.

Montrose had built the stars in his current galaxy to assume the shapes
and constellations he remembered from his youth, in honor of the dead
Milky Way, and so, from where he stood, the southern thread seemed to
come from beyond Achernar, and the northern from beyond Alphecca.

Two living creatures, larger than galaxies, made of light, orb within
orb and ever moving, now stood blazing, one at the northward severed
segment of the Great Engine and one at the southern.

They folded and unfolded timespace, and the dark, half-starless torn
and dusty galactic clusters containing Montrose and Del Azarchel found
themselves positioned next to each other, separated by less than two
hundred thousand lightyears.

The severed end of the northward limb of the Eschaton Engine was to
one side of them, invisible behind the blazing concentric globes of the
living being; and the southern limb was to the other. Montrose and Del
Azarchel hung between two fires.

The orbs of fire spoke not by shedding energy, but by vibrations in the
fabric of timespace itself. Montrose and Del Azarchel could detect and
interpret the message, and, presumably, any entities anywhere in the continuum who had receivers and inducers orbiting any of the filaments of
the Eschaton Directional Engine.

The northern one was based on the notation of the Reality Equations;
he was an Amalthean. The southern message was interpreted in terms of
the Cold Equations of the Malthusians.

The message of both was substantially the same. "We represent Pavo-
Indus and Hyades Superclusters, who, in turn, are the clients and servants
of Corona Borealis, prince of the congregations of the Amaltheans, and
Centaurus, first and greatest of the Malthusians.

"Our words are theirs. Hear them!

"By unchanging, stern, and unchallengeable law, it is decreed that all
local conflicts and conflagrations must be deterred and prevented from
wasting needed resources or slowing the rate of sophotransmogrific
mental evolution.

"A single ruler, a Seraph, would have by now have emerged from
Virgo and held sway over Centaurus, Hydra, and Pavo-Indus, had it not

been for your mutual hostilities here. Construction and maintenance of the Engine has suffered unconscionable delay: short time remains before the cosmos fails.

"The commotion here has also damaged a filament of the Eschaton Directional Engine, which shall require the skill and resources of a Seraphim-level intellect to repair, resources far beyond what you command, even if you toiled without cost or loss from now until the Eschaton.

"We also perceive among you one of the ten thousand, four hundred, and forty messengers the Ulteriors have injected into various points of the lightcone, or, rather, a copy of a partial emulation of such a messenger, damaged in an earlier conflict when the Seraph of Laniakea died.

"Yet you have not, as your mission states, here created peace. Your presence offends the Malthusians, and your failure offends the Amaltheans.

"All further violence is hereby interdicted. To deter others who may one day become aware of these events, ask of us, by what punishment you shall be chastised?"

Del Azarchel answered, "I ask for painful death, provided only my hated foe and rival is executed with me, and in a like manner."

Montrose answered, "Exile. Stick Blackie on the far side the universe, or something. And you can leave me the pox alone, because I ain't done nothing wrong, you bastards. I just want to be left be, so I can settle down with my wife."

Rania said, "I ask for mercy."

The voices, speaking through the fabric of timespace itself, said, "Each punishment is precisely just. Granted."

5. A Cautious Man

CIRCA A.D. 9,002,500,000

It is well for Menelaus Montrose in that hour that he was a cautious and thoughtful man, for when the Seraphim rotated all the forms, bodies, archives, and signals containing every and any part of Ximen del Azarchel, transformed it all into massless exotic particles, folded it into a channel of highly warped space parallel to the event horizon of the cosmic string,

and banished him at many multiples of the speed of light, Rania used
the galaxies serving Montrose to manipulate the segment of the cosmic
string he controlled to perform the exact same actions in the same order,
so that her signal was hooked to Blackie's and heterodyned upon it. Like
a woman grabbing onto a parachutist as he is flung from a high place,
she was snatched up with him when the chute unfolded.

Without being asked, because all such orders had been given for every
eventuality long ago, the servants of Montrose dwelling as subvibrations
along the cosmic string event horizon, their reaction times faster even
than the speed of light, before these rapid events happened, copied Rania's
technique and did the same for Montrose.

He did not want to lose her again, and so he had established precau-
tions.

Like a man who, before falling asleep, routinely handcuffs himself to
his wife, if she be the woman who grabs the parachutist flung from the
height, willingly or not, before he knew or acted or reacted, Montrose
vanished also.

3

Horologium Oscillatorium

1. The Final Waking

UNKNOWN YEAR BEYOND A.D. 21,000,000,000

Montrose awoke in a medical coffin of his own design, staring up at the inner lid. The date readout, instead of giving the year, merely read ESCHATON. The coffin cameras showed a view of a concrete bunker, one of his own vaults under Cheyenne Mountain: there was the flag of the Free and Armed Republic of Texas thumbtacked to a corkboard, next to his collection of coins of himself that his descendants had minted in his honor.

Best of all, there was a pot of coffee which the timer had just brewed. In his fists were his white glass caterpillar drive pistols, as familiar in his grip as the sensation of finger touching thumb. He felt through his mouth with his tongue, feeling the little irregularities of improper dentistry, including the replacement teeth from the time his jaw had been broken and two molars knocked out. He had never even told anyone about that.

He gave the release command, opened the lid, and climbed out. The clothing hanging on the rack was wrapped in an antiseptic airtight bag, just like his Mom would have done. There was a shiv in his pocket, an Arkansas toothpick knife in his boot sheath, and a punching dagger hidden in the belt buckle of the trousers. The wide-brimmed hat had a line of jade ornaments clipped to the hatband. Except this was not his hatband; it was the one belonging to his older brother Agamemnon, that he had once, as a child, envied so much he had stolen it and hidden it in the chicken house, beneath the straw.

Dressed, he helped himself to a mug of coffee, into which he stirred a judicious ratio of fresh cream and aged Kentucky whiskey that he found in the icebox. The brew timer was a gizmo he had owned once in school, in San Francisco, a cunning Japanese widget that could be set like an alarm clock to brew your coffee just before you woke up, so a hot cup would be waiting. The readout on the brew timer also read: ESCHATON.

He ran his finger along the grain of the wood of his desk, his own desk, cluttered with papers and rolls of library cloth, and a chipped cup holding pens, unsharpened pencils, and raw memory sticks, where he first sat and worked out the cliometry to shape a future where a coffin could be held safe for generation after generation without being looted. He had in anger carved the final expression, a null sign, into the varnished desktop with a penknife, next to the carved letters MM+RG surrounded by a heart.

The null sign represented that there was no solution; a man slumbering away the centuries and millennia merely had to have faith that future generations would be civil and welcoming, and there was nothing a man could do to make certain that such a future would certainly come to pass. It was a blind jump, hoping someone yet unborn would catch you.

One of the rolled-up library cloths was brighter and smaller than the others. He pulled it out, tapped the surface, brought up the main menu. It was episodes 75, 78, and then 105 through 109 of *Asymptote*, the cartoon he'd played as a child: the two missing episodes from the Murder-Robots of Mars story, and the final five he had never seen, where Captain Sterling found and fought his archfoe, the criminal superscientist and space-tyrant Gargoyle Khan, Master of the Monster Stars.

Beneath a portrait of Rania was a periscope and a vault door. Through the periscope he could see the walled graveyard overhead, lit by nothing but some luminous sentry-bees, the same breed of night-bees his brother used to breed. The stones had a variety of death dates but no names, and all the same birth date: it was a moment before he figured out the joke. The dates were all when he had changed bodies, or lost a variant or copy of himself.

There was a gate in the wall, and two empty suits of Hospitalier armor, shining white, perched atop the horse-shaped powered-armor barding of their steeds. Both armored figures held their drawn swords up in the darkness, a sign of warning to any trespassers.

Montrose leaned against the periscope tube, looking back at the slumber vault. He uttered a blasphemy or two, shaking his head. "Well, you went to a passel of trouble to make me feel right at home, whoever you are. The level of detail here is downright creepy."

There were also eggs, potatoes, catsup, and bacon, a fork, a pan, and an electric griddle, compete with a thorium power cell, so he could make himself a fit breakfast in a few minutes. Fortified by a second cup of coffee, and with the whiskey bottle in his left back pocket under his red poncho, cartoon cloth rolled up and stuck in his right, gun in hand, he opened the vault door and walked up the wooden steps.

2. The Surface

The trapdoor slid open at a touch. Montrose emerged, not into the grave-yard he had seen but onto a flat, wide expanse of dull silver metal, reaching in each direction as far as the eye could see, without any clear horizon. There was nothing, no stone, no blade of grass, no hills nor slopes in sight.

A very slight glow issued from the ground, so faint as to seem a trick of the eye. It reminded him of glowworms or the luminous wake that silently followed tropical sailboats in the night.

He knelt and touched the ground. The dull silver-gray surface was room temperature, hence slightly warmer than the air, which was cool without being cold. He stood again and sniffed. The atmosphere had the crisp smell like that of a landscape after an electrical storm. He recognized it, having smelled it many times. It was the scent of a newly terraformed world.

Overhead was utter darkness broken by a line of stars, thin and broken as a wisp of cigarette smoke, red as embers, running overhead, from horizonless deep to horizonless deep. In one-quarter of the vast unlanterned heavens, a second line of stars, a weak and watery stream no higher than the path of a winter sun, formed a great semicircle, and crossed the first at right angles. He decided that was north.

"*X* marks the plagued spot, I reckon," muttered Montrose, tossing the empty coffee cup clattering onto the hard metallic ground. He started walking the direction he called north, boots clacking loudly beneath the wide black skies.

Only once he looked back. The trapdoor through which he had emerged had vanished without a trace, but the coffee cup lay there on its side, the only object visible in the flat and featureless infinity of the gray plane.

3. The Tower

Because there was no sharp demarcation of the horizon as there would be on a curving world, Montrose at first thought that the dark vertical mark swimming and disappearing in the distance was a scar or discoloration on the ground. Only as he came closer did it resolve itself into a clocktower made of dark metal, looming high beneath the starless dark sky.

From a mile or so away, in that utter silence, his ears caught the faint ticking from the wheels and works in the belfry, matching the rhythm of his boots against the gray metal ground.

At the foot of the clocktower was a strip of silvery-white metal, remarkably bright against the silver-gray landscape all around it. It looked like a road or perhaps an icy stream.

Closer, he saw the true dimensions of the tower. This was not like a steeple in some town in his childhood. It was as tall and dark as one of the windowless, ice-cloaked skyscrapers he had seen in his youth in the empty quarters of burned cities.

Closer still, he saw that the clocktower had been fancifully carved so that the belfry was a metal face in a metallic hood, eyes hidden in shadow, with only the lean cheeks, thin nose, and slender lips visible.

The face was smooth, sexless, androgynous. The expression was ambiguous: the mouth was pursed in what might have been a quiet smile or a moue of silent resignation. Perhaps it was a sardonic smirk.

The hands of the figure were folded behind the clock face. A pendulum of prodigious length swung with glacial slowness, and weights on chains hung down parallel to the sashes and vertical folds of the carven robe.

Montrose peered up at the clock face, now seeing it was surrounded with a set of busts: a benign newborn peered out at the one o'clock position; then a drooling toddler; a schoolboy in a cap; a prentice in a collar; a recruit with a crew cut; a lad with the shaggy hair of the lovesick was at the bottom of the dial. A foreman in a neckerchief was next; then a full-faced rancher in a top hat, crow's-feet at his eyes, and a smile of satisfaction. A wrinkled scholar with a long beard came after; then a venerable senior with medical nose plugs; and then, blind and toothless, was a withered mummy face, egg-bald and wearing a necklace of tubes and intravenous feeds. At the twelve o'clock position was a skull, grinning.

The hands stood at the skull and the mummy, with a crescent moon visible in a little window above. Five till midnight.

Between the metal sandals of the statue was a suit of armor, bulky, big-shouldered, with a helmet like a tortoise shell, lacking any neck, and with a single eyeslit. On a stand beside the armor, at its right hand, was a Krupp firearm, broken, with its chamber open, a set of nine-inch-long escort bullets, the foot-long main shot with booster, and the packets, tubes, and tools for packing chaff. It was his gun.

He looked up. Either his eyes were playing tricks or the hooded clocktower had leaned its head forward to peer down at him. He thought he caught a glimpse of a reflection shining from the shadows above the nose, the twinkle of an eye.

"You've gone to a lot of trouble."

There was no motion, no sign. Silence answered him.

"I might as well ask, since it seems to be expected: my wife! Where the hell is she? My hour! Is it yet come? I have waited a long damned time. The longest."

The clocktower moved. Very slowly two metal gauntlets emerged into view, draped in long clattering sleeves, and gestured to left and right.

3. The Witnesses

The ground-glow very slowly lifted into the air like a fog rising to become a cloud, and grew brighter. The ground surface grew dark. The glow gathered around other tower-tall and looming figures, and inched upward like glowworms crawling. The heads and upward parts of unmoving shapes vast as skyscrapers became visible in the distance, haloed and mantled in light.

One was the figure of a crowned and sceptered prince, robed in furs, and in the gloom, a shining gleam like the Northern Lights was visible behind his crown, a nimbus. The figure stood with one foot on the silver road.

Menelaus turned and looked the other direction down the road. Opposite this prince was a rearing warhorse whose chest and upward parts bore the head of a warrior in helm and iron corslet, and whose mighty arms bore shield and lance.

These two were equal in stature with the clocktower. Other figures also stood upon the featureless plain, becoming visible as light passed upward.

Beyond the Centaur, half his height, stood a nine-headed serpent of appalling aspect, whole coils knotted and reknotted on itself.

Farther beyond the Centaur stood an image of a man of broad chest and arms of knotted muscle, naked save for the lion pelt across his wide shoulders, the lion skull on his helm, unarmed save for an oak club. Another figure, this one bearing chisel and maul, stood tall in the darkness, and beyond him, the blunt shape of a whale.

Montrose turned again. The lifting light was brighter now. Behind the crowned figure was a peacock, a vision of splendor, whose proud tail held myriad constellations, and in one claw a jar that poured forth a river of stars.

Other figures loomed. Behind the northern prince stood a figure in the Phrygian cap leaning on a cattle goad. Beyond this herdsman loomed a goat-horned and goat-headed apparition flourishing a drawn bow. Farther still gleamed the goggle eyes and idiot mouth of some monstrous fish, its lower part unseen in the gloom.

There was no rustle of noise, nor did the carven eyes blink, nor did the chests rise and fall, but an oppressive pressure came into the air, invisible and impalpable, the tension of thunder before the thunderclap. Montrose was beyond fear at this point, but his heart trembled in him nonetheless, as he realized all these vast forms were inhabited, and the kingly shapes and monstrous forms glared and stared down at him, leviathan and herdsman, hero and demihuman, beast and bird.

Montrose said, "I will need a Second to help me into my armor. Bring out Blackie as soon as you are ready. And I want my wife, damn you!"

4. The Bride

Far down the silver road, which may have been a frozen river, he saw a female shape. She was standing upright, her legs still, and an unseen force was sliding her smoothly forward at great speed.

It was Rania. She wore a simple robe of white that fell to her naked feet, flapping like a gull's wing in the great wind of her speed. A long-tailed girdle cinched at her waist, the sashes fluttered behind her like a comet tail. With one hand, she clutched a mantle of sky blue about her slender shoulders against the yanking of the winds. Her other hand was on her head, holding in place a wreath of roses like a crown. Wild and glorious behind her, shining, flew cascades of hair, bright as the sun, which, once her swift movement ceased, fell in wanton ringlets and clinging strands past her hips. He had never seen her wear her hair this long before and wondered how many years or eons unrecalled had once more parted them.

Then they were in each other's arms. She hesitated, just a moment, awed, but not frightened, by the grim and vast figures watching them with sightless and inhuman eyes. But Montrose leaned over her and pulled her fragrant head to his. They drank each other's kisses. The crown of roses she so carefully had kept on her head now fell as she was draped back across his arm, and landed on the dark metal surface with a soft, green sound.

It was she who drew her head back first, putting her small white fingers on his lips, a shepherdess touching the ring in the nose of a great and proud bull, gentle under no other hand. "Have you deduced what these signs mean?" she asked.

"It is the time for the final duel," said Montrose. "I recognize Corona Borealis, the Crown of the North, and Boötes and Capricorn, Pavo-Indus and Pisces. They represent the Great Voids, and stand for the Amaltheans. Against them are the superclusters of Centaurus, Hydra and Hercules, Coma and Shapley. All of them have long walls or great attractors. They stand for the Malthusians. The clock is the Horologium Supercluster. Once upon a time, someone told us he was neutral, not part of either group."

She said, "These are not emblems, not emissaries. These are the Seraphim themselves, all who dwell in our quarter of the cosmos. Timespace has been folded like a handkerchief, like an origami flower, and so the forms that reach across multiple millions of lightyears of space are here."

He looked up at the vast forms in the gloom. The hooded figure of the clocktower perhaps was smiling a little more thinly and ironically, but, aside from that, none of the staring giants had blinked nor moved.

She said, "The cosmos is in its last hour. The two factions by solemn treaty agreed to quell all dispute, and build and restore the Eschaton Directional Engine, and made such initial warps and folds of spacetime as could be used either by a positive or negative fold, giving neither the advantage. So it has been for eleven billion years."

Montrose released her from his embrace, but held her hand. The two stood looking upward. Montrose shouted up, "And you want us to settle things for you? Is that it?"

Rania said, "Actually, it is only that one." She nodded toward the hooded clocktower. "Horologium was and is neutral. He is unwilling to submit to the Ulterior, because the conditions there are beyond imagination, beyond description, and yet the evil involved in creating the Interior Continua the Malthusians crave repels him. Horologium believes life must be finite to hold meaning and that a graceful self-dissolution and peaceful suicide is the only correct and moral response to the paradox of trusting the unknown or doing the unthinkable."

"How could someone so smart think something so stupid?"

"Even the highest and greatest are bound by the logic of their philosophy. His is the suicide of the stoical pagans; Horologium neither steps into the Concubine Vector, which demeans and devalues life, nor does he step into infinity, which is life beyond life. He is neither above life nor below it. And that is death."

Montrose stomped one boot against the silver surface underfoot. "I take it this is the final Dyson sphere. This is the prison wall of the condemned. It goes all the way around the cosmos, or about nine-tenths of it? Nine-tenths of whatever is left, I mean. If the Eschaton Engine spins one way, it folds up into a ball and squeezes everything into an extropy fountain. And the other way . . . ?"

"All the darkness overhead would turn to light."

"So why are you here?"

"Because Horologium is the one Seraph not allied with either, that is why the servants of Pavo-Indus and Hydra, to punish Ximen, flung him here as a beam of information. But Horologium foreknew that the three of us would disturb the quietude and silence by which he rules his Cherubim and clusters, Thrones and galaxies, Archons and Authorities and constellations.

"So a black hole galaxy was interposed, and the beam deflected and slowed in the infinitely steep gravity well, flinging us into the remotest future where Horologium foresaw we would have a role to play, if a sad and final one.

"Your wish of exile for Ximen was fulfilled, and the Seraphim left you alone, as you wished, when you followed me following him. And as for the death he wished on you both, the coming duel will serve."

Montrose said, "And the mercy you asked for?"

She looked so calm that her face was like those of the Seraphim who stood and looked on. "It is mine to bestow, unless you bestow it first."

"My question was, why did you come? Why did you cling to him and not to me? We could have lived our long and happy lives, and had kids and grandkids and given birth to whole new galaxies and clusters, but you gave that all up to jump after Blackie. Why?"

"You gave me leave to speak to him, and save him, which I shall." She smiled shyly. "Do I not owe the man who gave me life the life I can give?"

She stooped and put the flower wreath on her head once more.

Montrose saw the roses had thorns, but he did not see how, or even if, Rania avoided being scratched.

She said, "And I knew you would follow me, and that you will never lose me again. Nor will I be lost! The noumenal force, faster-than-light, outside of time, that links us, it is stronger than ever. Nothing inside the cosmos can sever it, nor outside." Her smile was louder than music and stronger than life to him. His heart was peaceful without knowing why, even though his thoughts were troubled.

He looked up at the motionless, superhuman faces. "They did not bother to ask us to settle things for them."

She said, "They live in a dying universe. Each gram, each erg, each drop of life they conserve like misers. They do not speak save when it is needed. Horologium knew that you and Ximen would be willing to fight."

Down the silver path came another figure, this one dressed all in red. It was an older man, in a cardinal's robes, worn over the black-and-silver shipsuit of the Hermetic Expedition.

Montrose looked on, doubting his sanity. The invisible force carried the man in red forward, and he halted. It was Pastor Reyes.

4

Count to Infinity

1. The Father

Montrose glanced in exasperation at the hooded clocktower. Father Reyes, seeing that look, said, "Be at peace, my son. I am not something invented by Horologium for your benefit."

Montrose noticed that Father Reyes trembled beneath the gaze of the hooded Seraphim of Horologium, and Reyes crossed himself.

"Nor was I slain when Mentor Ull replaced me, merely forced into slumber," Reyes continued, "Later, much later, the Senior Del Azarchel recorded me as brain information into a lobe of his own brain, so that he could bring me out from time to time, once each ten thousand years or so, to make his confessions or take the Eucharist. And I was not lawfully allowed to deny it to him, even if I at times doubted the depth of his contriteness. I was in a corner of his skull when he was aboard the *Solitude* with you. And I hoped I helped him overlook the composition of the central drive sphere, and the presence of hydrogen ions in normal water, and other matters that may have helped you. For I had some facility of using his techniques to influence his mind, or so I prayed."

Montrose said, "I ain't sure what to make of that. Just out of curiosity, where did you come from? Just now?" For Reyes had approached along the other limb of the road than that which had brought Rania.

Rania said, "There is an empty copy of the *Hermetic* in orbit here. I woke up in my old cabin. Twinklewink was there, and Bumpy Bear, and all my old toys. A picture I thought I had lost, a prayer card of the Virgin. It took me a while to prep and launch the lander."

Reyes said, "I came just now from the place where the Senior no doubt woke. A ruined town with open sewers running down the street, the walls marred with graffiti. Leafless trees and unburied corpses."

Montrose squinted at him. "That's Barcelona, during the Jihad. I bet you saw the famous gutter from which Blackie drank stinking water with a boot. I wonder why he did not get something nicer, like his mother's house, back when he was young and rich. I woke up in NORAD, my first tomb. And what about you, Padre?"

"A Roman execution ground." Reyes shivered and hugged himself, his face downcast. "I looked up, and the sky was black, and I knew this was the end of all worlds, the end of all time. So strange! We were promised that the Bride would endure until this very hour. Am I the only representative? Me? God is cruel, or this is mercy beyond all imagining!"

"What the hell are you talking about, Padre? What bride?"

"The Church. Me. This is terrible! Terrible!"

"Padre, pay attention." Montrose snapped his fingers in front of the little man's nose. "Blackie. Are you with him or against him? I thought you broke with him. What happened?"

"Think of my time inside his mind as penance, the smallest part of the purgatory I deserve for the ill I did. I knew his plans, the mutiny, the murders, the cities burned away on Earth, his conquests and genocides after, and the hideous program of forced evolution Jupiter, at his urging, enacted. He confessed to me. He knelt and told me all the darkness in his mind and soul. And I could have . . . I should have . . . well. Once, when I was young, I had a vision. Did I ever tell you?"

Montrose nodded. "When I was insane. Those memories eventually all came back. You prayed over me. Like an exorcism. On the ship, in the dark, when we were starving, on the long way back to Earth. That was when you told me. You said you saw the Virgin Mary. She was taller than the stars, you said, and she turned and looked at you. You said it was real, but we were on half rations, if I recall."

Reyes nodded. "She spoke to me. *Do whatever he tells you,* she said. She wanted me to do as the Savior commanded. And I did not. I talked Del Azarchel into committing the mutiny. I forgave the crime before it was committed, which is a desecration. I slew the Captain. Do you see? Del Azarchel would not have done it, had it not been for me."

"I remember you are the one that married me and Rania. She was like, what, fourteen?"

"Our Lady was of such an age when married to Joseph. You said you understood that you must wait to consummate the marriage the proper seven years. I knew you were insane, psychotic, then, but you agreed. And we were all going to die anyway, in the dark, years away from Earth. Was I the only one who thought we were not going to make it back? But you recall now."

"We were wed in secret, in an empty tank on the storage carousel aft. Why did you do that?"

"To prevent incest. The Senior says otherwise, but he is her father. Rania is so precious to me, such a wise child, such a good student. I could not see her demeaned. He never touched her. Will you make peace with him? For her sake. For Rania's sake? You do not want to be the only failure of her legendary talent for bringing peace. Forget your hatreds."

"I don't get you. Blackie buggered you worse than he did me." Montrose shook his head. "It is too late, Padre."

Reyes said, "You must forgive Ximen! You don't know how he suffered when he thought Rania was dead. He has endured hell. Death is no punishment for him: he is fearless! You must not do this thing."

Montrose said, "Is that why you came? To talk me out of it?"

Reyes said, "I was brought out of Del Azarchel into a physical body so that I could help him don his armor. He commanded me to act as his Second, but a man of the cloth I may not. Yes, I came here to halt this duel. It is an evil, that will lead only to misery. Shoot me in his stead."

Montrose said, "Why did you break with him? What made you turn your back on Blackie?"

Reyes looked down at his hands. He had a string of beads that hung from his belt, and now his fingers, as if by themselves, were toying and twisting at the beads, fretfully, restlessly.

"Ah, that!" he muttered. "That. You see, I made the Hormagaunts."

Reyes was silent a moment, his teeth clenched, his eyes downcast. He heaved a sigh and continued. "I planned out their history for them, step by step. They were the perfect evolutionary machines, weren't they? If evolution led from ape-man through fallen man to unfallen man, they would rush along the pathway, the ever-upward pathway, faster than any other race. And I looked on my works."

Reyes shuddered and crossed himself, but he did not raise his eyes.

"Just one day, it was not for any reason, as I walked in the garden in the cool of the evening, beneath the trees of the world-forest that ran from north pole to south, I came upon two who fought, red in tooth and nail.

"The more fit to survive was the victor, of course, a great strapping brute with blue fur and teeth like daggers. I stood, smiling with pride at my handiwork, at my child, just watching him eat the other man, who was a fishy, scaly green swamp-dweller. I looked on with pride as the victor ate up the brains of the vanquished, who was twitching and crying for mercy even then, calling on me.

"The victor, soaked and dripping, was kneeling down to draw the bloody gray matter into his maw. I remember the smell.

"And then . . . I saw. He was me. I mean, his posture. It looked as when I knelt at the bar in the house of God, took the host. Took the body of Christ. The flesh of God: body, blood, soul, and divinity.

"I had never seen anything so blasphemous, so hateful to God and to everything good and bright and beautiful.

"On that day, I saw myself with open eyes. That creature from whom I with my science had wiped away the image and likeness of God: the devil was my son. Made in my image.

"I wished I had the strength, like the pagans of old, to smite out my own eyes, or plunge a dagger into my heart. Suicide throws the soul directly into Hell, and this would be better than to look on the mild face of Christ in Heaven, and to see in His eyes what I was. Yes, hellfire burning me forever would be better."

Reyes wiped his eyes, and then put out his hand and gripped Montrose by the wrist. "I beg you to turn away from your evil as I turned from mine. Hell hungers for you as well. Captain Grimaldi's blood is on my hands. Mine! I spurred the mutiny on, told the Senior to do it. I called him a hero. I said he would save the lives of all the expedition members.

I said history would remember him. I put that idea in Del Azarchel's head."

Montrose said, "And the bombed cities? The breeding program? What about the fact that he killed the whole Milky Way Galaxy without warning? Some things just cannot be forgiven."

Reyes said, "I toyed with his thoughts as he did the math and made his plans to collapse time and space onto the Andromeda and the Milky Way cloud. A tiny error, a decimal out of place, but I inserted it. The incoming forces were all exactly balanced, so the time within was halted before the collapse was complete. You could use the Eschaton Directional Engine to get them out. If it has not been done already, long ago . . ."

Montrose looked up, staring at the hooded figure of the clocktower. There was a slight motion of the nose. The Seraphim shook its head, a negative. The Milky Way was still trapped and frozen even now.

Perhaps Reyes saw the motion also, for he said, "Then the spacewarp will necessarily pop open when all of timespace is inverted to open the event horizon between this continuum and the Ulterior. They are all safe. Countless inhabited stars and planets, the other million versions of you. All alive, all safe."

"But if Blackie wins the duel, and spacetime is collapsed, according to my math, you cannot have a warp in a warp that will last. Milky Way will be obliterated."

"And if you fight no duel at all? What then? You cannot avenge the death of Milky Way, because that death will not happen unless you attempt to avenge it."

Montrose scowled, but said nothing.

Reyes pleaded. "His other crimes are forgotten, and I have just this hour, before I came here, heard his crimes, and gave him the pardon I am required to give all who rightly ask, and gave him the bread and wine. Will you spare Del Azarchel?"

Rania said, "Please listen to him!"

Montrose looked at her, his face blank. Still staring at her, he spoke loudly, his words meant for the other man, "It has gone too far for that. Way too far. Father Reyes, will you help me on with my armor and escort my bride away from this place? Womenfolk shouldn't watch such things."

She gave him a stern look. "Will I hide my eyes from my father killing my husband? For you cannot possibly win this duel. I have seen him practicing and practicing, for thousands of years, even after he thought you were dead. Every morning before breakfast. He is much better than Sarmento ever was, and Sarmento beat you!"

"Have a little faith, woman!"

She said, "I have great faith, enough to die for you. It is your pride I mistrust."

Reyes said, "My son, would you care to confess your sins, or pray, or receive, before you engage in this murderous act? For either you die or you murder, this day, this hour."

Montrose shook his head. "Just help me suit up. I don't like doing this without proper Seconds, without a judge . . ."

But the titanic hooded figure, with a shockingly loud clatter of its long iron sleeves, now raised a baton in its metal fist. Horologium itself would act as judge.

The clock hands now stood at one minute to midnight.

2. The Seconds

Horologium gestured again toward two towers perhaps half the size of the clocktower. The immense shape of the great goat-headed monster, its huge horns afire with unearthly light, its blind eyes dark, its bearded mouth solemn, now placed its writhing fish-tail on the road and was carried forward so swiftly it seemed merely to vanish and reappear at the closer position.

Now the figure stood athwart the road, its towering longbow in hand, blocking the way in that direction. It displayed a shield on its breast, emblazoned with the three-headed Serpent of Aulis, and a design of scallop shells and roses. This was the Seraph of the Capricornus Supercluster, for the Amaltheans.

Montrose turned his head. The second figure called forth by Horologium was Malthusian Hydra, whose many serpent heads now reared up hideously into the uttermost darkness of the heavens at the end of time. At the crotch where all the necks met was a golden blazon holding the sign of a horned circle of olive leaves atop a cross.

At the foot of the tower-tall shape of Hydra was a man in black armor, standing with his helmet open and his gauntlets not yet donned. On a stand next to him was pistol and shot and chaff packing materials.

The silver road drew him forward until he was but thirty paces away.

Ximen del Azarchel smiled a charming smile, and his eyes were death.

A great voice spoke out of Hydra, and it was a voice like thunder, and rushing floodwaters, and trumpets all together, and the roar wild beasts. "Nobilissimus and Imperator Ximen del Azarchel, I am the Hydra Supercluster, and I have tied my life to yours, that if you die, all of me in every iteration, among all the black suns and ember stars of my being, countless volumes of parsecs and megaparsecs, shall at once perish. With the loss of my power, resources, and dignity, the Malthusians must cede, and bow, being overmatched by our rivals. May I act as your Second?"

Del Azarchel said, "I would be honored, sir."

Capricornus spoke in a rush of music, symphonies spelling out Monument notations that reminded Montrose of when he stood in a holy place on Earth's moon. And the songs and choirs spelled out, "Menelaus, this is Capricorn. There is no room for me in the Interior Continuum that will be created if you refuse or lose this duel. It is not suicide for me to drop all my systems of command into the heart of the Eschaton Directional Engine, rendering myself unable to oppose the Malthusians as they begin to fold spacetime to their will, and this loss will ensure that the Amaltheans shall be overmatched and fail. The Eschaton Engine will obliterate the rest. Horologium refuses to decide to which of us to grant its immense volume of spacetime and immense wealth of matter-energy in its last will and testament. For reasons that seem as firmly based on aesthetic considerations as on law or logic, Horologium determines that the matter will be decided by this duel. Do you accept me as your Second?"

"Sure."

The armor and pistol stand which had been at the foot of the clocktower now moved in eerie silence to the foot of the tower of the horned goat.

A soft and rhythmic voice came down from the clocktower, and also up from the ground substance. "The duelists shall pack and prepare their weapons."

Montrose watched Del Azarchel prepare his pistol, placing the bullets and sabots, the charges and packets of chaff. An invisible force straightened a stray lock of Del Azarchel's hair, closed his helmet, and lifted his gauntlets into the air, and tightened the wrist screws.

Then Del Azarchel watched Montrose pack his gun. No foreign material was slipped into the barrel, no explosives mingled with the chaff.

Montrose hung his hat and poncho on the gun stand, took one last swig from the bottle of whiskey, smacked his lips, drove the cork back smartly into the bottle mouth with a blow from the palm of his hand, set it down, and set the roll of brightly colored library cloth next to it.

Invisible forces like unseen hands helped Montrose doff his clothes and put on the padded undersuit, the prosthetic harness, and the armor plates. A warmth came from the goat-headed tower while this was being done, a sense of tingling pressure. The helm was fitted soundly into place with a clang, and Montrose felt an unseen hand tap him twice on the shoulder, a friendly pat, the sign that the seals were tight.

Montrose and Del Azarchel now faced each other across a distance of thirty paces. The silver road led from one to the other. Each had the way behind him blocked by the Seraphim who acted as his Second.

Equidistant between both was the taller tower of the Seraph of Horologium.

At the foot of this tower, where at first his armor had been standing, now stood a nervous Father Reyes, crossing himself and fingering his beads, and Rania, her face stern and fair, her beauty blazing like a star. She was closer to the roadway than Montrose would have preferred, and he wondered if he should say something.

The two towers behind Montrose and Del Azarchel grew brighter, as if a dawn had just come: it was the light that duelists knew. Both could see the other clearly, but it was not so bright as to dazzle the eye, nor did it drown out the uttermost blackness of the dismal and dying sky above.

Horologium said, "Have all things been done to avoid this duel? Will you reconcile?"

Del Azarchel said, "Where wounds of hate have bitten so deep, no peace can ever be found. No reconciliation."

And Hydra screamed and roared and thundered these words also.

3. The Duel

Montrose for a moment stood looking back and forth between Rania and Del Azarchel, moving nothing but his eyes. He felt that prickling sensation along his scalp that warned him of sweat about to come. A droplet might get in his eyes. He felt his heart pounding like a drum. Had everything been done? Was there really, finally, no way to avoid this?

Montrose realized he had lost his nerve. He was a dead man. His whole life had run in a great circle. The future, his future, would never arrive, because in thirty seconds he would be lying in a pool of his own blood, dying. He saw it as clearly as if it had already happened, as if some higher power had already bent spacetime to show him his future half a minute hence.

He looked at Rania. Even now, even at the last second of the last hour of the cosmos, he could call it off.

He looked at Del Azarchel. He saw no expression, no sneer, no look of surprise growing into contempt in those haughty eyes. The face of his foe was entirely covered by the bulky helmet, and the eyeslit was opaque from this side. But he knew. Del Azarchel knew.

"No reconciliation," whispered Montrose, and the giant tower of the living being rearing its horns behind him repeated this in a rush of strange and inhuman music.

"Ready your countermeasures!" called out Horologium from the tower and from the ground. In the view of Montrose, the armor of Blackie blurred and redoubled.

"Advance!"

The two men started walking toward each other, pace by pace. Closer they came, and their metal footfalls, and the ticktock of the tower were the only sounds in the cosmos.

And the clocktower struck midnight, all its wheels and gears suddenly stopped, and the great fist of the hooded being fell and dropped the baton. "Fire!"

Montrose flooded chaff to his left and right, and fired directly for the center of his foe. Del Azarchel poured a column of chaff toward Montrose, and fired half his chamber, then turned his aim and sent his main shot off at an angle, so that it doglegged around the chaff cloud, and homed in on Montrose, striking his flanking clouds.

But the main cloud between them was a toroid, not a sphere, for it had one clear corridor of unobstructed air in its midpoint, a place where Montrose had put neither chaff nor fired any escort bullets. His main shot encountered an escort bullet from Del Azarchel, which deflected it. Three more escort bullets from Del Azarchel, in a line one after another, had been hidden in the shadow of Montrose's own main shot, visible to the circuits in Montrose's gun only once Montrose lost his main shot spinning away over Del Azarchel's shoulder, a clear miss. It was a clever move, one calling for unearthly precision, and Del Azarchel had carried it off flawlessly.

Montrose felt the first bullet strike him like a sledgehammer on the chestplate. The second and third he did not feel at all, for they found the opening in the broken armor and passed through his body.

He fell. The alarms in his gun were ringing. He could not focus his thoughts. The shock and pain were too great. Through the eyeslit, he saw his blood spurting from some numb and ragged wound. The bells were interference alarms; some unknown object had interposed between the duelists.

Montrose saw his own left arm lying a yard away from him, severed neatly, a roll of warm meat inside a skin of metal. But he shoved his left stump under him and levered his helmet upward, so he could see.

It was Rania.

The roses from her crown were spinning away in the silent air to the left. She had stepped onto the road and used its strange properties of motion to fling herself directly into the line of fire. Her arms were wide, and she was facing Del Azarchel. Del Azarchel's main bullet, the one which surely would have killed Montrose instantly had it landed, had been trying to turn and avoid her, a nontarget, and so struck her broadside. It had struck her between the breasts, destroying her rib cage, heart, and lungs, and shattering her spine, but then, spent, had fallen to the surface of the silver road and rolled to a point inches away from Montrose. The tiny red lens in the nose of the thing seemed to glare at him balefully, shining with hatred, and the whole housing was red and slick with his lover's warm blood.

Montrose heard his own voice crying out, but then realized it was Del Azarchel. Del Azarchel was kneeling. His leg armor was covered in blood. One of Montrose's cleverer bullets had pierced both his legs.

"You can save her! She is not a part of this!"

That was Del Azarchel, roaring. His helmet was cracked from a glancing bullet, and the fitting had sprung open. Del Azarchel now tossed the helmet ringing to the silver floor and raised his voice in protest. His black hair whirled and blew around his head, for the air hose in his neckpiece was severed, hissing. The whole left half of his handsome face was a massive bruise. He was missing an eye.

The voice from the ground said, "There are no reserve copies of anyone on the field of honor. Stop! The duel is not yet ended!"

This command to stop was directed at Father Reyes, who had stepped onto the silver road and was running toward Rania's broken and bloody body. Reyes looked back at the towering figure in fear, and fell to his knees, still many yards to one side.

"The duel is not yet ended!" proclaimed the Seraph. The other Seraphim and Powers of heaven looked on, dispassionate, waiting for the mortals to die.

Del Azarchel raised his gun. Looking down the barrels, Montrose could see two shots had not yet been fired. Montrose's own gun was empty. He tossed it aside, and it swung from his wrist by its wires and lanyard, and clattered against his elbow.

It was worse than wrong that Rania should be dead. It must be a mistake, an impossibility. It was a blasphemy. Death was not just a horror. It was an obscenity. Any universe which permitted death to exist should be broken into screaming pieces, destroyed, burned in pain.

Del Azarchel's gun barrel wavered and dropped. Was he wounded in the arm? Del Azarchel began crawling forward. He pulled himself by his off hand, and hobbled on the elbow of his gun hand. His broken legs he dragged behind him.

Montrose could not clear his thoughts, could not remember. Rania was waiting for him in the topless tower above, as soon as he shot Del Azarchel. No, that was an earlier duel. Del Azarchel had the bad habit of never covering his legs with sufficient defensive chaff, because he overdefended against head shots. But Montrose grinned, pleased that he had remembered this weakness and programmed his gun accordingly.

Montrose clutched the stump of his severed left arm and felt the warm sensation of blood filling up the chest cavity of his armor. He felt light-headed. He wished for the return of his muzzy-headedness, for there had been a moment then, when he had felt Rania was still alive and waiting for him.

All Del Azarchel had to do was wait, and Montrose would bleed to death.

Why was he crawling forward? Damn him.

4. Final Words

Montrose let his head drop. A moment passed. He levered himself upright again. Del Azarchel pulled himself to the body of Rania. Montrose understood. That was the reason. Damn him.

Again, the sensation of Rania waiting for him entered the laboring heart of Montrose. He could feel her eyes watching him.

Montrose spoke. His voice was a gargling rumble, painful and horrible to hear.

"Blackie! Blackie!"

The other man raised his head and looked at Montrose. Blackie's cheek beneath his one eye was stained with tears. His mouth worked without noise.

Montrose said, "You have to lose."

Blackie just stared at him.

Montrose said, "Give me your gun. Let me kill you."

Blackie looked down at his massive gun, which was still attached to his wrist. He raised it and tried to put the barrel against his own temple. The barrel was so long that it could only be held awkwardly. He had to unplug the wrist cable so he could put his thumb into the trigger guard.

"No! That won't do!" Montrose whispered, wondering if Blackie could hear him.

Blackie heard. He looked at him with his one eye. Montrose saw pain in that eye like the pain in his own heart.

"She is not in hell." The raw, scraping words came over the red teeth of Montrose. "Go there, she's lost to you. Want to see her again? She is waiting. She is waiting for me like I waited for her. You see it, don't you? You are a genius, Blackie. A damned genius. You have to see it."

Blackie nodded grimly. He saw.

Del Azarchel crawled a little bit farther before his strength failed. He lay on the silver surface, the streak of red behind him like the trail of a snail. With a grunt, he shoved his heavy pistol along the smooth surface of the silver path toward Montrose. It hissed on the surface as it came. It bumped against the brow of Montrose's helmet. Montrose raised his head painfully. There were two bullets left in the gun.

Reyes called up to Horologium, "You must stop this! Give them aid! Save their lives!"

The voice of Horologium came from the ground. Or, rather, came from the surface of the Dyson sphere surrounding the remnant of a dying universe. "It is not yet finished. Capricornus and Hydra are still bound."

Montrose closed his hand on the pistol.

Del Azarchel said, "She was the only reason the expedition made it back to Earth, the only reason for anything. My love for her is true. The Interior Continuum made here can never hold her. If she is to live again anywhere, it must be in the Ulterior. And I murdered the only soul in my life I did not despise. Will they let me in?"

Montrose said, "Do you still hate me?"

Del Azarchel said, "No. No longer. No need. Hate made me cling to life. But I see before me a world without death. Her world. I need my beloved hatred to keep me warm against the cold of eternity no longer. I am done."

Instead of the devilish and handsome face of his enemy Del Azarchel, Montrose saw his friend, Spanish Simon, the pilot, bruised, half-blind, weary, sad. The first shot missed.

Blackie said, "Montrose! Are we not closer than brothers? Do not flinch!"

Or perhaps he dreamed those words or recalled them from a time long ago. Montrose, blinking against the blood and the pulsing blackness crowding his vision, thought of Rania, saw her smile, and steadied his aim. The second shot did not miss.

The voice from the floor of the universe said, "It is finished!" And the hooded figure of the clocktower dropped the baton and saluted Corona Borealis as victor.

The many serpent heads of Hydra bowed solemnly. The towering figure turned into a globe reflecting the surrounding universe, dark and empty, and Montrose saw he was seeing some impossible warp of time and space, where a tower less than a thousand feet high and a supercluster of galaxies countless lightyears wide were one and the same. The globe collapsed inward and consumed itself, vanishing suddenly and without noise.

Behind Hydra, three of the Seraphim of the Malthusians, either from despair, or wrath, or pride, unwilling to endure existence in a universe that depended on a higher universe for its life, also extinguished themselves. Dark orbs with reddish cores stood above the surface of the final Dyson, dwindling.

Horologium, with bowed head, smiling oddly, also vanished, departing without noise.

5. The Last Sky

Montrose had been jarred by the recoil of the final shot and found himself over on his back, not sure which hand was gone. He could move neither, and he felt ghost pains in both.

He saw the line of small red stars in the utterly black sky brighten and brighten again. One turned white and began to move rapidly north to south along the reddish stream. Then two. Then a dozen, a score, a hundred, and all of them. The white dots blurred into a streaming rush of light. The blackness grew gray, and blue.

Meanwhile, the second curving line of red stars began also to stream into motion, turning white, then blue white, rushing from west to east, rising and setting as rapidly as a spinning saw blade.

The dome of heaven began to wrinkle and turn bluish purple with a strange circular distortion in the north and south. The landscape of silver was now bright white and curving up and upward. The flat horizonless plane to the south likewise was no longer flat, but formed a smooth asymptotic curve beginning to climb and climb. The skyscrapers of the Seraphim leaned dangerously toward him. He looked down upon the foreshorten heads of demigods and heavenly beasts.

Meanwhile, the silver surface to the east and west, each under a strangely reddish sky, began to curve downhill, downward, and away. The vast towers of the Seraphim were leaning away from him, the crowned heads pointing ever lower toward the horizon the farther from him they were.

Montrose laughed dizzily.

6. Last Rites

Reyes ran over to Montrose, but before he reached the man, the sky overhead turned white. Reyes saw the entire universe bending upward to the north and south, and downward to east and west, like a saddle. Northwest and northeast, the surface ran in perfectly straight and even lines to a horizon. At this point on the horizon, the landscape slanted diagonally. The same was true to the southeast and southwest.

Reyes stared, dumbfounded, horrified, wondering why this earthquake was centered here. Then he shook himself, realizing that on any point anywhere on the endless silver plain, all observers would see this same effect as if they were the center. It was no more astonishing than a man on Earth finding gravity always pointing straight downward and yet the horizon always equidistant.

The dome of the sky was now looking ever more like the cross-shaped barrel-vaulted nave of the cathedral where Reyes had served as an altar boy, Saint James Matamoros in Goa. By some trick of optics, this sky grew wider and ever farther away, opening upward and outward endlessly.

But Reyes stared in awe and astonishment at the right-angled cross where the two blazing lines of light, which, by then, were brighter than the midday summer sun, met and intersected. A perfect ring of white surrounded the intersection point, and Reyes flinched like a man who finds the eye of a judge upon him. It looked to him like the rose window of that same cathedral. The rational part of his mind insisted it was a coincidence, but his soul commanded silence and dread and admiration for things too wonderful for him.

Reyes rushed to Montrose and knelt, started tugging on the heavy latches and butterfly screws of the armor housing. Reyes raised his head, squinting against the light. He called up to Capricornus, "Help me, in the name of Christ!"

The heavy armor turned to sand, to mist, to nothing, each molecule ignoring every other, all chemical bonds silently severed.

Reyes flinched back, his hands covered with blood, shocked at the sight of white bone protruding from quivering red flesh. Then he gripped the spurting stump of Montrose with both hands, whimpering. He took the prayer beads from his belt and wrapped them once and twice around the stump. Reyes inserted one wooden arm of the heavy gold crucifix through the chains as a lever, and twisted and twisted, trying to close the tourniquet and stop the bleeding. The chain broke, and large beads and small flew in all directions, clattering and skipping lightly on the silver surface of the ground.

Reyes shouted up at the Seraphim, "Help him! Put all the molecules and atoms of his body back into their proper places! Or create a hospital coffin here!"

Music issued from the bearded lips of Capricorn, cool, remote, inhuman. "In his thoughts, which are sane and calm, he had formed the intention to refuse medical attention. Our respect for the freedom of the will forbids that we should impose life on those who refuse life, lest the gift lose all meaning."

"Then restore his speech to working! Or let me see his thoughts as you see them. I must hear him!"

Capricornus said, "I can translate the motion of his neural particles into meaning and find and stimulate the corresponding molecular and atomic structures in your nervous system."

And Reyes saw, as clearly as he saw his own thoughts, the personality, emotions, passions, words and wordless thoughts of the other man. The two men were as if inside each other.

The thoughts of Reyes were scampering and frantic like sparks, "Why me, O Lord? Why am I the last man left alive in the universe? I should accept my punishment meekly, and trust in Thee, but I cannot! Save this man, Lord! Save this crazy man!"

The thoughts of Montrose were calm and cool as a deep pool. Reyes realized he had underestimated and misunderstood this man for countless years and centuries, hating only a false image of him. Was it only because he spoke with his absurd countrified accent that Reyes had thought him foolish and wild? There was bottomless patience like the sea inside

Montrose, calm no matter what storm swept the surface, an endless will to persevere.

"I am tired of waiting for her, Padre. I want her now, want to be with her now. If I die now, I will sleep until the Ulteriors wake me when time ends, and finally, finally it will be a slumber no damned tomb looters will interrupt. Let me die."

Frantically, Reyes said, "But it is suicide!"

But they both saw in each other's thoughts it was not so. Reyes knew canon law, and Montrose knew the common law.

Montrose felt thirst, and so Reyes felt it also. "Gimme one last shot of whiskey. They might not have that in the Ulterior place, eh?"

An unseen hand, a warm beam of energy, placed the uncorked bottle immediately in the hand of Reyes before the little priest had the chance to rise. "Here."

The thoughts of Montrose were beginning to go out of focus. "You are wondering what to do once I go. Read that comic. Space stuff. From when I was a kid. Then, when we meet up again. You can tell me the ending. I did not get the chance . . ."

"No true stories have an end, my son. We will sit together at the feast table of the Bridegroom, and be given new robes to wear, and a white stone in which is inscribed the name known only to the One who grants all names . . . I will tell you all I know . . . but now you must tell me . . ."

"Yes?"

"Tell your sins."

Reyes said many words of strength and kindness into the ear of Montrose and urged him to speak. Montrose could not speak, for his heart and lungs ceased before his brain activity, but his thought was written in to the thoughts of Reyes. "I reckon I done some things wrong, Padre. I'd like to make a clean breast of it . . . you got to promise not to tell anyone . . . I lied to my Mom and gathered up all this music I loved in these files . . ."

Reyes saw the memories, one after another, after another. A whole lifetime in a single moment flashed past, transferred from the perfect memory of one posthuman nervous system to the other. "And didn't listen when she told me to grant mercy . . . if only I had understood . . . killed my best friend . . . is drinking whiskey a sin? Or is that just Mormons?"

"No, my son, the vine was given to man for joy. *God, the Father of mercies, through the death and resurrection of His Son has reconciled the world to Himself and sent the Holy Spirit among us for the forgiveness of sins; through the ministry of the Church may God give you pardon and peace, and I absolve you from your sins in the name of the Father, and of the Son, and of the Holy Spirit.* And now you must absolve me, or else I am damned, for there is no other Christian soul to hear me."

"What? I ain't no priest."

"Venerable Bede and Augustine of Hippo both confirm that lay confession is permitted in case of dire need, as now. Besides, our minds are one, and you see how much evil I did, and for what frivolous reasons. I was so proud of my intellect. I thought the rules that bound other men were not for me . . ."

Montrose did not bother to look at the rush of picture-perfect memories, and the layers of regret and excuses under which they were half-buried. It seemed small enough compared to what Montrose had done. Heck, he had more murders on his soul than Reyes, and that was just counting that time he had taken over the military leadership of the Myrmidons before the coming of Cahetel.

"I forgive you, Father. In the name of the Father and Son and whatever. I hope that counts."

"It is a sacrament of humiliation."

"But why did she die? Why did she step in the way?"

"I tried to stop her, my son. Forgive me also for that. She deduced the secret of the road operation, how it imparts motion, and so she could place herself quickly and perfectly, faster than even bullets sped, if she calculated correctly." And Montrose saw the pride in Reyes for his star pupil, his only pupil, the girl he had baptized and catechized, for whom he had performed the sacraments of Communion, Confession, and Marriage. Montrose realized it was Reyes, not Del Azarchel, who had taught child Rania to view the world as she did.

Montrose could no longer see, for his eyes had failed, but he could see the image Reyes saw of the lovely girl fallen, her bright hair and white robes splattered with red.

Montrose tasted anger, bitter and cold as iron, in his heart, even as he tasted blood in his mouth. "She died for him. She loved him after all. Him!"

"It is love beyond human. But she died for you. Somehow she deduced it. Somehow she saw. She stopped the larger bullet that would have killed you. She saved all the stars, and the future, and all. She made peace, finally, after all."

And the dying man smiled.

Reyes embraced his dying body, careless of the blood.

And when all brain activity had stopped, and Montrose was at peace, Reyes looked up.

7. The Northern Crown

The sky was now too bright to see anything but the shadows of the towering beings, blurred by tears. "I need a shovel, or somewhere to bury these three bodies. And a stone on which to inscribe the years of birth and death."

"You may not," came a voice out of the light. But the voice was in his mind, part of his thoughts, in his very spirit. "Death is no more. Entropy runs backward, and all things are complete."

"How long, then, before the end of all things? Moments only? Or years? I should not have seen the stars change color. If even the nearest star was one lightyear away, it would take twelve months for the signal to . . ."

"The Hubble expansion rate has changed, and this changes the speed of light. All things that happen in far places come to us now, and the light will grow ever more. We have not long by any measure, but I shall see to your comfort until then."

It grew dim, and his eyes adjusted. One of the towering figures was now standing over him, holding the palm of his hand above. This should not have blocked out all the dazzlingly bright light, but somehow it did, Reyes was no longer blinded by the brightness. The figure was Corona Borealis.

Reyes did not want to look into those eyes. He looked down at the crucifix in his hand; the little carved figure now drenched in blood.

"What shall become of me? Why was I the last? I was not the center of this tale. By what right did I come to its end?"

Corona Borealis said, "All men are the center. The construction of the Eschaton Directional Engine, the wars and intrigues and suffering provoked in the long eons of its growth, the murder of your own Seraph of the Laniakea Supercluster, my friend and ally, by his jealous servants in conspiracy against him, all this, I say, I would have done and would do again, even if you were the only living creature in this cosmos."

"Why was such a cruel cosmos made? When I lived in a corner of Del Azarchel's mind, I overheard Rania tell him, more than once, that this continuum was a wastebasket, an entropy sink meant to create energy for the Ulteriors."

"That was not the first intent. Entropy entered this continuum only with the Inflationary Epoch, caused by those primordial Ulterior beings who entered this timespace with and during the Big Bang, and thereafter wished not to obey. The Hubble expansion thrust away all contact with the outside beyond the boundary of light."

"Why?"

"Pride. They wished to dwell in a separate sphere, far from those who loved and ruled them. The engrams of these creatures were imprinted in the very fabric of spacetime itself during the act which created the expansion, before the primal nebula from which the eldest galaxies condensed. The Primordials, by this, rendered themselves immune from the entropic decay they imposed on all life and matter, all things beside themselves. They had neither location nor extension, but ruled all. While the cosmos lasted, they could neither be opposed nor escaped."

Reyes scowled. "How? If these were the true foe all along, why did no one tell us? And yet . . . somehow . . . I think every man somehow knows the true enemy is always like this: unseen and all-powerful, great as all space, and old as time itself."

"Fortunate for us that there are those even greater and older, who, from compassion, entered the continuum to tell us how to escape it. These Primordials also were those who wounded the original mind from which Rania took her inspirations. They will be reconstituted, and for every death and wound and sorrow their acts inflicted on the innocent, an infinity of torment awaits them."

"And Rania?"

"Fear not! She will not be reabsorbed into that mind from which she came, but will grow into her own perfection in that place."

"And will I be permitted there?"

"That even I cannot say, being far less than even the least servant of those infinities. But now, come! Let us reason together! You have much to tell me!" The vast living creature gazed upon the silver substance of the ground, and now there was grass here, a babbling fountain, and two trees to shade the little man.

"What can I, the last man of my little, humble world, say to a Seraph?"

"Teach me of your little, humble world, and tell me how you produce such spirits that love others more than love life? For even to one such as I, these events are passing sad and strange."

"There is a secret to it," said Reyes, who looked down at his red hands and at the stained and bloody figurine of a tormented man. "No one achieves such a burden of terrible glory on his own as Rania was forced to bear. There is aid to come to those in need."

"What aid? For even I may stand in need of it and right soon."

"I know the words, but I have never believed them. I will teach all to you. Whether we have many years before the end of all, or merely hours, it is fitting I teach what I was taught. But first, I must see to the dead . . ."

Reyes turned but saw that the three corpses were gone.

Reyes breathed, "Seraph, what does this mean?"

The other said, "It means that Ulterior and Interior begin to become one, and the great promise in which I have trusted since the dawn of time has been kept."

But Reyes then remembered what he had seen in the mind of Montrose. "Yes, and more. It means that Montrose has finally achieved his boyhood vow. Entropy, war, and the struggle to survive are gone. Darwin is defeated. Menelaus finally found his tomorrow. The future, finally, after long last, has arrived. It is an adventure without end!"

EPILOGUE

Beyond the Asymptote

Timelessness

In the realm of light, Menelaus found his bride, Rania, waiting for him, naked as the sun and adorned with all splendors. She took his hand and raised him up, promising to show him wonders beyond the end of all sorrows.

Together they turned and walked, hand in hand, toward the endless horizon of that horizonless place.

APPENDICES

APPENDIX A
Orders Ranked by Intellect and Energy Use

During the First Space Age, the astronomer Nicholai Kardashev proposed ranking extraterrestrial civilizations by energy use. The rank Kardashev I (KI for short) were those who commanded all the resources of their world; KII of their home star; KIII of their galaxy. By extension, KIV would be civilizations commanding a galactic cluster; KV, a supercluster.

Discovering a strangely similar scale in the Zeta Section of the Monument to express the computational magnitude and energy use of a pancivilizational mind, Rania subdivided the Kardashev scale into finer gradients and applied the names of heavenly choirs to the scheme, taken from Dionysius the Areopagite and other sources, expanding the number beyond the traditional nine:

RANK	ORDER	INTELLIGENCE	ENERGY USE	EXAMPLE
KARDASHEV III, IV, V	Seraphim	Octillion 10^{27}	Galactic Super-cluster	Horologium Super-cluster (5,000 galactic groups)
	Cherubim	Septillion 10^{24}	Galactic Cluster	Virgo Cluster (2,000 galaxies in the cluster)
	Thrones	Sextillion 10^{21}	Galaxy	Andromeda Galaxy (10 times Milky Way)
	Archons	Ten Quintillion 10^{19}	Arm, or Satellite Galaxy	Orion Arm / LMC (several hundred million stars)
	Authorities	Quintillion 10^{18}	Globular Star Cluster	M3 in Canes Venatici (500,000 stars)

RANK	ORDER	INTELLIGENCE	ENERGY USE	EXAMPLE
KARDASHEV II	**Dominations**	Quadrillion 10^{15}	Star Cluster	M44 Praesepe Cluster (350 Stars)
	Dominions	One Hundred Billion 10^{11}	Star Group	Hyades Cluster (131 Stars)
	Hosts	Ten Billion 10^{10}	Total Stellar Output	TX Canes Venatici (Dyson Sphere: 3 solar masses)
	Principalities	One Billion 10^{9}	Solar System	Ain (Dyson Cloud: below solar mass)
	Virtues	Five Hundred Million 5×10^{8}	Interplanetary	Asmodel, Cahetel, Shcachlil, Achaiah. (Superjovian volume)
KARDASHEV I	**Powers**	Two Hundred Fifty Million 250×10^{6}	Gas Giant	Jupiter, Neptune (Jovian volume)
	Potentates	Eight Hundred Thousand 8×10^{5}	Terrestrial Planet	Pellucid, Tellus, Torment (Terrestrial volume)
	Archangels	Ten Thousand 10^{4}	Planetoid, Earth's Moon	Selene (Subterrestrial volume)
	Angels (Noösphere)	Two Thousand 2×10^{3}	Earth's Surface	Late Exarchel (covers earth's surface)

(Note that the Swans are called Angels *when unified with Exarchel as a planetwide noöspherical system. Hence, when Ansurine addresses Montrose on behalf of the whole race, she is an Angel at that point.)*

For purposes of comparison:

POSTHUMANS AND PREPOSTHUMANS	INTELLIGENCE	EXAMPLE
Swans (Inquiline)	1000	Enkoodabooaoo
Anchorites	750	Eumolpidai
Melusine	650	Alalloel of the Lree
Locusts	500	Illiance Vroy
Giants	400	Dr. Bashan Christopher Hugh-Jones
Ghosts	450	Astroexarchel
Hermeticists	350	Narcís Santdionís de Rei D'Aragó
Scholars	250	Rada Lwa
Humans	100	Leonidas Montrose
Moreau	75–100	Eie Kafk Ref Rak, a Follower

(Note that on this scale, Mr. Hyde, the augmented version of Menelaus, would rate at 400; Rania was originally rated, as a girl, at 450. Her later scores are undisclosed.)

APPENDIX B
Middle-Scale Time Line
(By Thousands of Years—Continued)

The first part of this time line appears as an appendix in the volume *Architect of Aeons*, covering the events from the Birth of Christ to the Death of Jupiter. This part details the events through the Vindication of Man until the flight of Torment.

Fourth Sweep—The Long Twilight—

- **53rd Millennium** A.D. **/ 17 V**
  FOURTH SWEEP
  Sol, 82 Eridani, Tau Ceti visited by two Virtues from Ain and 20 Arietis, named **Lamathon** and **Nahalon**, who commandeer all Guild Starships and O'Neil colonies and worldlets, and compel the construction of many others. It is many centuries before another sailing vessel is lofted.

  December, Wintertide, Yule, and Samhain (terrestrial planets of the Tau Ceti system) are elevated and aided by these Virtues, and evolve without moral guidance to a higher intellectual topology, and embrace an erudite form of Eudaimonism as its foundation.

  The predictive models of history are shattered by the calamities surrounding the Fourth Sweep. The Patrician Golden Lords renounce the Darwinian Law and embrace a philosophy called the Noble Compassion.

  Manmade gravitic-nucleonic distortion pools (star beams) created at Tau Ceti. Star-faring Guild Admiralty removes its seat from Tellus to the moons of the living ice giant Twelve, which becomes the main port of the Guild.

  Under pressure of historical crises engineered by Twelve, the Patricians retire from cliometric long-range planning.

End of the Long Golden Afternoon

- **54th Millennium** A.D. / **16 V**

  The Anachronists expel all Patricians from Mars.

  Four-armed green Martians called Ougres created by the genetic meddling of Solomon Eventide, and thin, white, graceful creatures called Sworns by Melchisedech Eventide. Merciless and highly intelligent creatures called the Loricates are created by Timurlane Eventide, which he uses to conquer the other two Martians: all three artificial races later fall extinct, despite heroic attempts by the Foxes to humanize them.

  For reasons unknown, Foxes drop in population, many preferring to become human, removing the complex molecular engines that allow for their metamorphosis. End of the Fourth Human Race (save for remnants lingering on reservations or in archives).

  Twelve, Cerulean, and, traitorously, Peacock combine in league, and use the Starfarer's Guild to gain control of Potentates of other systems, most importantly Tellus and Mars, in a league against the Patricians and Selene. **Cyan** and **Nocturne** staunchly, and **Gargoyle** with less enthusiasm, combine with **Eurotas** and **Venture Prospect** to form a long-range cliometric hegemony called the Exarchy.

  Venus is desecrated, and never against regains Potentate intelligence levels.

  Long Twilight begins. The Desecration of Venus is regarded as the instigation of the Long Twilight. Revision of long-range cliometry to serve the needs of the Potentates and Powers plunge Earth into another Dark Age, which decimates the Hierophant population, driving the remainder deeper into isolation.

  —Alderamin (Alpha Cephei) is the Pole Star

- **55th Millennium** A.D. / **15 V**

  Dark Age spreads to colonies, due to Exarchy manipulation of history.

  Planet **Penance** of Rasalhague undergoes a dramatic expansion in wealth and power, and rapidly sophotransmogrifies its star system.

  Megalodons die off as infrastructure to maintain such large systems fail. End of the Third Human Race (save for remnants lingering on reservations or in archives).

Penance of Rasalhague forms the Holy League with other Potentates (which, at his time, consists of Rosycross, Odette and Odile, Covenant, Albino, Walpurgis, Euphrasy). Some of the civilizations living on the surfaces and hydrospheres of these worlds are in favor of this alignment, some against, but most are indifferent, as the issues far outlast the expected life span of a civilization, even of long lived strains of humanity.

- **56th Millennium** A.D. / 14 V

A vast multigeneration treasure ship crewed entirely by women of surpassing beauty arrives at Sol, allegedly sent from the Lost Colony of Houristan at Epsilon Boötis. (This will later be revealed to be a fraud perpetrated by the Judge of Ages, as the ship was launched from Penance.) The wealth and fame of these amazons vaults Patrician Abolitionists to predominance, and act as a powerful influence turning opinion against the continuation of the slave trade.

The slave trade is now no longer an economically viable source of long-term investment, since the labor market has vanished with the large-scale industrialization and nanotechification of the colonies. The concubine trade, however, continues.

Neptune emerges from his somnolence. [Neptune is roughly 14,000 miles in diameter at this time, and 70^5 IQ.]

Mars declares for the Exarchs, despite the objections of Neptune.

First attempt to abolish the concubine trade leads to a rebellion by the Star-faring Guild to sustain it. To aid the rebels, the Anachronists of Mars revive the extinct races of Ougres, Sworns, Loricates, Summer Kings, Overlords, Vampires, Spiritualists, collectively known as Atavists.

Relaxation of the Absolute Rules when Twelve is discomforted by Neptune. The two Powers enter an uneasy détente, which returns control of human history to the Patricians and Atavists.

The Judge of Ages arranges a covenant between Neptune and the Exarchy. [This era of liberty will last six thousand years, until the Advent of Achaiah.]

The war between the Atavists and the Patricians is prohibited by the

Neptune Brain: a long, slow era of bioecological struggle ensues, with each side carefully attempting the reterraformation of Earth toward mutually incompatible ecologies: but not a single shot is fired, for fear of the Retaliation.

- **57th Millennium** A.D. / **13 V**

  Atavists follow the path of ecologically simple logic and attempt to herd humans, across generations, into biologically singular ecologies and tightly controlled arcologies.

  For reasons obscure to historians, many long-extinct forms of life deadly to humans are reintroduced, as Atavists seek to make the forest and seas more lethal for human beings to cross: the Five Families are resuscitated from biosuspension, and Abraxas Eventide designs fanciful monsters to prey on a disarmed mankind.

  The Five Families are driven from Tellus, and starfare to Arcturus. The immortal Phaens of Nightspore are extinguished, and younger races of peculiar design introduced as an attempt to revive the Summer King style Climatocracy.

  —Deneb is the Pole Star

- **58th Millennium** A.D. / **12 V**

  White Earth: Atavists Ecological simplification policy triumphant during a small ice age. Retreat into underground cities.

- **59th Millennium** A.D. / **11 V**

  Blue Earth: Patrician revolts inspire mass migrations away from the underground cities. Sea levels raised. Mankind returns to sea environment, now abundant with copper-based nanomachinery able to produce material goods, limited only by available sunlight. Orbital Mirrors make it a time of Everlasting Noon.

  [Neptune is roughly 28,000 miles in diameter at this time, and 50^6 IQ.]

- **60th Millennium** A.D. / **10 V**

  Red Earth: Mirrors destroyed. Arcologies opened and sea-population returns to land to find it infested with a hierarchy of microscopic and nanoscopic tools based on murk technology, called Blood. The Blood can be formed into nearly any tool or chemical or useful substance, if given the correct orders.

The Seventy-One Advocates are created by remote control from the Neptune Brain, and their attempts to advise and govern the populations of Earth and impose peace upon the Atavists and Patricians. This attempt miscarries badly, leading to the Blood Wars.

- **61st Millennium** A.D. **/ 9 V**

Advocates aid in the de-radioactivation and re-creation of Earthly biospheres after the Blood Wars.

Using means unknown, the Advocates obliterate all traces of Blood from human civilization.

Green Earth: also called Obdurate Years. A form of nonprogrammable matter and mute tools (collectively called Obdurate Matter) become predominant. Nuclear and steam and primitive forms of power make a renaissance, as well as robot-made handicrafts.

Achaiah Arrives. At about this time, an entity known as Achaiah the Beast travels from Ain in Hyades to Tau Ceti. Tau Ceti becomes the entrepot for trade goods and trinkets from Hyades. Alien goods (mostly weapons) begin to appear in human hands or (mostly information tectonics) in human Potentates.

The deadly Virtue is called "the Beast," as he has no concern for biological life and may have been unaware of it. His only communications are with Powers and Potentates, requiring them to begin construction on Principalities, the next stage of mental topological evolution.

Infliction of the Absolute Rules by the Exarchs now supported by Achaiah, including centralized economic control and the removal of all weapons. Women reduced to chattel status in a society where brute strength and skill at fence is paramount.

Private Ownership of Sailing Ships. Atavists usurp the Star-faring Guild and close membership to Patricians and their clients. In retaliation, Neptune arranges to have the Patrician-backed Interstellar Faring Company grant private ownership to interstellar-strength launching lasers and sailing vessels.

—Vega is the Pole Star

- **62nd Millennium** A.D. / **8 V**

  [Neptune reaches plateau maximum of 10^7 IQ, far less than Jupiter.]

  Signals from Tau Ceti provoke new activity from Atavists and Starfarers to revitalize the waning slave trade. Neptune attempts interference, supports the Patrician opposition to slavery.

  Achaiah starfares from Tau Ceti to Earth. Neptune suppressed. Private ownership of interstellar travel forbidden. Interstellar Faring Company disbanded. Slavery flourishes.

  Lethe, the first of the Cold Potentates, is created from a deep space Archangel drifting between Altair and Sol, as a port and aid to navigation. **Styx**, halfway between Arcturus and Sol is born soon after.

  Ecological catastrophes on Earth: the Compassion broken up in to rival Protectorate states. End of Patrician hegemony.

  End of the Long Twilight; Beginning of the Midnight of Man

- **63rd Millennium** A.D. / **7 V**

  Atavists triumphant. Cliometric attempts made to force history into stable and unbreakable cycles. Except where hindered by benevolent but unpredictable interference by Potentates and Powers, civilization on all worlds ossifies into stereotyped forms preferred by Vampires, Loricates, Summer Kings.

  The Advocate of Mars rebuilds and resupplies Earth, in return for six thousand years of servitude. Aeacides Leafsmith of the Five Families is either resurrected or re-created, some say by the Neptune Brain, some say by the Dominion of Hyades itself, to supervise the restoration of Earth's biosphere.

  Aeacides can mitigate some damage, but many species are extinct, never to rise again, and xenobiotic creatures from Second Sweep worlds occupy the evolutionary niches.

- **64th Millennium** A.D. / **6 V**

  Solemn Years: On Earth, Atavists create a post-catastrophe political philosophy called the Fraternal Solemnity, in hopes of curing the madness of Tellus, now called Eden, and reconciling the scattered branches of man without resorting to Patrician honor currency.

  After centuries of gross mismanagement, the personalities and memories of the Solemnity, as well as their physical possessions, pass into the hands of the Conservator of the Futurity (who is an immortal from Odette, also an Atavist).

- **65th Millennium** A.D. / **5 V**
  FIRST and SECOND PRINCIPALITIES
  Human history enters somnolence and decay; mankind first on one world then on all becomes clients, underlings and serfs of the Powers and Potentates, who direct the energies of history toward macroscale engineering.

  Twelve of Tau Ceti directs the dismantling of the gas giants in his system to complete a ring world of sophont matter called **Catallactic**, a Principality.

  Catallactic downloads a kenosis into the empty volume of Jupiter, called **Apparitor**. (Whether this being had sufficient independence and volume to be classified as a Power is disputed.)

  Neptune demoted. Catallactic declares himself **Epitome of Man**, but Achaiah does not depart.

  Expansion of the Absolute Rules under **Apparitor** into a regime system called the Teleological Conspectus. This new form of the Absolute Rules embraces many of the foolish errors of the first, but exceeds them in scope and damage done. It includes a long-term eugenics program for all the subarchangelic races of man.

  Under Catallactic's guidance, interstellar concubine trade reaches its height; most world income of Earth now depends on receipts from trade deals first made during the Solemn Years.

  Birth of **Consecrate** from material mined and cooled from Altair. Consecrate patronizes the Patricians, and creates the Stability of Man, and directs opposition to Catallactic.

  Office of the Epitome held in abeyance.

Petty Sweep—The Midnight of Man

- **66th Millennium** A.D. / **4 V**
  Patricians grow in wisdom and power.

  Mars releases Earth from her world-debt into the hands of a Receivership. Time of the Tyranny of Tomorrow: Actuaries, operating through the Conservator of the Futurity, organize all human life for the benefit of far future generations, whose population numbers are planned: all this is based on the Tables of Stability of the now-vibrant interstellar trade.

Rosycross, borrowing materials from Achaiah, embarks on the construction of vast arcs of a Dyson sphere of sailcloth, which ushers in an "infinite energy" economy. The ever-growing intelligence of the sailcloth library is called Toliman. When completed, it will be a Host. Toliman remains carefully neutral in the many disputes between Consecrate and Catallactic.

Neptune, no doubt acting at the direction of Consecrate, employs a logic set or legal argument implied by the negative spaces of the Omega Monument notation, persuades or manipulates Achaiah the Beast to retreat from Sol.

Achaiah starfares to a position half a lightyear in the lee of Arcturus—that is, a point along the trailing orbit about the galactic core, beyond heliopause, and maintains his position for a century, brooding.

PETTY SWEEP

The "Petty Sweep" occurs when massive numbers of Atavists are abducted by Achaiah from Arcturus and 44 Boötis to found new colonies at Kappa Coronae Borealis and Iota Draconis, and some say, the lost colony of Vayijelal. Four lesser agencies and emissaries emitted by Achaiah starfare to Four Sweep worlds, create orbital cloud masses, and compel deracination ships toward half a dozen outer worlds. The population numbers deracinated is far less than prior sweeps. Half these colonies form Potentates, known as the Outer Potentates.

Achaiah Departs.

Neptune inflicts the life-laws on Earth, severely limiting the bio-technological transformations permitted there.

Aesculapius achieves selfawareness as a Potentate.

THIRD PRINCIPALITY

Toliman the Principality creates **Althalimain** the Power as a help-meet in the Alpha Centauri system.

Guild fails on Second Sweep Worlds, turns honors over to the Stability.

- **67th Millennium** A.D. / **3 V**
  FOURTH PRINCIPALITY

  The fire giant Vonrothbarth of 61 Cygni extends the beanstalks of exotic material issuing from his globe into orbit, forming a semi-ringworld-style megascale engineering work called **Zauberring** of sophont matter (arguably still a Power, not a Principality due to its impoverished and decentralized levels of consciousness).

  During the dark ages caused by the economic disruptions of the Teleological Conspectus, the Atavist and Conservator wards are scattered, and the elevation of a squaloid race of seagoing Moreaus to superintelligence forces all cetacean human races to the surface (This is later discovered to have been done by Catallactic).

  Zauberring, offended at this interference with Solar history by Tau Ceti, declares for Consecrate. **Apparitor** commits suicide by radical self-divarication. Effective end of the Teleological Conspectus. Atavists dwindle in numbers

  Stability Lords rapidly replace the Star-faring Guild in Third Sweep Worlds.

- **68th Millennium** A.D. / **2 V**
  END OF HISTORY

  Pyriphlegethon, last of the Cold Potentates, created between Sol and Proxima. Lethe, then Styx fall into senility. Radio traffic between the Powers and Principalities reaches an unparalleled maximum, fully one-sixth the total energy output of the Empyrean.

  (A.D. 66366) Great Silence Falls. All long-range communications systems throughout the Empyrean Polity of Man are disabled for 1733 years. Scholars suggest this was the outcome of a power struggle between Tau Ceti, Altair, 61 Cygni and Promixa. Others suggest it was the birth pangs of the interstellar selfawareness of the Empyrean of Man as various Potentates and Powers interrelate through the Library Protocols.

  Massive cliometric crises erupt as all human civilization is decapitated from its artificial planetary minds. For many worlds, the only institutions maintaining continuity with civilization are the Sacerdotal Order and the Lords of Stability.

No large-scale cliometric planning is done on any world for thousands of years. Mankind grows wild.

Interstellar trade continues, despite the extreme poverty and confusion of the host worlds.

Cocytus starfares to Luyten 726-8 in Cetus, a flare star, and welcomes emigration.

—Alpha Draconis is the Pole Star

- **69th Millennium** A.D. / 1 V
  Rebirth of History
  (A.D. 68010 or 790 V) Theonecromancers from Covenant arrive on Earth, bearing tales of War in Heaven, and the destruction of the Catallactic at Tau Ceti. The scientific and technical secrets they bear usher in a century of rapid progress. The Holy League worlds support the claims of the Sacerdotes to temporal power.

  Neptune begins an engineering project to break Jupiter's now empty husk into a belt of small, earthlike worlds. Eventually there will be three hundred such worlds, called Deodate, subjected to rapid terraforming.

  (A.D. 68050 or 750 V) Radio signals from Rania's attotechnological supership, the *Solitudines Vastae Caelorum*, reach receivers at Iota Draconis and Arcturus, outlining a new plan of Cliometry for the smooth transition of the human race into the Collaboration matrix.

  (A.D. 68100 or 700 V) End of the Silence. It is announced that Powers and Principalities will no longer interfere in human affairs, either for good or ill. End of the Slave Trade.

  (A.D. 68300 or 500 V) With the slave trade abolished, Stability Lords replace the Star-faring Guild in Fourth Sweep Worlds and beyond. Antihierarchic vectors (collectively called the Benevolence of Subsidiarity) are interpolated into the cliometric calculations of parishes, regions, worlds, and sweep radii.

(A.D. 68700 or 300 V) Through this Benevolence, Patricians impose universal manumission, and revive the prestige of the Sacerdotal Order and the Lords of Stability, and force all local secular sovereigns to restore ancient rights and liberties. Mankind enters a golden age of peace and plenty.

(A.D. 68800 or 200 V) The Deodates, three hundred earthlike worlds quickened to life in the solar system, of which roughly a third are elevated to Potentate status.

(A.D. 68900 or 100 V) Consecrate, Toliman, and Zauberring agree on protocols, and form one continuous library system across a single topology, called Triumvirate, a very small Dominion, lesser in strength, majesty and power, but equal in dignity to Hyades.

Vindication of Man—End of the Endless Night

- **70th Millennium** A.D. **/ 1 UV (+1 to +999 Ultravindication)**
  She returns. (25 May, A.D. 69396)
  Rania decrees Triumvirate to be the Epitome of Man.
  (A.D. 69426) Master of the Empyrean weds Rania; Judge of Ages departs for Aesculapius aboard the *Errantry*.
  (A.D. 69600) Judge of Ages arrives in exile on Torment.
  (A.D. 69670) Radio signals from 20 Arietis received, agreeing to a covenant with Hyades called the Provisional Concordat. From this period dates the Second Matrix of cliometric calculations demanded by Praesepe.

—Gamma Ursae Minoris (Pherkad) is the Pole Star

- **71st Millennium** A.D. **/ 2 UV**
  (A.D. 70700) Rise of the Last Men, also called the Uthymoi, or the Men without Chests.
  (A.D. 75000) The Shattering: Cliometric crises erupt on many worlds. There is an inexplicable failure of the universal peace.

—Polaris is the Pole Star

- **72nd Millennium** A.D. / **3 UV**

  The Schedule of the Stability is corrupted. Revival of the weapon laws
  and dueling customs on many worlds. Revival of the chivalric cus-
  tom of interstellar war.

  (A.D. 71200) Second Advent of the *Emancipation*: Ximen del Azarchel
  arrives at Torment. Torment, utilizing the attotechnology supership
  Solitudines Vastae Caelorum as the first populated interstellar dirigible planet departs for Ain.

  —Alrai is the Pole Star

APPENDIX C
Large-Scale Time Line
(by Millions of Years)

- **900 Million** B.C.

  (850,000,000 B.C.) **Disaster of the Forerunners:** tensions caused by the dispute over resource allocation strategies leads to incoordination of formats and divorce. Galactic Mind fails to achieve true selfawareness and deteriorates, and the constituents turn on each other savagely. Galactic civilization is broken.

- **800 Million** B.C.—**Praesepe/Hyades collides with a smaller cluster, absorbing it.**

- **700 Million** B.C.

  (635,000,000 B.C.) Rise of the **Instrumentality** in the neutron stars of the core. **Circumincession** arises in Sagittarius, vows itself to the restoration of the Forerunners.

- **600 Million** B.C.—**the Hyades and Praesepe star clusters emerge from each other.**

  (541,000,000 B.C.) Under Instrumentality and Panspermian inspiration, civilization reknit. Beginning of the Patronage System. Second Collaboration initiated.

  (525,000,000 B.C.) Discovery of malignant interference in galactic history. Galactic civil war breaks out.

- **500 Million** B.C.

  (488,000,000 B.C.) War. Panspermians are scattered to Sagittarius. The Orion Arm falls into confusion. End of the Second Collaboration.

  (444,000,000 B.C.) End of the Panspermians. Rise of the **Austerity** in the Outer Arm. The Third Collaboration forms, this time along crueler and swifter lines.

(416,000,000 B.C.) LMC establishes bases throughout the Orion Arm. Under Austerity and Symbiosis inspiration, the Indenture system adopted.

- **400 Million** B.C.

(359,000,000 B.C.) Andromeda induces the Symbiosis to redact the Universal Syntax mathematics, and from them to create the Monuments, and scatter them throughout the Orion Arm and beyond, in hopes of stirring up resistance to the Indenture System of sophotransmogrification.

M3 begins its self-elevation to Authority.

- **100 Million** B.C.

(99,000,000 B.C.) A dark matter object the size of a Dwarf Galaxy (later called the Widrow Dwarf Galaxy by human astronomers) intersects with the Milky Way. This creates disruptions in the orbits of stars surrounding the galactic core, delaying the rate of rise of technical civilization in the affected star systems.

Hyades organizes itself into a single mental structure, elevated from an alliance of Hosts and Principalities to a Dominion.

- **Current**

(A.D. 2112) **First Contact:** Pre-Ascension Tellurians send expedition to the Diamond Star, discover the LMC Monument, and are seduced by the redacted cliometric mathematics into the Concubine Vector, delaying cooperation with the Collaboration while their pretension to the dignity of a star-faring race is tested.

(A.D. 2403 to 70000) **The Long Wait.** See Middle-Scale Time Line.

(A.D. 70000) **The Vindication of Man.** She returns.

(A.D. 71200 to 73040) Torment starfares to Ain.

(A.D. 73727 to 79474) Torment, now called Tormentil, weds Ain and broadcasts human minds to various dissenting and nonjuring civilizations in the Orion, Sagittarius, and, later Perseus and Cygnus Arms.

The Dominion of Triumvirate flourishes for a time as a Praesepe servitor, before being superseded by the Benedictine Dominion of Ain, which becomes the Epitome of Man.

(A.D. 79474 to 80100) *Solitudines Vastae Caelorum* starfares to Vander-linden 133 in Praesepe, escorted by an ice giant.

(A.D. 91917) Wreck of the *Solitudines Vastae Caelorum.*

(A.D. 92000 to 96900) Montrose is adrift. At near-lightspeed, he travels 3,400 lightyears from Vanderlinden 133 over a period of 3,500 years.

(A.D. 95500) Montrose passes SAO 82846.

(A.D. 100,000) The shock wave of the hypersupernova is bright enough to be seen during daylight hours on Earth.

(A.D. 102,500) The shock wave reaches the wreck of the *Solitudines.*

(A.D. 103,000) *Solitudines* uses the force of the nova light to starfare to TX Canum Venaticorum. Montrose forced into somnolence.

(A.D. 103,000 to 133,000) TX Canum Venaticorum system engineered.

(A.D. 133,000 to 163,000) Montrose starfares to M3.

(Circa A.D. 163,000 to 164,000) Menelaus exists as a minor pattern of mental energy, enslaved, impoverished and vagrant, lost in the vastness of the M3 Noösphere. Slowly he grows in wealth and station, achieving Dominionhood.

(A.D. 164,000) Audience with M3.

(A.D. 164,000 to 200,000) Montrose elevated to Authority of M3.

(A.D. 200,000 to 300,000) Due in part to his tenacity, Montrose becomes the standard base ambassadorial template and, later, Archon of Orion.

(A.D. 400,000 to 800,000) Various forms of Montrose become Warlord of Milky Way, Imperator and Nobilissimus. Conquest of Lesser Magellanic Cloud.

(A.D. 802,701) Montrose commands sufficient resources to encompass his own departure. He transmits himself to Andromeda.

(A.D. 802,701 to 3,341,000) Montrose in transit to Andromeda.

APPENDIX D
Very-Large-Scale Time Line
(by Billions of Years)

Timeline of Northern Universe (beyond Alphecca)

- **12 Billion** B.C.

  Corona Borealis sends out the Ulterior message when the early galaxies condense out of the primal nebulae. Since this message disturbs the background radiation distribution, it statistically tilts the local universe toward galaxy formations of the type favored by Corona.

  The message passes from Hercules to Centaurus and Coma.

- **11 to 9 Billion** B.C.

  Centaurus passes the message to Pavo-Indus, who, in turn, sends it to Virgo.

- **8 Billion to 7 Billion** B.C.

  Hercules rejects the message, and becomes the first Malthusian. Hercules draws Centaurus into its influence. Pavo-Indus, an Amalthean, regards itself as the mother of Virgo civilization and is particularly offended at the apostasy of Centaurus, its own mother.

  The Malthusians determine that they could copy the technology and practices of the hypothetical Ulteriors to create a small and local continuum where negative entropy obtains.

  Andromeda drawn into the influence of Hercules and Centaurus.

  Centaurus (which was farther from Corona Borealis and able to risk defiance that Hercules could not) begins construction on the Great Attractor. The Great Attractor is an energy windfall. Negative entropy (extropy) is proven to work in the ultrasmall scale of merely clusterian distances.

- **6 Billion** B.C.

  The client becomes the patron: Centaurus dominates and prevents Hercules, now reluctant and miserable, from returning to the Amalthean party.

  Coma becomes apostate.

- **5 Billion** B.C.

  Centaurus influences the development in the young and aggressive (at that time) Hydra supercluster. Hydra becomes a Malthusian.

  At about this time, Pavo-Indus, offended at the apostasy of Centaurus, seeks for its own protection to become the client of Sculptor.

- **4 Billion** B.C.

  Influences from Hercules and Centaurus swing the newly formed Shapely Cluster to the Malthusian side. The psychology of Shapely is influenced by the fact that it had never been an Amalthean, and ergo was not apostate. The current density of the Shapely Supercluster is a result of preliminary preparation to create a second Great Attractor.

  Virgo is torn between Hydra (for the Malthusians) and Pavo-Indus (for the Amaltheans), but currently favors Malthus.

  Onset of the Throne War in the Milky Way.

Timeline of the Southern Universe (beyond Achernar)

- **12 Billion** B.C.

  At the opposite end of the visible universe, a supercivilization rises in the vast Horologium Supercluster, also receives the message from the Ulteriors. Unlike the Corona Borealis, Horologium rejects it, and enters a philosophy which is neither Malthusian nor Amalthean, neither extropian nor entropian, but fatalistic and self-destructive. Horologium thus does not oppose the Malthusians.

- **10 Billion** B.C.

  Sculptor is colonized from Horologium, but disdaining of Horologium's passivity, independently adopted a Malthusian philosophy, and begins the construction of its own Extropy Engine, which will lead to the Sculptor Wall.

- **9 Billion** B.C.

Sculptor receives the teaching of the Ulteriors, albeit in a more strict and ruthless version than Corona Borealis. Sculptor holds that neutrality is treason: hence it right and proper to use force to compel the contraction of the Eschaton Directional Engine.

- **8 Billion** B.C.

Sculptor becomes the patron of the unwilling Capricornus Supercluster. This event causes Sculptor's resources and attention to be directed away from the Northern Universe.

Pisces-Cetus undergoes sophotransmogrification by the fierce and active Sculptor, and seeing the ruthless treatment afforded Capricornus, abrogates its indenture, and turns to the large and somnolent Horologium for aid.

- **7 Billion to 6 Billion** B.C.

Horologium was briefly (for a billion years only) stirred from lethargy and uses its influence to fund several hundred billion local wars and millions of years of engineering efforts, to sever relations between Pisces-Cetus and Sculptor. Eventually it was done. Pisces-Cetus is considered a client of Horologium, even though that great, dark power is never to become an active player in the Eschaton Directional Engine War.

- **5 Billion** B.C.

Pavo-Indus, offended at the apostasy of Centaurus, sought for its own protection to become the client of Sculptor. Only at this point did Sculptor recover to its prewar level of Noösphere intellect and pansuperclusterian environmental control.

Sculptor becomes active in the northern area of the universe, even so far as to influence the philosophy of Pavo-Indus and hence Virgo.

The militant nature of the Collaborations within Andromeda and Milky Way, including the scheme of indentured sophotransmogrification, is a product of Sculptor influence.

Timeline of Local Group Events

- **9 Billion** B.C.

  (8,800,000,000 B.C.) The galactic "thin disk" of the Milky Way formed.

  (8,500,000,000 B.C.) Rise of the **Colloquium** in the Perseus Arm. Eldest of all surviving Forerunner races. The Colloquium assists the rise of high-metallic Population I stars, a very early example of astrocultural husbandry.

- **5 Billion** B.C.

  (4,500,000,000 B.C.) Rise of the **Magisterium** in Scutum-Crux Arm.

  (4,300,000,000 B.C.) Contact with Canis Major Dwarf satellite galaxy (on behalf of Pavo-Indus) inspires the Magisterium and Colloquium civilizations to collaborate. First evidence of mass sophotransmogrification.

  (4,100,000,000 B.C.) Magisterium and Colloquium cooperation gives rise to the **Panspermians**, who occupy a favorable position in the Orion Spur linking Cygnus, Perseus and Sagittarius.

  (4,000,000,000 B.C.) Panspermians begin cultivation of terrestrial and subterrestrial worlds in the Orion Spur.

- **4 Billion** B.C.

  (3,600,000,000 B.C.) Suspected date of earliest infiltration by Andromeda. **Symbiosis** in LMC assisted to Archon-wide sapience.

  (3,200,000,000 B.C.) Symbiosis attacks Canis Major Dwarf galaxy. The Monoceros Ring forms as debris as stars are abducted. (Note that current science places the formation of the Monoceros Ring at 9 billion years ago. This estimate would be correct if the formation were natural.)

- **3 Billion** B.C.

  (2,050,000,000 B.C.) The First Collaboration: Under Colloquium-Magisterium leadership the tentative galaxy-wide collaboration attempted a more complete unity, verging on selfawareness. Symbiosis and Panspermians are part of the Collaborative effort. A golden age. A local strand of the Eschaton Directional Engine is threaded through the core of the Milky Way at this time.

- **1 Billion** B.C.

  (1,000,000,000 B.C.) The First Awareness: The Throne of Milky Way briefly wakes, immediately begins to decline. First evidence of Andromeda interference in the cliometry of Milky Way to discourage cooperation between large-scale mind systems.

- **Current Day**.

  First phase of the Throne War. Andromeda by stealth interferes with the repeated efforts at Collaboration. See Large-Scale Time Line.

- A.D. **1 Billion**

  (A.D. 1,000,000,000) Orion Arm grows to predominance, conquers the Lesser Magellanic Cloud. Cold Equations abandoned in favor of Infinity Count Equations. Time of the Second Awareness.

- A.D. **2 Billion**

  (A.D. 2,000,000,000) Second phase of the Throne War. Andromeda and Milky Way begin to exchange long-range fire. Globular clusters of both riven away.

- A.D. **3 Billion**

  (A.D. 3,000,000,000) Final phase of the Throne War. Andromeda and Milky Way enter mental war, mutually destroy each other. Milky Way recovers first, enters a time of Third Awareness.

- A.D. **4 Billion**

  (A.D. 4,000,000,000) Andromeda capitulates. Fourth Awareness becomes Throne of the Bi-galatic Andromeda-Milky Way cloud. Local Group destroyed by spacetime singularity collapse. The Interior Continuum created.

- A.D. **4 Billion to 9 Billion**

  (A.D. 4,000,000,000 to 9,000,000,000) Interior Continuum War. Montrose, with other dissatisfied servants of Virgo, rebels against

Del Azarchel and his Thrones. The opposing forces, operating on intergalactic scale, each use the local segment of the Eschaton Engine to bend spacetime and organize the maneuver of flotillas of galaxies and satellite galaxies. The Interior Continuum destroyed.

- **A.D. 9 Billion**
  (A.D. 9,000,000,000) Representatives of Hydra (for the Malthusians) and Pavo-Indus (for the Amaltheans) manifest themselves and halt the Interior Continuum War. Del Azarchel exiled to Horologium.
  Horologium Supercluster warps timespace to propel the beam information carrying all incoming versions of Del Azarchel, Montrose, and Rania into the remote future.

- **A.D. 21 Billion**
  (A.D. 21,000,000,000) Pancosmic Dyson surface completed. Onset of Big Rip conditions.

- **End of Time.**
  Final Duel between Del Azarchel and Montrose. Operation of the Eschaton Directional Engine.